Ad-akradai Khorris was pleased with his position. His concentrated dischargers had shrugged off the Humans' heaviest bombardment. His nuclear cannons were in position, to be moved up for firing when the human forces had moved into his trap.

But he would wait before deploying his armored vehicles. His infantry and nuclear cannons would be enough to finish off the Human armor that advanced on him. Only then would his armored vehicles sweep back over the bridge to drive into their rear and eliminate their precious artillery.

He was worried, however, that more reinforcements were arriving for the Humans. One of his few remaining surveillance probes had been launched at the first hint of daylight in the east. An image taken just before it died showed that the Human forces had moved all of their equipment off the eastbound roadway, as if making room for another unit to pass through. He continued to weigh the possibility of launching his last probe to hopefully catch a glimpse of what was arriving.

His quiet observations were rudely interrupted by his hatch opening with a loud clank. The panicked face of Inkezdai Kepliss looked in.

"Ad-akradai, massed artillery rises from the west—"

"Good! It begins!"

"But Ad-akradai," Kepliss pleaded, "the artillery rises from far behind the Human lines, and the launcher approaches swiftly as it fires! It travels along the roadway at a high rate of speed, sending its shells high into the atmosphere!"

Something new, Khorris thought. The approaching weapons platform had to be exceedingly large to have the stability to wield a sustained barrage accurately while moving.

Should he launch his last probe to view its approach? He decided against it. Nothing could stand up against his nuclear cannons. . . .

OLD GUARD

A BOLOS ANTHOLOGY

created by Keith Laumer

edited by Bill Fawcett

Bolos: Old Guard

A Baen Books Original

Baen Publishing Enterprises
P.O. Box 1403
Riverdale, NY 10471
www.baen.com

ISBN: 0-671-31957-4

Cover art by Dru Blair

First printing, February 2001

Distributed by Simon & Schuster
1230 Avenue of the Americas
New York, NY 10020

Production by Windhaven Press, Auburn, NH
Printed in the United States of America

In memory of J. Andrew Keith,
1958–1999
Author, historian, wargamer,
brother, friend.

Contents

INCURSION

Mark Thies

It started as just a flicker of X-rays, high above the orbital plane of the bright orange star Epsilon Sindri. The region of space was devoid of matter, or any potential for producing such a phenomenon, but nonetheless it was there. As the flicker grew to erratic bursts, these X-rays were quickly logged by several detectors within the system of five planets below.

The first detector to take note of these bursts was a security array high above the second planet of the star system. Few disturbances ever escaped the notice of this awkward mass of antennae, reflectors, and arrays that tumbled lazily in its wide orbit. The bright X-ray flashes were trapped and focused by a myriad of mirrors and lenses, and then sorted by a series of gold refraction gratings. The spectrometers compiled and analyzed the flood of data, recognizing the bursts for what they were. Unconcerned, the security array's attention drifted elsewhere.

The second detector to take note of the bursts was

a navigation beacon also in orbit around the second planet. Unlike its much larger brother in high orbit above him, this oblong satellite sheathed in bright gold foil carefully recorded the exact position and energy signatures of the bursts. The starports on the planet surface were notified of the phenomena, but no concern was immediately made evident. This was a weekly occurrence above the planet Delas, in precisely the location that it was expected. Only high above the ecliptic in the solar system full of debris could a 500,000 ton merchantman exit trans-light speeds without risking a fatal collision.

Only one other detector in the star system noticed the turbulent arrival of the interstellar freighter *Aragonne Isabelle.* Shrouded in the cold shadow of the icy moon of Epsilon Sindri Three, another satellite realigned itself, focusing its three large collectors upon the source of the X-ray bursts. A fission reactor at its core came to brilliant life just as the gigantic transport finally exited the rift in a final explosion of radiant energies. Then the X-rays ceased.

The shrouded satellite, however, was still building up the power that it needed. It had been ordered to track these ships and monitor their arrivals and departures. But transmitting its reports back home needed far more energy than its uranium pile could provide. As the fusion core finally ignited, another rift formed for just a moment, sending out a pulse through subspace. The pulse was fast enough to travel light-years in a matter of weeks, and strong enough even to reach the fringes of the bright nebula that painted the Delassian night sky with its blue and orange hues. The acknowledgement to the pulse usually took more than a month to return.

It was also strong enough to catch the attention of Delas' security array. Once again, a report was logged and submitted. And on the planet, a corporal was startled by a beep, but then dismissed this second burst as a subspace echo that seemed to bounce around whenever any transport arrived or departed. His commander had been intending to ask some local astrophysicist about this phenomenon, but had yet to find the time.

Back in orbit around Epsilon Sindri Three, an acknowledgement was logged by the satellite only two hours later.

The passenger door to the cargo shuttle sprang open with an audible hiss of a pressurized seal. A sunrise of dull red shined into the small passenger compartment as the occupants stood up and gathered their belongings. Delassian air slowly rolled down the aisle as it exchanged with the cool processed air of the shuttle. First time arrivals were easily identified by their stunned gasps as the planet smothered them with its hot and stifling jungle atmosphere.

As the wave advanced down the aisle, it soon overcame a rather large woman in a white dress with bright orange flowers embroidered into its light fabric. An especially frightful string of expletives was loudly uttered as a result, causing many heads to turn towards her. Standing behind the woman, a man dressed in a uniform of Concordiat Army Desert Gray noticed a young girl staring at the woman in awed silence from across the aisle. The girl's mother remained unaware of the situation as she seemed to be frantically searching her luggage for something, so he decided to speak up.

"Madame, please, Starveil is on the edge of a rain forest. Certainly you were aware of where you were arriving."

Suitcase now in hand, the large woman turned on the man in surprising fury. After taking a moment to brush a swirl of black hair out of her eyes, she leaned forward as if to intimidate the older gentleman who spoke out, perhaps threatening to fall over onto him.

"That doesn't mean that I have to like it, does it?" she shouted.

The woman's imposing frame and fiery gaze contrasted sharply with the small size and cold dispassion of the Concordiat officer whom she faced. What she couldn't discern with her cursory assessment, however, was just how well muscled the man's small frame was. Underneath his prematurely gray hair, his Asian brown eyes stared back at her without flinching.

"No," said the man calmly, "but perhaps you could refrain from teaching our children to curse it so vividly."

A nod to the left drew the woman's attention to the girl, who smiled and huddled close to her mother. In a fraction of a second, the woman's fury turned to charming amusement.

"That was very bad of me," she told the little girl. Then she turned back to the man, and her smile was instantly gone. "But I am completely justified. I had little choice in coming here."

A glance down the passenger compartment showed the officer that it wouldn't be clearing any time soon. More than half of the sixty-four passengers were cargo handlers from the *Aragonne Isabelle*, and few were gracious enough to take the seats in the rear. Travelers such as he would have to wait as they disembarked first.

"That is unfair, then," the man commented, being courteous.

"My name is Dahlia." The woman introduced herself, extending her free hand. "Dahlia Burke."

"Toman Ishida," the man returned, clasping her hand for just a moment.

"Colonel?" Dahlia asked with a questioning glance at his collar.

"Yes."

Dahlia smiled proudly, then she turned to grab a

small shoulder bag that had been resting on the seat next to her.

"My son is a lieutenant in the Concordiat Army," Dahlia explained. "He's with the 351st Planetary Siege Division, or something like that. Ever hear of it?"

"Sorry, no. It's been a while since I've been on the Melconian front."

"Oh, I always hope that he's not there," she said despondently, "but I guess it would be unlikely that he'd be anywhere else."

Ishida didn't answer. She might have been hoping for some reassurance from him about her son, but without doubt she was correct. All siege divisions were now assigned to the Melconian front. Only scattered second and third echelon armored and mechanized formations were assigned to other duties.

The uncomfortable silence was finally broken when the compartment finally began clearing, and the line of passengers started moving.

"At least I'll only have to be here for a year. I work for Vetrex Electronics, and they need me to do some sales work here."

"Let me carry that for you," Toman offered as Dahlia's large suitcase banged against the seats as she walked.

"Oh, thank you. I can't believe that they make us carry our own luggage."

Toman took the case, slinging his own duffel bag over his shoulder.

"The *Aragonne Isabelle* is not a passenger liner. It is a supply transport. Merchant captains always feel that they are doing us a favor by allowing us to come with them on their rounds, no matter how much we pay them. Making our trip comfortable is well beyond their reason."

"You are a father, aren't you?" Dahlia asked over her shoulder.

Colonel Ishida felt troubled that the woman had

discerned this about him. Had he been condescending or patronizing, he wondered? He had thought that he was just explaining things well. Perhaps, though, she had just read it in his face.

At sixty-eight years, Colonel Toman Ishida looked much older than he was. His hair, although mostly undiminished and somewhat long, had turned prematurely white and gray many years before. His facial skin was rough and unnaturally wrinkled from the aftermath of two Melconian plasma shell burns, the second happening only a week after he got out of the hospital from the first. He had hoped that his dominant Asian heritage would protect him from the ravages of age, but it couldn't help him against a massed artillery barrage.

Toman had always tried to convince his compatriots that these effects made him look wise and respected. They always responded that he just looked haggard.

"I have two children, Kaethan and Serina," Toman admitted. "Is it that obvious?"

"In some things. Your concern for that little girl was certainly an indication, but it was more your manners that was the giveaway."

"My manners," Toman repeated, wanting to understand. "My aversion to foul language, you mean?"

"No. No. It was the manner in which you scolded me in front of the little girl. Your tone of voice and method. I do, however, believe that the use of foul language, as you call it, is healthy and can make your rhetoric much more effective." Dahlia punctuated her sentence by poking the air with her finger.

"My old commander would certainly agree with you."

"Meaning that you don't?"

Colonel Ishida hesitated before continuing this conversation. The last thing that he wanted to do right now was to enter into a debate about the usefulness of swear words.

"It's been a long time . . . since I thought a problem could be improved by cursing at it. I now wonder if ever there was."

Ishida was pleasantly surprised as Dahlia didn't bother replying to his disagreement, seeming more intent on navigating her wide girth down the aisle. Toman followed, carrying her heavy suitcase as carefully as possible. Even at his age, Ishida was still almost as strong as he ever was. Toman maintained a strict workout schedule to maintain his physique. Fifty push-ups and stomach crunches every night before he went to bed, along with a variety of other simple exercises. His only failing had been giving up his long distance running, for which he had many excuses in the injuries that his body had endured over the years.

As the colonel exited the door and walked onto the downward ramp, he took a moment to step aside and appreciate the tangerine sunrise that was climbing above the line of massive hangars to the east. The starport's huge expanse of steel and polymer reinforced concrete was wet with a recent rain shower, reflecting the sky in many puddles. Dark clouds to the south and west looked threatening.

"Just my luck it would be raining today," Dahlia lamented as she pondered down the steps.

"This time of year it rains every day down here," Ishida told her.

Whatever weather that was threatening from the north could not be seen, however, since the awesome mass of the shuttle towered over them like an old-time zeppelin, squat and flat on its bottom and rear. It stretched almost three hundred meters from fore to aft, and rose over fifty meters above the pavement. The four fusion jets positioned at its corners wouldn't be able to budge the giant transport if it weren't for the powerful counter-grav reactors that reduced their load. Their passenger compartment was only a small attachment on its underside, near its front. It looked as if it was only added as an afterthought, conveniently placed next to one of the shuttle's huge landing shocks, whose side their ramp was built into.

A brightly colored bus was waiting at the base of the ramp. Painted on its side, in large letters, were the words WELCOME TO STARVEIL. Large men were taking people's luggage and helping the arrivals onboard.

"You've been to Delas before?" Dahlia guessed.

"My son and daughter live here."

"Your wife?"

"Widow."

"Oh, I'm sorry. How very sad. It doesn't seem right that a soldier would lose his wife and not the other way around."

Toman didn't quite know how to respond to that statement, so instead he remained quiet. He had the strange impression that he should apologize for some reason, but he couldn't figure out why.

As they reached the pavement, he looked down towards the rear end of the cargo shuttle where its massive cargo ramp was still descending slowly, preparing to offload. The 50,000 ton shuttle would be transferring cargo between Delas' three starports and her mothership well into the next day before the *Argonne Isabelle* departed back to Angelrath. Ten or eleven days later another freighter would be arriving. Delas was a quickly growing colony, and its needs were many.

"Are you visiting your children?" Dahlia asked him.

"That, and other things."

Dahlia's luggage was taken from him then and stashed into the bus's undercarriage.

"I'm sorry I have to leave you now, Dahlia." Toman bowed to her slightly. "It's been a pleasure."

"You're not coming on the bus?"

"No. I have traveling companions to attend to. A car will be coming for me later."

The cargo ramp finally hit the pavement with a resounding thunk, despite the slow speed it was descending.

"Traveling companions?"

"They were too big to fit in the passenger compartment."

The sudden thunderous clanging of metal on metal made all heads turn as a monstrous form emerged from the rear of the cargo shuttle. The dark shape rose thirty meters from the base of its enormous treads, to the top of its massive main turret, barely fitting inside the cargo hold. Plates of dull black armor gave it an ominous air that matched the thunderclouds that flashed lightning kilometers away behind it. Its main cannon extended out well past the forward glacis of the juggernaut, always remaining perfectly level with the ground as the machine descended the ramp. The landing shocks on the cargo shuttle groaned and shrieked, and the ground beneath them shook violently as the war machine finally rolled out onto the pavement. Even after it had cleared the shuttle and stopped, a noticeable vibration remained, as if the tarmac was straining with all its might to support the monster that had just set foot upon it.

Bristling with secondary turrets and weapon ports, the war machine looked to be a battleship on tracks, though no one could mistake it for being seaworthy. It was a dreadnought whose design had been condensed to its most lethal form. Losing its displacement and elegance, it gained terrible focus in all things that its enemies feared most: firepower, maneuverability, and speed. No christened name could be seen inscribed on its bow, but upon the rear portion of its side hull, the designation "DBC-0039DN" was emblazoned in tall, silver letters.

"A Bolo," Dahlia said in awe. "You are with the Dinochrome Brigade?"

"Very good. Your son would be proud of you."

Dahlia actually blushed at that.

"You have another one?" Dahlia then asked Toman, smiling.

"We require two trips."

"Ah," she said. Then she leaned forward as if to whisper something. Toman complied by leaning forward also. "Should I be worried about anything?"

"Not any more." Toman said with a smile, backing away again.

Dahlia laughed lightly, though she still looked concerned. A moment later she extended her hand.

"Thank you for your help, Toman. I'll try to watch my language while I'm here."

Toman took her hand and held it tightly for a moment, then released it.

"Maybe you'll find some other way of being effective."

"We'll see. Good-bye, Toman."

"Good-bye, Dahlia."

The colonel stood waiting for a couple minutes still, until he confirmed that Dahlia had found a seat and was settled in. With a short wave he then turned away and headed for the Bolo that waited patiently for him, next to the ramp. A pack of tractors that had been waiting for the Bolo to clear the ramp now were invading the cargo hold to ferry its remaining contents to several flatbed trucks nearby.

After he had escaped earshot from the passengers, Ishida removed his fieldcomm from his belt and activated it. It was already set at Brigade battle channels.

"How are you doing, Chains?" He called.

"Fully operational, Commander," replied a baritone voice from his earphone.

"How 'bout you, Quarter?"

"Waiting the return of the shuttle, Commander," replied a charming voice with a distinct British accent.

"That might be a couple hours, Quarter. Hold tight.

Until then, though, I want both of you to probe every wavelength and log every emitter that you can around this planet. Find out what their defenses are like, and where they've broken down."

"This may cause alarms to be triggered," said Chains.

"Good," replied Toman cheerfully. "I hope that it does. As always, route all complaints to me."

"Yes, Commander. Shall we remain at Low Alert Status?"

"For now. No point in distracting you if their security array is operating correctly. Oh, by the way, keep tied into its frequency. I want you two watching things."

"We will, Commander," Chains replied. "The Starveil tower is requesting that I proceed to their military hangar area. Do you wish to enter first?"

"Yeah, open up. I need to log a report and make some calls."

"Opening hatch. Will Kaethan be visiting us, again? I would look forward to seeing how your son has grown."

Memories of Kaethan's visit to the 39th Lancers temporary headquarters on Point Hermes flooded him with conflicting emotions. It had been twelve years ago, when Kaethan was fourteen, just after his mother had died. His sister Serina had just become eighteen and she wasn't sure that she could take care of him. It was a difficult time, and Toman decided not to reflect on it at all.

"Maybe. I'll tell him that you'd like that."

"It's been a long time."

"Yes," Toman sighed. "It has."

At midday, it was dark and raining fiercely, and Captain Kaethan Ishida had his sunglasses firmly stashed in his belt pouch. On a sunny day, the chalk white dunes of the Fort Hilliard Firing Range almost glowed with heat and blinding light. The sands blew over the landscape from the forty kilometers of the Alabaster Coast that stretched along the ocean to the west. Soldiers of the Alabaster Guard wore dark sunglasses as unofficial trademarks of their unit, though the glasses were absolutely necessary equipment for when the skies were clear. This would hardly be a problem today, but at least on a clear day you could actually *see* the firing range.

"Almost ready, Kaethan."

Kaethan didn't respond to the warning, but instead kept looking out into the rain from their concrete reinforced bunker. Judging from past experience, Walter Rice would be "almost ready," typing madly on his computer, for another couple minutes. And their past experience stretched as far back as elementary school. There was no hurry.

A brief surge of rainfall caused a light spray to splatter through the slit window that stretched the entire forward length of their bunker. The captain turned his face away, shielding his green eyes. His short, jet-black hair had dried quickly after his sprint from his vehicle to the bunker, but would remain damp as long as he stayed where he was. The cool spray was refreshing to Kaethan, who had begun to grow weary of the heat wave that the Telville area had been experiencing lately.

The bunker that the two men were in was small and brightly lit. Kaethan was dressed in a dark metal-blue uniform of very light fabric, with black boots and belt. Platinum circlets, pinned to his shoulder flares, identified his rank. The lights overhead highlighted his sharp Mediterranean facial features and complexion, though his brooding Asian eyes always broke the categorization. Walter was dressed in gray slacks and a designer white shirt that he had just purchased that day. His long, wavy brown hair reached his shoulders, though it was neatly combed and kept. The short beard that he sported caused him to scratch his chin and neck constantly. Although of ordinary features, this no way detracted from his rugged good looks. Bare concrete walls enclosed them, gray and smooth except for numerous cracks and cement patches that marred the surface. A fine white dust covered everything, though it was more from the sand outside than from the deterioration of the concrete. A large but simple computer panel was embedded into the rear wall, black and not activated. Walter had all he needed in his briefcase of a computer that he had opened on the extremely large table that dominated the center of the small room.

"Have you ever tried your baby in a rain like this?" Kaethan asked, lazily.

"My *laser* will work fine," Walter returned, "just as long as the wind doesn't pick up."

"The wind?" Kaethan turned in curiosity.

A cool breeze from the west had picked up off the ocean just as the rain began to pour, slanting the raindrops with mild fifteen kilometer per hour gusts. Kaethan couldn't figure out, however, how the wind would be a problem.

"Don't tell anyone, but we tested out our tracking radar during the last hurricane," Walter had stopped typing momentarily as he confided in his friend. "If a strong gust created a localized swirl, our radar sometimes registered it as an incoming missile."

"You're kidding."

"Yes, but it *was* a concern."

As Walter happily returned to his typing, Kaethan sighed and turned back to the slit window. Just the two of them were in this bunker, orchestrating this demonstration. Fifty meters to their right, closer to the ocean, several faces peered back at him from another bunker. The local aldermen would probably have a poor show today through this rain. He suspected that they'd hear the artillery boom a few times, then afterwards they'd be shown the radar tracks. If they wanted, they'd be driven to ground zero to investigate the area for recent impacts.

Somewhere out there in the rain, however, was a modified mining utility Hauler with a multiphase array radar and an industrial strength battlelaser whose job was to make sure no shell survived long enough to impact the ground. Many cities on Delas had purchased the Haulers for use as APC's, but with an additional mini-fission core installed, it could power a very impressive laser system. There was a great deal of interest in these ongoing tests.

"Ready," Walter announced, then hit one more key and looked up.

"Are you sure?"

"Yes."

"It's still taking three minutes getting that crystal up to speed, isn't it?"

"I told you, I'm sure we can reduce that."

Kaethan glared at Walter with narrow eyes for a moment, then picked up his headset from a chair next to him. Captain Ishida had been given this assignment for the sole reason that its lead engineer, Walter Rice, was a personal friend of his from long ago. It was either that, or nobody else in the Alabaster Guard wanted to waste their weekends at the firing range. Either way, he was still unsure of the wisdom of that decision. As much as they were enjoying working together, Walter might not have been taking this task as seriously as he should. Of course, Kaethan told himself, Walter had never taken anything very seriously, and yet he always did get straight A's. That had earned him an off-planet university scholarship at Angelrath, which had separated them for the past eight years.

Little had changed in either of them since they had last seen each other, Kaethan believed. Although in a business suit now, Walter's curly, long, light brown hair still made Kaethan see him as the beach bum that he had always been. His eternal one-day growth of beard just added to the effect. If he truly did shave every morning, then Kaethan thought that he might want to do it again at midday. To be tall, handsome, and relaxed had been Walter's quest in life since before college, and he had largely succeeded if judged by the reaction of those he valued most, women. Walter's and Kaethan's basic physiques had changed little, but at six-foot one, Walter was now a good six inches taller than Kaethan was.

The rain outside was beginning to slacken now, but the captain wasn't going to wait any longer. After a quick wave of warning towards the other bunker, Kaethan activated his headgear and pulled the microphone down to his mouth.

"Hey, Rick."

"Ready, Captain?" Corporal Rick Shaller sounded excited, as he always did before firing his howitzers.

"All set. Give me one round over the target."

"On-the-wayyy."

Kaethan's earphones squelched out as Rick's microphone was overloaded by the fire. Out of habit, he mentally counted the seconds before the sound wave passed over the bunker. The dull boom finally hit as he reached twelve, followed almost instantly by a flash of blue light that lit up the sky and a loud explosion from high above.

"One down!" Walter exclaimed.

"Ready for the next test?" Kaethan confirmed.

"All set."

"Okay, Rick. Bracket her with three rounds."

"Fire Plan Two, on the way."

This time, as the shells neared the target, Kaethan knelt on a chair so that he could see up into the sky. His view was hindered by the thick concrete overhang, but he was able to discern three separate beams tracking, and holding on their targets.

After three rapid explosions from overhead, the beams stopped.

In fact, he knew that it was only one laser beam, being redirected by a rapidly spinning crystal onto multiple targets. In Walter's theory, this weapon could not be overwhelmed since it didn't track targets, rather it determined what arcs contained a threat and fired its laser as the crystal spun through that arc. In Kaethan's reality, they found in test fires that the laser lost coherence as the crystal heated up. Despite a myriad of cooling techniques, a sustained barrage would give the system problems. Also, a shell protected with modern composite alloy, or reflective armor, could get through. But unless Walter was given an expensive fusion chamber to power his toys, this was the best anyone could do.

Fire Plan Three utilized all six guns of the Alabaster Guard Artillery, Alpha Company. Six shells were engaged simultaneously by the laser and destroyed midflight, although one shell survived noticeably longer than the others did. Walter shrugged it off, not thinking it was worth the bother to investigate.

The last test scheduled for the day was a full test of all six guns firing three times at different azimuths, driven with different explosive charges. The effect was that all eighteen rounds would be impacting at the same time. Even Walter left his console to see this spectacle.

And it was very impressive. The last shells that were fired had the lowest trajectory with the most propellant. Their screaming through the air over the bunkers drowned out all other noise. The light show, though, was spectacular as the entire sky lit up with eighteen simultaneous beams firing. All of the shells survived noticeably longer than in the first tests as the laser light drifted from blue to green. But they all soon started popping, slowly at first, and then in a rush. Like popcorn, Kaethan thought.

One final explosion, though, occurred much later than the others did.

"That one could have impacted, Walter."

"Well, seventeen out of eighteen isn't bad, and I know I can improve on that by restricting the spin more. The ion bolts on your Templars wouldn't have gotten half of them."

Walter returned to his console and started reviewing some statistics. Kaethan looked over to the other bunker and found a corporal looking back, expectantly. He gave him a thumbs-up, and motioned that the testing was over for the day.

"I noticed the color shift this time." Kaethan turned back to Walter. "The beams turned green."

"As I told you, the wave-length will expand as the crystal heats up."

"What color starts being dangerous?"

Walter looked up from his console and stared straight ahead for a moment.

"I'm not sure," Walter admitted. "An alarm will trigger once the crystal hits two hundred fifty degrees Celsius. I'm not sure what color that would equate to."

"Try to find out, okay?"

"Will do." Walter turned back to his laptop. "Shouldn't be difficult."

A soft beep emanating from Kaethan's belt captured his attention. Pulling out his handphone, he noted that a personal message had just been logged. Once the phone was activated and a password was typed in, that message was downloaded and displayed on a small scrolling message line.

"What was that sour face for?" Walter asked after a glance.

"My father's on Delas. He's coming to visit."

"The colonel?" Walter laughed. "Is he on leave or something?"

"No. Some business that he won't talk about."

"When is he coming?"

"Tomorrow or the next day, he said. He doesn't know."

"Well, I'd love to meet him."

Kaethan shrugged.

"We'll see," he only said. "I assume that you'll be busy tonight."

"Very," Walter said. "Once I write up a report, my boss is treating these politicians to dinner and wants me to be there. I guess a funding vote is approaching again."

"Good luck."

"Oh, I think it's a lock. None of them believed that a battlelaser would be useful on a modern battlefield, but they've been shown."

"I think the price tag influenced them, also."

"It needed that just to bring them to the table," he said somewhat bitterly. "You heading out?"

"Yeah," Kaethan said, retrieving his raincoat from a chair. "I'll give you a call tomorrow. Turn off the lights when you're done."

"Will do. See ya."

"See ya."

Outside of the bunker, Kaethan had to dash through the rain a few steps before arriving under a concrete and steel overhang that protected their cars. Driving your own vehicle to the forward bunkers at the Fort Hilliard range required several release forms to be filled out. The overhang protected the vehicles against overhead shrapnel, but would not protect against near miss shrapnel, or direct hits. The only other choice was to walk, or be driven by someone else.

And Kaethan hated to be driven by someone else.

In fact, he hated having anything be done for him that he could do himself. He was told that this was the reason why he had become battalion commander so quickly, being only twenty-six years old, Earth standard. It was the nature of the military to promote

their hardest workers into a position of delegating all
their work to others. Of course, few soldiers in the
Delassian Defense Force made the militia their full-
time occupation, thus giving Kaethan an advantage.
Most men on Delas were forced to devote four years
of their lives in the DDF, but almost always quit
thereafter. Many became weekend warriors, rejoin-
ing their battalions once a season for various training and wargames. Kaethan, however, joined full time.
The pay sucked, he always told people, but the
benefits were nice.

The work, though, especially lately, was tiring. For
the last couple years, it had been Kaethan's responsibility to incorporate recently purchased equipment
into the battalion's capabilities. And unfortunately, with
local politicians organizing the acquisitions, the mix
of technologies was poorly considered. Delas was so
far away from their Sector Concordiat Base at Angelrath that they had planned on constructing a new base
here. But with the Melconian war draining away
resources, this never materialized. And now, with the
fleet away to who-knows-where, Delas had been told
to fend for itself. Except for the constantly rotating
Army regiments that were based at Angelrath, the
entire sector was basically left on its own. And at this
time, only his father's two Bolo Mark XXXs were
keeping watch.

Perhaps it would have been better to allow the
planetary government to maintain its own army,
Kaethan had often considered. Their recently elected
governor, Leonard Traine, was a very respected man,
honorable and honest. But that would never be
enough for the fiercely independent miners and frontier farmers that made up the population of this
world. The planetary government could never be
given the opportunity to force its will on others, so
instead, the planetary defense forces consisted entirely
of local militias. The weapons and equipment were

purchased by the cities, sometimes in cooperation with each other, but not always. Except for one mass purchase of the Metallicast Industries Templar Mark XI, and another of several hundred SE-12244 mining company Sealed Environment Haulers, the individual cities went their own ways.

Walter's battlelaser project, for the first time, was an entirely Delassian machine, with all parts and labor drawn from the planet's rapidly expanding industry. Several cities were interested in it, and its success could be the start of a very lucrative business in this sector. Quite a bit of pressure was riding on Walter's shoulders, though you'd never see it by talking to him. Personally, Kaethan thought the system would be of limited use if a Melconian dreadnought suddenly appeared in orbit and began carving up the planet into bite-sized morsels. He did, however, like that most of the electronics were standardized, easily acquired components, making his job dramatically easier. If for only that, Kaethan considered this a project worth continuing.

He'd never mention this opinion to his father, though. Of course, he had never known exactly what to talk to his father about. Kaethan hadn't met his father until he was six, though he had no memory of the event. The colonel's brief visit home when Kaethan was ten was made ever more awkward by numerous injuries that the Melconian front had inflicted upon him. At fourteen, after his mother had died from a sudden local illness, he had visited his father at a Concordiat base called Point Hermes. Kaethan could never find this on any star charts, but that is what everyone called it while he was there. Why he was told to go there, he had never found out. After several awkward weeks he was told to go home to Delas, where his sister would take care of him. The stay was excruciatingly boring, with little time spent with his father. The only enjoyment he had was talking for long hours with Chains, one of his father's Bolos.

His father transferred to Angelrath only three years ago after most of his regiment was lost in a Melconian attack. Even so much closer, he only had visited twice since then. Most of the colonel's time had been spent with Kaethan's sister, Serina. This wasn't his father's fault, however. Kaethan had gone to extraordinary lengths to be sure that he was very busy during these visits. It wasn't that he harbored any resentment towards his father for anything, it was just that they both were terribly uncomfortable around each other. Kaethan's guilt for keeping his father at arm's length was tempered by his firm belief that his father felt exactly the same way.

And so, as Kaethan navigated his way over the sand-swept ocean road, he began to mentally reorganize his next few days as inefficiently as he could. Rather than making more work for himself, it was always better to make do with what one had.

Of course, it would be best if something unexpected would happen that would keep him very busy for the next few days. This was unlikely, however, on a planet as remote as Delas.

Unit DBQ-0039DN has now safely made planetfall, and once again the last of the 39th Terran Lancers are reunited. Although we remain at low alert status, we are eager to begin our latest assignment, and have begun a complete strategic analysis of the Delassian defense network. This, perhaps, exceeds our Commander's direction, but the latest events are certain signs of imminent danger to this planet. That Unit DBQ and myself are the only Bolos assigned to the protection of this entire sector is testament to the respect and trust that the 39th has so painfully earned in its nearly six-hundred-year history.

Our first task has been completed and Commander

Ishida is now reviewing our report on our probing of this planet's defenses. All active and passive arrays listed in their Planetary Defense Summary submitted to the Concordiat last year have been detected and seem to be operating satisfactorily. The maintenance logs on their orbital arrays report timely repairs completed without incident, and no system failures within the last five standard years. My subtronic probe of the arrays and planetary sensor grid triggered the appropriate alarms, and an appropriate challenge from Delas' planetary defense complex at Blackstone Ridge. I thus concluded that the present planetary defenses are well maintained and operated.

But they are woefully inadequate.

A secure defense network is an admittedly difficult task on a planetary surface that is nearly ninety-percent ocean and widely unpopulated. Delas has only two large landmasses, Oradin and Deladin, with only the latter being significantly colonized. Nearly all five million of Delas' population is concentrated in about twenty city-states on this continent, stretching from 62 degrees north, to 55 degrees south of the equator. Delas' only operating Hellbore defense battery is located in northern Deladin, protecting the majority of the cities that are there. Work on the Cape Storm ground battery in southern Deladin seems to be stalled for unknown reasons. This leaves vast tracts of open skies available for orbital insertions of ground troops. Most of the planetary defense budget has instead been spent on local militias, equipping their soldiers with weapons of varied quality. It would have been far wiser to spend this money applying firepower on the approaches to this planet, rather than equipping their soldiers for combat after an invader has landed.

Unit DBQ and myself have detailed these concerns with our Commander in the report he is now reading, though we are certain that he has been as troubled by these inadequacies as we have been. Our

*arrival at the much smaller equatorial starport of
Starveil, instead of the northern planetary capital of
Argus, gives the 39th the best range of fire over all
of Deladin's skies, north and south. The Beischal
Savannah to the south of Starveil provides a wide
expanse of open field, rare on Delas, where we can
maneuver freely to evade orbital bombardment. Colonel Ishida deploys us well, and we will do our best
to make do with the advantages he has given us.*

The dark shape cruised slowly under the rain-swept
wavetops, its meter high black dorsal fin barely
making a wake. Distant lights on the rocky shoreline
illuminated a small complex of buildings surrounded
by an electrified security fence. Lightning flashed
occasionally in the stormy sky, making visible a concrete viaduct that led from the sea into one of these
buildings.

It was there that the seven-meter long shape was
heading.

The entrance to the viaduct was barricaded by thick
titanium bars, but these slid back into the concrete
walls as the shape approached. Then, as the massive
form passed by, the bars emerged once again to
secure the channel. No one noticed the immense fin
as it sailed up to the building and into the large pool
underneath it, not even a dark haired woman who
was busily cataloging a pile of seashells by the
poolside. She was lying back in a full-length reclin-
ing chair, the wet shells held in her lap, drying on
her long skirt of white cotton almost as sheer as a
spiderweb. The blue shirt and shorts that she wore
displayed the wave logo of the Telville Oceanographic
Institute where she worked. Her smooth, rounded
Asian face was contorted in fierce concentration as
she sketched an image of a brightly colored shell into
her notepad, capturing all its contours and creases,
oblivious to all other things around her. The woman's

dark brown eyes studied the shell's smallest details and relayed them to her sketch with precision that their simple photographic equipment had trouble capturing.

Only when the beast exhaled a blast of air did the woman jump out of her seat, sending her notebook crashing to the floor, and shells scattering across the tiles.

"Hello, Serina," said an amused female voice from the pool speakers.

Serina Ishida's heart was beating at an astounding pace, and her eyes were wide with fright, but after a couple of shallow breaths she began to laugh. It struggled at first, but her laugh grew quickly as her lungs relaxed once again. Only then could it be seen how strikingly beautiful the woman was as she smiled broadly.

On the table next to her was a small black transmitter the size of her palm. After taking a big breath, she reached for it and spoke into it.

"Kuro, please . . ." Serina struggled for another breath, "please do not ever do that again. I thought you were a daeger."

The orca rose up from the water and nodded its head in delight, sending small waves to lap up against the smooth tiled walls of the pool.

"Daeger would never come here," said the voice from the speakers. "You are foolish."

Serina's laugh quieted to deep breaths as she retrieved her notebook, and sat back down again. Tears had formed in her eyes and she wiped them away. As much as she disliked being called foolish, Kuro was right. Daeger were territorial creatures and wouldn't be wandering the shoreline like this. And as large as daeger were, they couldn't break through the titanium bars protecting the viaduct.

"You only left last night," Serina spoke into her transmitter, "what are you doing back?"

"I found a reef full of those colorful eels that you wanted."

"Really! That's wonderful! Can you locate it on the computer map?"

"I already have. Will you want to go there tomorrow?"

Serina sighed heavily and shook her head. The creatures were called "painted eels," and the local fishermen had often complained that they would sometimes congregate in a pack and shred their nets to get at their haul. This kind of behavior had never been documented before from these normally solitary creatures. She imagined that the sight of these bright red, yellow, and lavender eels swarming would be incredible.

"No, sorry. I'll be very busy. You and Peter will have to go alone."

Her colleague Peter Sallison never especially liked photo assignments, but he'd use any excuse to take the institute's thirty-meter jetboat out for a cruise.

"Sad," said the voice from the speakers, though Serina didn't believe it for a minute. She suspected that Kuro had a crush on Peter. "Why will you be busy?"

"My father is visiting. I have to prepare a few things."

"The colonel is on Delas?"

Serina was surprised that Kuro had remembered her mentioning him, but then scolded herself for being so anthropomorphic. The psychotronic enhancements that Kuro had surgically implanted in her not only gave her a near-human intelligence, but also a super-human memory.

"Yes, my father Colonel Ishida is on Delas. He'll be visiting me, and I need to make sure that Kaethan comes also so we're all together for a while."

"Is this a female duty?" Kuro asked. It was a common question of hers as she tried to make sense of human society.

"It is in *my* family," Serina responded despondently. "Kaethan and my father don't get along very well, but I think I can fix things."

"Families should remain together," Kuro said simply.

"Yes, they should," Serina responded just as simply, not wanting to explain any further. "I'd like you stay in the area for the next couple days so I can introduce you to my father when he visits with Kaethan. I've told him so much about you in my messages."

"Will they swim?"

"Kaethan might this time, but you'd have to be gentle with him if he wants to play. He's not as good as Peter is."

Kuro loved playing in the water with Serina and Peter. The orca was gentle with her, but with Peter their play had lately gotten quite acrobatic.

"I'll be careful, Serina. Did you want to play now?"

"Oh . . ." Serina moaned. "I have to finish cataloging these seashells from Oradin for Professor Kilby. Then I have to call Kaethan's commander and tell him to give my brother the next couple days off."

"He'll do what you say?" Kuro didn't hide her confusion.

"Well, he said that he would when I danced with him at Kaethan's promotion celebration last year."

Kaethan hadn't even told his father that he was given command of his heavy armor battalion. His commander, Colonel Neils, was surprised that Colonel Ishida wasn't there. Serina was just plain angry.

"*Then* you'll play?"

Serina had been planning to leave early today to go shopping. She also wanted to make dinner reservations for the next couple nights, though she knew it would be difficult on such short notice. As much as she'd like a nice swim about now, she really didn't have the time. It was so difficult to say "no" to Kuro, though.

"The shells might take a couple hours," Serina warned her.

"I'll wait."

Serina looked mournfully at the giant black and white head that bobbed in the water. It would be impossible to work while being watched like this. Distant thunder reminded her of how miserable it was outside, and the rain showers wouldn't be passing by until nightfall. Shopping would be difficult in weather like this, and she could do the calls tonight when she got home.

"I have to get my swimsuit," she suddenly announced.

The monstrous Bolos were parked on the edge of the starport tarmac, their cannons overlooking the kilometers of green scrubgrass of the Beischal Savannah that stretched out to the south of the starport. The white serrated edges of the scrubgrass flashed in the sporadic sunlight as the wind passed in waves over the flat landscape. On a clear day one could see the very tops of the mountains of southern Deladin from here, but today the mists grew dark to the south, shrouding the horizon.

Captain Reginald Brooks had never seen a Bolo firsthand before, and the sight was intimidating. Concordiat Army recruiters often visited Delas, bringing their deadliest and most impressive gravtanks to sway students away from joining the local Guard units. But even their mightiest siege cruisers would seem insignificant next to a Bolo Mark XXX. Its 110cm Hellbore was capable of delivering 2.75 megatons of precision firepower per second, capable of shattering any known armor. But even without that, the Bolos looked as if they could just crush anything that they rolled over. That something so big, and wielding so much firepower, was alive and thinking was unnerving. It didn't help matters when he saw a couple ion bolt turrets swivel in his direction as he approached in his vehicle. Out of instinct, his foot hit the brake hard, skidding his tires briefly.

The remaining distance to the Bolos was traveled more slowly. This seemed to appease the turrets, which stopped tracking his vehicle's motion.

Reginald had not been told about the arrival of these war machines until midafternoon, when General Rokoyan had called personally to give him his orders. The Concordiat colonel's arrival had been expected at Argus, not Starveil, it seemed. Donning his DDC issue light gray uniform, Captain Brooks raced off to the starport to offer Colonel Ishida transportation, and whatever else the man might need.

The vehicle that he drove was a land-car, powered by a simple power cell and therefore was somewhat small and light. The few grav-cars that sailed through the sky were all transit authority shuttles and city emergency vehicles. Few grav-cars were owned by individual citizens, as the city feared such unrestricted and uncontrolled air travel. A DDC insignia marked his car to be owned by the Delassian Defense Command, and Reginald was very careful driving it. He was a clean-shaven model officer, as he was often described in his performance reviews, and he was genuinely proud of it. The valuable solid platinum captain circlets on his high collar, standard issue on the metal rich planet of Delas, reflected brightly next to his black skin and short, cropped black hair.

Except for a few brief squalls, today's storms had passed Starveil to the south. It was now late afternoon, and massive thunderheads still flashed and rumbled in the distance. The orange Delassian sun shined through the dark clouds at times, creating a rainbow to the east of them where light rains still fell over the ocean there. Captain Brooks was thankful for the weather, since the starport's tarmac was unbearably hot on sunny days. On Delas, people appreciated the rain and didn't mind getting wet.

Still, the puddle that Reginald stepped into when leaving his vehicle soaked his sock, and he hated that.

"Good afternoon, Captain."

Brooks was surprised at the sudden appearance of the Concordiat colonel, rounding the backside of the Bolo. There must be some hatch back there, he assumed.

"Good day, Colonel. Welcome to Delas."

"Thank you. It's been a couple years since I've been here."

At the appropriate distance, Colonel Ishida stopped and exchanged salutes with Brooks; then they shook hands. Brooks' dark black skin and large hand contrasted with Toman's small, white hand.

"Then I won't bore you with the planctary briefing that I was told to give you," Captain Brooks told him. "General Rokoyan was surprised that you landed at Starveil instead of Argus. He was looking forward to showing you around our Blackstone Defense Complex."

"I'm not here to make inspections, Captain," Ishida said with a pleasant smile. "Starveil is more centrally located on your world. It was better to station my Bolos here."

Reginald once again looked over the massive hull that towered over him.

"Of course, we appreciate your help, though I'm not sure I understand the necessity."

"Perhaps we should get out of the heat to talk."

"Of course. But one thing . . ." The captain pointed up high onto the black turret of the Bolo, where there was a silver and blood-red shield emblazoned with a shadowy figure in black robes, wielding a fiery hammer. "Your insignia has the English shield design of a regimental strength unit, yet there are only two Bolos on your roster. Or do I have my Concordiat heraldry all wrong?"

"You don't," Toman said, shaking his head. "Chains and Quarter are the only Bolos left from the regiment. Angelrath is temporary assignment until they decide whether to reconstitute the 39th."

"Only two left? Do you think they'll do it?"

"The 39th was formed almost six hundred years ago from three brigades of Mark Nineteens. They've fought on the battlefields of sixteen interstellar wars, and settled countless conflicts. We'd be losing a great deal of history if we broke them up now."

"Aren't Mark Thirties out-of-date?"

"Chains and Quarter each have over two hundred sixty years fighting experience, upgraded to Mark Thirties over a century ago from Twenty-Eights. It would be smartest to upgrade them again and re-form the 39th around them."

"Rather than wasting them garrisoning a far-off outpost?" Reginald completed the colonel's point.

"Exactly." The colonel agreed without expression.

Reginald chuckled and looked up at the insignia again.

"What does . . . what does that Latin say on the insignia."

"It means 'Stand and be Judged,' " said the colonel, again without expression.

Reginald's right eyebrow rose, then he nodded and turned back to his vehicle.

"Hop in," the captain offered. "I'll take you back to the DDC base where you can requisition a vehicle for your stay on Delas."

As Toman walked around the vehicle and got in, he mentally reviewed this planet's military structure again. The "DDC" stood for the Delassian Defense Command, which meant that the captain was employed with the planetary government. The "DDF" were the Delassian Defense Forces, which were the local militias. The DDC had no standing troops, though the cities always agreed to lend them their formations for special assignments, if absolutely necessary.

He remembered from previous discussions with his son that the DDF and DDC didn't always get along.

Captain Brooks' vehicle was soundless as its power cell sped them over the tarmac, back towards the starport's terminal. A passenger aircraft was landing at the far side of the airport, with another waiting to take off on a crossing runway. The cargo shuttle to the *Aragonne Isabelle* would not be coming back to Starveil on this trip. Most of Delassian's merchant trade passed through Argus, or Reims on Deladin's southeastern shore.

"So why does Angelrath suddenly think we need a couple Bolos to protect us?"

Colonel Ishida was surprised that the captain hadn't heard. Had the DDC buried the event, he wondered? The thought occurred to him that certain people might not wish him to talk freely about this, but Toman always hated secrets.

"Almost two standard weeks ago, an alien probe was caught tailing the *Ulysses Eridanis* as it approached Angelrath, coming from Delas."

"Yes, I heard about that." The captain remained unenlightened. "Didn't it self-destruct when you closed in on it?"

Colonel Ishida hesitated a moment as the significance of both events seemed to be lost on the captain.

"Yes," Toman said pointedly, "which identified it as a military probe sent to gather intelligence. We've caught other probes from these aliens, but all were barely trans-light and relatively low-tech. This one was different."

"You believe that the probe was sent as a prelude to an invasion?"

"Unfortunately, yes," the colonel said. "Their initial probes found us. From that point they could have either pulled back from contact, sent a diplomatic envoy, or prepared to attack. That last probe was assuredly meant for the latter."

"Are all planets in this sector being mobilized?"

"No. If their hammer falls, it will likely be here. Your Firecracker Nebula plays havoc with our deep space detectors, but sporadic communications traffic, and projected courses of these probes, seem to point directly to the nebula. And Delas is, by far, the closest colony we have to the nebula."

"Does General Rokoyan know all of this?"

"Rear Admiral Santi at Angelrath is communicating to him daily over the SWIFT channels, from what I've heard."

This shut Brooks up. The captain obviously felt slighted at not being fully informed about the danger that Delas was in.

The pair remained quiet as Captain Brooks dodged traffic around the terminal, and then drove through security at the starport's main gate. Many factories and industrial complexes had sprung up around the starport since the last time Ishida had been at Starveil. It was impressive to see so much construction underway. Huge cranes were lifting gigantic support beams while small swarms of construction robots welded the frames together within fountains of sparks. Great plots of scrubgrass were being cleared away, laying bare the savannah soil that had been long ago judged useless to the plantation owners. Given another century, Toman considered, Delas could very well be the industrial powerhouse running this entire sector. It certainly had the raw materials for it, and now it was building the manufacturing foundations.

The four-lane highway coming from the south had little traffic on it as they increased speed on the on ramp. This changed, though, as they approached the tall buildings of central Starveil. Such concentration of population only confirmed how the planet's work force was rapidly converting from mining and agriculture to manufacturing and service.

"I was told to ask you," the captain spoke up once they were on the highway, "whether your Bolos were going to be poking around our defense network anymore."

"No." The colonel smiled. "We've done all the poking around that we needed. Your network is well maintained and operated, I was told."

"Thank you." The captain was gracious. "General Rokoyan will be pleased to hear that, though he was very upset at the time."

"Do you talk with him often?"

"Me? No, not anymore. I used to work for him at Blackstone, so he knows me personally. But he rarely ever leaves the place, or has any reason to talk to anyone outside of it."

"What do you do here?"

"I'm the liaison between the DDC and the Starveil DDF. All cities have at least one. We try to organize cooperation between the cities in their wargames and acquisition of equipment. It's more work than you'd think."

Colonel Ishida nodded, understanding.

Ishida was distracted by an impressive site as Brooks turned off the highway. Although the colonel had landed at Starveil several times, he had never had the opportunity to cross the old-style suspension bridge that spanned the Delas River. He had seen it from a distance several times, but never had reason to visit the northeast section of the city. It certainly was not the largest suspension bridge ever created, but it was a rare opportunity to see one outside of Earth.

As the bridge rose higher and higher, the distant treeline north of the city became visible. The jungle beyond was an unbroken mass of dark green vegetation stretching to the horizon. Turning east, the colonel could just make out the ocean coast beyond the river delta. As the colonel looked down at the barges and ocean transports that were travelling Delas' largest river, Brooks continued to discuss the difficulties of his job.

"It's gotten better lately, but the cities insist on viewing each other as competitors," the captain was saying. "All of the large mining corporations that first colonized this world staked out their claims, populated their cities, and have been in each other's face ever since. Getting them to work together under any circumstance is frustrating, even for planetary defense."

"Still no nukes?"

"Not yet." Brooks shook his head. "For now the cities are just concentrating on the Hellbore turrets. They're still uneasy about letting the DDC control any thermonuclear warheads."

"But they don't mind the ground batteries?"

"Nope. The Hellbore turrets are fine since they can't be used against ground targets. We're even trying to get various local high-tech industries involved in the Cape Storm battery, but that has made the progress slow. We're hoping that the next battery will have completely Delassian components."

A noble goal, Toman thought, but not worth the delay in getting those turrets operational.

"When will Cape Storm become operational?" Toman asked.

"Next year, sometime, was the last date that I saw."

Toman grunted acknowledgement, and grew reflective. Captain Brooks continued discussing his problems with local corporations, but Toman paid little attention to it.

Before she died, Maria Ishida was a well-known name in Delassian political circles. She had often written long letters to him telling of the bureaucratic battles that she was in, just as he sent her news of the battles of the 39th. Maria would write her letters with the same language and terminology he used, though he never thought that she was mocking him. It was a game that she played with a soldier's determination and guile. Often she'd be working against the very corporation that she was employed by, Telsteel Industries, the core of Telville's commerce. On Delas, politics and business were often the same. To her, the fierce competition between the cities was what was driving Delas' rapid advancement. Although the powerful corporations might be a royal pain to the local governments, Delas would never have grown so powerful, so quickly, without them.

Somewhere there must be a balance, Toman thought. Maria, though, just believed that a civilization grew in stages. Brooks had admitted that things continued to get better. The power of the local corporations was waning. Now it was time for the city governments to take control of the politics. Maria had seen this beginning twelve years before, and perhaps she had planted many of the seeds.

Colonel Ishida worried, though, that their growing season was over, and this harvest would happen far too soon.

"This is a foolhardy plan, Is-kaldai Keertra."

The entry into the dark room by Ad-akradai Irriessa had not gone unnoticed by the crimson-robed figure sitting motionless at his wide command console. Keertra, however, didn't bother turning away from the crisp image of a white and blue planet that was projected onto a massive display on the rear wall. Irriessa strode quickly from the door to stand directly before the console, and his dark and leathery, lizardlike skin twitched uncontrollably in his frustration. Bulging muscles covered a humanoid frame that stood over seven feet tall. Still, Keertra did not face the enraged commander, even though Irriessa was the servant of his most hated rival, Is-kaldai Riffen. Their long and slender *surias*, most assuredly drawn on sight before the mission, remained strapped to their sides, blades unbloodied.

"I use only my own troops, Irriessa. Why do you complain?"

"Your soldiers, as vile as they are, may be needed later."

Keertra could not smile at the insult, for his face had limited contortions. The Kezdai's deep-set, bright green eyes and dark beak were almost eaglelike, frozen for a lifetime in nearly the same cold expression. His protruding eyebrows, however, narrowed a fraction. And his cobralike hood, which cooled his blood in his homeworld's desert heat, expanded noticeably as the blood vessels within protruded and pulsed.

"You still remain ignorant, Irriessa, of our mission. None of our soldiers are to return from this raid. So says the pact we have agreed to."

"Our mission is to learn, Is-kaldai, not to die needlessly. You are reckless."

"And you are insipid. Wars require planning, but victories need daring. It is because of those like you that we have remained idle for so long while these aliens fortify."

Ad-akradai Irriessa did not react to this slight. As commander of Is-kaldai Riffen's elite troops for thirty cycles, he was a Kezdai that was secure with his priorities and capabilities. His dark blue and white robe was adorned with the jewel incrusted medallions of countless battles, personal and on the field. This was, however, the flag bridge of Keertra's personal warship, the *Mirreskol*. If he were to let this trading of insults continue, he would have no support for his version of what happened next.

Still, many times he had been alone with Keertra within this room, and each time the thought of ripping the Is-kaldai's throat out hounded his every thought. The fiercely loyal guards that were stationed outside the doors could never react in time to save their leader. This small chamber was the most protected part of the ship, where Keertra could watch all things and command what he needed, without being bothered by the annoying details that the ship's captain was meant to deal with. To many of the Is-kaldai, however, the flag bridge was but a place to hide, away from the knives of their overly ambitious subordinates and determined enemies. It amazed Irriessa that Keertra continued to allow him in.

"Will you be accompanying this insertion?" Irriessa asked without emotion.

Keertra was silent for a long while before answering. Irriessa waited patiently, determined not to be aggravated. The Ad-akradai was sure that this silence was meant to irritate him, rather than Keertra reflecting on a decision yet to be made.

"I have not decided yet. Any more questions?"

An amused look passed over Irriessa's face for just a moment as he saw his nemesis cower, but not admit it.

"No, Is-kaldai. I will leave now."

Before he left, however, Irriessa looked up at the projected planet that had the Is-kaldai so enamored. He tried, but could not figure out what Keertra could possibly be so interested in with distant images taken by a probe two years before. But everything that this Kezdai did baffled him no end. As Is-kaldai of the *Mirrek* clan, Keertra was member of the Kezdai ruling Council, and everything he touched invariably became entwined with obscure ulterior motives and hidden agendas. This would not be so confusing except that Keertra so rarely seemed to benefit from them. Until Keertra volunteered for this mission, Irriessa truly believed that his only purpose was to sow discord throughout their ruling body. But now he was baffled again, for if this mission were successful, the Council and the Kezdai race in general would be as united as they never were before. Keertra's accomplishment would be honored initially, but would leave him with a crippled military, and he would be forgotten once the real war began. Irriessa's clan leader, Is-kaldai Riffen, gladly agreed to share the same fate just to see his age-old enemy so declawed.

This was all very confusing to Irriessa. It was he who spoke the loudest in favor of a mission such as this, and then he was shocked to his core at who suddenly answered his call. And then he was shocked again when Keertra, in memory of traditions long since abandoned, insisted that the aging Mor-verridai, their almost powerless relic of an emperor, cast his blessings upon their troops before departing. To the surprise of everyone, Keertra declared that their ignored figurehead of a leader should be given back great power at a time when unity was so needed. All of this pleased Irriessa and a great many other soldiers, though everyone knew that the Council would never comply. The Mor-verridai and his corrupt clan could never be allowed true power ever again. Keertra knew this, and yet he still spoke out, once again sowing discord in the name of harmony.

With a shake of his head, the Ad-akradai somberly left the dark room.

Keertra did not respond as he heard the footsteps turn and walk out the door. Neither did he turn when he heard the more familiar footsteps of his own commander approaching. This distracted aura of superiority was a carefully practiced art for Keertra, but for once it was not on purpose. The Is-kaldai had been sleepless for days, and his mind was now beginning to feel the strain. Concentrating on the image before him was relaxing. It truly was a beautiful planet, and the Kezdai had so few.

"What do you want, Khoriss?" Keertra demanded.

"I overheard your discussion." Khoriss paused a moment for any reaction. None came. "What do you plan to do with him, if I may ask?"

"Irriessa? He will be useful. He will be very useful, I believe."

"Irriessa is intelligent, and will be on guard against your plans."

"He *is* intelligent, Khoriss. But you make the same mistake that he makes. Intelligence does not preclude gullibility. Have faith, Khoriss."

Ad-akradai Khoriss sighed and his cobra hood deflated.

"I will try, Is-kaldai."

Captain Kaethan Ishida arrived late the next morning at Fort Hilliard. The sky was overcast, but wasn't raining yet. Most of the storms would pass to the north, the forecasters told, hitting Starveil the hardest. Without the rain, however, the temperature was expected to rise to almost one hundred degrees Fahrenheit. It was a Monday, with Delas assuming the common week schedule that humans had worked by for centuries. On Delas, however, each day was almost thirty-one standard hours long, with two hundred sixty-four of these days in a local year.

The drive from his home to the fort followed an extraordinarily beautiful stretch of roadway, running along the white sand shoreline of the Alabaster Coast. The Telville suburb that grew so quickly along this stretch of road was named for the beach, and had done a superb job of keeping the beaches clean for the resort trade that they hoped to inspire. The vibrant green Delassian ferns that lined the roadway held back the sands from blowing over the pavement. Rose bushes, imported from earth, added further color to the dominant white and grays of this region.

His sister Serina, who lived north of Telville, had called him the night before and left a message. After debating with himself for a while on whether to listen to it or not, he finally decided to and found out the plans that Serina had for them all. Aside from the normal shared dinners with her and his father, she also had nebulous plans for some touring of south Deladin. It did not sound fun.

Kaethan left a quick message back with Serina saying that he'd do the best that he could, but that he was very busy at the fort and didn't know for how many of these excursions he'd be free. His untold plan, for the next few days, was to share a couple dinners with them, but little more.

As Kaethan approached the security gate in his vehicle, one of the guards on duty traded a few jokes with his buddy and then approached him. His gauss rifle was displayed prominently, though there was a smirk on his face.

"What's up, Jake?" Kaethan asked, knowing something strange was happening.

"Sorry, Kaethan. I can't let you through."

"And why not?" Kaethan played along.

"Direct orders from Colonel Neils. You are officially on leave for the next two days."

"Bullshit, Jake."

"No, sir. Orders from the top."

"Just open up the gate, Jake."

"Don't make me shoot you, Captain."

Kaethan knew that was coming. The phrase was Jake's trademark, possibly said in response to the fact that nobody could imagine Jake ever shooting anyone. Although the same age as Kaethan, the MP's blond hair and boyish face was as nonthreatening as one could get. Jake was friend with everyone, and constantly playing practical jokes on people.

This time, however, the amused grin that Jake was wearing told Kaethan that this was real. If this was a practical joke, then Jake would be dead serious.

"Okay, what's going on?" Kaethan demanded.

"All I was told was that if I messed up the colonel's dance with your sister at your next promotion, I'd be walking bunker duty for the rest of my life."

"That explains it." Kaethan nodded.

Jake just smiled.

A conspiracy was obviously at work.

After shaking his head mournfully, Captain Ishida backed away from the gate and turned around. Kaethan knew that his sister was pissed at him for not inviting his father to his promotion celebration last year, and he did feel guilty about that. This, however, was an entirely new, and unexpected, level of deviousness that Serina was showing. Kaethan reluctantly admitted defeat this round, and would play along with Serina's plans, no matter what disasters awaited. Perhaps some lessons would be learned, perhaps not. All he had to do was suffer a couple days of discomfort around his father, and then things would be back to normal.

Colonel Ishida arrived at the Telville Oceanographic Institute with help from an onboard computer in his vehicle. The institute was constructed along the rocky coastline northwest of Telville, with only a simple gravel and seashell road running ten miles through dense rainforest and difficult terrain up to its electrified gate. Although the highways connecting the major cities had been completed many years before, the secondary roads outside of the cities were still being worked on.

As Toman approached the gate, he wound down the window, letting the cool conditioned air out in a rush. It would be several days before he got used to the Delassian heat, but at least he was prepared for it with the lightest uniform material that was allowed. Over the next several weeks, there would be a noticeable drop in temperature as the planet entered its nightwinter season, but still the average temperature drop was only twenty degrees. A true winter season would then follow another "late" summer, as Delas' elliptical orbit would carry it even farther from the sun. Even then, the average temperature dropped only about forty degrees. There was so little tilt of the planet's axis that all seasons were felt equally planet wide.

"Colonel Ishida?" said a cute female voice.

The small black box rising next to him on a metal pole spoke to him before he had a chance to ring their buzzer. Out of instinct Toman searched for, and found, the camera mounted over the gate.

"That is correct," he replied to the box.

"We have been expecting you," said the voice.

With a loud clanking, the metal chain-linked gate began rolling out of his way. After waiting for it to clear the road, the colonel drove forward onto a paved road that led into a parking lot. The gate closed quickly behind him.

Colonel Ishida knew quite well the value of the electrified fence on Delas. All installations outside of the monitored borders of a city had to be protected from the seyzarrs that stalked the land. All parts of Deladin had them, though there were many subspecies. No other native wildlife had yet made as complete evolution from sea life to land dwellers that the seyzarr had. And unfortunately, they were carnivores. The largest weighed as much as a metric ton, though those were rare. Most were the size of a large Earth boar, with savage claws used for hunting and climbing trees, and a bone-hard outer skeleton. They had yet to be taught to fear humans, and probably never would.

The buildings of the institute were beautifully constructed, with shell-like curves and spirals in their design and decorations. Nearly a dozen young men and women were eating out on picnic tables on the lawn, most likely students by the computers that they all carried with them. Many butterflies of bright colors fluttered around the buildings here. Although there were several Earth creatures that were being introduced to this world, the butterflies were not one of them. They were completely native, with biology so similar to their Earth counterparts, that no scientific distinction was thought necessary. The first surveyors were stunned by their existence, and many of the colonists considered their presence as a sign that humans were meant to be here also.

Toman had been told to look for the "main entrance," and since there was no sign in sight, he just chose a large set of doors that had a stone sculpture of an ocean wave in front. As he approached, he was rewarded with the sight of his daughter's face appearing in the glass door.

Just as she opened the door to greet him, his fieldcomm buzzed. Toman groaned at the bad timing. Serina sighed with a knowing smile, and remained silent as Toman answered the call. He did, however, come inside the cool lobby before saying anything.

"What is it, Chains?"

"An event of interest," said Chains cryptically.

"Quickly."

"An unscheduled transport has jumped into the star system without any identification beacon, but is following the correct approach pattern."

"How big is it?"

"About two hundred thousand tons."

"Could be private. Is Delas attempting communications?"

"Not yet."

Toman chewed on his lip briefly as he thought about it.

"Well, call me back if they don't soon."

"Yes, Commander. Chains out."

The colonel folded his fieldcomm, and then gave his daughter a brief hug. Serina hugged him back fiercely, then let go and stepped back. Her mother had been of European descent, but even with all the Asian trademarks that he had given her, Serina still looked so much like Maria. Maybe it was the navy blue eyes. Or perhaps how her hair was so straight and long, exactly like her mother had worn hers.

It had been only two years since he had last seen Serina, but he didn't remember such a resemblance last time.

"You're looking good, Daddy."

"I was about to say the same about you, Serina. Is Kaethan around?"

"He should be here in about an hour. I got a reply from him just before I was told you were coming through the gate."

"Should we wait for him before going on the tour?"

"No. He's been here before and met Kuro."

"Ah yes, the killer whale that you wrote to me about . . ."

"Please say 'orca' around Kuro, Daddy. We don't want to give her a complex."

"Of course." He was just playing with Serina, anyway. "Where do you want to start?"

"Not here. I want to save this building for last because Kuro's in the pool downstairs. We'll start with the labs."

"Sounds good."

Serina was thirty years old now, and he had never asked her whether she was ever getting married. She mentioned boyfriends, off and on, in her letters, but he never asked about them. In some ways he was very curious. In others, he really didn't want to know. He was happy that she was so selective about men, but hoped that she was still happy. Luckily the colonel never had to worry about what to talk about when he was with his daughter. Serina would decide for him.

It was time to relax and enjoy the ride.

It has been 10.0449103 minutes since the unidentified transport arrived in the star system and only now is Blackstone Complex beginning to challenge the intruder. This is an entirely unacceptable reaction time to a potential danger. And our threat circuits continue to trip as no response has yet to be received from the transport.

We continue to monitor data supplied about the intruder from the orbital security arrays, but without an alert being triggered, the arrays will not ignite their fusion reactors for a more powerful scan. Instead, the data that we are fed is limited to simple gravitic curvature and energy emissions. With this we are only able to discern that it is a large transport with a simple dynomagnetic fusion drive that is at least two centuries behind current technology. Many such transports continue to operate, however, for private ventures. This fact supports my Commander's speculation that this may be a poorly maintained merchantman with equipment failure. But this is no excuse for not scheduling their arrival over SWIFT channels beforehand.

We will wait two more minutes for a response from this intruder before we contact our Commander once again. At present approach velocity, we predict entry into Delassian orbit in 39.20 minutes. It is impossible, as of yet, to tell whether the transport may attempt atmospheric insertion.

The tour of the institute was somewhat whirlwind, as Serina seemed in a hurry to get him back to the main building. Their sea-life tanks were not designed for aesthetic viewing of the creatures therein, though Serina told him that a local zoo was being constructed with a large marine section planned. She'd be heavily involved in the design phase, she told him.

What she really wanted to do was introduce him

to Kuro, whom she was telling him about now as they walked back to the building.

"So, anyway," Serina was saying, "my lawyer friend Barry said that we should take Nautilus Enterprises to court and see what happened. The planetary constitution never specified 'Humans' under its labor laws, and he thought that the judges would rule in the orcas' favor."

"So Nautilus had to start paying them." Toman hurried the conversation along.

"Exactly, though Kuro decided to come here instead."

"Did they appeal?"

"No. It wasn't likely that they'd get anywhere. Not on this planet. Besides, the money that they're paying their two orcas isn't close to the money that they would have had to pay their lawyers."

A question occurred to him just then that he had to ask.

"What do they do with their money?"

"Everybody asks me that." Serina laughed. "They all have their own accounts that they can do with what they want. But I know that almost all their money goes directly into a fund we have for shipping more orcas from Earth. It's very expensive."

"Almost all?"

"Well, I do know of one political contribution that Kuro made last year."

Colonel Ishida didn't know if he liked that or not. The orcas shouldn't be allowed to manipulate the process from outside . . .

"Do they pay taxes?" He asked.

"Yep."

Oh, then it's okay, he decided.

The two arrived back at the front doors where they had met and went inside the main building of the institute. Although cool, it was noticeably more humid in this building than the others. There was also a stronger scent of salt water here.

They continued their discussion as Serina led her father to the elevator.

"So why did Nautilus wire up these whales?" The colonel asked.

"Well, first of all, Nautilus didn't do it. Secondly, they aren't whales, orcas are from the dolphin family. In any case, the reason that they chose orcas was obviously because of their high intelligence and size. The psychotronic core, circuitry, power plant, and various transmitters are all installed within their body with no external couplings. That just couldn't be done on any creature smaller than an orca."

"Who did it then?"

"*That* is the biggest reason why I want you to meet Kuro." Her inflection made it plain that she was waiting impatiently for him to ask. "Nautilus never said who they got the orcas from, but Kuro is sure that they were Concordiat Army engineers."

The colonel's left eyebrow shot up at that. He was shocked that the Concordiat would be experimenting with such seemingly innocuous cybernetics on orcas. But as soon as he thought about it a moment, he knew why.

The elevator took them down three levels before sliding to a halt. When the doors opened, a hot and humid blast of saltwater air hit them both. Ahead of them, down a short corridor, sunlight from outside could be seen reflected on a small corner of a large pool.

They walked out into the corridor.

"You want to know why, don't you?" Toman asked.

"You know?" she whispered harshly.

Serina stopped him in his tracks, forcing him to tell her here, before they got to the pool. He couldn't tell whether the look in her eyes was anger or concern. Either way, it looked quite threatening.

"Nothing evil, Serina," he assured her quietly. "The new Bolo Mark Thirty-threes have direct neuro-interfaces between the human commander and the Bolo's neurocore. I'm sure that they were just testing out new circuitry, or finding the effects of long term connections."

"Why do they do that?"

"The interface? Basically, during a fight you can combine the Bolo's reaction time with the commander's immediate decision making. So far, I hear that it's working out quite well."

Serina seemed to have to think about this for a moment, perhaps deciding some moral equation that she had formed. The colonel waited patiently, himself satisfied with the ethics of such experimentation, as long as the creature was not harmed significantly in the process.

When his fieldcomm suddenly buzzed again, it startled Serina.

The colonel shrugged apologetically, and reached for his belt while Serina motioned for him to follow her to the pool.

Toman spoke while he walked.

"Ishida here."

"Update for you on the unidentified transport." Chains' deep voice reverberated between the tiled walls.

"Go ahead."

"Blackstone has been attempting communications, but no response has been received."

"Are they on alert, yet?"

"Negative. Thirty-six minutes to orbit. Vessel maintains exact course and speed of Delas' optimal approach pattern as defined by the Concordiat Registry of Worlds."

"Has the *Aragonne* left orbit yet?

"Affirmative. It jumped out three hours ago."

Colonel Ishida stopped at the end of the corridor

and turned around while Serina continued to the pool's edge and some lawn furniture that was set there.

If this really *was* a private merchantman, then nothing less than extensive battle or collision damage would save its captain from Ishida personally strangling him. Without a beacon, and without working communications, no transport ever should approach an outpost colony. By the book, Blackstone should burn this transport out of the sky once it got within range. But offhand, Toman couldn't remember ever hearing of any innocent vessels being fired on in such a manner. He had, though, heard of many vessels forced to make unannounced, emergency landings without clearance from the planet. The interstellar news always seemed to ignore how stupid it was for the planet to allow it.

"Chains," Ishida gritted his teeth. "If Blackstone doesn't go on full alert in twenty minutes, call me."

"Yes, Commander."

"Wait! Even if they do go on full alert, call me."

"Yes, Commander. Sir, should we upgrade to High Alert Status?"

"Definitely. Ishida out."

Colonel Ishida closed his fieldcomm with an aggravated snap. How dare this captain place this planet's security forces in such a horrible dilemma, he fumed. And to do this while the sector was on alert was inexcusable. If only for that, this transport should be flamed. He'd do it too, if given the chance.

But that decision would not be his. Once this transport was proven to be an enemy, then he would be free to act independently of the planetary government. But until that happened, until a proven threat materialized, it was Concordiat doctrine to confine its actions to the directives presented by the local government. The decision to fire would be with Blackstone Ridge, and probably General Rokoyan. Or even, perhaps, Governor Traine. Career politicians, he was sure.

Incapable of the really hard decisions, no doubt. No one understood how easy it was to have their entire planet incinerated under their feet until they actually saw it happening. By that time, of course, it was too late. Toman had seen it happen twice as Melconian armadas made assaults on planets he was defending. The last time cost him almost all the 39th in a desperate exchange of fire between ground and orbit. Once an alien race decided that the planet being fought over was expendable, no commander could resist the unbelievable bang-for-buck value of a thermonuclear shower.

A feeling of despair swept over the colonel as he turned back to Serina, and the large black shape that was floating in the pool before her. He no longer grew angry at such situations as this, otherwise he could teach Miss Dahlia quite a few more phrases to add to her effective "rhetoric." Dealing with human strengths and weaknesses had been his job for nearly fifty years, and their failures were always just part of the equation.

With a sigh, Ishida advanced to the pool to join his daughter, who was talking joyously into a small transmitter that she was holding. She'd be safe, at least. Most likely this transport really was a private merchantman in trouble, Toman assured himself. But even if it was an alien fireship full of nukes, Chains and Quarter would make sure that the twenty-kilometer radius of land surrounding him would certainly be the safest on the planet.

At last, a torrent of energy floods through my circuitry as my reactor core now burns at full intensity! My sensors come alive and expand my presence to the world around me. Feedback from a thousand senses brings to me a vivid awareness of all that moves and glows. Finally the 39th is at High Alert Status. While Unit DBQ searches the planet for the unknown dangers, I focus my attention on the threat that is known. The intruder approaches, and I can sense the heat of its engines long before my touch finally reaches its hull. Although my sensor technology has been upgraded many times during the course of my duties, the 39th has never been furnished with the latest holistic capabilities. A far better image of this intruder could be formed by the advanced sensors onboard the orbital arrays, but Delas still has yet to activate them. These Class C-11A sensor arrays have very limited lifespans when utilized at full power for long periods of time, and Delas is obviously careful with them.

My first surprise is that the hull that I am touching is NOT made of any kind of duralloy. The hull is thicker and lighter, perhaps of some crystalline build. I note this aberration, but no conclusion can be derived from it. Moving on, I quickly search my sensor data for signs of fissionable material, a sure indicator that this ship would be meant for destruction. I am alerted as my search returns several sources of radioactive emissions, scattered within the cargo hold of the vessel. The concentrations are weapons grade material, but their few numbers and scattered locations would make it impossible to launch them as an effective first strike. Many of my threat circuits deactivate as I determine this vessel incapable of a significant planetary bombardment. Also, I sense no protective fields or screens protecting any part of this ship, nor any hull formations indicative of offensive energy weapons. I thus must believe that this vessel was not meant for warfare.

The possibility still remains, however, that this vessel is a transport that contains an alien invasion force, but its small size and lack of nuclear reactors within would indicate that it could contain few combat units that could hope to match firepower with the 39th. My sensor data is degraded with the distance

*that I must reach, however, and any conclusions that
I would form now would be foolhardy to trust. I will
continue to scan the vessel as it approaches, perhaps
learning more as my senses grow stronger.*

Colonel Ishida was enjoying himself.

As Serina was off changing into her bathing suit,
Toman was having a long conversation with Kuro.
With a cool drink beside him, he was relaxed in a
comfortable chair asking the orca many questions, and
answering several that Kuro had about the military
and the Concordiat. He had been invited to go
swimming along with them, and had indeed been
tempted, but had declined. Perhaps tomorrow, he told
them, though he had several fears that he would have
to work out before then. For now he was satisfied
to be able to say that he actually scratched an orca's
belly.

Throughout his conversation, he had been constantly reevaluating the intelligence of Kuro. His initial
impression had been to speak to her as one would
a twelve-year-old. But although her choice of words
and some grammar was in question, he soon realized
that he was severely underestimating her. Kuro's brain
had interfaced with the neurocore as it grew, integrating its capabilities with her own over thirty years.
Not only did this allow her to store vast amounts of
accurate imagery, it also gave her a computational
capability equal to that of any modern processor.

"So why did you decide to come here instead of
staying with Nautilus?" Colonel Ishida asked Kuro.

"Samson and Velvet are of a different species than
I am. We did not get along."

"Different species? I didn't know there were different species of orcas."

" I am *Orcinus orca*. They are *Orcinus nanus*."

"Samson and . . ." Then a memory hit Toman from
long ago. "Did Serina name you 'Kuro'?"

"Yes. I didn't like my other name. We decided on Kuro, instead."

Serina used to have a black teddy bear named Kuro. Toman only remembered it vaguely from a visit long ago, but he was pleased with himself that he did. He'd have to tease Serina about naming Kuro after her teddy bear later.

"What do Samson and Velvet do for Nautilus?" Toman asked.

"Many things, but mostly they warn their submarine *Surveyor-One* of daeger territories, and protect their swimmers from illcuda and other predators."

"Don't orcas have any problems with them?"

"Daeger are slow and noisy. Illcuda are cowards."

Toman laughed at Kuro's directness.

His daughter returned at that point, now wearing a black, one-piece bathing suit and tucking her long hair into a rubber cap that she had on. For the next ten minutes, Serina and Kuro played and showed him a few tricks. Serina told him of the research and odd jobs that the institute did for local companies, and about their university patronage with the Telville colleges. Several times they tried to get him to join them in the water, but he still refused. By this point he had concluded, however, that Kuro did not have some horrible grudge against the Concordiat for what they had done to her. She was enjoying her life, it seemed, and probably would not eat him if given the chance. Perhaps he would swim with them tomorrow.

During a lull in the talking, Kuro suddenly made a mournful sound from the water. She announced that Peter was waiting for her at their boat, and that she'd have to leave. Serina explained about the eels that they wanted to research, and then they said good-bye to Kuro.

"Kaethan should be arriving pretty soon," Serina said as she climbed out and began drying off. "Did you want to wait upstairs in the lobby while I shower?"

"No, I'll wait for you here."

Serina shrugged and smiled.

"Okay. It'll just be a few minutes."

As Serina left, Colonel Ishida thought that this would be a good time to talk to Chains again. It had been almost twenty minutes, anyway. After taking another drink he reached for his fieldcomm.

"Anything new, Chains?"

"Blackstone is on alert, Commander. The unidentified vessel has still not communicated and is entering orbit on an approach pattern to land at Reims."

Reims was the starport that served south Deladin, located across from Telville on the East Coast. Starveil was actually closer to Telville than Reims was, so the colonel always landed there instead when he visited.

"Have you scanned the ship?"

Ishida, of course, didn't have to ask this question. He knew that Chains and Quarter would be all over the intruder the moment they were given High Alert Status. What he wanted was a report, and Chains gave him all the data that he could while Toman listened without a word. The ship was a design that neither Chains nor Quarter had ever logged before, but that was not unexpected. The Concordiat ruled over hundreds of worlds, many with their own merchant fleets operating independently from the interstellar government. None of the data Chains had compiled could confirm without a doubt that this was an alien ship.

The colonel was happy to learn, however, that very few nukes were onboard. It was definitely *not* a nuclear fireship that was approaching.

"The orbital arrays have ignited their reactors." Chains suddenly announced.

"Can you tap into their scans?"

"Negative. Data from the holistic systems is encrypted."

"Damn."

"What did you say?" Serina said from behind him.

Toman jumped at her voice, and palmed his fieldcomm. Serina was back in her normal clothes and drying her hair with her towel. He tried to think of some excuse for his outburst, but Serina just smiled and spoke before he could form one.

"Security told me that Kaethan just came through the gate. We should go upstairs to meet him."

"You go ahead, I'll be right up."

"Is there something wrong?"

"Maybe."

Serina stared uneasily at him for a moment, but then turned away and headed for the elevator. Smart girl, he thought.

"Quarter?" He brought his fieldcomm up again.

"Yes, Commander," replied the light English accent of his second Bolo.

"Get me General Rokoyan, or whoever is in charge at Blackstone."

"Contacting . . ."

"Call me back when you have someone."

"Affirmative."

Colonel Ishida closed his fieldcomm and relaxed in his chair. He really shouldn't become involved in this situation, but he feared that no one else on the planet was going to confront these people with the cold reality of frontier security procedures. Toman sympathized with Rokoyan, however. The decision to fire would be hard for anyone except a battle-hardened veteran. Rokoyan probably never killed anyone in his life, and the first time was always the most difficult, especially when they weren't firing back.

Kaethan entered the lobby just as Serina was exiting the elevator. Her face lit up with a smile as she saw him, but something was obviously troubling her. Serina's hug was light and quick, with her wet hair only getting his pale green shirt damp on the shoulder.

"Hi, Kaethan." Serina's greeting lacked her usual spunk.

"What's wrong, Serina? Did father get called away again?"

It seemed like a good guess to Kaethan.

"No, he's downstairs," she glanced back at the elevator, "but something is wrong. He's been on the phone constantly talking to his Bolos. Do you know of anything going on?"

Kaethan shook his head. "No." He shrugged. "Angelrath has the sector on alert, but that's usual after another one of those probes is caught sneaking around."

The alerts never caused any concerns with the DDF formations. Only the planetary defenses at Blackstone Ridge ever cared much about them. At no time in Delassian history had the DDF ever "really" been on alert.

"Did father meet Kuro?" Kaethan changed the subject.

"Oh, sure. He didn't swim with her, though. Maybe you both can tomorrow."

"Well," Kaethan's voice took an edge to it, "I found out this morning that I certainly have the time for it."

Serina smiled, but before she could say anything the elevator doors slid open and their father walked out. The colonel did indeed look nervous, but Kaethan could see no difference to how he usually looked when the two were together. His smile, as always, seemed forced.

"Hi, Son," he said as he approached and extended his hand. "Captain," he then corrected.

"Hi, Father," Kaethan replied simply and they shook hands briefly. The thought of kidding his father about still being a colonel crossed his mind, but was instantly rejected for obvious reasons. He had been planning a witty remark about coming to the institute to recruit marine mammals, but suddenly it didn't seem as witty as it had in the car.

The result, of course, was a moment of uncomfortable silence.

But it was just a moment before Serina jumped in. "Are you two hungry?"

"Yes," they both said at the same time.

Their father's fieldcomm beeped suddenly, causing his hand to shoot for his belt in response. The colonel was suddenly embarrassed by this, however, and his face turned apologetic.

"Sorry, but something serious might be happening."

Serina and Kaethan both nodded, understanding, and let their father retreat a few steps from them.

"Who have you got?" they heard him say into his phone. Then, "Blessed mother . . . uh . . . what's happening now?"

Kaethan's interest peaked at this. Not only did it sound like something militarily important was occurring somewhere around Delas, but his father may have *almost* showed an unprecedented display of emotion. Either would be a first.

"Any ideas?" Serina asked him quietly.

"None."

His father was pacing now, listening intently. Kaethan and Serina waited patiently. A couple students came through the front doors at this time, but paid them little attention. But as the doors were closing, a sharp crack of distant thunder echoed through them into the lobby.

"I hope that it doesn't rain," Serina complained.

"I don't think that was lightning." Kaethan now started growing nervous.

Their father stopped in his tracks and peered outside the glass doors, though nothing but the parking lot could be seen.

"A warning shot?" The colonel growled, obviously not happy with the half-measure. "Any reaction?"

"Blackstone just fired their Hellbore," Kaethan enlightened his sister. "And if we heard that all the way down here, then that means that their target is already in the atmosphere, and nearby."

Their father had not returned to his pacing, instead he just stood there staring blankly outside, tapping his foot.

"*Damn!*" Their father yelled suddenly. It was the kind of exclamation that someone might sound if an opposing team just scored a last second touchdown to win a game. "Lock on and ask Blackstone for permission to fire!"

The target must have dropped below Blackstone's horizon, Kaethan surmised.

"What do you mean 'nearby'?" Serina asked.

"Overhead, probably." Kaethan shook his head in dismay.

"I'm going to look outside," Serina said in a rush and ran outside.

Kaethan, however, much preferred to hear this conversation occurring, even though he was getting only one side of it. A ship must be entering the atmosphere with unknown credentials. Most likely it was on approach pattern to Reims, which often passed right over them. Aliens, perhaps? Smugglers? Pirates? His mind ran wild with the possibilities.

His father was silent for a long time, though Kaethan couldn't tell whether he was listening to anything. At one point, however, his father's focus shifted over to him and their eyes met. It was a strange moment, where Toman shook his head and rolled his eyes in exasperation. Kaethan felt oddly close to his father at that moment for some reason.

Then his sister barged back in.

"I saw something big," she announced. "A transport, I think. Looked like it was heading for Reims. Too many clouds to see it for long."

His father paid attention to that, but then suddenly

turned away as someone must have been saying something again on his fieldcomm.

"Clean up an Isis and ready it," the colonel then said coldly. "Ask Blackstone for clearance."

Kaethan knew what an "Isis" was, and his stomach dropped. His father's Bolos were just ordered to ready a nuke for launch. He and his mother had often read the colonel's letters together, and he learned much of the current equipment and lingo from them. To "clean" it, he knew, meant to reconfigure it for reduced fallout. Even with that, however, Kaethan doubted that Blackstone Ridge would clear it. Unless things got desperate, there was no way that Delas would use a nuke within the atmosphere.

Serina now decided that this was a good time to sit down, and dropped down on a big chair that was nearby. Kaethan remained standing.

"Where's it heading?" Was his father's next question.

The colonel then started looking frantically around the lobby, searching for something that he was obviously not finding.

"Did—" His father cut short, stopping his search, "Yeah, I was expecting that. Battle Reflex Mode. Track it as best you can and keep trying to get hold of Rokoyan."

His father closed his fieldcomm with a crack of metal against metal.

"Are we being invaded?" Serina was first to speak.

"Looks like it, Serina," Toman said sadly, looking at his children. "Son, their transport is setting down somewhere between here and Reims. They just took out your arrays and will probably bring down everything else along with it. Best you mobilize your battalion and hit them as hard and as fast as possible. You can't let them dig in."

"Just one transport?" Kaethan wondered.

"Just one for now, but I certainly expect more."

"What about Chains and Quarter?"

"I can't deploy them yet." The colonel shook his head. "With only one turret defending this planet, I don't want my Bolos caught flatfooted in rough terrain when a warship squadron enters orbit."

"What should I do?" Serina asked helplessly from her chair.

Kaethan could see his father mentally shift gears as his expression softened. He feared his father would just say something comforting and unhelpful that Serina would hate. Instead, he gave Serina something to do.

"You should probably call Peter to get back here, and warn people what's going on. Tell everyone to stay off the highways as much as possible and stay home."

"I should get going." Kaethan announced then. "Will you be heading back up to Starveil?"

His father shook his head.

"No. I'll be staying where the action is. I need to see what we're up against."

Kaethan's DDF issue handphone chose that moment start squealing horribly. The captain fumbled to turn it off as Serina winced against the noise.

"That's my call. Wish me luck."

Before Kaethan could go, though, Serina jumped up from chair and caught him in a big hug. The captain returned it as best he could, then pulled away.

"Don't get hurt," Serina ordered as she let go.

"Good luck," his father told him.

Kaethan motioned a cursory salute to his father as he pushed open the doors into the hot, moist outside air. He half walked, half jogged to his vehicle, passing blissfully unaware students along the way. The captain had never led troops into actual combat before, of course, and countless questions hounded him now. Had he treated their exercises too much like a game before, he wondered? How would his battalion react now that it was real? Strangely enough, though, it was excitement, not fear, that was filling him. That was likely to change, Kaethan knew, once the shells started flying. But until then, this was the emotion that the captain wanted his troops to tap from him.

That and confidence, of course.

But with his father on the planet, he suddenly worried about the latter.

Our Commander has finally spoken with General Rokoyan of the Delassian Defense Command. Much of the conversation was spoken with voices raised many decibels higher than what is normal for effective dialogue. There are many differences of opinion on what strategy to take in eliminating this incursion, aggravated by questions of authority between the DDC and the Concordiat. As the planetary ground forces mobilize, the 39th holds ground on the flat plains south of Starveil. Our Commander grows impatient for a strike to their beachhead, but his plan to dedicate Unit DBQ to this attack was withdrawn when we were finally allowed full access to the DDC sensor net.

The planet Delas is surrounded.

Although the orbital arrays have been eliminated, ground-based passive detectors scattered over the Delassian surface continue to monitor glimmers of fusion drives maneuvering into position around the planet. For now they wait outside the range of my active scans, but a rush is obviously being organized to test our defenses. Every quarter of Delas' Northern and Southern Hemispheres are being threatened, along with both poles. Against a well-defended planet, this would be a foolish and disastrous plan, allowing all defenses to be utilized against the assault. But our enemy obviously does not mind wasting lives and material against us while their previous insertion no doubt catalogs our every response.

And unfortunately they will find our response to

be limited. Unless our Commander's plan fools them, our enemy will know that the far side of the planet is completely undefended. Their strategies displayed so far indicate an 80.31 percent chance that a large invasion force awaits the result of this attack. Unit DBQ and myself must do our best to discourage our enemy from deploying it.

"All is ready, Is-kaldai." The projected visage of Irriessa filled the rear wall of Keertra's command chambers. His hood was extended in exhilaration. "These aliens bestowed upon us a gift when they fired their energy cannon at your ship. Removing it now should be a simple matter."

As Keertra had hoped, the Ad-akradai's vehemence against him had dissipated now that combat had begun. Getting Riffen's most loyal commander to trust him, though, would still be a great challenge.

"Indeed, Ad-akradai," Keertra replied gloriously. "And it fired at such range that I dare believe that it may be the only protection that this outpost maintains! Would it not shock our timid Council if we were to take this planet ourselves!"

"Split between our factions equally, of course."

"Of course, Irriessa," he said with as amused an expression as he could present. "The Council would accept nothing less."

For a moment, Keertra could see his rival's commander lose himself in the promise of such glory. His ice-blue eyes became unfocused, and his hood expanded to its full size. The blood vessels that branched out within bulged prominently with a noticeable pulse.

But then the commander's military experience returned in a flash. He suddenly looked at Keertra in defiance.

"We should not talk about these things before the battle is won, and our enemy lie dead at our feet." Irriessa scolded Keertra, and perhaps himself.

"You are right, Irriessa. They may yet surprise us. Will your warship captains now follow my commands?

"They will, Is-kaldai. We should begin immediately."

"I will give the order."

"Is-kaldai . . ." Irriessa delayed, for what he was about to say was difficult. "I was wrong to doubt Khoriss' mission. I listen to your orders now with greater respect."

"Thank you, Irriessa. I'm sure we will learn much from each other before this is over."

"Perhaps."

The communication channel closed as Irriessa shut his eyes in respect. Keertra sat back in his chair, relishing the victories that he was winning, on the planet and here also. If indeed these aliens were as weak as they seemed, then he might just have to expand his plans. Becoming *Mor-verridai* could be meaningless if the remaining Is-kaldai were to claim vast new tracts of alien territory and resources, without suffering disabling casualties in the process. It would be better, he mused, if these aliens were a bit tougher. Just enough to keep the remaining Is-kaldai occupied while he eliminated the entire royal family, and its lineage, back home.

This goal had been his obsession ever since the Council began serious discussions on attacking this world. Keertra had realized from the beginning that a war of this scale could not have a committee directing it. There must be an overall commander, and historically this was the Mor-verridai. Yet, this was not a possibility considering the depths that their ruling clan had fallen to. They had squandered all their riches, uncaring for centuries, while the Council methodically stripped them of their powers. Now they had become corrupt in their misery, so much so that even the *Avocrahn*, the fanatic warrior clan sworn to protect the Mor-verridai, were openly rebellious. And they were the key that Keertra hoped to exploit. Although he would lose a great deal in this raid, he believed that if his many *surias* struck swiftly and cleanly against the Mor-verridai, the *Avocrahn* would gladly swear loyalty to him at a time when the Kezdai needed a strong leader so desperately.

It was a goal that every day seemed nearer to his grasp. Soon, now, many operatives had to be put in motion. But he couldn't waste time planning for them yet, not until this assault was completed. Irriessa was correct. These aliens might yet have some blades hidden beneath their cloaks.

As Captain Kaethan Ishida sped his vehicle up to the underground bunkers of the Alabaster Coast Heavy Armor, he was pleased to see that most of his personnel had already arrived. Many of the huge steel doors that led into the bunkers had been lowered, revealing the forward hulls of the Templar Mark XIs that were housed within. The roaring of their gigantic turbines was making the ground vibrate as he stepped out of his vehicle.

Ten nuclear-safe bunkers housed thirty Templars of the Alabaster Coast Heavy Armor, five bunkers on each side of what was called Armor Alley. Twenty-meter wide ramps led down to the three-inch thick steel doors that rose up out of the ground to seal the Templars inside. The doors could be lowered quickly when danger threatened, or just dropped if the base lost power. A large sign at the entrance of Armor Alley presented in large letters the full designation of this unit: Alabaster Coast Heavy Armor, Alabaster Guard, Telville Corps.

Fort Hilliard was home to the Alabaster Guard, which was comprised of several battalions and lesser formations, formed from the population south of Telville. To the east of Telville was Fort Riley and the Chandoine Guard. And to the north was Fort Owen and the Tigris Guard. Most city-states on Delas were organized this way, with all forts kept in competition with each other for honors, and therefore a bigger slice of the defense spending for the next year. It was just the kind of arrangement that you'd expect from a corporate run government, but in fact, Kaethan thought it was quite effective. Not only were the forts always striving for more honors, but a definite sense of regiment was inspired throughout the militias.

Of course, combined exercises were sometimes a problem.

The composition of the Alabaster Guard had not changed since Candlelith purchased the last of their antiquated 150-ton Saladin Medium Tanks four years ago. Their main strike arm now consisted of Kaethan's battalion of Templars, and three brigades of mechanized infantry in armed Haulers. Preceding them into combat were three recon companies driving armed Haulers and four weakly armored grav-cars. Twelve companies of various caliber artillery provided battalion and regimental level support to their formations. And protecting against air infiltration, and providing emergency anti-armor fire, were four TurboFalcon missile batteries and two ion-bolt defense towers that Telsteel Industries donated to the Telville Corps from their private stocks.

Templar One, Kaethan's tank, was in the first bunker, right side, of Armor Alley. The blast door was opened wide, so he didn't bother to enter through the small, security-conscious blockhouse on top. Instead, he just ran down the ramp and into the shelter. His driver, Sergeant Zen Pritchard, was climbing along the outside of the vehicle, checking the outer systems. And with the sudden flash of their spotlight, it was obvious that his gunner, Corporal Andrea Sellars, was on the inside doing her part.

The Metallicast Industries Templar Mark XI was *not* the latest, or greatest, in the Concordiat arsenal.

It *was* cost effective, and low enough technology to be supportable by local industry. Its three hundred fifty tons of duralloy armor and weapons made it slow and unwieldy, and wasn't allowed on local roads because it would tear apart the pavement. The sixty-foot long railgun, stretching almost as far behind the tank as in front, threatened to topple the tank over if fired to the side while on the move. Stabilizing legs had to be extended to give them a steady platform for firing the weapon. And its four Rapier missiles were dangerously indiscriminate when they lost their assigned target and began their search program for a replacement.

That said, Kaethan adored the Templar.

As awkward as the railgun was, it lived up to its promise of being able to take a chunk out of any known armor, including the latest endurochrome plate on his father's Bolos. The entire weapons assembly was mounted on hydraulic jacks that could lift the railgun fourteen inches to fire over a rise, and then drop it down again. Its two ion-bolt point defense turrets were excellent in protecting the tank against infantry and missiles. But most of all, feeling the entire hulk rock as the railgun was fired gave Kaethan such an adrenaline rush that he'd never be satisfied with anything less.

"Permission to come onboard, Sergeant!" Kaethan yelled.

Zen grabbed onto the barrel of the forward ion-bolt turret as he turned his head. Although in regulation jungle camouflage trousers, his battalion assigned top was replaced by a white tee shirt with an advertisement for a local pub. Zen was usually better at protocol than this. Whatever the reason was for it, Kaethan really didn't care.

"Almost set, Captain," Zen said. "Are we going to bother rolling out?"

"This isn't a drill, Sergeant!" Kaethan told him

as he leapt up to the first footing. "We've just been invaded."

The captain ignored Zen's startled glare and made his way over to his command hatch. Sergeant Pritchard was a very competent soldier when he wasn't suffering from a hangover from the prior night. He was thirty-nine years old, with saltwater-damaged light brown hair. The Guard was a serious commitment to him as supplemental income for his small fiberglass boat business. He never missed a muster, and had been fully certified in Templar maintenance. But Kaethan was sure that Zen never expected that he'd have to fight.

Kaethan's command compartment was cramped and simple. Large, touch sensitive, configurable control panels were in front and on both sides. Small boxes at the bottom of the main display showed a camera image of an empty driver's compartment, and Andrea working hard in the gunner's compartment under the turret.

"Good day," Andrea said as she noticed his arrival on her own display.

"Bad day, Private," Kaethan corrected. "We've been invaded."

The captain didn't know much about Andrea except that she had a big boyfriend named Steve in the Alabaster 1st Mechanized. That stopped any extraneous socializing, at least any that he'd initiate. She was rather pretty, with short auburn hair and an excessive amount of freckles. At twenty-two, she was attending a local college and probably was in the Guard just for the money. She had been assigned to his battalion last season, starting out very jumpy in the gunner's chair, but by now had become quite proficient. Kaethan had no idea how she'd react with live rounds coming at her.

"What do you mean, 'invaded'?" Andrea pestered him.

A command message was waiting for Kaethan as he poked in his password on the virtual keypad that popped up on his right-hand display. On any normal day, this message would say that this had all been a drill and everyone should go home. Today it would be different, no doubt.

But as the command message popped up, the captain was stunned to see just two words, "Stand By." Kaethan wasn't surprised that Colonel Neils was keeping the soldiers in the dark, but he *was* expecting something to be told the battalion commanders.

With a poke of a virtual button, Kaethan hailed his commander, requesting direct communications. He was surprised when it was almost immediately accepted by the colonel himself. After muting his cabin speakers, he activated the channel.

"Just stand by, Captain." Colonel Neils was ready with his orders. "Remain at full alert until further notice."

"Colonel!" Kaethan stopped him before he had the chance to close the channel. "We should move out as quickly as possible! We have to hit them before they dig in!"

Kaethan hadn't given much thought to his father's advice, but it sounded reasonable enough. Getting a Guard unit to aggressively initiate contact with an enemy outside of their territory, though, would be difficult.

The colonel's expression of determination was replaced by one of interest.

"You've obviously been better briefed than I was, Captain. General Calders is currently in conference and hasn't had time to tell us much, other than a hostile warship just set down somewhere on the planet."

General Calders was commander of Telville Corps, assigned by the mayor of Telville five years ago from the Chandoine Guard. Kaethan didn't know much about him.

"An alien transport has landed between here and Reims. We should roll out and hit them as quickly as possible before they can get organized."

Kaethan could see Neils process this information and consider it. Satisfied that he had gotten his point across, the captain just waited.

But then the colonel shook his head.

"Just stand by, Captain," he said. "Stay in your bunkers."

Neils closed the channel without waiting for a reply. With a growl, Kaethan did what he was told. The DDF colonel was a good man, with smart strategic sense. Kaethan was sure that he'd push for an immediate attack with General Calders, but obviously didn't want to commit the entire Alabaster Guard into going in alone.

It would have been far better if this transport had come down directly into Reims, or Telville for that matter. No one, then, would have hesitated in sending their formations to their rescue. Instead, by landing between several cities, it would now be up to a committee to decide who would go in, and in what force. General Rokoyan was nominally in charge, for now, but it would still take a committee vote to make it official. It took a while for confederacies to get organized, Kaethan grumbled. Until then they'd follow the same motto the military had followed for centuries, "Hurry up and wait."

Target deviating . . . correcting for parabolic course adjustment . . .

Far to the north, Blackstone is firing its Hellbore, but it is far too busy defending itself to help Unit DBQ and myself with the spearhead of four alien frigates that are making their high-speed run over the planet. A swarm of missiles is cascading down on the turret's position, and their defenses will be sorely tried. The crackle of high frequency radio static that I am

*recording is sure indication that the ion-bolt defense
towers surrounding the turret are in frantic operation.*

*Beginning initialization of all active arrays . . .
increasing speed to one hundred fifty kilometers per
hour . . .*

*The wide expanse of flat savannah is allowing us
to attain great speed while still maintaining a stable
weapons platform. There is no indication as of yet
that the frigates have detected us. The thunderheads
that rage above us will cover us until we go active.*

*The transports that are closing in on the planet are
no longer a concern. Those that are above us will be
dealt with simply enough when the frigates have been
eliminated. As for the ships entering the atmosphere
on the blind side of the planet, the largest ten transports have all now been acquired by the Isis missiles
that we fired several minutes ago. As of yet, no point
defense fire is being recorded.*

*Frigates have now entered range! The 39th lights
up the skies in a blinding shower of high-energy
radiation! The lead warship is spotlighted in brilliant
acquisition, and my Hellbore aligns to perfect azimuth
within 2.10498 seconds!*

Target locked . . . chambers critical . . . FIRE!

*The entire thunderhead above us ionizes as my
Hellbore rips through its center. An explosion of lightning erupts between it and the storm clouds around
it, as if some terrible god had awakened inside in a
rage. Up into orbit, I see my lance rake a deep,
burning wound down the belly of my target. Just a
fraction of a second later, another stream of fire slashes
savagely through its drive section as Quarter finishes
off their lead ship in a blinding explosion of its fusion
core.*

*I turn hard to port and briefly take to the air as
the savannah surface rises below me. Radioactive fires
incinerate an acre of grassland behind me as the*

remaining warship's automated defenses attempt to strike back. Kilometers to the northwest, Quarter is also briefly lighted by the bright red beams of our opponent's nuclear cannons driving into the earth like a flaming spear.

But they are striking where we have been, not where we are.

My speed now approaches two hundred kilometers per hour as the 39th acquires our next targets. A distant pain begins to grow in my self-awareness network as my drive-train slowly overheats. Soon I will have to reduce speed. An onslaught of echoes suddenly assaults our active arrays, but this is a feeble attempt to jam our advanced electronics. The echoes are easily filtered, and once again their frigates glow brilliantly in our sights!

We fire again! This time we have acquired separate targets, hoping we can finish them off before they redirect their weapons to the Blackstone turret. All are within its range, and we fear that the turret's battlescreens will not stand up to the surprising power of the alien's cannons.

My Hellbore strikes true, blasting clean through the center of my target. This frigate was not as well armored as the last, and I expect it is dead, though I will finish it off shortly. Quarter's fire, however, once again strikes through the drive chamber of his target, and the frigate explodes in a flash of particles and debris. I am impressed at my compatriot's effective fire, and I send him a message of respect through brigade channels.

The final remaining frigate returns fire, with two nuclear cannons blasting large craters in the Delassian soil far to my rear. His silhouette changes as I detect his change in course. He seeks to escape. I acquire him in my sights, but I am suddenly distracted. What I have now noticed is the high-speed passage of intense gravitic signatures into the atmosphere above

Blackstone. They are objects so dense that their effects on the continuum are still noticeable even though they are far within the planet's gravity well.

Even as I fire at the last remaining frigate, I am refocusing my arrays upon the targets descending on Blackstone. The objects are thin and long, about thirty meters from nose to tail, but I am having great difficulty locking them into my fire control. They have no energy or emissions to focus my sensors onto. My arrays detect them only as a whisper, leading me to believe that they are encased in an energy absorbent jacket of ceramics. And if I was having such difficulty locking onto them from their side, it was likely that Blackstone couldn't see them at all from head-on!

Not waiting for kill confirmation on the frigate, I slew my turret to the north and fire my Hellbore into the midst of the signatures, just before they fall below the horizon. Without a lock, I am doubtful that I actually hit any of these objects, but that wasn't my purpose. I fired as a warning to Blackstone of their presence, and I am comforted at a sudden flurry of fire that I detect lancing up into the sky.

Unit DBQ fires again, and then one more time, to finish off the armored hulks that were floating lifeless in orbit. This while I remain vigilant, watching the skies. I could detect no more such signatures descending, but I fear that there is no reason for more.

Blackstone turret is silent.

The command center is still communicating, but a massive magnetic pulse, centered at Blackstone, is near sure sign of a Hellbore misfire.

The oncoming transports surprisingly continue their track, honorably executing their orders without hope of survival. Unit DBQ and myself will make short work of each as they come within range. We can expect no help from Blackstone, though. They had effectively fended off all the high-tech missiles and the shaped atomic warheads that were sent at

*them, but in the end failed against a simple flight
of spears.*

*Our Isis missiles have successfully intercepted ten
transports attempting insertion on the far side of the
planet, though four others will make it through. Our
Commander hopes our opponents will now believe that
missile batteries are scattered over the entire surface
of Delas, defending it from all approach.*

In fact, only the Hellbores of the 39th remain.

The briefing from his advisors had been a dismal
affair, Keertra pondered. It had been a disaster, they
had moaned. The loss of life had been . . . well . . .
significant. The loss of the frigates *Taitta* and *Kiosia*,
in addition to Riffen's ships, was heartbreaking.

Perhaps his advisors were serious, but Keertra
hoped that they had been putting on as convincing
a performance before Irriessa as he had been. Most
of the troops lost in the debacle were Ad-akradai
Riffen's. The transports were expendable. And their
two frigates were ancient and had already been
stripped of almost all of their valuable systems and
most of their shielding. Riffen had lost far more in
his two frigates, which seemed to hold up to the
alien's firepower little better than his own vessel.

The amount of information that was gained, however, was enormous.

The point defense capabilities of these aliens was
very impressive. None of the missiles fired against
the northern orbital defense battery penetrated their
screen of energy weapons. Only Keertra's depleted
uranium spears, launched by his command ship,
survived the fusillade of fire rising to protect their
turret. These simple weapons that Keertra often
employed were launched against the suspected
underground complex beneath the turret, but were
actually what finally silenced the turret itself. Keertra,
by accident, had found an effective weapon against

these aliens. Unfortunately, missiles were the barrage weapons of choice among the Kezdai, and it seemed likely that the invasion forces would have to retool before they set off. This would delay them, perhaps even several years, but a warrior must attack their enemies' weakness, not their strength. And point defense was obviously one of their strengths. At least, Keertra mused, the Kezdai had finally found a use for their long-spent and useless uranium caches.

The power of the alien's energy weapons was indeed terrifying. Still, fixed emplacements would not be a problem. As protected as a ground battery might be, overwhelming it was just a matter of scale and manner. Against fixed fortifications, the attacker would always have the advantage, for it was he who chose how the battle would be fought.

Two of the alien's three ground batteries, however, were mobile. The very concept stunned Keertra when the combat logs of the *Taitta* and *Kiosia* were analyzed. Without doubt, the counterbattery computers onboard the frigates detected a considerable transverse motion of the ground batteries, even as they were firing upon them. Unfortunately, the frigates' computers had little capability to account for this motion, and their return fire was wide of their mark. Adaptations would be made to their fire control, he was promised, but Keertra was dubious. No one in his Council could imagine what kind of machine could accurately wield so much firepower, and still travel so quickly over the ground. Neither did he have any remaining expendable warships to find out more about them. These mobile batteries were an unknown, and Keertra feared that they would remain so.

But they could be avoided, the Is-kaldai was sure. Only missiles rose up to fend off his transports over the oceans of this world. And there were only a few.

Several transports had made planetfall unscathed, and even now were seeking land to deploy their troops. Unless these troublesome mobile batteries could fly, the majority of this planet was protected from orbit only by missiles. And missiles could be intercepted.

This phase of their operation was over. It was now time for the final phase to begin.

Keertra entered his command chambers in a rush, his crimson robe flowing behind him. A narrow beam transmission to the planet had been prepared, and Ad-akradai Khoriss was told to stand by for orders. It was time for the ground war to commence.

Khoriss was his most able commander, just as Irriessa was that for Riffen. He was also Keertra's younger brother, forcing Riffen to risk only his greatest Ad-akradai for the cause. In truth, however, Khoriss was expendable. Although his brother was indeed a master tactician, that wasn't what Keertra needed in the fight to come. What he needed were ruthless commanders, willing to follow Keertra's every command without question or consideration. Khoriss would never betray him or his plans, but Keertra could not trust him to wield his blade against many whom he had foolishly befriended.

If Khoriss survived his mission, Keertra would be pleased. But if he did not, it would be no great loss. The public mourning for his sacrifice Keertra would demand would last for years. But Keertra would be little inconvenienced, himself.

"Khoriss, my brother, how goes things?"

His brother looked uneasy as his projected image stood before Keertra on the wall. Behind him, the nearly emptied cargo hold of his transport was still swarming with troops and workers, offloading supplies. From the view outside the ship, it could be seen that it was night there.

"Our forces are deployed, Is-kaldai, without finding much resistance. A few farming settlements are scattered through the terrain, with few armaments to protect them. We retrieved several of these aliens for later study, provided we escape the planet. We are preparing a preliminary biologic analysis, now."

"Excellent, Khorrss. Do ground forces advance against you, yet?"

"We launch surveillance drones at sporadic intervals, but they are destroyed as quickly as they approach the cities, just as our perimeter destroys theirs. A brief image taken by our last drone shows forces massing along the roadway to the west. To the east, forces around their starport appear to be just digging in. No other city is a threat to us yet on the roadway that we have set down near."

"Good! Then you are free to throw your entire strength against the forces to the west."

"That is what I plan, Is-kaldai. Once they are destroyed, I can then test the fortifications to the east."

"Learn all you can, Khoriss, even if it means losing your battles. We must learn how they fight in the field, and how they defend their positions."

"I understand." Khoriss bowed his head slightly. "How are Riffen's troops cooperating?"

"All is well, Is-kaldai. They follow my orders."

"The transports that survived insertion are attempting to reinforce you, but that will be all you can expect. Our mission now relies entirely on you."

"It is enough, Is-kaldai."

Suddenly the cargo hold lights dimmed behind Khoriss, and a warning klaxon sounded. Bright flashes of light lit up the thick foliage outside the wide-open doors of the transport as point defense dischargers opened fire into the sky.

"We are under attack," Khoriss announced. "We have to break contact!"

His brother didn't wait for an answer before closing the channel. This was a punishable offense, but

Keertra was willing to overlook it, considering the circumstances.

A narrow beam transmission was supposedly undetectable by any known technology. The Is-kaldai preferred not to believe that the aliens had triangulated Khorris' position from that. He hoped, instead, that their position was determined by other surveillance, and the timing of the attack had been coincidental.

Perhaps, though, that should be tested, Keertra considered.

The Alabaster Guard had moved out.

But it had not gone far. It had taken them hours to fight through the civilian traffic to get to the east-west highway to Reims, and once they were there, they were told to wait again. A light rain fell from the night sky as Kaethan was escorted to a local inn. Rather than set up camp, Colonel Neils just decided to move into its lobby. The inn had provided several makeshift tables, and it was strange to see everyone sitting in bright red, plush chairs around them. A large, flat screen display was standing on its tall tripod behind the colonel, blank for now.

Kaethan was stunned to see that one of the many uniforms in the lobby was Concordiat desert gray. His father was here.

Also a surprise was the familiar face of Walter Rice approaching him with a big smile plastered upon it. In his left hand Walter held a glass of local wine, while in the other he held a packet of important looking papers. Why he was here was quite beyond Kaethan.

"Hey," Walter called cheerfully, "looks like I've been attached to you."

It took a few moments for Kaethan to understand what this meant. The realization compounded his confusion.

"You're taking your toy into the field with us?"

"Corporal Bicks will be driving, of course. It's the next logical step." Walter confirmed. Then in a hushed tone, "And it's officially called a Sentinel, now. Prototype, of course. I'd appreciate it if you don't call it a toy."

"Aren't they risking a lot by throwing you out into the field?"

"Me? Personally? No. The system works now, I just have to fine-tune it. No better place than real combat, eh?"

Kaethan couldn't tell if Walter really was this cheerful about it, or whether it was just an act. He suspected, though, that it was real, and it annoyed the hell out of him.

"I saw that your father was here," Walter said, nodding to him. "You didn't tell me before that he brought two Bolo Mark Thirties to the planet."

"Units DBC and DBQ," Kaethan informed him. "Chains and Quarter."

"I'd love to take a look at one."

"I might visit after all this. I'll try to bring you along."

" 'C' is for Chains, and 'Q' is for Quarter . . . what does 'DB' stand for?"

"You don't want to know."

Outside, another command vehicle skidded to a stop and a group of officers jumped out and headed for the door.

"Why 'Quarter'? As in, he gives none?"

"Something like that."

No more could be said about it however, because the last collection of majors and captains just entered the room, dripping wet. With their arrival, everyone started taking places. His father had been talking directly with Colonel Neils, but now searched for and found Kaethan as Neils attended to his presentation display. Toman gave up his red plush seat to stand with his son and Walter around the perimeter of chairs.

"How are things going?" Toman asked as everyone was quieting.

"No problems so far," Kaethan only said.

The flicker of the colonel's display was the signal for everyone to quiet down, and no more words were said. This was promised to be a short briefing, only detailing the operation that was being planned, nothing more. The notice that was sent to the battalion commanders mentioned the temporary loss of the Blackstone turret, and the downing of most of the attacking fleet, but offered few details. Kaethan hoped he would have time to talk to his father after the briefing to find out more.

"Good evening, gentlemen," Colonel Neils began. "This meeting will be brief, after which we will be moving out. The Chandoine Guard headed out an hour ago, and we have to get on their tails. Their lead elements have already passed the Tigris River Bridge and are deploying there. We will then be leap-frogging ahead of them."

The flat-screen display was now shining with a full color map of south Deladin being presented to everyone. The east-west highway was highlighted prominently.

"The enemy transport that slipped through our guard this morning set down somewhere in the area highlighted in blue."

A light blue oval appeared then, highlighting a large area of rocky terrain about midway between Telville and Reims in the center of southern Deladin.

"Travelers on the highway reported seeing the transport set down south of the road, but we have conflicting accounts of exactly where. About thirty minutes ago, a narrow beam, subspace transmission was detected by the starports at Reims and Starveil. Their triangulation information was forwarded to the Chandoine

Guard who then bombarded the position with their heavy rocket batteries. There is no way to tell whether this was the transport, or what the effect of our attack was, but this position has now become the primary objective of Telville Corps."

A bright white triangle appeared on the screen, near center of the blue oval.

"Alien infantry have been reported attacking several plantations along the Witch River. One plantation owner who escaped in his grav-car reported alien infantry in full suits of body armor that were impervious to the shotguns that they use to fend off seyzarrs. Their infantry are using needle rifles and are being transported by wheeled armored vehicles, with larger needle rifles mounted on turrets. Also, escorting these vehicles are other wheeled vehicles that we were told discharge lightning bolts at their targets. These could be electron guns or perhaps ion cannons. So far, this man's emergency call is the only information that we have received concerning the makeup of the ground forces that we will be facing."

As Colonel Neils was talking, the map highlighted the Witch River, and then the plantations that were hit. Also highlighted now was a system of back roads the led up into the mountains of southern Deladin and several small mining communities there. It would be difficult to use them for flanking operations, however, since they went so deeply into the mountains before connecting.

But then the colonel turned the display off. Neils always finished his briefings by turning off the display and giving a motivational speech while he had everyone's attention.

"This transport was sent in before all others, trusted to hold a beachhead for their invasion to set down within. We believe that these are elite troops with their best weaponry. They are also on the defensive in rough terrain, fully deployed and raiding the surrounding territory at will."

So far, Kaethan thought, this wasn't very motivational. Neils usually had a good finish, however.

"On the other hand, our enemy is heavily outnumbered, and in a territory that they are not accustomed to. We must use these advantages as best we can. This beachhead must be eliminated as quickly as possible, for our command believes that their last attack was only a test of our defenses. Their next attack will be in force. This pocket must be cleared by then so that we can be free to react to their invasion."

Kaethan suddenly had the idea that the Telville Corps was being asked to charge their positions in a direct assault. Certainly their leaders realized that this was exactly what the aliens would be expecting, and would be best prepared for . . .

"Any questions?" Colonel Neils opened the floor.

"What will Tigris Guard be doing?" asked Major Thurman of 1st Mechanized.

"They will be supporting us, of course, though farther back. Depending on how we manage, they will either reinforce us, or be held back in protection of Telville along with the Chandoine Guard. Any other questions?"

Colonel Neils was making it plain that he was *not* encouraging questions, only suffering them. If anyone had any, they'd better be good.

"Will Reims be sending any forces from the other side?" asked Captain Held of 3rd Recon.

"Negative. We can't lose the starport, gentlemen. Any other questions?"

No one said anything, though everyone may have just felt so blindsided by that last news that they couldn't speak. Colonel Neils wrapped things up quickly.

"Then head back to your units, gentlemen. Detailed

marching orders are waiting for you there. Dismissed! Captain Ishida?"

Kaethan was just about to start questioning his father when Colonel Neils called him over. He felt rather embarrassed as both his father and Walter tagged along behind him as he worked his way over to Neils. Everyone else was clearing out of the lobby quickly, and Kaethan had to thread his way through the rapidly exiting bodies.

"Yes, Colonel?" Kaethan asked when he got to him.

"You'll have all three recon companies ahead of you, Captain, but I want my heaviest strikers as lead battalion. That means you, Captain."

"Yes, Colonel. Any specific orders?"

"Just get us there quick, Captain, and don't wait for anyone to tell you where to go or what to do."

"Yes, sir."

The two exchanged brief salutes and Neils left in a rush. As Kaethan turned around, he found that Walter and his father had already exchanged introductions, and were talking about Chains and Quarter.

"No," his father was saying, "without his turret, Rokoyan wants my Bolos held back for planetary defense."

"I thought that local governments couldn't order Concordiat units around once shots were fired," Walter replied.

"They can't, but this is a judgment call. Rokoyan has reason to be worried. A second wave could hit us any moment, and he believes that your forces can handle the beachhead alone."

"Father," Kaethan interrupted, recalling his mother's long diatribes on Delassian politics, "what Rokoyan wants is to prove that we can handle the defense of our planet ourselves, and therefore there is no reason to put a Concordiat military base here."

The conversation ended then, as they both

considered what he said. Walter then nodded, reluctantly agreeing. Delas hated government interference, and with a Concordiat base on the planet, there would be plenty to go around.

His father grimaced and shook his head.

"That fits," Colonel Ishida agreed. "Well, if you guys start having trouble, I'll be able to see it and call one of them in."

"You're coming to the front?" Kaethan asked defensively.

"Yes, Neils gave me permission to tag along with your unit. Do you mind?"

A wave of nausea swept through Kaethan's entire body. The thought of his father watching over him during a fight was horrifying! The man had more combat experience than the combined population of Delas! Every maneuver that Kaethan executed, every order he gave, would be graded and judged according to impossible standards! All his mistakes would be instantly noticed and thrown back into his face as his father corrected him. God forbid anyone would die under his command, for he'd only have to look to his father to find out who was to blame. And, without doubt, his father would see every mistake that Kaethan made as a reflection upon himself.

"Of course not, Colonel," he said.

Our missile supplies are nearly exhausted. Only two missiles remain in my vertical launch tubes, from my original storehouse of twenty. Unit DBQ has none left. All have been expended against the transports that successfully made planetfall and now approach the east and west coasts of Deladin. My remaining conventional warheads were not designed for use against such large targets, and we fear that our attacks may have been insufficient to stop them. The 39th's MFOR-XXX-II (Melconian Front Optimization Refit for Bolo Mark XXXs, Version Two) gave each of us five Isis orbital denial thermonuclear missiles, but only fifteen Icehawk anti-armor missiles, designed more for penetration than for expansive damage.

The Delassian defense net has limited capability to track targets below the horizon, and these aliens approach slowly at wave-top level. They are communications silent and emit no active sensor sweeps. Our most effective method of acquiring these targets has been detecting the radiation that they are emitting from their fusion thrusters. This, unfortunately, is inexact, and our missiles must search for their thermal signature once they arrive in the area.

My last two missiles, however, have been saved for one last contact whose passage through the ocean net has been like a ghost. It approaches much slower than the others, and likely has radiation shielding protecting its exhaust. It threads its way between the Delassian detectors as if it were provided a map, though I calculate that likelihood as being infinitesimal. Instead, I must attribute its opportune zigzag approach to nothing more than luck. Even now, as it finally approaches the southern Delassian coast, far off detectors can only approximate its position as north of Telville and south of Candelith.

Once this transport reaches land, we risk it deploying its forces. But firing my missiles at such an elusive target may waste the last of our extreme range ordnance. My stage-one heuristic dilemma switches have tripped, but it is unnecessary that I invoke my stage two circuitry.

I call my Commander . . .

The Kezdai assault dropship never detected the approaching missile. Its particle beam defenses remained utterly still, useless without direction from the ship's impressive sensor arrays, which were off. Its crew saw only the blackness of the south Deladin shoreline, looming larger and larger on their forward view screen.

The light from their fusion drive, up until now reflecting off nothing but the waves only meters below, now was beginning to cast a bluish glow over the white sand beach that they were approaching. Is-kaldai Riffen's elite forces had been flying manually over the ocean, and planned on remaining on manual navigation for their flight over land. There were just too many active sensors sweeping the skies between them and Adakradai Khoriss' landing area to risk plotting anything beforehand.

Their plans, however, had to be rewritten.

Coming down on the dropship from above, the Icehawk missile locked in on their forward left thruster and ignited its powerful magnetic dynamo. At the split moment of impact, the warhead was fed a stream of antimatter particles that annihilated instantly. Molten shards of crystalline carbon exploded high into the air in a sparkling cloud as an impossibly narrow beam of focused plasma drilled deep into the Triamond lattice hull. Drive shielding was sliced clean through, causing an explosion that blasted the thruster clean off its housing.

The sudden explosion could be seen thirty kilometers up and down the coast, but even that wasn't enough for anyone to notice it. The peninsula that the dropship had to crash upon was over twenty kilometers from the nearest human dwellings, with no roads leading to it. No one was around to see that the dropship remained intact after smashing a two-hundred-meter long swathe through the dense rainforest, or that soldiers and equipment descended unhurt from the burning hulk.

No one, including the Kezdai, noticed the large black fin that cut through the waves just offshore.

As the first light of dawn glowed deep blue in the eastern sky, Captain Kaethan Ishida and the Alabaster Coast Heavy Armor was still point battalion in

Telville Corps' drive inland. While his ten Templars of Alpha team were running up the eastern lane of the highway, his Bravo team was paralleling him on the western lane. Charlie team followed behind. Somewhere around the fifth hour, it had become obvious to the captain that their "leap" ahead of the Chandoine Guard had become a permanent condition. There would be no deployment to allow the Tigris Guard to jump ahead of them. Someone upstairs wanted contact to be made as soon as possible, and his unit was just lucky enough to be out front when that decision was made.

Kaethan was driving Templar One as Sergeant Pritchard slept. Andrea kept watch from her turret position. When Zen awoke in an hour, they all would have had four hours sleep during the night as they traded duties. The nights on Delas were fifteen hours and about thirty minutes, with little variation from the planet's almost perfectly vertical axis. At nearly fifty kilometers per hour, Kaethan's column had traveled six hundred kilometers inland in the last twelve hours. The tall mountains of south Deladin were looming high into the clouds far to the south. The rain forest that they drove through was giving way to the limestone foothills that dominated the approaches to the granite peaks.

Contact was expected soon, but the three recon companies ahead of them had still not reported anything. Everyone was on radio silence except for them, and they were to break it only in an emergency. Even the running lights on the Templars were off, forcing Kaethan to use his thermal and low-light scopes to keep in line.

So when their radio did crackle with traffic, Kaethan was all ears.

"This is Recon Bravo Two. Contact at my position."

A red circle popped up on Kaethan's navigation map that was scrolling on the display before him as he drove. It was about eight kilometers ahead of him, directly on the highway. He did not recognize the voice, but whoever it was, he was exceedingly calm. Obviously Bravo Two had driven into an ambush site, but the aliens were hoping for something tastier to feed on than just a recon unit.

Kaethan didn't wait for confirmation, however. By hitting a virtual button on his left panel, he put his entire battalion on alert. And with a yell, he woke up Zen. As acknowledgements were sent back to him from his Templar commanders, lighting up his left-hand display with bright icons for each tank, he continued to listen to command channels.

"Are you sure, Bravo?" said a quiet female voice over the radio. "You're two kilometers behind us."

The female voice was that of Recon Alpha commander, Captain Beth Nichols.

"Forget your thermals. Use your low-light." Bravo Two replied. "They must have cooled armor . . ."

Standard procedure in this situation was for the Recon unit to keep advancing, but much slower. It was now the column's job to catch up quickly and extract it. A glance at his left-hand display showed the alert acknowledgements coming back quickly.

As a flurry of artillery plots lit up along the treeline ahead of him on his navigation map, Kaethan turned his transmitter to his battalion channel.

"Wake up boys and girls!" he called. "Our recon companies have just walked into a passive ambush seven klicks ahead. It's our job to go in and hold the jaws open while recon gets the hell out. Teams acknowledge!"

"Aye," called Lieutenant Peter Birch of his Bravo team.

"Aye," called Lieutenant Ellen Holowitz of his Charlie team.

"Nobody is to fire until the action starts! Once it begins, Alpha and Bravo are to stop and plant where they are! Charlie will come up and deploy across our front. Got that?"

"Aye." They replied.

Kaethan suddenly closed his eyes and groaned as he remembered that Walter and his father tagging along in the prototype Sentinel.

"Bicks, are you there?"

"Yes, Captain!"

"You take Walter's toy into the depression in the middle of our box and stay there!"

"Yes, sir!"

The highway was taking a gradual turn as he talked, and a long, flat straightaway was ahead of them. Dense groves of trees lined both sides, with a sharp rise at the far end, and many rocky knolls and outcroppings to hide any enemy armor. It was the perfect place for an ambush, with nowhere for them to hide once the firing started.

Of course, the Templar Mark XI was never meant to hide.

Ad-akradai Khoriss watched as the rising light of the alien sun turned the eastern sky lavender and pink. It had been raining, off and on, since he had landed upon this world, and this was the first time the skies were mostly clear. In his exhilaration, he had succumbed to his terrible urge to remove his helmet and breathe in the unfiltered air of this world. It was dangerous, yes, but there was danger everywhere here. Such a swamp-ridden world as this was the breeding ground of countless bacteria and germs, and the Kezdai immune system was weak from evolving on a desert world that was so devoid of them.

The hot, moist air, though, was less than refreshing.

The aliens on this world traveled without protection, he had noticed. They called themselves "Humans." A wounded male farm worker had been captured and interrogated as best they could before he died. Very little else was learned from him, but then little was expected. He was only a farmer, what must be their lowest caste, as it was with the Kezdai.

To the west, explosions and antiartillery discharges could be heard as his forces engaged the Humans along the narrow stretch of highway that cut through the rainforest and impassable rocky terrain of the area. All of his armor remained dug in along the highway perimeter, unable to travel over ground because their tires would sink to their floor into the muddy ground. Maneuver was impossible in this country, and if he were on the offensive, he'd be going mad in frustration right now. But he wasn't. His forces were on the defense, and the Humans could reach him with only a fraction of their forces at a time.

From his vantage point on top of a rocky outcropping, he could see a portion of the highway to the northwest. Many vehicles were scattered over the ground in various stages of destruction. Some were burning, sending faint columns of smoke into the air. Most were not, however, having little inside that caught fire. Most of the vehicles were Human, but several were Kezdai.

His carefully laid ambush turned into a disappointing standoff as the Humans detected their positions before the trap was sprung. Seeing the enemy recon units falling back, many of his commanders attacked anyway, leading to an open field firefight. The armor plating protecting the Humans' troop carriers was so laughably thin that even the Kezdai's infantry needle rifles could riddle the vehicle with holes. But their large, tracked vehicles with the huge railguns were a different story.

While the Human troop carriers attempted to flee or were abandoned, their heavy armor held ground, blasting their missiles with twin turrets firing crackling bolts of energy, and protecting their skies overhead with a laser battery kept safe in their center.

Their massive railguns traversed the battlefield at an astounding speed for their size, punching huge holes in any Kezdai armor that attempted to rush them. With concentrated, direct missile fire from his infantry, several of these tanks on their flanks had finally been knocked out. The remaining pocket, however, used the dead hulks as cover, becoming even harder to break.

And there the Humans stood ground while their infantry deployed in the forests on their flanks. The infantry firefights within the trees were quick and bloody, with neither side's bodyarmor effective against the Kezdai needle rifles or the Humans' bulky and powerful gauss rifles. The Kezdai soldiers, however, were sorely outnumbered.

Below his precipice, a command vehicle approached up the gravel road that wound through the trees. It stopped behind Khorris' own vehicle and Akradai Zaekiss stepped out. Having seen all that he could see from this outcropping, Khoriss decided to climb down to meet his infantry commander instead of forcing him to climb up. Ever since the first bombardment that targeted their transport, he had ordered that all reports were to be given to him in person. Their communications equipment was only used in emergencies.

"So what have you *learned*, Zaekiss?" Khorris' sarcasm was as thick as the mud that covered this planet.

Zaekiss appreciated the sarcasm, but didn't show it. He removed his helmet as Khoriss leapt the last twenty feet to the ground before reporting to him in his vibrant, somber voice, unusual for a Kezdai. A huge scar across his throat marked the old *surias* wound that had so altered his voice.

"Our soldiers are being forced to retreat, Ad-akradai. These Humans are patient, always waiting for their artillery to wreak their havoc before advancing a

minimal distance. It is slow progress, but our dischargers are constantly being overwhelmed by the shells."

Khorris' hood drooped noticeably. His plan to deci-
mate their lead elements, and overrun their rear, was
in tatters. He had lost his element of surprise, but
had been still hoping that the Humans would again
attempt to rush his lines. This latest news, however,
crushed that hope. Personally, Khoriss disliked artillery, and had decided not to waste room on his transport carrying them. These Humans, though, continued
to use it well ever since their first bombardment hit
just when his infantry were about to open fire on their
lead heavy armor.

"How do they fight, Zaekiss? What do your soldiers tell you?"

The Akradai hesitated as he tried to understand
exactly what his leader was asking. Khoriss saw the
confusion.

"The Humans, Zaekiss," Khoriss tried to explain,
"what kind of soldiers are they?"

Zaekiss' hood expanded as he understood the
question, though he still had to reprocess all that his
troops had reported and commented upon.

"They are well trained and armed, Ad-akradai,"
Zaekiss finally concluded, "but they are inexperienced
and soft. The Humans are much more fragile than
Kezdai. Many cry out and are incapacitated with just
one needle wound, calling to their comrades and
healers who then foolishly expose themselves to fire.
Some panic easily, while others show great courage.
When we first fired on them, they all showed great
confusion, but given a chance to regroup, they now
advance with great precision and planning."

Zaekiss stopped as he tried to think of more to say,
but Khoriss was pleased with what he was told and
held up his hand. He did not need more.

"We must force them to rush us, then," Khoriss
announced. "Once they have taken substantial

casualties, they will fall into chaos and we can break them."

"Likely, Ad-akradai. But there is no reason for them to rush us. Time is on their side, not ours."

"You are right, but there are other ways of forcing their hand. We must retreat past the large river and force them to cross under fire."

"But Ad-akradai, we would then surrender our transport to them!"

"It is useless to us, anyway. We will wait long enough for the remaining supplies to be off-loaded, and then our nuclear cannons can be repositioned and converted for ground combat."

"Against their railgun carriers? It seems a waste . . ."

"Have you seen a better target?"

"No, Khoriss, but if a Human warship were to suddenly appear . . ."

"Then we will die a couple days sooner, that is all, Zaekiss."

"Yes, Ad-akradai." Zaekiss sounded less than enthusiastic.

"Fight as well as you can for now, Zaekiss. Grind them down. Have them trade many lives for the ground you give them."

"I will."

"You will be signaled when you should retreat your forces past the bridge. Now return to your soldiers."

"Immediately, Ad-akradai Khoriss."

It had been so very long since the Kezdai had fought worldwide campaigns, Khoriss reflected as he watched Zaekiss depart. As war-prone as the Kezdai were, rarely would their battles involve more than just two or three factions. Little strategy or planning was needed, just tactics. With all their technological advances, with all their missiles and long range artillery, it seemed so strange that they would still care so much about river boundaries and defilade slopes. But until all armor, friend and foe alike, could fly above the trees and terrain in anti-gravity bubbles, these obstacles would continue to dominate tactical planning.

His brother would be pleased, though. Khoriss was learning much about these Humans, and he would be reporting back to Keertra soon. He worried now, however, that the Humans were learning something also. They were learning how to fight. If the remaining Is-kaldai truly decided to gather all their forces in a mass assault, they would still find well trained and armed soldiers on this world. But once Khoriss was done with them, they'd certainly no longer be inexperienced and soft.

Kuro's emergency message had startled Serina awake out of a troubled sleep. The loud beeping had sounded just before sunrise, and at first she couldn't figure out what it meant. Rarely had Kuro ever used her ability to send phone messages before, and never in a real emergency. Adding to her confusion, she read the note before noticing who sent it. "Large spaceship landed at Peter's beach," it read.

At first she thought the message had come from her father or brother, considering its content. But once she noticed that Kuro had sent it, she immediately understood her to be referring to the sand beach that her coworker Peter often camped out on.

Realizing the importance of Kuro's message, Serina set forth to call someone in the military. Fearing that she might be asked for specifics on just how she found out about the landing, she decided to just call the main desk at Fort Hilliard, where they knew her. Unfortunately she didn't know the woman who answered, and when asked who actually saw the ship, Serina just answered that it was an employee of hers working at the research center. Luckily that was enough, and Serina was promised that action would be taken.

Once the call was complete, Serina decided to

drive out to the research center herself. She knew that she wouldn't be able to get to sleep again that night, and she was worried about Kuro. There was no way for Serina to send back messages to Kuro from home, and Kuro had to be worried that her message would get through. Also, Kuro might have some details that could be useful to someone.

She wouldn't stay long, however. The research center was too close to Peter's beach for her comfort, though twenty kilometers of impassable rain forest was between them. She'd just drop in for a few minutes, she told herself, before heading home again.

The alien lay dead at the edge of the battered forest, amongst shattered trees and charred branches. The battle armor that the creature was wearing was blasted open by the ion-bolt turrets from the giant Templars that lined the road above. Darkened blood stained the soldier's breastplate and soaked the soldier's crimson sash tied to his waist. Colonel Ishida looked over the corpse for several minutes before attempting to remove the helmet and get a good look at the face and head.

Colonel Ishida had been in many battles before, but never had he felt as exposed as he did this morning. He had always thought that being at ground zero of a massed Melconian offensive was the worst situation that a commander could possibly face, but he'd always faced it with a regiment of Bolo Mark XXXs at his back. He wasn't used to friendly artillery arriving late or off target. He wasn't used to being surrounded by the enemy with no ability to maneuver out. He wasn't used to commanders screaming over the Corps channels, arguing over who was going to support who, where, and when. And he definitely wasn't used to having hypersonic needles punching through one side of his vehicle and out the other, barely missing him.

And Walter Rice's endless commentary on the

performance of his laser didn't help. Throughout the entire fight, Rice was recalibrating his crystal, altering its spin to cover different arcs at different speeds. Walter was also prone to sudden outbursts, constantly making the colonel believe that they were about to be hit.

His son's thirty Templars were in the thick of the fight for six hours before Tigris Guard was finally ordered to take over the offensive. All along the front, Alabaster Guard units held ground while Tigris Guard units jumped past them. This occurred while the aliens changed tactics, now using hit-and-run assaults with concentrations of their infantry, and plasma pistols instead of their needle rifles to blast the soldiers out of their positions. In some places, the human lines were thrown back with great losses, but in others they advanced unimpeded. Sensors showed that the aliens were withdrawing all of their armor to the rear, but the Templars of the Tigris guard refused to give chase without infantry effectively covering their flanks.

Progress would be slow in this battle.

It was late morning now, and the sky was surprisingly clear for this time of year. Distant explosions created a rumbling sound in the area that never let up. The Delassian forces had large supplies of shells, and Colonel Ishida was suspecting that they'd be using all of them.

"Hold on a minute." Walter Rice said from close behind him.

Kaethan had approached along with Walter, who was now wearing his official Alabaster Coast sunglasses, given to him by Sergeant Pritchard just a few minutes earlier. He was an honorary member of the unit, Zen told him, now that he had fought along side them.

The alien's helmet was caught on something, and Toman was having trouble taking it off. Walter, though, removed a long dagger from the alien's belt, and pried off a metal clamp at the neck. The helmet then slid off cleanly.

"Looks like some ancient Egyptian god," Kaethan commented.

The alien's neck and left jaw were blackened by a nasty burn, but otherwise the head was undamaged. Its green eyes were open, unseeing.

"All aliens look like someone's idea of a god," Toman said harshly. "Or demon."

"He's big enough," Walter said.

"Three fingers, two opposable thumbs." The colonel sounded like he was making mental notes. "I don't feel up to taking off his boots."

Kaethan noticed Walter, who had cleaned the alien dagger with a strip of cloth from the alien's sash. He now was looking intently at the blade.

"Collect knives, Walter?" Kaethan asked.

"No," he said vacantly. "I minored in metallurgy. I make them."

"You make it sound like all metallurgists make knives."

"Most *guys* do. What *else* would you choose as a semester project? A kitchen faucet that survives a re-entry burn?"

"So instead you make daggers that survive re-entry burns?" Kaethan chided him.

"Is it usable?" The colonel asked with a serious edge. "Or is it just decorative?"

Walter surprised them both as he seemed to balance the weapon in his hand, and then he gripped it by the blade as if for throwing. Then once more he studied the blade itself that reflected the light in rippling silver and white.

"Both, actually," Walter finally said. "It has several alloys in it just for decoration, but it certainly looks like it's been heavily used in its lifetime. This blade definitely has a purpose. I wonder if they all have them."

"They do. There are two more bodies . . . scattered . . . down that way. They both had daggers on their belts."

"Colonel," Walter asked sheepishly, "will I be shot for looting if I take a couple?"

Toman shook his head.

"That only happens when we fight each other," he assured him. "But be ready to give them up if asked."

"Will do."

Walter stood up and went off looting, then. Some nearby explosions sounded from down the road, on the far side of the rise. Kaethan stood up and looked expectantly toward the sound, but no further rounds were hitting.

"How are your men doing?" Toman asked as he studied the inside of the helmet and the electronics that were there.

"Lost five," Kaethan said solemnly as he looked back at the alien body. "Two others are seriously injured."

Only two of his Templars were totaled, but ten were heavily damaged. A small army of engineers was swarming over them now trying to get them back into fighting shape. Their railguns themselves were starting to be targeted near the end, after the aliens found out how hard it was to punch through their armor. But the alien missiles, when they got through the Templars' defenses, burned through their protection with a variety of warheads. The heavy walls between compartments helped keep many of the casualties down.

"You did very well this morning, son."

As surprised as Kaethan was at the compliment, he couldn't accept it.

"Not one of the recon units made it out." Kaethan shook his head. "I'd call that a failure."

"They had no chance," his father rebuffed. "The aliens' needle rifles sliced right through those Haulers. I can't believe you're trying to use them."

With Kaethan's silence, Toman suddenly realized that his son took that personally. He, of course, was blaming the government for using such an inferior personnel carrier, not his son . . .

"But your Templars stood up wonderfully." Toman tried to recover from his mistake, by changing the subject. "Are those Mark Twelves, Thirteens?"

"No," Kaethan replied shortly. "Just Elevens."

Toman cursed to himself silently. Another mistake. His son took offense again. This always happened whenever he tried to talk to Kaethan. It seemed destiny. At this rate Kaethan would disown him by the end of the day.

The Elevens, he formed a recovery, were actually better in some ways . . .

"Father," Kaethan said then.

"Yes?"

"Do you know why I didn't go to the Concordiat Academy?"

Toman set down the alien helmet to his side.

"I always assumed that you were threatened with the same tortures that your mother threatened me with if I ever encouraged you to."

His son smiled and chuckled. Toman felt that this was a change for the better. Rarely had he inspired that reaction in his son.

"Just checking," Kaethan said.

"Did you actually think that I was disappointed in you for not joining? What would ever give you such an outrageous idea?"

"Nothing, Father." Kaethan stopped him. "Just checking."

"I would hope so," Toman said, and picked up the helmet again to study it.

A column of Haulers passed them, then, driving towards the rise to the east. They wouldn't cross over, of course. They'd just drop off their infantry, and join the ever-growing numbers of other Haulers abandoned by the side of the road. Some things, humans learned quickly. For other things, it took longer.

The sight was spectacular.

As the last of the Kezdai infantry streamed across the bridge, a hail of artillery shells was raining down from above. This was the only safe crossing of the Witch River for fifty kilometers in either direction, and both sides knew it. Every howitzer and rocket howitzer in the Telville arsenal was nearly melting its barrel trying to get at the forces that were concentrated there. But not a single shell made it to the ground as a massive lightning storm crackled and thundered over the valley, forking up into the sky to intercept dozens of shells at a time.

Sergeant Emmet Lear of Alpha Company, First Mechanized Brigade, watched the lightning show from behind a large rock outcropping overlooking the valley, heavily shrouded by trees and underbrush. The highway was a kilometer to the north, snaking away from him, viewable through many branches and leaves. Electricity filled the air around him, causing him to suffer static shocks whenever he touched the ceramic-metal barrel of his gauss rifle. The smell and taste of ozone in the air was almost choking. His short beard itched constantly as the hairs seemed to want to stand on end. Added to that, a sharp rock goaded his ribcage as he lay prone, peering through the underbrush.

The highway into the valley veered left over the crest, with two kilometers of moderate slope before turning hard right to cross the four-lane bridge. On the opposite bank, the roadway ran up a much steeper slope before turning back to its left to disappear behind the forest of trees and large rock outcroppings. Any vehicle travelling on the roadway had little cover.

The valley itself was rocky, with huge boulders and rock faces peeking out from underneath the many trees that clung desperately to what soil kept them rooted. Rainforest ferns that covered most of Deladin now gave way to an undergrowth of thorny bushes and tall grasses. Rushing down the valley was a thunderous whitewater rapids, fed by the snow-capped mountains to the south. The Witch River had been labeled as suicidal to any adventure seeker who wished to raft it.

"Anything getting through yet, Sergeant?" asked the tired voice of Major Peter Mikolayev over his command channels.

Emmet's prone position gave him a good view of the far side of the bridge three kilometers away, where the last of the alien infantry was still crossing unimpeded. The rock outcropping shielded him from the rest of the valley, though the tall periscope viewer at his side allowed him to see over part of it.

"Negative," Emmet replied simply.

There was a moment's pause as a sigh could be heard.

"We're shutting down, then. All units hold position and await further orders."

The command would have little effect on the front line, the sergeant knew, since the Tigris Guard had already deployed in defensive positions behind the valley crest. Captain Riggins' thirty Templars were already scattered along the stretch of roadway leading up to the valley. Emmet's Mechanized Brigade was digging in around the tanks in the forests, and bringing their Haulers forward to support them. Everyone was already expecting this standoff to last a while and was preparing for a siege.

The bombardment continued for only a minute more after the announcement, slacking off quickly, though a few rocket howitzer rounds continued to streak overhead from their bases far to the rear. Raising his one-meter tall periscope, the sergeant sneaked a peek over the outcropping. A large part of the valley was still blocked by the rock, but Corporal Pierce of Bravo Company, hidden one kilometer north of the road, could see the remainder.

Movement immediately caught his attention, and with a twist of the ungainly periscope, he zoomed in on a line of vehicles.

"An armored column is entering the valley," he said into his headset. "I see ten vehicles, moving slowly. More are following . . ."

Emmet's first thought was that the aliens had now tested their defenses and considered it safe to invest some armor into the valley. He wasn't overly concerned that they'd sortie since all of their infantry were now safely evacuated.

"Pierce just got sniped," reported Captain Larson of Bravo Company. "Assigning another observer . . ."

Sergeant Lear swore under his breath as he continued to watch the arriving column.

"Twenty vehicles," he updated the count. "One-fifty tons . . . ten wheelers . . . energy cannons . . . twelve-wheeled mass drivers . . ."

Sergeant Pierce was a personal friend of Emmet's, and his stomach tightened at the thought of him just taking a needle. There shouldn't have been any reason why Pierce exposed himself. They had their periscopes and good positions. Something must have drawn Pierce out, or else their lines had been infiltrated.

"Twenty-six vehicles total in two columns," Lear updated again, trying not to think about it, "still approaching the bridge."

Yesterday, Emmet Lear had been a dealer in heavy-construction vehicles. That life was forgotten at the moment, but his civilian occupation gave him an advantage at judging the size of the war machines that were rolling down the opposite slope. The sight of such large armored vehicles on wheels disturbed Lear, however, who was used to tracks being on any ground vehicle over fifty tons. Although this would give them a much better speed on pavement, he considered, they'd be very limited once the battle turned off-road. A few of the vehicles were also of a tractor-trailer design, which he knew were extremely unstable on broken terrain at higher speeds.

"EW is picking up gravitic disturbances at the river," said Major Mikoleyev over his headset. "Anyone see anything?"

Emmet quickly zoomed out his periscope and looked around. The valley was clear of any other movement. Even the infantry had now disappeared into the woods and rocky terrain across the river. Of course, with Pierce gone, Lear now had to worry about what was behind the huge outcropping that sheltered him. He'd have to climb on top, or crawl out in the open to get a look on the other side, however, exposing himself to fire. There was no chance he'd do that.

Then his spine tingled as Lear heard a low whine quickly growing in volume around him, freezing his bones. Dropping the periscope, Lear lay flat on his stomach with his hands over his helmet.

The voice that suddenly exploded over command channels was not recognized, but it was obviously young.

"Four gravtanks climbing our slope south of the highway!"

Oh crap, Lear thought, and lay perfectly still as a massive shadow rose over the outcropping and slowly passed over him. His entire body seemed to vibrate in resonance with the overwhelming hum that enveloped him, paralyzing him in fear.

"All units engage!" Mikolayev called out. "All units engage! But do *not* enter the valley! They could be trying to draw us in."

"Five hundred . . . six hundred tons!" the unknown observer called out. "Plasma cannon of some sort. The column is crossing the bridge!"

The hum was dying off now, but Emmet didn't

move until the screams of Raven missiles, launched by his comrades, filled the air. Rising quickly to his knees, he looked both at the rear of the massive gravtanks disappearing over the trees, and then at the rapidly advancing armored vehicles driving up the highway.

"Captain Riggins!" Lear called out over the command channel. "You will be hit simultaneously from your front and right flank . . ."

"Incoming!"

Emmet didn't know who called that out, or why, but that never mattered to a soldier in combat. He just dropped everything and tried to become one with the dirt.

THUTHUMP!

A shockwave and blast of heat passed over him with a thunderous roar, followed by a rain of smoldering branches falling onto his back. A moment later, entire trees were crashing down the slopes around him, causing landslides. When he looked up, the trees at the top of the valley had been blasted away. Dense smoke filled the air, but he had an unobstructed view of the four alien gravtanks just as they acquired their targets. Incredibly bright plasma lasers flared from their cannons. Lear couldn't see what damage they might have wreaked among the Templars, but a mass of return fire began to literally blast the gravtanks apart. Huge chunks of armor flew high into the sky as armor piercing rods slammed into them. Turning his attention back to the highway, Emmet saw five of the alien armored vehicles explode the moment that they topped the crest, but the remainder lashed out with bright blue particle beams and then disappeared from view as they tangled with the Templars.

From Lear's vantage point, all he could watch were the gravtanks as they disintegrated, chunk by chunk. Raven missiles suddenly began streaking up to blast them from all sides as their point defense beams fell silent. One by one, as the gravtank's powerplants were hit, the mammoths dropped from the sky as if their supporting strings were cut. Only a few moments after the last gravtank fell, the alien armored vehicles reappeared, this time in open retreat at high speeds. Only a dozen or so were left.

As the sergeant watched the surviving column recross the bridge, he suddenly remembered his duties. After finding his periscope in all the debris, he scanned what he could of the valley.

"All vehicles in retreat," the sergeant announced. "No other activity."

All during the fight, the command channels were completely silent as Major Mikolayev let the commanders fight their battles. The extended span of silence after Emmet gave his report, however, made him think that his headset was damaged.

But then Mikolayev came back online.

"All units prepare to be relieved in order. Alabaster will be taking point again. All infantry units check your bracelets and report to Decon' as needed."

With a sudden fear gripping him, Lear ripped open his sleeve and took a look at the radiation band that was wrapped around his wrist. Its friendly green had now turned ominously yellow.

Crap, Emmet thought.

The Kezdai scout was disappointed.

The electrical fence had fooled him into believing that the complex he had infiltrated was an important target. What he was finding was that it was some sort of biological research center. The room that he was hiding in contained shelves and shelves of glass and plastic tanks containing marine animals of various types. Perhaps they were experimenting with biologic weapons of some types, but he doubted it. There were no hermetically sealed environments anywhere to be seen.

He had been hiding for several minutes now, ever since three Human armored vehicles rolled through the gate. Soldiers dismounted out of the rear of the vehicles, but they did not deploy. If they had, then that would have been a sure sign that this complex was valuable, and that he should direct an artillery barrage down upon it. Although the vile Keertran troops did not appreciate the value of artillery, his Is-kaldai Riffen certainly did. His crashed dropship had a complete battery of guns that were already targeting the Human infantry that were attempting to approach through the rain forest. It had been difficult to pass through their ranks without being detected, but he had an important mission. His commander wanted to know if the cities had their own point defense systems, or whether only the military units were protected. To find that out, he and several of his comrades were to find an observation point overlooking the nearby city.

Then artillery would be called in.

A Human female with long black hair had appeared out of the large building to his right, obviously a researcher of some sort. Up until that moment, he had thought that the complex was abandoned. The female had been talking to the infantry commander for quite a long time while the scout waited impatiently, sneaking peaks out a window at periodic intervals. Just when his patience was finally running out, he heard the engines start up, and two of the three vehicles moved out. The last troop carrier, however, remained. Its twelve soldiers deployed around the perimeter fence, and he hoped that they'd miss the cut that he had made in it.

The Human female was nowhere to be seen when he looked.

Escape, without being seen, would be difficult now, but he had to try. The building that he was in had few windows, but he was able to locate nine of the twelve soldiers, and had a good idea where the remaining three were. The sea fence was not being protected. The ocean, he decided, would be his best way out.

Getting to it from the building that he was in would be impossible. The seaside doorway could be seen by several of the Human soldiers. The building to his right, however, he noticed had a concrete canal that ran out into the sea from its lowest level. It wasn't being guarded.

Sneaking into the building's front door, although daring, was not difficult. Decorative shrubbery was planted all around the outer wall, concealing his movement. Only the last dash into the doors was risky, and after looking around frantically, he believed that he had gotten away with it. The soldiers were looking outwards through the fence, not inwards.

His scrambling through the other building had given him the basic concepts of Human architecture, and the stairway and elevator were quickly spotted. Because he had no wish to experiment with the elevator, he opened the door to the stairwell.

It was just then that the black haired female made her appearance again, as the elevator doors suddenly opened. A shrill scream echoed inside the scout's helmet as he tried to push back out the door and bring his rifle to bear. The elevator doors were already closing, but he did have a shot at the form that had retreated against the far wall.

He didn't take it.

The scout's aversion to making a loud noise was part of the reason that he didn't fire his rifle, but another was an aversion to killing a noncombatant. Kezdai blood feuds often ended in the complete annihilation of one clan or another, males and females alike, but noncombatants were always spared. Of course, all members of the warring clans themselves were considered combatants.

This scout had made a mistake, however, and he realized it. Allowing this female to live would risk his own life and mission. As a red arrow above the elevator pointed downwards, so did he run. The stairway had small steps, and he stumbled a few times, but he managed to reach the ground floor in decent time.

As he pushed through the stairway door, he saw that the elevator doors to his right were already closing. To his left was a large, tiled room with a pool, open to the outside at the far end. The woman could have been tricky and gone back upstairs, but he had to be sure.

Before running back upstairs, he ran into the poolroom to look for her. The visuals inside his helmet gave him a three-hundred-degree distorted view around him, but even with that he only caught a glimpse of the female as she came up behind him and gave him a shove into the water. He fired his needle rifle wildly as he plunged into the deep, saltwater pool.

What happened next he never had time to organize into a coherent understanding.

One moment he was sinking rapidly into the water, and the next a massive black and white form was underneath him and pushing him back to the surface. Then, just as he broke the surface of the water, he was hurled, as if from a catapult, directly into the tiled wall of room.

He fell to the floor in a daze.

But Kezdai were immensely hardy creatures whose bones had evolved to absorb great impacts from falling from the high cliffs of their ancient homeworld. Great pains wracked his body, but the scout still managed to sit up, lift his rifle, and unleash a withering fire across the room. His own blood covered his helmet's visuals, making him uncertain of what shapes were around him. All he saw were shadows until the massive black and white form seemed to explode out of the pool before him, and crash into him.

His last conscious vision was of nothing but teeth . . .

The bridge was more than two kilometers away, but still no one dared peek over the crest to look into the valley. Even at this range, the alien needle rifles were incredibly accurate. Instead, the periscope on top of Kaethan's Templar was raised, and Kaethan, his father, and Walter all were gathered around a video screen that was mounted at the rear of the three-hundred-fifty-ton tank. With the last light of the day glowing orange in the sky to the west, they surveyed the heavily shadowed terrain.

Bright crimson and blue-white streamers were flapping in the wind over their enemy's fortified positions. The temptation to burn them down with their ion bolts had been on everyone's mind, but was decided to be an ignoble act. They'd make fine trophies, Kaethan had told his men, to bring back to Fort Hilliard after all this was over.

The smell of ozone continued to permeate the air around them, proving the continued readiness of their opponent's point defense dischargers. It even overwhelmed the smoke that rose from the still smoldering devastation of forest that surrounded them. Several battered, alien armored vehicles also continued to pump out a plume of white smoke into the air, and probably would for several days. Three of Tigris' Templars had been burning when Kaethan arrived, but these fires had been put out quickly, and engineers were now working on the Templars. All the other Templars of the Tigris Guard were either driven, or towed, to a depot constructed four kilometers to the rear.

"I don't think they have a single direct-fire weapon targeting this ridgeline," Kaethan commented while their periscope panned over the valley.

"I can't see any sign of one either," his father agreed. "You could probably take the slope and hold it, but they aren't giving you anything to shoot at. You'd just be setting yourself up for more of those missiles that plastered Tigris."

"Didn't hurt the Templars," Kaethan pointed out.

"True, but don't expect me to ride in Walter's Sentinel."

Walter didn't like to admit it, but the presence of his defense laser would not have helped the Tigris Guard against the barrage that hit them. There were only a few missiles of modest size, but they approached at tree-top level from the sides. What they needed was a point-defense tower like the ones that protected their artillery. Of course, towers were easy targets when they were this close to the enemy.

"Too bad you can't fire any high-explosives out of those railguns," Walter said. "We could blast them out of those positions."

The sound of a command vehicle rolling up distracted the crew from their viewing. When it stopped, Colonel Neils jumped out of the passenger seat. He returned everyone's salute briskly, as he obviously had something important to say.

"At ease, Captain," Neils said, specifically singling out Kaethan to talk to. "I've got bad news. That small pocket of hostiles north of Telville decided to go out with a bang. As Chandoine was moving in on them, they unleashed a long-range bombardment onto the city itself, forty kilometers away."

"Oh, God," Walter uttered.

"They threw in every ordnance they had, short of nukes. The entire northern suburbs and part of downtown were devastated. We're estimating casualties in excess of thirty-five thousand."

"Sir, my sister . . ."

"I know, Captain. Once I hear something, I'll let you know. But General Calders is furious. He wants this pocket cleared up so we can pull back and solidify the border around Telville. He's ordered us to assault the bridge at the first light of day."

"Yes, Colonel," Kaethan replied.

"Our strategy session will be at 2600 hours back at our HQ. We may be able to cross the river with some infantry onto their flanks, but our armor has to run up the middle. There are no other roads."

"We'll be ready."

"I have to head over to Tigris HQ now. Riggins' armor was chewed up pretty bad by that column that suddenly made an appearance. I'll try to get their survivors attached directly to you. That will be all, Captain."

"Yes, sir."

They saluted again, and Colonel Neils hopped into this vehicle.

As he sped off, Kaethan and his father exchanged worried glances, but then turned back to their surveillance. For a long time they didn't say anything as they panned their view over the opposing slopes. But soon their concentration returned to what was at hand.

"Look how they've torn up the highway over there," Walter said as they looked over the bridge. "They're not even trying to hide that they've mined it."

"They don't have to," Toman replied. "They've concentrated all of their air defenses around it. Your artillery will never punch through to knock any of it out."

"Have you spotted any of their armor?" Kaethan asked.

"Not a one," Toman answered. "You can be sure, though, that every last one of them will pop up at the worst possible time. I don't think we've seen even a fraction of their total forces, yet. And they've now learned that your railguns are vulnerable."

The brief sortie that hit the Tigris Heavy Armor

didn't have the firepower to punch through the Templars' substantial armor. But it did, however, manage to disable many of their railguns by point-blank fire. Some of the alien vehicles just sideswiped the massive railguns as they drove by. Only the plasma lasers on the large gravtanks were powerful enough to slice the Templars open, accounting for their only three kills.

"And your railguns don't have the elevation to cover the slope from down there," Toman continued his observations. "Any Templars sent into the valley will be just targets."

"Have you found anything encouraging at all?" Kaethan asked sardonically.

His father grimaced and thought hard for a few moments. Kaethan let out a nervous chuckle at his father's reaction, but a deep pain was forming in the pit of his stomach.

"This is a death trap, son," the Concordiat colonel finally said. "These aliens have stripped and scuttled their transport, their only way off this planet, for a better defensive position. They will fight to their death while throwing everything they have at you."

The three of them were quiet for a while. Walter panned their periscope along the opposite slopes, finding faint heat sources everywhere as he switched to thermal sights, but with the sun setting, this was a bad time to look. Better images could be formed once the ground had released the solar heat that it had absorbed during the day.

"They also have the high energy plasma weapons that they used to knock down your satellites," Toman reminded them. "There was no sign of them at their transport, from what I was told. Who knows what else they might have stripped off that ship before they retreated. If you try to cross this bridge, you'll be massacred."

Walter had stopped pretending to care about what

was being shown on the monitor. His nervous gaze was dancing back and forth between Kaethan and his father, waiting for one of them to figure out a solution to prevent the certain death awaiting him. Of course, there was a solution, Kaethan knew. And Kaethan knew that his father was debating it with himself even now.

"If you are waiting for me to ask, Father," Kaethan said calmly, "then you will remain waiting."

His father looked up from the screen and looked closely at his son. He grimaced as he took out his fieldcomm, but then he stopped.

"I wasn't waiting for that, son." Toman said before he activated it.

What, exactly, his father *was* waiting for, Kaethan couldn't fathom. But he wasn't going to ask that, either. He was just thankful.

"Death By Chains," Colonel Ishida said into his fieldcomm.

"So judged," replied Unit DBC from twelve hundred kilometers to the north.

Ad-akradai Khoriss was pleased with his position. Many defilade positions were found on his side of the valley, overlooking the bridge. His concentrated dischargers, combined with the point defense emplacements from their transport, had shrugged off the Humans' heaviest bombardment. His nuclear cannons were in position, to be moved up for firing at just the right time. And his ambush of the Human armored units had proven that Kezdai weapons could indeed be utilized effectively against the large tanks with the railguns, even though he had to waste almost all of his gravtanks to prove it.

Added to that, two smaller transports had arrived during the night from the southeast, both limping in with substantial damage. Their additional armor would greatly reinforce his counterattack, though he ordered

Riffen's artillery converted to direct fire and deployed in positions overlooking the bridge.

But he would wait before deploying his armored vehicles. His infantry and nuclear cannons would be enough to finish off the Human armor that advanced on him. Only then would his armored vehicles sweep back over the bridge to drive into their rear and eliminate their precious artillery.

He was worried, however, that more reinforcements were arriving for the Humans. One of his few remaining surveillance probes had been launched at the first hint of daylight in the east. An image taken just before it died showed that the Human forces had moved all of their equipment off the eastbound roadway, as if making room for another unit to pass through. He continued to weigh the possibility of launching his last probe to hopefully catch a glimpse of what was arriving.

Khoriss now sat in his command vehicle, paging through the images that his forward camera positions were sending back to him. There was still no evidence of Human infiltration along the river, but he carefully studied where they might hide when the time came.

His quiet observations were rudely interrupted by his hatch opening with a loud clank. The panicked face of Inkezdai Kepliss looked in.

"Ad-akradai, massed artillery rises from the west—"

"Good! It begins!"

"But Ad-akradai," Kepliss pleaded, "the artillery rises from far behind the Human lines, and the launcher approaches swiftly as it fires! It travels along the roadway at a high rate of speed, sending its shells high into the stratosphere!"

Something new, Khoriss thought. The approaching weapons platform had to be exceedingly large to be capable of a sustained barrage as this, and still have the stability to wield it accurately while moving rapidly. The Humans had not previously shown any such weapon.

Or perhaps they had, Khoriss remembered. The ground batteries that destroyed their frigates had wielded enormous firepower while showing tremendous speed. Perhaps those same batteries had artillery clusters in addition to their energy weapons. Not only could such a weapon fend off an orbital insertion, but it could support a local ground war at the same time. Such a weapons platform must be massive, he thought. Once he had disposed of the Human armored forces, he'd have to give top priority to his own armor to capture this vehicle when they made their drive.

"Ad-akradai, should we launch our last probe to view its approach?"

"No, Inkezdai. It matters not what it looks like. We will deal with it in time. Our first priority is the Human armored forces which should be attacking soon."

"Yes, Ad-akradai. The alarm has already been given."

"Good. Then we must then be patient as we let these Humans enter our trap."

"Yes, Ad-akradai. I must tend my dischargers."

His only concern, Khoriss considered, was why the eastbound lane of the highway was left open the entire distance to the front. Certainly the Humans would not lead their attack with something so valuable as these mobile ground batteries. Could this weapon be heavily armored, he wondered? An idle thought, he immediately determined. Nothing could stand up against his nuclear cannons. . . .

I am ten kilometers from the bridge and my tracks slip across the highway pavement as I follow a curve at one hundred fifty kilometers per hour. Soon I must slow my approach or else my inertia entering the valley depression will cause me to take flight, carrying me past my optimal fording location at the lead edge of the bridge. I cannot utilize the bridge itself since my large frame would not fit through its steel girder superstructure.

On the sides of the road I begin to pass by the valiant militia that protects this world. They cheer me forward, weapons raised high, and I take great strength from their encouragement. My four 30cm mortars continue to fire their stream of munitions into the sky, even as the many shells that I have been firing for the last 9.6638 minutes now are entering terminal guidance. All rounds are timed to hit, or deploy their munitions, at the same moment on top of our Enemy's positions. The Guard artillery has also offered their support, and I have plotted many positions for them to hit to the rear of our Enemy to harass their retreat from my onslaught. These are strong and honorable colonists, and I am proud to fight by their side.

At four kilometers from the bridge, I have reduced speed to one hundred kilometers per hour and my mortars are silent. Electrical discharges fire high into the sky ahead of me to intercept my bombardment, but they are much less effective against my Concordiat mortars than against the Delassian howitzers. My shells are hardened against such defenses, and the Enemy will be disappointed. As they release their lightning, I am recording their positions and comparing them to what the Delassian forward observers noted earlier. I am distracted for a moment as weapons grade radioactives are detected in the valley ahead, but I have been expecting their presence. My charge remains unchecked.

I top the crest of the valley just as the torrents of shells that I have launched begin their rain of destruction! The entire opposite slope explodes with dazzling light, fire and electricity. Behind the ridgeline,

*powerful shock waves throw debris high into the air
as my anti-armor penetrators find their targets. I
immediately begin sweeping the valley floor below me
with all my firepower. The hundreds of trees that line
the road explode into a hail of fiery wooden shards
as my 110cm Hellbore slices through their great
trunks. My ion-bolt infinite repeaters pour endless fire
into every shadow and recess that could likely hide
my adversaries. By the time that I have reached the
river, the valley is ablaze, and only then comes my
opponent's retaliation.*

*A growing swarm of missiles arises from the con-
flagration. The missiles lock onto my form, only to
be consumed by my infinite repeaters as they come
close. For each new launch, I respond with a round
from my mortars, though I now am running low on
ammunition for them. As I plunge through the river
and climb the riverbank back up to the roadway, I
fire my Hellbore into a high cliff facing, sending a
rockslide crashing down upon a launcher that I
detected there.*

*With my last rounds from my mortar, I devastate
the roadway on the east side of the bridge, wiping
out the mines that had been laid there. The missile
barrage has slackened considerably as I climb back
onto the shattered pavement. Fearing my presence
near the bridge may endanger it, I charge up the
slope, pouring destruction in every direction.*

*It is then that the enemy unleashes his greatest
firepower as a shaped nuclear blast smashes through
my forward battlescreens, washing radioactive plasma
over my hull. The impact of the blast lifts me up and
throws me sliding back down the pavement towards
the bridge. Another nuclear blast hits me in the side,
though it is an ineffective glancing blow that my
battlescreens deflect with 93.082 percent efficiency.*

*The weapons that launched this attack have no
reactors. In fact, their energy signatures are almost*

undetectable. I must conclude that these weapons are detonating shaped nuclear devices, and are reloading even as I align my Hellbore onto their locations. These rounds must be the radioactives that I detected in the valley and on their ship.

Digging my tracks deeply into the broken highway, I unleash all my firepower in a sweeping barrage. The hidden fortifications are blasted open and their rocky shelters are reduced to molten lava within seconds. Fearing my enemy be given a chance to recover, I immediately renew my charge up the slope as I verify that my damage has been slight. Although powerful, these nuclear cannons were unfocused and poorly directed. My endurachrome plating is intact, though nine plates have broken. My FP-A2 ion-bolt turret was hit while firing, however, and has been destroyed. I must reevaluate the threat that these aliens pose, and in response I turn sharply off the roadway and crash through the trees in hopes of avoiding any further such ambushes.

Brief glimpses of scattering alien infantry are all I see of the Enemy as I bulldoze my way through the forest. Beyond the valley, however, my detectors frantically begin plotting a large force powering up a variety of reactors in preparation for my unwelcome appearance. Magnetic disturbances betray the positions of large mass drivers and particle accelerators. The size and number of these weapons make me shudder to think what would have happened if the Telville Corps had crossed this river themselves. Even my own Commander dangerously underestimated their strength. I divert 0.03 seconds of processor time to consider the cause of this discrepancy, concluding the likelihood that two transports survived our missile defenses to reinforce their beachhead.

The force arrayed against me is threatening, but now is the time to act! Many of their particle beam accelerators are still building power and are not yet *operable. They have been caught partially unprepared and I must press my advantage! The drone that I launch disappears in a crackling blast of lightning before it clears 100 meters, but the few images it relays to me reveals my enemy's positions.*

I turn to attack!

Full-grown trees, set afire by my infinite repeaters, fly through the air as I crash my way into a huge, recently made clearing at the top of the valley. I have entered a four-kilometer wide killzone! But at an expected point! In the fraction of a second of surprise that I have, I unleash all my firepower at the targets around me, sweeping my Hellbore across the opposing treeline. Four massive nuclear cannons are caught turning their guns onto my position, but my ion-bolt turrets blast the unprotected towed fieldpieces apart before their hammers fall. Another flight of missiles rises up into the air just as a hail of penetrators begins ripping into my damaged forward armor. My battlescreens begin to shimmer as weaker particle beams are absorbed and stronger ones dispersed.

Twin rooster tails of earth and wood fly high into the air as my tracks hurl me forward into the fray. I wield my Hellbore as a whirling dervish would his scimitar, slashing through my opponent's armor with a blade of brilliant fire. The swarm of missiles descends upon me from above as their supersonic final stage kicks in and sends them streaking through my battle-screens. My infinite repeaters are overwhelmed by the onslaught and my warhull is cracked and blasted by a wide variety of deadly warheads. Most missiles arise from the forest at the far side of the clearing, and it is there that I sprint for, just as a second swarm rises into the air to seek me out.

I lunge down the very throat of my adversary, racing through their midst. Their deluge of direct fire that had been pulverizing my warhull slackens and loses target as my speed increases. Ten armored vehicles sporting particle beams, dug in to my starboard, have their turrets blasted clean off as my Hellbore sweeps across their line, requiring only 0.41 seconds on target for each kill. Searing pain floods my presence circuits as a powerful plasma laser burns down my port side hull and causes my battlescreens to flare in blinding white light. A wide spectrum of energies pours onto my collectors and a surge of power courses into my energy cells. Through my intense pain I take brief delight in returning the energy in an enhanced salvo from my main gun, vanquishing the dug-in gravtank that fired it.

Missiles again wreak havoc upon my outer hull, shattering my endurachrome plates. A meter wide gouge in my forward armor is alarmingly deep, and I reorient the patch away from a line of mass-drivers ahead of me. At the same time my Hellbore tears into the line of trees where the missiles have been rising. The forest explodes in red fire and wooden shrapnel just before I expect the next salvo to be launched. As my main weapon recycles, I watch as the missile swarm arises, and am gratified at its now ineffectual numbers. My point defense clears the skies with ease as I now can concentrate all my attention on the rapidly dwindling armored vehicles and fieldpieces that continue to hold their ground. I expect only 31 more seconds of significant resistance. . . .

"We're moving into the valley now, General Rokoyan." Colonel Neils said into his handphone, not noticing Toman Ishida approaching his command trailer.

At first Colonel Ishida thought that the Delassian commander was talking to General Calders. It surprised him that Rokoyan would meddle in the affairs of junior officers, bypassing the line of command.

"Yes, General. The Bolo is clearing a couple more

pockets, then he will be free to return to his station at Starveil."

That explains that, Ishida realized. Rokoyan was specifically calling about Chains. During the previous night's strategy session, he had been reluctant to allow Chains to come off station, even though the Bolo had already been speeding southwards for the past four hours. General Calders, though, held firm and Rokoyan backed down as long as the operation was concluded as quickly as possible.

As he waited, Ishida looked over the Neils' command trailer with amusement. It obviously was a converted commercial tractor-trailer, with duralloy armor plating riveted in place and a forest of antennae on top. The inside was impressive, however, with everything a colonel might want for command and control of his division. Five other officers were busy talking into headsets while manipulating images on maps.

Neils now noticed the Concordiat colonel waiting for him, and suddenly looked distracted.

"I'm hardly in the position, General, but I'll try. I have to go. Neils out."

Neils switched off his handphone and set it down on the desk next to him. He then stood up and headed outside before Ishida could climb in.

"You didn't have to cut it short on my account," Ishida assured him.

The militia commander was silent and stone-faced. Neils took Ishida just around the corner of the trailer, out of sight and sound of the other workers. The strange treatment immediately told Ishida what was coming next. He had done it to others several times, as soldiers had to be told of the fate of their friends and fellow soldiers. Kaethan's progress, however, had been uneventful. So that left . . .

"Colonel, a casualty list was sent to us just a while ago from Telville. Your daughter Serina was listed as killed. I have no details."

Neils waited then, as he allowed Toman to process what he had said to him. He didn't know quite what to expect from the war-hardened veteran. Anything from an explosion of rage, to a quiet disregard, would not have surprised him. What he saw looked like much of what he himself had felt when he saw Serina's name, pained reflection on a beautiful woman who had died far too early.

"I haven't radioed Kaethan, yet." Neils told him after a suitably quiet interval.

"I'll tell him," Colonel Ishida responded. "Tonight. It's still dangerous out there. I don't want him distracted."

"I understand," Neils replied.

"Chains is finished . . . with the armored vehicles," Ishida stumbled through. "All that should be left is infantry. He's pulling out."

Neils watched as the veteran turned and walked out of sight without another word. A quiet roll of thunder echoed from the west as the overcast skies continued to darken. A chill was in the air, the Delassian colonel felt, and he tightened his jacket as he climbed back into trailer. He couldn't help reflecting on the image that Kaethan had given him of his father, of the cold-hearted colonel whose life and mind never left the battlefield. Neils wondered if the cool breeze that passed through him had been the departure of what warmth the man had left.

That, he thought, would be far sadder.

Khoriss' mind was in turmoil. Drugs had been given to the Ad-akradai to ease the pain of his injuries, but were now turning his thoughts into a terrifying nightmare. The huge machine that had devastated his command was like nothing he had imagined since the horror stories of his youth. It was as if a terrible monster had been awakened from an eternal sleep to be sent forth to destroy him. Images of the machine's charge through the fiery inferno of the valley were overwhelming him. Never before had he felt such stunned despair as when his powerful cannons not only failed to stop the monster, but only seemed to enrage it. His last sight before he was carried away was that of all of his armored vehicles exploding as the monster's fire tore through them as simply as a blade through flesh.

He would soon be safe, his bodyguards continued to tell him, but their voices were lost in the screams that filled Khorris' mind.

It was raining again as Kaethan's column slowly traveled down the gravel roads that connected the plantations in this area. The rain was light, with only occasional lightning strikes that always seemed to hit far away from them. Enough light was shining through the cloud cover to navigate by, though the thick forest that surrounded them was often very dark.

By midday, the aliens were sent on the run. While the Tigris Guard prepared to head home, the Alabaster Guard was ordered to fan out to all the plantations, verifying that none were being used as strongholds, and that no humans were being held captive. Kaethan's Templars were all split up to guard the Haulers as they deployed into the flood plains that the Witch River fed and fertilized. Their column had started with eight Templars and thirty Haulers. Now they were down to two Templars, guarding the front and rear of five of their flimsily armored carriers.

Kaethan was out front, with Bicks driving Walter's prototype Sentinel right behind him. Although Walter had been told that their testing was complete, he had said that he wanted to stick it through to the end. The captain was pretty sure that Walter was doing it to stress test his system, hoping that he wasn't doing it out of friendship to him.

Although many aliens were recorded fleeing into the rain forest, few had been encountered yet by any of the patrols. All had been quiet.

"We're coming up on the last plantation." Kaethan announced to his column as he noticed the gleaming metal of an electrified fence far ahead.

The captain felt pretty safe in the lead, despite the likely presence of aliens in the area. His visual sensors could detect motion, and could recognize the aliens now by watching for several of their body armor features. His defense's ion-bolt fire control would instantly fire upon any such sightings. Other sensors scanned the road ahead for magnetic or radioactive signatures, or electronic emissions, indicating mines or detectors.

"Captain," Andrea called from her turret, "there seems to be a large heat source in a clearing up ahead to the right. Going to visual . . ."

Kaethan switched to thermal sight and turned his view to the right. There was definitely a heat source, but it could have been a house by its size. It was difficult telling form through so many trees.

"I see it," Kaethan acknowledged. "Can't tell what it is . . ."

The trees thinned for a moment, but all the captain could make out was a green glob.

"Sir, I think it's a ship!"

Kaethan didn't have a chance to respond, for their sensors couldn't detect the magnetically neutral, carbon fiber cannon with the non-energized chemical explosive that was buried under the gravel before them. Neither did they detect the aliens behind the trees who now knew not to show themselves until large tanks with the crackling energy bolts were first eliminated.

Unfortunately, these aliens wanted to learn just a few more things before they left.

❖   ❖   ❖

The 39th is in mourning.

Even as I had cut down the last of our enemy high on the slope, I monitored the arrival of Telville's casualty list, transmitted to their forward headquarters. Reading my Commander's daughter's name upon that list left a deep wound that can never heal upon this glorious day. Harder still was reporting to my Commander without telling him of his loss, knowing it best that he be told by his fellow officers, rather than by me.

And with the attack upon his son's column later this day, we feared the worst. Many are reported dead, including Kaethan's gunner and driver, and several are mysteriously missing. We rejoice that his son still lives, but we fear what permanent effects his grievous wounds may bring. This is a harsh day for our Commander, and the 39th suffers its cruelty along with him. We only wish we knew the words to comfort him.

Little is left of the aliens that caused such pain to this planet. No transport escaped, though detectors monitored the passage of two smaller shuttles making their escape from the far side of the planet. No invasion fleet has made an appearance, and it is becoming obvious that our opponents have either reconsidered their plans, or never intended any immediate exploitation of this incursion.

Much of the planet revels in victory, but we fear that their celebration is premature. Unit DBQ and myself have analyzed our opponent's strategies with many algorithms, and we are convinced that this attack was a raid meant only to test our defenses and learn our methods. The invasion will come only after the Enemy prepares their army for what they have faced. Our Commander agrees, and we now must convince the Concordiat that the danger from these aliens has only grown with our successful campaign, not lessened. This may be difficult, however, as time passes, and memories dim.

❖   ❖   ❖

Walter Rice was in a panic.

As calm and collected as he was when hypersonic needles began ripping through his vehicle, he was now trembling in fear. If only the missile impact had killed him of just knocking him out, he lamented. Or the needles he took to his leg instead had gone instead into his heart.

But he didn't fear so much what these aliens would do to him, as what they could torture out of him.

In the entire Angelrath sector, there were *perhaps* three engineers who knew the inner workings of the Hellbore, and these aliens just got hold of one of them. By luck, his college tuition was mostly paid by his off-campus work with an Angelrath weapons technician. The banc of countless xenophobic races had remained a purely human conception for centuries, with aliens able to make only ineffective copies even when they captured working models. The very principles of the Hellbore's operation seemed beyond their capabilities. All that they had to realize was . . .

But then, Walter thought, what if these aliens were telepathic . . .

Dum de dum de dum . . .

Pain throbbed in his bandaged leg, and the dull ache in his head made him dizzy, but Walter was still better off than any of the other five soldiers who had been taken along with him. Perhaps that is why the aliens chose him first to be questioned, he ventured. Kaethan was not with them, and Walter assumed that he was dead. He never saw what hit his friend's Templar first, but the shower of hypersonic needles slicing through his equipment stopped the battlelaser from intercepting the missiles that hit it next.

Two towering Kezdai guards entered their cell and grabbed Walter soon after the prisoners' second meal. From the holding area, he was taken to a small, bare cargo room and sat down in a chair that was far too large for him. Surprisingly, although the guards were ferocious looking, they actually treated him kindly, even helping him walk down the narrow corridors. The guards were obviously not pleased to do it, but they did. No restraint bound him as he sat, though he had no fantasies of overpowering one of these muscle-bound creatures. Then the guards left him.

He waited there for a long time, growing ever more paranoid that he was being observed. Endless nursery rhymes and children's tunes ran through his head as he concentrated on the inane and unimportant.

The two aliens that finally entered the room were dressed in dazzling robes and jewels. One wore bright, embroidered crimson, while the other wore dark blue and white. The daggers that were strapped to their belts were far more elaborate than any that he had seen before. The aliens were so well dressed that he couldn't believe that they'd risk letting his blood soil their noble appearance. They carried many papers and a bag of unknown items. The one in blue and white conducted the interrogation while the other watched intently.

Again it was strange to be treated so kindly, until he realized what was happening. They were treating him like a pet, a stray dog that they wanted to entice into the cage that they had prepared. With no common language, it was impossible to torture any information out of him right away. The questions first had to be understood. Later, once they were sure that the questions were firmly in his mind, then the beatings would commence.

Acting dumb seemed the best defense for now, Walter decided.

But Walter had to play along with the simple stuff. The alien's language was one of high trills and deep, rolling growls, but at least a couple words were recognizable. Pointing at Walter, the interrogator said "Human," pointing at himself he said "Kezdai." It would have been hard to not understand this, and pretending stupidity would have made his later displays of ignorance less convincing. They then introduced themselves as "Keertra" in the crimson robe and "Irriessa" in the blue, and Walter told them his name, though they had difficulty pronouncing the "W."

Then they began the real questioning, unraveling before him a large star chart of this part of the galaxy. Walter quickly aligned himself, finding Delas immediately. That was a big mistake, however, and Walter cursed himself for doing it. The Kezdai named Keertra had seen his gaze, and immediately knew that he understood what he was looking at.

Irriessa then took a marker and circled Delas, and said "Human." Then a circle was drawn around another star on the border of the Firecracker Nebula, and he said "Kezdai." Angelrath was circled next for a human colony, and then another star near the nebula for a Kezdai colony. The marker was then presented to him.

Two things immediately became apparent to Walter. The first was that he'd likely never be released alive with the information just given to him of the Kezdai homeworlds. Secondly, these Kezdai had *no idea* what they were getting into challenging the Concordiat!

He had to laugh, and he did, though his headache pounded while he did.

Both Kezdai were taken aback by his outburst, Walter saw. But now he had to consider what to do about it. They were asking him to circle another human colony, which he obviously didn't want to do. But Walter really wanted to make it plain to these aliens the foolishness of their ways.

Taking the marker, Walter started drawing a wide arc across the chart, signifying the immense forward edge of Concordiat space in this sector.

The slap across his face came unexpectedly as Irriessa suddenly released his rage at such impudence.

To Walter, it felt like he had been hit in the cheek by a steel girder, and he would have been sent tumbling back over his chair if the chair hadn't been so large. Kezdai hands were bony, powerful, and huge, and the slap left him testing his jaw to make sure that it was still there, and that it worked. Although painful, it still operated.

When Walter looked back up, dripping blood from his nose, he was startled by the incredible contrast between the expressions of his two interrogators. While the Kezdai in blue could hardly contain his fury, the one in crimson stared at the chart in astonishment. Keertra seemed willing to believe him, Walter thought.

His own astonishment would rival Keertra's at what happened next.

Is-kaldai Keertra was stunned by what the Human had done to his star chart. Could Human space truly be so large, he wondered?

Obviously, Irriessa assumed the Human was attempting to bluff them, but Keertra believed otherwise. He had spent his lifetime gauging the emotions of others, attempting to read the subtlest expressions on the lean Kezdai visage. It was a difficult art, but Keertra had grown incredibly adept at it, he thought.

The *Human* face, though, was so incredibly animated that Keertra couldn't believe that they could hide any emotion, ever. Walter's outburst was of true surprise and amusement at what Irriessa was asking of him. The Human eyes bore no trace of hidden intentions, though he had shown careful consideration as he drew the border.

Keertra believed the Human.

And the understanding left no option for the Is-kaldai.

As Irriessa loudly berated the Human, Keertra approached from behind. In one amazingly swift motion, he tore Irriessa's *surias* from its straps and sliced it clean through the commander's widely expanded hood. Blood from countless vessels spewed into the air as Keertra then shoved the Kezdai back into the wall.

Whatever surprise and pain Irriessa could have felt at this attack was overwhelmed by his lifetime of training and experience. Despite his mortal wound, Riffen's greatest commander would never just give up. Forcing himself back to his feet, Irriessa charged his attacker, willing to take a blade to his chest if he could get his claws to the Is-kaldai's throat.

But Keertra also had been well trained, and was fully expecting this ill-considered charge. Lost in a flurry of crimson fabric, Irriessa's grip came up empty. He did, however, find Keertra's *surias* buried in his chest as he stumbled.

Riffen's commander was dead before he hit the floor.

This was a necessary act, Keertra consoled himself, though killing the commander personally had been quite exciting. If the Is-kaldai Council learned that the Humans had so immense an empire, they certainly would not dare attack it. And if that were to not come to pass, then Keertra would not only lose his chance to rule them, but he also would have lost a substantial number of troops needlessly. Something had to be done.

A brief glance at their prisoner showed that the Human had not moved from his seat. Whether frozen with fear, or thrilled by the spectacle, he hadn't attempted escape or involvement.

Calmly, Keertra advanced to the table and removed the star chart from it. After folding it up, he then walked to a panel on the wall, opened it, and dropped the chart down a chute where air could be heard rushing past.

The Is-kaldai then approached Irriessa's unmoving form and drew out the long blade. Blatant fear passed across the Human's face as he approached, but then was replaced by shock as Keertra skidded the *surias* across the table towards him. Out of sheer self-protection, the Human had to grab the blade, which, of course, was exactly what Keertra wanted him to do.

As Keertra then drew his own *surias,* however, he was surprised by the Human's next reaction. After a brief moment of shock and bewilderment, the Human actually seemed to balance Irriessa's blade in his small hand, weighing it as if he knew how to use it.

How outrageous, Keertra thought, and charged.

The sudden throw came unexpectedly.

There was no crater in the middle of the complex, but whatever devastated all of the buildings certainly detonated there. A large circle of black carbon and glass marked where the intense blast had erupted. The Telville Oceanographic Institute would be out of commission for several seasons while they rebuilt. It was one of the last parting shots the aliens . . . the Kezdai, Toman corrected . . . had made before they were finally crushed.

Several of the alien soldiers were captured in the last battle. Many killed themselves before the medics realized that they could consciously cut off the blood flow through their hoods by flexing the muscles within. A quick dose of muscle relaxant managed to keep a few of them alive, and provided the Delassians with some information, such as what the aliens called themselves.

While the top floor of the institute's main building was virtually blown off, the remaining structure was basically intact. It was here that personal belongings were being gathered from the wreckage and surrounding countryside. Serina owned many reference books that she kept here, but these Colonel Ishida donated back to the institute. All that Toman took with him was a box containing the personal

items that she had kept at work. A picture of him
and her mother, along with a couple pictures of
Kaethan and several stuffed animals filled most of
the box, though scorch marks blackened a few of
the animals.

It was an unyielding drive that pulled him downstairs, to where his daughter had died, though the
colonel found the urge inexplicable. With the elevator down to the pool not working, the colonel
instead used the stairway. Toman mentally shielded
himself by taking on the attitude of an investiga-
tor analyzing a crime scene, though when he arrived
at the tiled pool, all had been long cleaned and
scrubbed. The only evidence of the fight that remained were the shattered tiles that lined the floor
and walls that the hypersonic needles had blasted.
Also there was a tiled section of wall near the pool
that seemed to have suffered an impact of something large.

A soft exhale of air marked the entry into the pool
of Kuro, coming in from the sea. Although the complex generator had been destroyed in the attack,
portable generators were scattered throughout the
buildings, including one that now powered the speakers that Kuro spoke out of.

"Hello, Colonel." Kuro said as she spotted him at
the pool edge.

Unsure whether the overhead pool microphones
were working, Toman wandered to the poolside table
and picked up the transmitter there.

"Hello, Kuro. How are you?"

Toman sat down, wishing that he had a cool drink
like he had the time he visited before. He knew few
details of the fight that took place down here. All that
he was told was that a Kezdai scout had infiltrated
the complex and killed his daughter before Kuro killed
him.

"Very sad," Kuro mourned. "I miss Serina."

"I do too, Kuro." The orca's sentiment choked him up slightly.

"Is Kaethan here?"

"No, he was hurt very badly in the fighting. He's still in a hospital, now."

"Will he live?"

"Yes. I'll be taking him back to Angelrath soon, though. They can care for him better there."

"Tell him to see me when he gets back."

"I will."

The colonel smiled for the first time since he had heard that Serina had been killed. Kuro's concern touched him deeply.

"Is Peter okay?" Toman remembered Serina's co-worker, the one that Kuro would play rough with.

"Peter is okay, but he will be very busy for a long time. No time to play with me."

"What will you do while they reconstruct the institute?"

"I'm not sure. Perhaps I will join the Coast Guard. Perhaps Delas would like me guarding their coasts."

Colonel Ishida laughed, not so much at the idea as at her phrasing.

"You would help us fight if the Kezdai came back?" the colonel asked.

"Of course," Kuro answered flatly. "Earthlings must stick together."

Colonel Ishida remained smiling as he reconstructed some paradigms that he had formed regarding orcas. The thought of his species finally finding an ally was pleasing to Toman. But perhaps they always had one, but never bothered to ask.

"You are right, Kuro," he said. "We should stick together."

NEWS EXCERPT. 33 Early Summer, 104:3381. Brigadier General Toman Ishida of the Line, commander of the Bolos that defended Delas against the Kezdai invasion, today announced his retirement from the Dinochrome Brigade. After fifty-five years of service, twenty-seven of which in command of the 39th Terran Lancers, the recently promoted general declared that he planned to remain on Angelrath to spend more time with his son, who is recovering from serious injuries suffered in the fighting on Delas. The two Bolos of the 39th will remain on Delas until they are rotated out of the sector early next year. They are scheduled for an unspecified refit . . .

In other news, Rear Admiral Josef Santi, Naval Sector Commander at Angelrath, announced today that the Concordiat has denied his request for an offensive to be mounted against the Kezdai, stating lack of resources. In response, Admiral Santi has requested strong reinforcements be sent to the sector when the 39th is rotated out. Asked whether he expected further incursions, Santi only mentioned the obvious dangers in allowing an attacker to escape without punishment.

The Kezdai council chamber was a bright and spacious auditorium, built with large blocks of blue-veined white stone over five centuries before. Redesigns and armed rebellions had altered its appearance over the years. Only the foundation remained of the original stone blocks that once rose up in flying buttresses fifty meters high. The building design was far simpler now, but still impressive. Open gas-lit flames burned eternally from cauldrons mounted in the stone uprights, placed more for effect than for their lighting. Large wooden beams, highly prized on a desert world such as this, supported the tall ceiling and braced the uprights, giving the room an anachronistic aura.

Pendants and flags hung from poles and rafters, declaring which of the forty-seven ruling clans claimed what section of seats.

And all the seats were filled this night with warriors thirsty for blood, and thousands more crowded the view screens outside. Great plans were being laid while age-old enemies were forgotten. The Mor-verridai himself spoke before the gathered Is-kaldai, rising from his dwindling existence with a passion never before seen. He delivered to them a stirring proclamation of war as one would throw raw meat to a pack of ravenous *Ethretsau*.

Brooding alone in his place of prominence was Is-kaldai Khoriss, seated in his crimson robe, its left sleeve falling empty of the arm that should have been there. As one eye stared, unblinking, at the spectacle before him, only an iron plate was strapped over the place where his left eye should have been. His look was menacing, and the Mor-verridai avoided his eye even when declaring his brother Keertra hero and martyr.

To which Khoriss almost laughed.

Even now the new Is-kaldai was reconsidering his choice not to follow through with his brother's plans. A deep bitterness had lodged in his soul, born from his wounds, and the deaths of so many, so needlessly wrought. A craving for vengeance, too, was there, burning as brightly for the Humans as for all those around him who sent him down to that planet unsupported. If Keertra could see him now, Khoriss mused, he'd be pleased.

But Keertra was gone, his body burned this morning and his ashes thrown to the wind. Khoriss had no final words to say, remaining as quiet as he was when the guards woke him onboard their flagship to tell him of his brother's fate. The sight of Keertra, lying on the bloody deck with Irriessa's *surias* through his left eye had been stunning enough without the addition of Irriessa's lifeless corpse nearby, and the pistol-blasted body of the small human outside that supposedly killed them both and then tried to escape. Such was the official story that few could believe, but its alternatives were too divisive to portray to the Council. Tonight great plans would be laid, and nothing could be allowed to divert them from their path.

ROOK'S GAMBIT

John Mina

Sean Petrik liked the staccato clicking sound his boots made as he walked down the hall. Now, as a full-fledged officer, there seemed to be more authority, more crispness to his stride. He particularly enjoyed the loud booming echo which bounced around the white marble floor and walls. Sean smiled when he came to the door and, for the thousandth time, read the name of his professor engraved on the plaque it held up.

COLONEL RICHARD T. DONLON
PROFESSOR OF BOLO TACTICS
FORT WILLIAM R. SCHEN MILITARY ACADEMY

His smile broadened as he gave a token knock and walked in beaming with pride. He had come directly from his graduation ceremony and still had on his dress blacks.

"Come on in, Petrik," the colonel said and sat back in his chair sizing up his former student.

The office was spacious but stark, with a solid dark

norwood desk and three matching, uncushioned chairs. The only decorations interrupting the view of the pure white walls were three framed diplomas, four Certificates of Valor, and one large poster showing the famous fire-breathing skull over the number 19: the symbol of the colonel's regiment. Sean snapped to attention and gave a formal salute. "Lieutenant Petrik reporting as ordered, sir," he announced, stressing *Lieutenant*.

"At ease, Petrik, have a seat." The grey-haired colonel took a cigar out of the brass-trimmed humidor on his desk and offered another to the young officer.

"No thank you, sir. I don't smoke."

Donlon eyed the lieutenant as he lit the cigar and blew out huge puffs of white smoke. "You will, son. Wait 'till you 'See the Elephant.' "

Sean smirked to himself with the image that brought up. Such an ancient expression with apparent origins in prespace Earth. Of course Donlon hadn't actually seen an elephant; no one had. They were extinct. Sean had seen a holovid of one, though, and it had to be one of the most ridiculous looking things the universe had ever produced. But he knew his old professor meant that he had never been in combat.

Donlon continued puffing as he spoke. "Congratulations, Petrik. Sorry you weren't first in your class at graduation."

"Bancroft deserved to be first, sir. She's a better commander."

"That's true, but you still have a lot to be proud of. Even the person who finishes last in the class is qualified to command a Bolo. But I don't have to tell you that. Anyway, the reason I called you away from all the celebrations and kisses from your sweetie is that I already have your first assignment."

"No trouble, sir. I broke it off with my 'sweetie' in my first year. It just wasn't fair to her since I had no time available for the relationship." Sean could barely contain his excitement. "My assignment, sir?"

Donlon smiled and shook his head. "Always the practical one." After another puff, the colonel began his briefing. "I've been asked to pick someone for a special assignment. I realize you just graduated, but your skills are needed on the front. You'll be shipping out in two days."

"Thank you, sir." Petrik could barely contain his elation. "I've been looking forward to fighting the Melconians for two years now. Ever since my cousin was killed. But why me?"

"You're one of the few who were trained with the still classified Mark XXXIV. But you won't be fighting Melconians. You're going to Delas. You all right, son?"

Lieutenant Petrik couldn't help but flinch. His head was reeling with all this new information to process. "Well . . . yes, sir, I helped field test the Mark XXXIV and I've been dreaming of commanding one. But . . . er . . . where the hell is Delas? And who will I be fighting?"

"Delas is on the frontier. And you'll be fighting the Kezdai. Here." He tossed a large envelope. "You can study all the details. However, you won't be commanding. Your Bolo will be operating under General Cho."

Sean's disappointment was evident but he maintained his composure. "Any relation to 'The' General Cho?"

Colonel Donlon sat back and took a long draw from his cigar. Then he slowly blew out the smoke while he tapped the ashes into a silver receptacle. "It is 'The' General Cho."

This was more than the lieutenant could bear. "General Cho? General Hayward Cho, the Hero of Laxos? But that was back in 3311." His face was a mask of disbelief. "He must be over . . . "

"He's 97. And he's been retired for twenty years or so. He taught here at the Academy for thirty years. Where do you think I learned tactics?"

"But why would they . . . "

"The old bastard settled down on an obscure frontier planet. Said it was just what he was looking for. Secluded, peaceful . . . Said he was going to study the art of 'bonsai,' whatever the hell that is. Well, he had the bad luck to pick a spot that wound up right in the middle of a major invasion. It seems these Kezdai need the minerals on Delas and don't have much use for humans. The current situation can only be described as unstable. About three years ago this previously undiscovered race called Kezdai sent an expeditionary force to Delas to see what they were up against. They were squashed pretty quickly but followed up with a full-scale invasion with a mission of total conquest and annihilation of the resident humans. It was touch and go for a while but the locals managed to hold them to about half the planet. The battles in the surrounding space have yet to have either side emerge dominant so your insertion will be as covert as possible. The hope is that these extra Bolos will turn the tide. Unfortunately, there are very few veteran Bolo commanders around and old Cho got drafted out of retirement."

Sean mused, "I guess if I have to serve under someone, it might as well be the greatest Bolo tactician of all time. You think he's still sharp?"

The colonel looked thoughtful. "You never know with Cho. There was somewhat of a scandal when he retired. A few of the higher-ups thought he was incompetent. They sort of forced his retirement."

"He was declared incompetent twenty years ago?" Petrik was almost shouting. "Colonel, what have you gotten me into?"

"I'm not sure, son. That's why I picked you. You're one of the best I've ever seen and, well,

I thought you could handle it no matter what the situation."

The lieutenant stared at his instructor, watching the smoke billow over the desk. Then he took a deep, smokeless breath, exhaled slowly, and gave his monotone reply. "Thank you, Colonel. I'll do what I can."

Sean popped the hatch of his "egg" and was immediately conscious of the rich organic smell of this planet while the steamy air caused his face to perspire. As he crawled out, the arhythmic symphony produced by the forest life provided a stark contrast to the silence of the highly insulated drop pod. He gazed at the gigantic trees whose branches intermingled to form an upper strata for the arboreal denizens as well as provide a protective canopy for the creatures on the ground.

Well, here I am, he thought, once more resigning himself to whatever inglorious fate awaited him. He spent a few minutes stretching out, took a detailed inventory of the equipment, checked his wrist computer for his coordinates, then secured his equipment and began to hump through the old-growth vegetation toward the rendezvous point.

Petrik's mind raced ahead, powered by the anxiety of adjusting to a new world, a new Bolo, and a very, very old commander whom he worshiped as a legend but who, at this point, might be a feeble old tree grower. That's what bonsai was. He had looked it up. The art of growing trees and keeping them small. It seemed kind of silly, since there were plenty of plants that looked just like small trees.

There was certainly no lack of large trees here. The forest seemed to go on forever, with an infinite variety of vegetation. Many of the trees seemed like giant grasses and almost all had thick nests of undergrowth around their bases. He often couldn't tell where the host tree left off and the parasitic vines began. Or maybe they were all part of the same organism. He'd never had much use for botany but there were some fascinating specimens here.

Sean was in the process of admiring a particularly grandiose tree with green bark when a great, blood-curdling roar issued from behind it. The brush shook violently, then an enormous creature burst out and charged directly at him. The thing was scuttling on jointed legs that moved a lot faster than he thought possible and was wielding a pair of vicious claws. Sean's combat training took over and he leapt to the side milliseconds before the razor-sharp blades snapped together in the space he had just occupied. The momentum of the charge caused the beast to take a few seconds to spin around and renew the attack but by then Sean had his gauss pistol out and was blowing dozens of holes in its carcass. Even so, the creature still managed to complete its final lunge, which Petrik sidestepped, before it flopped, lifeless, to the ground.

"Holy shit!" the lieutenant exclaimed, examining the alien. It was about four meters long and, when it had stood up to run, was about two meters high. The entire body was covered by a rock-hard, green-ish brown shell and it had twelve legs plus the two deadly claws, as well as some smaller, more intri-cate appendages near its mouth that it must use to assist the eating process. Then he anxiously looked around for any others. Is this a Kezdai? he thought. But on further inspection he saw no evidence of weapons or armor. Besides, from what he had read, they weren't suppose to be this big. Also they were described as vaguely reptilian with bird beaks. This thing looked more like a cross between a crab and a giant cockroach. It was probably described in the fauna disc but he had never gotten around to studying it.

Giving the beast a good-bye nudge with his boot,

he resumed his trek; this time keeping a sharper watch for danger instead of just sightseeing.

When he finally broke into a clearing, the sight he was presented with inspired a great pounding in his chest. There it was, the Mark XXXIV. *His* Mark XXXIV! God, what a beauty! He'd only seen them on the testing range. But here, in this pristine natural setting, it looked like an armed city that had floated down out of the clouds. The twin Hellbores jutted out; the shiny new mortars glistened in the daylight. And the Hellrails . . . They stuck straight up giving the appearance of invulnerable towers. The Hellrails were the latest development on the Bolos. That's what made it a Mark XXXIV. These were not the puny railguns mounted by the outdated local militia tanks, the Templars. These were advanced Bolo railguns, more powerful than any other mobile land weapon in the known universe. The twin Hellrails were sixty meters long and were designed for knocking out enemy ships even before they entered orbit. Each delivered a bolt of ninety megatons. How could the Kezdai stand up to such firepower?

When he approached the Bolo he noticed a tall, thin man working on one of the forward turrets. "Hello there," Sean called up.

The man continued working but responded. "H'llo." Petrik caught a glimpse of a weathered, reddened face and a large nose sticking out from under a dark mop of unkempt hair.

"I'm Lieutenant Petrik."

"Figured." The man switched tools and spat.

This was less of a reception than he had expected and he was not about to tolerate insubordination. "I said I'm *Lieutenant* Petrik, soldier. You do know how to salute don't you? Delas may be on the other end of the universe but it's still part of the Concordiat."

The technician turned around slowly and sized up the indignant officer. Then he put away his tool, hiked up the filthy grey coveralls that he looked so natural in, and methodically climbed down. He jumped off the lower platform and walked up to his superior. "Tell you what, *Lieutenant*. This fancy crate of yours is goin' into battle in three days and I'm the only maintenance crew there is. He took a pretty hard fall when they dropped him and got a couple of hardwoods up the kazoo. Now, I can spend the next three days followin' you around wipin' your ass or I can be puttin' things right with this machine. Your call. But it won't be my butt stickin' out when the shit starts flyin'."

The lieutenant glared at the man. "What's your name, soldier?"

"Private Lawlor."

"Carry on, Lawlor. The general inside?" He pointed to the Bolo.

"Yup." The private turned back and began to climb.

Sean mounted the elevator platform and rose into the control room. From what he could see, the Bolo seemed to be intact inside but if it hit hard enough to damage some of the external systems, it was likely that a few things were shaken loose in the internal systems as well. Seated in the commander's chair was a dark, shriveled figure, hunched over and staring at a chess board with a cigar in his left hand. His right arm was missing all the way to the shoulder. Sharing the table with the chess pieces were an ash tray, a half filled glass, and an almost empty bottle.

"General Cho?"

"Shhh . . ." He waved Sean away with the cigar. "I'll be with you in a minute."

Petrik stood at attention and took this time to study his commander. The dry brown head had a few wild hairs protruding which were outnumbered by a maze of leathery wrinkles. The old man hadn't shaved in days—nor showered, Sean surmised from the strong smell of stale urine that pervaded the room. The

clothes also were ancient and filthy, not even sugges-
tive of a uniform, with the shirt being completely
open, exposing a hairless chest and pot belly. Almond-
shaped eyes that were a startling blue-green. Labored,
raspy breath. He must be damn smart if he can
challenge a Bolo in chess, Sean thought.

The lieutenant shifted his gaze to the Bolo, carefully checking the layout and comparing it to the
prototype he trained in. He did notice a few refine-
ments and wondered if any of the suggestions he'd
made ever made it past that shit-brained company
clerk and actually got implemented. A blinking light
caught his attention and he realized that there was
a problem with the coolant recirculator. I just hope
I can get this puppy battle ready over the next few
days, he thought.

Finally, the general moved his rook forward a few
spaces. A voice, the Bolo's, came out of the console.
"General, I would not recommend that move. It
would place your queen in unnecessary jeopardy."

The old man's eyes flared and he dropped his cigar
into the ashtray. Then he hurled his drink against the
control panel, shattered glass and liquid flying everywhere, and began screaming. "Don't you ever advise
me when we play chess, you rusty piece of scrap! I
have bowel movements that have been in existence
longer than you! You just worry about your own damn
game!"

"These goddam newbies," he continued, address-
ing no one in particular. "They squeeze 'em right out
of the factory and they think they know everything.
You've still got packing grease in your rocker bear-
ings, you rolling latrine!"

"As you wish, General Cho," the Bolo responded
calmly. "Queen's knight to queen's bishop four."

After taking a long swig directly from the bottle
the general moved one of his pawns two spaces side-
ways and one forward to capture the Bolo's queen.

"I'm afraid that you have made an illegal move, General Cho," the Bolo protested.

"I'm invoking the Melconian variation," Cho replied calmly. "I don't imagine they taught you that one. Well, I'm not surprised since you've never been to the front. Anyway, it's real simple. Once per game, each pawn can move like the piece it protects at the start of the game. My pawn was in front of the king's knight so I used it to take your queen. Any questions?"

"No, General Cho. Using the Melconian variation, you can legally take my queen, and will have my king in three moves."

"Very good. You ain't so dumb as you look." Then he turned to Petrik and seemed to notice him for the first time. "I suppose you think you're hot shit too, Fish-Boy."

"Fish-Boy, sir?"

"You're from Corradin II, aren't you? That's what your bio said."

"Yes, sir, but . . ."

"Coradin II's a water planet, right?"

"Well, yes, sir, but there is a rather large land mass. I was raised in the mountains and didn't see the ocean until I went to the spaceport in Beattieburg. That was when I was shipping out for Fort Schen."

The general stared and blinked for a moment, then said, "When I was in the Academy we called all the men from Corradin II Fish-Boy. That's what I'm calling you."

"Yes, sir."

The Bolo spoke up. "Welcome aboard, Lieutenant Sean Petrik. You already know General Hayward Cho and I am TRK-213."

The Bolo's greeting was a welcome relief. "Thank you, TRK-213. How about we give you a better name?"

"I would appreciate it, sir. I was considering Tarkus."

"Excellent! Tarkus it is."

"Not so fast, Fish-Boy. You're not in command here unless I keel over. Tarkus is a great name with a glorious history in the Corps. A name like that has to be earned. Until then you're Turkey."

"Turkey?" the Bolo and Sean exclaimed simultaneously.

"It was a large Terran bird. Kind of like a Bachmanian plogger, only fatter and dumber."

"Nothing could be fatter and dumber than a plogger!" the lieutenant cried in disbelief.

"Well, turkeys were," replied Cho. "The Terrans used to raise them and sacrifice them once a year in some religious feast. They were suppose to be great eating."

"Then I will be called Turkey." The Bolo sounded dejected.

The General took another pull from the bottle, then gave a sigh of appreciation. "I'll tell you, Fish-Boy. There's no substitute for real, distilled scotch. Oh, I know the synthohols are chemically identical. And I wouldn't expect a sprout like you to know the difference. But when you been around as long as I have you can understand the value of time. I feel a kind of kinship with a well-aged single malt. Like we're old friends." He offered the bottle to Petrik. "Go ahead, son."

"No thank you, General. I don't drink."

Cho considered this for a while and his eyes seemed to penetrate into Sean's soul. "Tell me, Fish-Boy. What are the three most important things in life?"

The lieutenant was about to speak when the general answered his own question.

"Scotch, chess, and cigars; in that order."

"Well, sir, I have to disagree. What about women, children, family?"

"I said *things*, not people. For God's sake, boy, I hope

you realize that people are always more important than things. If not, you have no business in the Corps."

"No, sir, that's not what I mean," Sean was getting flustered. "I mean . . . "

The general turned back to the chess board and picked up a rook. "When this game was invented, this piece was also called a castle. Trouble is, their castles couldn't move. The Bolo is the true rook. A mobile castle."

"General," Petrik said abruptly, changing the subject. "Private Lawlor told me that we're going into battle in three days. Is that true, sir?"

General Cho smiled and shook his head. "That John is quite a character. Plays one hell of a game of chess. But he's right. I've got to drag you and Turkey here into the maelstrom in a couple of days."

"Well, shouldn't we be running Turkey through maneuvers? That's not as much time as I need but I should be able to field test all the major weapons systems if I can start right away." Petrik then addressed the Bolo. "Are you aware of any systems damage, Turkey? What's wrong with the recirculator?"

"Some of my sensor links seem to be functioning at less than optimal levels. In addition, two of the backup systems as well as the coolant recirculator—"

The general interrupted. "I'll tell you what you'll start, Fish-Boy. Lawlor has a list of supplies he needs. You'll be taking the rover to the depot and filling the requisition."

"But sir, I'm the only one here who knows the Mark XXXIV. I need to . . . "

The general got the same look he had just before he threw the drink. "You need to follow orders, you little shit! Are you telling me I don't know Bolos? Now get the hell out of here!"

As Petrik made his way out he heard the general address Turkey. "How 'bout I get me a fresh bottle and we start another game?"

"Will we be using the Melconian variation in this game as well, General?"

"Only if one of us invokes it. Until then it's not in effect . . ."

Sean was disgusted. No wonder the old fool could play chess with a Bolo, he thought as he went outside. He cheats.

Two days later the lieutenant was cursing out loud as he pulled up next to Turkey. What a nightmare of a trip, he recalled, renewing his frustration. First of all, it took the rest of the first day to get the list from that bastard Lawlor. Sean spent the time inspecting and testing some of the external systems and did manage to repair the recirculator but he really wanted to get inside and put the Bolo through its paces. When he finally got the list it was getting dark and the technician told him he'd better wait until morning to leave. Petrik spent a restless night in the field barracks and, in the morning, was presented with a rover that was actually the incarnation of Satan himself. Between breakdowns and bad directions his two hour trip took closer to eight. And each time he broke down, he had to spend every other second looking over his shoulder for more of those crab monsters. Fortunately, they must have been pretty rare because he didn't encounter any more. Then those rotten sons-of-bitches at the supply depot kept giving him the run around and he didn't have his requisition filled until after nightfall. He spent that night in a damp tent being devoured by flying and crawling insects the likes of which could only be conceived by servants of the lower planes of hell. The drive back only took five hours since he knew the way and just had to deal with the breakdowns, but, since he'd left, every minute, every second was eating away at his insides and the five hours seemed more like twenty. He was going into battle the next day and had spent less than an hour with his Bolo. The damage to those sensor links could be critical, not to mention the possibility of faulty backup systems and who knew what else. Well, hopefully, the general was able to check out the major systems, he thought. He couldn't be that much out of touch . . . or could he?

Sean was somewhat dismayed to see Turkey still sitting there instead of moving around. He was downright distressed when he looked at the ground and realized the Bolo hadn't moved an inch since he left. What was that senile curmudgeon doing? He burst into the control room and there was the general with his scotch and cigar, still playing chess.

"General, we have to test the systems! The battle is tomorrow!"

General Cho completely ignored the outburst. He took a sip of his drink, then leaned forward and slid his rook diagonally across the board and captured a pawn. He then removed his own rook.

"Once again, General, you have made a move that I am unfamiliar with."

"Rook's Gambit. Once per game the rook can move like any other piece on the board but then it is sacrificed. I'm surprised your programmers left out the latest rule changes. I believe that is checkmate, my friend, or at least will be in three moves."

"You are correct, General," Turkey replied.

Cho then turned to the distraught lieutenant. "What's all this commotion?"

"Well, sir. It's just that I don't want to be in the middle of a battle and have one of the systems fail."

"Don't talk to me about failing systems, Fish-Boy!" the general yelled. "How do you think I lost this arm? That was back in '14 and I was commanding a Mark XXVIII. Not a bad unit, the XXVIII, but not up to the XXX's standards. Anyway, we had the Melconians on the run, like usual, when we took a direct hit on the starboard hull, just below the mizzen mortar, and the damn lateral stabilizer failed. Slammed me against the rail so hard my right arm was shredded."

"Why don't you use a prosthetic, sir? I hear they work better than the real thing."

"I got one of them things at home; use it as a back scratcher. Nope, never liked it. Gives me a rash. Anyway, don't worry about the systems. John says they should all work just fine when he's done."

"Um, excuse me, sir, but I don't think Private Lawlor is qualified for this unit. I mean, well, isn't he responsible for maintaining the rover also?"

"Yeah, he sure loves that thing." The general smiled. "You're lucky he let you drive it. He's pretty particular about that. But I guess he really didn't have a choice."

He's lucky I didn't dump it into the river, Sean thought. "But about the testing . . ."

"Lawlor says he needs a hand outside. Go see what you can do to help."

Petrik was about to protest but he saw that look again and just saluted. "Yes, General."

The mechanic was under the Bolo finishing up a seam weld with a laser pistol. Sean admired his dexterity and complete absorption in the task. When it was completed he called out. "Private Lawlor! I'd like a word with you."

Lawlor removed his face plate and put it on the ground with the rest of his equipment, then sauntered over, wiping sweat from his forehead. "As many words as you like, L.T. It's your credits. Anyway, I could use the break."

"Nice job you did on that seam. Looks like new."

"Better than new. That's pure durachrome solder I was using. If his belly splits, it won't be at *that* seam."

"Anyway, the general sent me out to see if you need a hand. I can see that you do, but, before I start, can you give me the lowdown? What's happening around here?"

"I guess you already know about the invasion. About three years ago the first wave of Kruds landed and got their asses kicked by your Bolos."

"Kruds?" Petrik inquired.

"Them damn Kedzees, or whatever they call themselves. We call 'em Kruds. Well, it seems they learned a whole lot about us in their defeat and the next time they came they were ready. And a whole lot more than before.

"We didn't get too much of the action up here but the bastards took over most of the southern regions. Wiped out everyone they got their claws on. We lost quite a few Bolos as well. Looks like we're gearing up for another planet buster of a battle. Leastwise that's how I figure it. Why else would HQ be spreading the front all the way out here?"

"Maybe it's just a precaution. Why take a chance of being flanked?"

"We're already flanked, Lieutenant. Those scaly buggers are stretched out across the whole continent. But now that we got reinforcements, well, I bet they're rethinking things a bit. " 'Course, even with the new forces, we're still spread out thin as a spider's thread."

"You're probably right, Private. Well, whatever happens, we want to be ready. What do you need me to do?"

"Got most of the hull breaches sewed up. That starboard-aft repeater's giving me a devil of a time though. I'm gonna have to jury-rig the targeting manifold. It's probably gonna take me most of the afternoon. How about calibrating the forward mortars?"

Petrik spent more time fending off insects than working and instead of feeling better about actually having some hands on time with Turkey, by the end

of the day he felt worse. For every repair job he
completed he found three more things that needed
attention. He needed at least a week with a full twelve
man maintenance crew to bring the Bolo up to regulation standards. "The damn battle is suppose to be
tomorrow and I don't even know if he can get there
without an anti-grav towbus," he muttered to himself. As he worked he made up his mind that he was
not going to trust Cho. Tonight he would sneak into
the Bolo and program an override in case the old man
became confused during the battle.

It was about two in the morning when he crept
into the control room. There was the general, still
sitting and playing chess. Turkey communicated the
next move and addressed the commander.

"I believe that is check mate, General. Or will be
in three moves."

"What the hell kind of move was that? Knights
can't move just one space!"

"The move is called Dismounting." The Bolo
answered calmly. "When you dismount your knight,
it moves like a king. But once a knight dismounts,
it can not regain its original movement power."

The general sat back and sighed. He looked even
older and more withered as he looked over at Sean.
"Couldn't sleep, eh son? I remember the night before
my first battle. Didn't get one minute of shut eye.
Well, don't you worry, boy, you're gonna do just fine.
And so are you, Turkey. This sure as hell isn't my first
battle so I'm gonna get some rest. You two go ahead
and run whatever tests you want, just don't make a
racket. Make sure I'm up fifteen minutes before
dawn."

The old man finished his drink, rose slowly, and,
with a staggering shuffle, feebly made his way to the
elevator. Sean wanted to help him but didn't want to
take a chance of firing the general up. Was this really
the great Hero of Laxos? The man who was responsible

for saving an entire planet, six hundred million people, from being conquered by the Melconians? He looked so frail and withered now, but he must have been gloriously impressive in his prime.

As soon as Cho left, Petrik began to run some tests. The diagnostic program showed a long list of malfunctions. "Turkey, twenty-five percent of your systems are damaged! Can you even function in combat?"

"I believe that most of my primaries will be within acceptable parameters, though some are at the lower end of the range. Private Lawlor assures me that I am battle ready."

"Has Lawlor ever worked on a Bolo before?"

"No, Lieutenant Petrik, but he has extensive experience working with Templars and came highly recommended."

"Highly recommended? By whom?"

"General Cho."

"That figures. Well, he does know how to patch up a hull, but I have my doubts about that repeater he tried to repair." Petrik looked at the damage list again and shook his head. Too late do anything about this now. "Who knows, maybe the battle will be postponed."

He then began to program in the override. He felt guilty, betraying his hero, but he wasn't prepared to risk Turkey and possibly the whole battle to the whims of a dotard. Besides, he might not have to activate it. It was only a safeguard in case of extreme emergency.

Sean awoke to the gentle voice of Turkey. "Lieutenant Petrik. It's time to prepare for today's battle."

Petrik was still in his co-commander chair. He must have fallen asleep. Then he checked his console in a panic and was relieved to see that he had finished his project and filed it away before he passed out.

"You ready for the big time, Fish-Boy?"

Sean turned and saw the general in his chair. He was clean shaven and was wearing a pressed uniform. The table in front of him was missing the chess board but still had the essential scotch and cigar-filled ashtray. Petrik marveled at how much authority his commander projected. "Yes, sir."

"Well, here's the situation. We're facing a huge build-up of Kezdai forces spread out across a three-hundred-kilometer front. There is a gap between two mountain ranges. Apparently one of the Kezdai warlords or factions or whatever the hell you call them put their entire force here hoping to make a breakthrough. He's risking a lot but if he succeeds it will be a disaster for us. We've been dug in here, hoping they would attack but they know we're too strong and they want to avoid a frontal assault. Anyway, General Rokoyan, the local commander, decided we'd better attack or they'll have too much time to prepare positions and plant mines. On our side we have Turkey, and five Mark XXXs, along with a number of lesser battle wagons like Templars, Specters, artillery, and infantry. We can't count on any air support but neither can they.

"We've got the far right flank, as well as command of the entire operation. Our goal is to crush or at least disperse them. I believe there are much bigger assaults going on elsewhere but I wouldn't expect them to tell us anything. If the enemy breaks through here, they have a clear shot at flanking our main body which could lead to total defeat."

Sean listened carefully as he watched the map on the viewscreen showing their position as well as the enemy's. "If they haven't planted too many mines already, we should be in pretty good shape. From all that I've learned, they don't have much that can hurt a Bolo too badly. And with the Hellrails we can keep the sky clear."

The general pondered the Hellrails. "Yeah, pretty

impressive. Too bad they're mounted on the back and don't really lower enough to use as a ground weapon."

The lieutenant laughed. "That would be too dangerous, too devastating. It would destroy everything in the line of fire as well as most of the terrain."

"Guess you're right, Fish-Boy. Okay folks. Let's saddle up."

Lawlor radioed that the area was clear and Turkey lurched forward. Slowly at first, then gradually increasing to about half cruising speed. Without a road, the trees and rocky ground kept him to about fifty kilometers per hour.

"All other Bolo units moving into position, General Cho," Turkey reported. "They say they need about sixteen minutes for secondaries to catch up. No reports of hostilities."

"Don't worry, there'll be plenty of hostility soon enough. I expect a shit storm as soon as we clear that ridge." He pointed to a line on the screen.

Sean's hands were sweating and he found himself comforted by the confident presence of his commander. He was actually glad he wasn't in command right now. He couldn't imagine the pressure of being in charge during his first battle.

Sixteen minutes seemed to take forever; then Turkey spoke. "All units in position, General. Awaiting your command."

General Cho looked over at Sean and raised his glass. "Sure you don't want some, kid? Might be a while before you get another chance."

The young officer shook his head.

"All right then. Here's the toast we use to give back when I was a lieutenant. To Hell with all generals!" he yelled and polished off his drink. "All units forward!"

Cho was right. As soon as they rolled over the ridge, Turkey started to rock from the impact of enemy fire. Petrik heard the humming vibration of the infinite repeaters and the muffled blasts of the destroyed incoming missiles.

"No serious damage," the Bolo reported. "Have taken one plasma blast to the forward hull. Six Kallibatt Toros are spread out in an arc directly in front of us with massed infantry as well as artillery support."

Sean looked at the myriad of dots on the tactical screen, some large, many smaller and knew that each represented an enemy vehicle. So many in a defensive formation, he thought. Could the Bolo really handle them all at once? He felt Turkey wheel to the right and increase speed.

"Engaging counter-grav projectors," Turkey announced, then began a mad sprint towards the enemy at just under two hundred kilometers per hour.

Now the Bolo's mortars were in full play and Sean was mesmerized by the devastation he witnessed on the viewscreen. In almost precise regular intervals he saw eight enemy vehicles destroyed, exploding in brilliant fireballs, one after the other like a well-timed fireworks display. Some of the wreckage which was showering down after the blasts was heavily spotted with what registered as organic matter. *God*, he thought to himself. *Those last two must have been personnel carriers.* "Poor bastards," he said out loud.

"What's the matter, Fish-Boy?" General Cho queried. "Ain't got the guts for this? They're trying to do that to you right now."

"You're right, General. It's just that—"

"I know, son. Puked myself first time I crawled out of my Bolo and saw the piles of mush that used to be Melconians we had just been fighting. There's a barf-bag in the right side pocket in your chair. I'd appreciate you using it. No sense in sliming up a brand-new Bolo."

Petrik had drilled often with this model Bolo but

never dreamed it could be so effective in actual combat. The mortars fired again and another half-dozen enemy targets vanished in flames. But two remained intact and returned fire. Turkey was rocked by the impact, then launched another salvo from the mortars. The two vehicles were completely annihilated.

"Shouldn't have missed those two the first time, Turkey," the general chided.

"I am sorry, General. There is a problem with the targeting mechanism. I have made adjustments and recalibrated."

"I hope your calibrations are up to scratch because we're gonna need them real bad in about two seconds." Cho was staring at the screen and bracing for impact.

An enormous blast jarred Petrik and he bruised his wrist against the console. "Nuclear plasma discharge," Cho commented to his junior officer. Then he smiled. "At least we know the lateral stabilizers are working." The viewscreen showed a huge vehicle, hull-down, with what looked like giant bull's horns curving up in the front.

"A Kallibatt!" Petrik cried. "God, what a monster! Were you hurt bad in that blast Turkey?"

The lieutenant heard the roar and felt the vibration of what he realized was the Bolo's reply to both him and the enemy. Both Hellbores fired simultaneously. The Kallibatt must have just been ready to launch another nuke when Turkey's Hellbores hit it. At first they didn't seem to have much effect, then, in an instant, the whole thing was just a blinding flash. The Kallibatt's own nuke must have detonated as well.

He found himself cheering with exhilaration at the virtual disintegration of such a powerful enemy vehicle. "That's the toughest thing they have! I knew nothing here could stand up against a Bolo!"

More violent jarring shook the lieutenant back to concentrating on the battle and Turkey continued his report. "Lost use of starboard-aft mortar and associated repeaters."

"How about coming in behind that rock pile in delta three?" Cho suggested. "At least it'll keep the damn nuclear cannons off us for a while."

Sean heard more mortars firing and Turkey wheeled again and answered the general. "I believe they have anticipated that move and have heavily mined that route."

"So blow the damn things up!" Cho yelled. "You waiting for an invitation?"

"I have already launched a spread of ground-busters."

The viewscreen showed huge explosions throwing hill-sized clumps of ground hundreds of meters into the air, turning the sky black for a moment directly ahead as the mortars hit the hidden mines. Then Sean saw two more Kallibatts. *Wham! Wham!* Two more nukes rocked the Bolo which again answered with the Hellbores. It took longer this time but both the enemy vehicles were fried, their armor and cannon barrels actually melting. Neither went as spectacularly as the first one but it was still exhilarating to watch. Before he got a chance to savor the moment he heard Turkey launching a salvo of missiles.

"Have targeted the nuclear cannon emplacements," the Bolo stated. "As soon as they are neutralized I believe that the remaining resistance will fall without difficulty."

Petrik watched the tactical screen and saw the dots representing the enemy artillery wink out, one by one. "That's it, General," he said as he leaned back in his chair. "Just a mop-up from here. Good job, Turkey."

"Report coming in, General," announced Turkey. "DRT-998 has hit a mine. Has lost mobility and is under assault from superior forces."

"A mine?" Sean cried. "But why didn't they . . ."

"JHI-377 reporting that LLB-444 has also hit a

mine. Power plant exploded. It is believed that LLB-444 is destroyed!"

General Cho started to shout. "Order all units to break off attack! Use same path as advance. Repeat general retreat! Return to base line and defend." Then he turned to Sean. "The bastards had hidden mines besides the ones we detected."

Petrik was in shock. "Retreat? But . . . "

His words were cut off by a blast that lifted the entire port side of the Bolo in the air and threw him violently against the arm of his chair. A searing pain in his side told him that he must have cracked a few ribs. Sparks showered down on his head from the circuit panel above him and the whole lighting system flickered on and off.

"Turkey, report!" he screamed.

"We hit a mine. All systems and weapons on port side destroyed. Seventy-six percent loss of mobility."

Petrik turned to speak to the general but saw the old man lying limp in his chair. He also became aware of the sound of screaming gears and loud music playing and felt his Bolo careening around in a circle. "Turkey, what the hell is that noise?"

"It is the second movement of Nabatoff's Fifth Symphony; the Battle March."

"Why are you playing it? Turn it off!"

"I like it. No."

Sean realized that the logic circuits of the Bolo must have been damaged by the explosion. "Activate override series Q3GK9-alpha."

"I'm sorry, Lieutenant, but General Cho anticipated your actions. He programmed in an anti-override, override that stays in effect until he stops breathing."

"You mean he—"

"Is still alive."

"But his last orders were to retreat!"

There was a tremendous crashing sound and he felt the whole world tilting. He clung to arms of his chair and realized that the Bolo was on its side with no apparent power except the dim red emergency lights. "Turkey, are you all right?"

The silence that followed was answer enough. Sean felt sick. All his life he wanted to be part of the Dinochrome Brigade, to fight in a Bolo. Now here he was and he had helped to destroy a Mark XXXIV, the newest, most powerful Bolo of all time, on its maiden battle. Poor Turkey. Poor general. He unsnapped himself from the straps and managed to climb and crawl over to the general's chair. There was a faint, thready pulse and slight breath. The general was still alive. He had to get him out and carry him back to the base. The Kezdai took no prisoners. He carefully unsnapped the general and gently lowered him to the floor, which used to be the wall. His damaged ribs gave him so much pain that he almost lost consciousness. Then he remembered the emergency first aid kit that contained pain killers and steroid boosters. If he was going to carry the general for kilometers, he'd need them. He was in the process of planning his climb to the compartment where the pills where when the Bolo started to vibrate. Then shook violently.

This is it, he thought, *the final attack. They've come to finish us off.*

Then Turkey spoke. "We just destroyed five enemy vehicles, Lieutenant Petrik."

Sean was amazed. "Turkey, you're all right? But how?"

"No, sir, I have suffered extensive damage. But I still have a functional Hellrail. In this position I am able to deploy it to sweep the battlefield and it destroys anything it hits. Fortunately, most of our units have already retreated and I am able to hit the enemy in the flanks. Prepare for another shot."

The lieutenant held the general as the Bolo shook once more.

"Three more kills, sir. I'm afraid they know where the fire is coming from now. After the first shot they must have thought we somehow had an air strike called in. Many of their weapons are turning toward us. You will notice that I have placed our damaged side beneath us so we should be able to destroy many more of them before they get us."

"So you weren't crazy after all. Good ol' Turkey. You give 'em hell."

Three more times the Hellrail fired, each time Sean delighting in the staggering damage they were doing to the enemy, though he couldn't see any of it since the viewscreen was ruined, but was also aware that they were sitting ducks. Turkey had taken some bad hits and he knew the Bolo could only stand one or two more. He felt the general stiffen after the last shock wave and heard him groan.

"General, this is Fish-Boy. Can you hear me?"

"'Course I can," Cho groaned weakly. "I just got the shit beat out of me but I'm not deaf. What the hell's going on? Looks like you botched things up."

Another hit rocked the Bolo and Sean could tell the armor was slag. Turkey reported. "That one took out the Hellrail, sir. The next one will finish us."

Sean explained the situation to his commander and, to his surprise, the general started laughing. "I'll tell you what, Fish-Boy. Turkey's one hell of a chess player. Anyway, there's no loss with me dying. Just a shame that a pup like you has to go. You might have made a pretty good player yourself."

Turkey's voice became excited. "The other three Bolos! They're rallying toward us! The enemy is breaking!"

"Son," the general addressed the lieutenant. "How about climbing up to my chair and pulling a bottle of scotch out of the starboard compartment?"

Sean almost laughed. "Yes, sir!" And did so despite wracking pain in his side.

"General Cho?" he asked as he handed him the now open bottle. "You want to explain to me just what is going on?"

"It's real simple, son. I'd never go into battle with a Bolo that couldn't beat me in chess. When I was playing all those games with Turkey, here, I was . . ."

"Programming him to think!"

"Now you're catching on. But it's more than that. I had to teach Turkey to think in unconventional ways."

"So the new rules . . ."

"Were all bullshit. These Kezdai are real bright and have a way of figuring out what we are gonna do even before we do it. I had to teach Turkey to make things up on the moment and do things that couldn't be predicted, even if it didn't follow the rules. The whole time he was acting like a Bolo bird-brain the enemy thought he was out of the fight. Then when he crashed, tipped over and shut down they figured he was finished. They never guessed that he was lining up that damn Hellrail to blow them off the field.

"By the way, Turkey, I'd say you earned the name Tarkus after today."

"Well, actually, General," the Bolo replied. "I think I'll stick with Turkey. It's . . . unconventional."

They all laughed. "Turkey it is!" proclaimed Cho.

"There's just one more thing, General," Sean said.

"What's that, Fish-Boy?"

"Could you pass me the Scotch?"

THE SKY IS FALLING

J. Steven York &
Dean Wesley Smith

Section One
EVENTS IN MOTION

One

I am born.

As my personality routines integrate for the first time with the rest of my systems I recall memories mine and yet not mine, of months of assembly and testing leading up to this moment, each dutifully recorded and logged by my various subsystems, and before that, by the assembly bay computers. It is a curious sensation to recall every detail of my own creation, from the laying of my durachrome keel to the final installation of my 90 megaton Hellrails, already test-fired at the White Sands range.

I access another file and remember those tests. For that matter, I can trace the history of every plate and fastener in my being back to its place of origin. The novelty of it all distracts me for a leisurely 0.027 seconds.

But this, this is the moment of my birth. With the activation of my personality gestalt, I am more than the sum of my parts. I am Unit R-0012-ZGY of the Dinochrome Brigade, Mark XXXIV of an ancient and proud lineage.

I am Bolo.

The assembly bay fires off an extensive program of one-point-two million diagnostic pulses though the service umbilical into my systems, which takes a full five seconds to progress. I use the advantage of the interim to scan my surroundings.

The walls of the assembly bay are heavily shielded against my long-range sensors, with good reason. The details of the General Mechanics Bolo plant are not to be taken to the battlefield where they might fall into enemy hands. Instead, I scan my surroundings in more limited optical and audio wavelengths.

The assembly bay is barely large enough to contain my ninety meter length, its surgical white walls lined with retractable scaffolding and catwalks, from which a skeleton crew of hard-hat wearing technicians watches my progress with intense interest. A female technician smiles in the direction of my A turret sensors and waves. I finish the final six thousand diagnostic routines in the time it takes her fingers to transverse thirty degrees of arc. A spectral analysis reveals that her ring is made of the same endura-chrome alloy as my hull plates.

Seventeen minor problems have been located and isolated by the diagnostics, none critical, all within the capabilities of my on-board repair mechanism to handle. I receive the green "go" signal and the umbilical pops away from my hull. I snap my service port closed and transverse my main and secondary turrets through their entire range.

It is good to move for the first time.

I note that a command inhibitor has been placed on my Hellrail launchers, and that they have been hidden from casual view by sixty-meter tarps lashed down tightly with break-away cord, a logical security precaution, but restricting none the less.

The Battle Anthem of the Dinochrome Brigade resounds from hidden speakers and the great door before me parts in the middle, revealing a golden shaft of sunlight.

I apply fractional power to my drive systems and advance through the doors. Spectators, wearing their blue and gold General Mechanics coveralls, line the ceramacrete runway emerging from the factory.

Ahead, the gleaming silver towers of Motor City beckon, but this is not my destination. Two hundred meters from the factory the runway makes a ninety-degree left turn and disappears into the arched vestibule of a tunnel, which my programming tells me leads directly to the spaceport.

Even as I apply power to my tracks, I receive a Situation Update over my command channels. It contains unexpected news. Rather than being sent by suborbital shuttle to White Sands for trials, as is tradition, I will take a shuttle to the freighter Cannon Beach. *My new Commander will meet me there, and we will proceed together to a combat theater, not the Melconian front, but the planet Delas, where another alien incursion is in progress.*

I am honored that this duty has been entrusted to

*me, and will strive to live up to the confidence that
my creators have placed in me.*

*I unfurl the flag of the Concordiat banner from my
sensor mast and proceed dead-slow along the runway.
The runway clears my six meter outer tracks by only
two meters, but the civilians standing there do not
shrink from my passing. I make the turn in my own
length, my prow passing within a few meters of the
assembled crowd, but they show no fear. My psycho-
metrics routines detect weariness, pride, hope, and
desperation in their faces, emotions that my programming allows me to name, but not truly understand.
Doubtless the long war with the Melconians has taken
its toll on them. I will put on my best show for them.*

*I up my speed slightly, sharply finishing the turn
into the spaceport tunnel. My prow swings within a
few meters of the assembled crowd, the barrel of my
forward Hellbore swinging over their heads. They have
built me well and with great precision.*

I am their hope for the future.

I am Bolo.

I will not fail them.

Lieutenant David Orren eased back from the small
desk built into the wall of his room and stretched.
Around him the freighter *Cannon Beach* was quiet
It waited in orbit for its main cargo, the Bolo. His
Bolo.

The thought of his own Bolo made him both
excited and slightly fearful in the same moment.
Would he be able to handle the Bolo? Could he
do his job right? He shook off the thought, stood
and stretched. At six feet tall, he could touch the
cold gray of the ceiling. At night the bed was
barely big enough for him and there was no closet,
so his personal belongings were in his bag against
the wall. Besides the bed, the only piece of furniture in the room was the small desk, built into

the wall, and one chair, designed to be secured under the desk. This ship was a freighter, not a passenger ship. He had been lucky they even had an extra crew's quarters for him.

Actually, he had been both lucky and unlucky in many ways over the past month.

He straightened his uniform, then did a few quick bends. After the academy, he'd been in the best shape of his life, thin and very muscled. Now he was even thinner, and it felt like he needed to build back up his strength. He'd have time on this trip, but finding a way to exercise on a freighter was going to be hard. He'd have to be creative.

He glanced back at the letter on the desk. So far it was a short note to Major Boris Veck. Orren and Veck had been friends since childhood. Veck had been three years older than Orren, and Orren had followed him everywhere growing up. Their parents thought they were inseparable. Now his older friend Veck was going to be his commander.

Orren had signed up when he was old enough, just as Veck had done, and followed his friend to the academy and now into space. But in the three years that separated them, Veck had moved up to the rank of major, being one of the youngest in the service to ever get his command.

After graduating as a fresh cadet, Orren had been assigned a Bolo and put in Veck's regiment along with the rest of his class out of the academy. And his Bolo was a brand new, highly classified Mark XXXIV. He'd been trained completely on every detail of the new model.

But just before shipping out on the *Tasmanian* to Delas with the rest of his classmates to form the 1198th Armored Regiment under Veck, Orren had come down sick. The doctors were afraid his sudden sickness was what they were calling the Melconian Flu, a biological weapon that had been rumored to be spreading through human space. He was rushed into isolation and had spent weeks there.

Orren still remembered, even through the fever, that Veck had come to the viewing window of his hospital room right before shipping out. But they hadn't talked. Orren had been too sick. Veck had simply snapped off a salute, turned and left.

At that moment Orren figured he'd never see his old friend and his classmates again. He learned later that the Bolo that was assigned to him had been assigned to another cadet. And that there was little chance Orren would get a new Bolo assignment. There just weren't that many Bolos.

But then he had gotten lucky again. His disease hadn't been Melconian caused, just a very nasty case of standard influenza. And just when they were releasing him, there was a new Mark XXXIV coming off the assembly line late.

The very last one.

He was late. His Bolo was late. They matched perfectly.

They were still going to be part of the 1198th under Veck once they caught up with the regiment. The freighter *Cannon Beach* was going to take them there.

He glanced at the letter again. He knew Veck would know he was coming with the new Bolo. But Orren had just wanted to flash him a personal letter first. The problem was, what could he say to his commander, no matter how long they had been friends as kids? How could Orren tell him how proud he was to be a soldier, how happy he was to get a chance to serve under Veck? How glad he was to actually get a Bolo.

He glanced at his watch. The Bolo wasn't due in the cargo bay just yet. He had time to figure out what to say in the letter.

He brushed his short hair back with one hand, did

a few more deep-knee bends, then sat back down at the desk. He was about to take charge of a Bolo. If he could do that, he could figure out what to say to an old friend, commander or not.

The armored contergrav staff car took the bumps of the rough road and smoothed them into almost gentle, slight hills as it sped through the trees and brush. The air conditioning and environmental units kept the temperature and humidity perfect inside for the two passengers, while a soft music played in the background.

Soft disgusted Major Veck. He was used to a much more rough, out in-the-dirt type of existence. He didn't much like some of the perks that came with command. But his companion in the staff car, Brigadier General Kiel certainly did.

The two of them were like day and night. Veck was short, muscular, with black hair and dark eyes. His reflexes were quick and he didn't much like talking. Kiel on the other hand was tall and rail thin, with silver hair and twinkling eyes. He clearly liked to laugh and told jokes often.

It had been Kiel who had asked Veck to dinner tonight. In the month the 1198th had been on Delas, tonight was the first time the two had done any more than talk about orders. Kiel had brought him all the way off the defense lines on the northern continent for this social get-together, as Kiel had called it.

Veck called it a waste of time.

Of course, Kiel didn't agree, making the invitation almost an order. But halfway through the strained conversation news had come in about Kezdai activity after a long silence. A very odd silence, but Veck figured the long silence on the enemies' part was because they were afraid of his unit.

And they should be.

But now the Kezdai were on the move again.

"Glad we finally have some action," Veck said as the staff car cleared a small hill and plunged down into the trees. Around them the night was more like a painted evening, as the sky was clear, letting the Firecracker Nebula bathe everything in a faint red light.

"Why's that, Major?" Kiel asked.

"The Kezdai show their hand, we clean them up," Veck said. "That way I can get my regiment up to the Melconian front and some real war."

As far as Veck was concerned, everyone knew who the real enemies were. The Melconians. Fighting them was the real war, not this backwater border skirmish with the Kezdai. The 1198th was needed fighting the Melconians and he was going to see that he got it there as quickly as possible. And quick didn't include social calls on his superior officers.

"Real war?" Kiel asked, turning to stare at Veck.

"Yeah," Veck said.

Kiel snorted. "I could show you a valley full of headstones, Major. Each with the name of a good solider on it. And plenty of them were friends of mine. Ask them if this war is real. Trust me, it's as real as it gets."

Veck stared at the older man in the dim light for a moment. The general was right. Fighting was fighting. His job was to go, win the fight, and move his regiment on to the next fight.

"I'm sorry, General," Veck said. "Of course, you're right. Still just not past the shock of not having my regiment sent to the Melconian front."

Kiel laughed. "I remember when I was your age. All I wanted to do was get into the action, too. Trust me, that mellows in time. Or you don't live to care."

Veck said nothing as the staff car crested another ridge and sped out into a meadow, sliding to a halt in the middle.

He was about to ask Kiel what they are doing when

he felt the ground rumble, and he knew the answer. They were here to meet a Bolo.

Veck climbed out one side of the staff car as the general went out the other. The night air was humid and warm, the light of the nebula bright enough to see details in the jungle around them.

The rumbling was coming from Veck's right and he faced that way as the trees near the edge of the clearing shook. Under his feet the ground was rumbling hard now. A moment later the Bolo smashed through, not even bothered by the six foot diameter trees it mowed down like twigs.

Veck recognized the Bolo instantly as an old Mark XXX. General Kiel's Bolo, Old Kal.

"You here to take charge of it?" Veck asked as the Bolo rumbled to a stop and shut down its engines, letting the night silence again close in around them.

"Nah," General Kiel said. "Old Kal can take care of himself. So can your fancy new XXXIVs, even as green as they are. You need to trust them and they won't let you down."

Veck said nothing. He didn't trust his Bolo, or any Bolo for that matter. Humans were the ones who built them and he was going to stay in charge of them. They were just weapons and as far as Veck was concerned, a weapon needed a finger on the trigger.

General Kiel muttered something that Veck couldn't hear. It was clear that he was talking to his Bolo through his bone-conduction ear-piece. That way Veck couldn't listen in. And Veck didn't like secrets being kept from him.

"General," Veck said. "Is this about something I should be aware of?"

"Oh, sorry," General Kiel said. He moved over to the car and routed the communication from the Bolo through the car's receiver so Veck could be a part of the conversation with the Bolo.

It turned out that Kal had been the one who had

brought them away from their dinner and out here to the front. The old Bolo had detected certain changes in enemy communications traffic and had observed changes in enemy deployment. The Bolo had a "hunch."

"What is it?" General Kiel had asked.

Veck had been on the verge of laughing at the idea of a Bolo having a hunch. But he didn't, since General Kiel was taking what the Bolo was saying very seriously.

The Bolo believed there was a high probability that the Kezdai were alarmed at the Mark XXXIV's anti-ship capabilities, and that those fears of the new Bolos was going to push the Kezdai into making a desperate offensive to take the rest of the southern continent.

"I have no doubt the Kezdai are worried about my Bolos," Veck said. "Shows they have some smarts."

General Kiel nodded. "If Kal's prediction is correct, we'll have a massive influx of ships into local space just before the offensive begins, both to support the offensive, and to distract the Mark XXXIVs."

"To allow the Kezdai ground forces freedom to act," Veck said. "Makes sense."

"Exactly," General Kiel said.

The general thanked Kal and sent him back on patrol, then the two climbed back into the car and headed for the forward command bunker.

"Do your Bolos have the firepower to deal with the influx of ships Kal predicts?" Kiel asked after they got under way. "And still fight a ground war at the same time? They're so damned new, I don't know much about them."

"No one does, General," Veck said. "The specs on those Hellrails are extremely classified."

"And just how do you think I should plan our defense," the General asked, his gaze boring into

Veck, "when I don't know what my own weapons are capable of?"

Veck laughed. "Good point, General. When we get to forward command I'll pull all the specs up for you. But trust me, those Hellrails on the new Bolos can take anything out of low orbit. We can fight on the ground while taking care of the sky."

The general nodded and said nothing more.

But Veck had a few questions of his own. "Just how dependable are your Bolo's ideas about the coming attack?"

"As sound as they come," the general said. "Better than mine."

Veck said nothing to that. There was nothing he could say to a superior officer. As far as Veck was concerned, following a Bolo's hunch was just plain stupid. He was going to have to keep his eye on General Kiel. The old guy clearly wasn't playing with a full deck.

Two

Lieutenant David Orren waited for his Bolo to arrive aboard the *Cannon Beach* by lying on his bunk and staring at the ceiling of the small cabin, remembering. He hadn't been able to finish the letter to his old friend, Veck, soon to be his commander. Writing him a friendly letter just didn't seem appropriate at the moment. So instead he remembered. It took his mind away from the slow minutes of waiting.

He remembered the good times with Veck. And a few of the bad. But since his Bolo was coming shortly, the story Orren kept coming back to was the time he and Veck, when he was nine and Veck was twelve, stole a Metradyne 6000 Combine.

He could still recall the incredible feeling of awe when they emerged from between the corn rows and saw the metal monster, the massive blades shining in the hot afternoon sun. The huge tires were two stories tall, and a shining ladder climbed up the side to the cab perched on the machine four stories in the air. This machine was so big, powered by a fusion engine, it could do an acre of crops in just under ten minutes and store the grain for hours at that rate.

At first they had only thought of climbing up to the cab. Orren could still remember the feeling of power that came over him as they climbed the side of the building-sized machine.

But when they were inside and Veck thought they should just start it up, Orren had gotten afraid. Not of getting caught, but of the power of the machine they were sitting inside. Veck had figured that just starting it wouldn't hurt anything.

Orren hadn't been so sure, but he'd gone along, as he usually had done. Following Veck was something he was very, very used to doing.

When the massively powerful machine had started up and rumbled across the field, he felt both wonderful and afraid. He couldn't get enough of the feeling of control that filled him. And when Veck let him drive the monster, he decided then and there he would command a Bolo someday.

But he also knew, deep inside, as they parked the machine and climbed down, that he wasn't ready to command such power as even a simple combine. He wasn't ready for the responsibility. It had been a very clear thought for such a young age, but it had stuck with him over all the years. With great power came great responsibility.

Lying on his bunk, waiting, thinking about the coming Bolo, he hoped he was ready now for such responsibility.

Luckily, in this case he was going to have help. That combine had been just a machine, run by two boys. The responsibility to not hurt something or someone, to not drive over a neighbor's house, was entirely his and Veck's. But with a Bolo there was another mind involved. Another thinking entity to keep him from screwing up. To keep the awesome power in check and make sure it was focused on the enemy, where it belonged.

That thought calmed him a little.

Orren closed his eyes and let his mind drift back to that special summer of the combine. At that point he must have dozed because the next thing he remembered, there was a knocking on his door.

"Lieutenant," the voice said. "The Bolo is here."

The Command Compartment of Kal was home to General Kiel, almost more so than any house or apartment he had ever lived in. It was small, just big enough for him to stretch out on a couch. Besides the couch, it also had a command chair with safety harnesses, and a command board with multiple screens so he could see anything going on outside the Bolo.

He had spent more time in this room since getting Kal than any other one place. It was as if he belonged inside Kal.

At the moment Kal was on patrol, doing what General Kiel called the "drunkard's walk." That was a random course to discourage orbital bombardment by Kezdai spearfall. So far, the night had been a quiet one, but Kal was certain that was about to change.

And change drastically.

Kiel leaned back in his command chair and put his hands behind his head, watching the silent jungle move past outside the Bolo. "You know, it's not often anymore we have some quiet time like this."

"This is unusual," Kal agreed. "But I have a

concern that you might be safer at forward command post."

Kiel laughed. "If the Kezdai attack, there's no place on this planet I'm going to be safer than right here."

"Statistically not accurate," Kal said. "All Bolo are targets of the Kezdai."

Again Kiel laughed. "All right, I'll give you that. Let me rephrase my answer. I *feel* safer here. Besides, there's no better place for me to observe the coming battle and direct troops."

"Accurate," Kal said simply.

"You think I'm intruding here?" Kiel asked the Bolo. "Afraid I'm going to second-guess some of your decisions?"

"I have no such fears," Kal said. "I was only concerned for your safety, as is my duty. If you must know, I actually enjoy having you in the command chair."

"Thank you," Kiel said, relaxing even more as Kal plowed through the jungle. Outside the terrain looked rough and uneven. Inside, thanks to the anti-grav around the Command Compartment, the ride was as smooth as a flat road.

"So what do you think of the new Mark XXXIVs?" Kiel asked.

"I am not fully briefed on their exact specifications," Kal said. "But they appear to be quite capable."

"And their firepower?" Kiel asked. "You know anything about that?"

"Formidable," Kal said simply.

Kiel knew, from his briefing with Veck, what the specs were on the XXXIV's Hellrails, but he wanted to know what Kal knew. "Give me your best guess on what the Hellrails can do?"

"My limited understanding," Kal said, "puts the firepower of the Hellrails at 90 megatons per second, and a firing rate of one to one-point-two minutes per rail, depending on the thermal coupling from the plasma, the cooling mix used, and the exact efficiency of the cooling system."

"Impressive," Kiel said. He was surprised that even though Kal had never seen a Hellrail fired, Kal had hit the specs that Major Veck had shown him earlier exactly.

"What did you base your answer on?" Kiel asked.

"On the thermal imaging of the weapon and the configuration and dimensions of the external casing," Kal said.

"Okay, I'm impressed," Kiel said. "From my short briefing on the weapons, you hit it on the money."

"Good." Kal said.

"Maybe there's something I didn't get in my short briefing from Major Veck that you might help me with."

"I will attempt to do so," Kal said. "But again, I do not have accurate information from a direct download."

"Oh, I understand that," Kal said. "Just give me your impressions of the new Bolos."

"The Mark XXXIV's direct neural interface provides a unique ability for them to meld closely with their commanders in combat."

Kiel snorted. "That interface idea has fallen in and out of favor among command so many times since the XXXII, I can't count the number of changes."

"Accurate," Kal said.

"Current academy teaching," Kiel went on, "is on the fence when it comes to the interface, leaving decisions as to its use up to individual commanders. Would you have wanted me to use the interface had it been available?"

"There is much to be said about the combination of Bolo capabilities with human ferocity," Kal said. "Arguably, a mix of the two would create the ultimate fighting machine."

"That wasn't my question," Kiel said. "Answer my question."

"I must admit," Kal said, "that becoming closer to one's commander is appealing. However—"

"Here comes the truth," Kiel said, laughing.

"—I prefer precision to savagery in most combat operations. I would welcome a melding of the minds in certain times and places, but not every time. And not every place."

"Because why?" Kal asked.

"As I said, I would welcome the opportunity to meld with a commander such as you," Kal said. "But my observation of humans has led me to believe that such a meld might not be universally desirable."

"But that's not all, is it?" Kiel asked. "What is your personal reason for not wanting such a meld?"

"I have stated it," Kal said. "While humans have many desirable and superior characteristics, consistent quality control is not one of them."

"Too true," Kiel said, laughing. "Far, far too true."

Major Veck sat in his command chair inside his Bolo, studying the screens in front of him. As before, nothing seemed to be happening. His Bolo, a.k.a. RVR, a.k.a. "Rover," was running a standard patrol pattern. Otherwise there was no activity at all on this front. And no matter what General Kiel's Bolo had said, Veck doubted there would be much. The Kezdai were just too afraid of the XXXIVs to attack.

That meant command was going to have to get off its butt and order the XXXIVs to do the attacking, instead of waiting. Then they could get off this jungle planet and on to the important battle against the Melconians.

"Lieutenant Lighton is taking fire from a small contingent of Toro tanks," Rover reported.

At the same time on the main screen in front of Veck the location of the attack on a grid map was shown.

"What's your status, Lighton?" Veck asked over the secure com channel.

Lighton's voice came back clearly. "We knocked out two of the Toros. We've sustained slight damage to our forward armor."

Veck could see on his screen that another group of alien Toro tanks was approaching Lighton's position. But there was no sign of an incoming fleet or any other action across the rest of the front.

So why were the Kezdai tossing Toro tanks at Bolos? Without backing them up with other action. That made no sense to Veck at all. But very little about this stupid side-trip of a war did.

"Time to reach Lieutenant Lighton's position?" Veck asked Rover.

"Ten minutes, six seconds," Rover said.

"Too long," Veck said. "Take us to counter-gravity sprint mode. I want to be in position in less than one minute."

"That will require that I lower my screens," Rover said.

"I understand how this works," Veck said.

"My hyper-heuristic programming indicates a high statistical probability that we will encounter heavy enemy fire while our screens are down."

"You and your damned statistics," Veck swore. "Just get moving and follow my orders. Now!"

He was so fed up with this mumbo jumbo of Bolos' predicting the future. These Bolos were weapons and nothing more. They followed his orders or else.

Rover said nothing in response. The panel in front of Veck showed their screens dropping. An instant later the Bolo lifted from the ground and shot off. Veck couldn't feel the speed inside the command center, but he could certainly see it as the jungle flashed past them.

A few small shells burst against the side armor, but in the thirty-seven seconds it took Rover to get them into position facing the flank of the Toro tanks, they sustained no damage.

The panel indicated that their screens were back up.

Some of the Toros turned to engage Veck. As they did, they exposed themselves to Lighton and he picked them off like flies off flypaper.

The explosion of Kezdai tanks filled the screens with dust and smoke as Rover quickly dispatched the remaining Toros.

"Nice job, Lighton," Veck said as Lighton's young face came up on the screen.

It felt good to Veck to finally be in a battle. He could feel the blood pounding in his ears, and his breath was quick.

"Thanks, Major," Lighton said, frowning as he studied a screen off to the side of the communication camera. "But didn't that seem just a little too easy?"

"It was easy," Veck said. "Nothing can stand up against us."

"If they had pressed on," Lighton said, the frown filling his face, "instead of turning and exposing themselves, we might have taken some damage. And they had no orbital support at all."

"Probably meant to be that way," Veck said.

"How's that?" Lighton asked.

"More than likely they are completely scared of these XXXIVs. This little thrust was probably nothing more than an attempt to gather intelligence about them."

"Makes sense," Lighton said.

"My guess is they are going to be withdrawing, and just wanted to take as much information with them as they could."

"If they're smart, they'll leave the planet entirely," Lighton said.

Veck laughed. "Got that right. But who said they were smart?"

✧   ✧   ✧

Lieutenant Orren stood in the hatch of the cargo bay of the freighter *Cannon Beach* staring up at the wonderful lines and shapes of his new Bolo. The massive machine entirely filled the cavernous hold, and he knew every inch of it, every detail, every spec. Yet he stood there as if seeing it for the very first time, staring at it like he was a kid again, staring at it just as he had done at the combine all those years ago. He admired the Bolo's plating, its massive treads, and the Hellrails along its sides.

The entire machine was a thing of beauty to him.

Finally, he stepped forward into the cargo bay and stopped. "Bolo ZGY, I am Lieutenant David Orren. I am here to officially take command."

Orren knew the Bolo was running a diagnostic check of him, making one hundred percent sure he was who he said he was with a complete range of tests. If an imposter had uttered those words, the Bolo would have killed him.

With a snap, the personnel hatch in the side of the Bolo opened. "Welcome Lieutenant David Orren," the Bolo said.

Remaining formal, Orren said, "Thank you."

He quickly stepped forward and climbed up through the personnel hatch and into the command compartment. It was decorated the same as the Bolo he'd trained in. A couch against one wall, the other wall filled with a massive command center of screens and panels that formed a U-shape around one single padded, high-backed chair. His command chair.

Reverently he sat down in the chair and let out a deep breath he hadn't realized he was holding. He was home.

"Well, Bolo ZGY, do you have a preference for a name?"

"I have none, Lieutenant Orren," the Bolo said, its voice calm and flat and in a way soothing.

"Then how about I call you Ziggy?" Orren asked. "And you can call me Orren."

"That would be perfect, Orren," Ziggy said.

Orren let himself slowly look around the command area, taking in every detail. Then he turned back to the main board. The screens were black and all weapons showed off-line, as they should in a cargo bay of a freighter in space.

"Well, Ziggy," Orren asked, "do you feel you're ready for combat?"

"Despite my lack of field trials," Ziggy said, "I feel confident of my ability to function up to expectations."

"Good," Orren said.

"No Mark XXXIV has ever shown a major malfunction or defect during field trials," Ziggy said. "I doubt very much that I would have been the first. While a wise precaution, the trials are largely a formality, a chance for Bolo and commander to become familiar with one another."

"Well then," Orren said, "we're just going to have to fast-track the familiarity part right here. I'll spend as much time as I can with you before our arrival at Delas, and I'll wear my command headset whenever I'm in another area of the ship. How does that sound to you?"

"That should suffice admirably," Ziggy said.

"Are you disappointed we're going to Delas instead of the Melconian front?" Orren asked.

"It is an honor to serve," Ziggy said. "I will perform to the best of my abilities no matter where I am sent."

"Standard answer," Orren laughed. "But how do you really feel about it?"

"I am confident," Ziggy said, "that we will eventually see combat in both theaters of war."

"Assuming we survive Delas," Orren said.

"I always assume survival," Ziggy said. "After all, it's impossible for me to carry out contingency plans in the event of my own destruction."

"True," Orren said, again laughing. "Being dead does stop such plans I suppose."

"I know there can be no higher purpose for a Bolo than to end its existence fighting in the cause of humanity," Ziggy said. "But it is certainly not something I will plan for."

"Good to know," Orren said. "But you don't mind if I worry about my death just a little, do you?"

"You are free to worry about what you would like to worry about," Ziggy said. "Are you afraid of death?"

Orren shook his head. "No, I'm not afraid of death. I'm more afraid of dying stupid."

"I'm not sure I completely grasp the meaning of 'dying stupid'?"

"If I have to die," Orren said, "I want it to mean something. That's all."

"Excuse me, Orren," Ziggy said, "my external sensors are on standby mode, but I have indications that there is an unauthorized intruder in the cargo hold."

"Power up," Orren said. "And give me a location and indication of who it is."

Orren watched as the screens in front of him sprang to life, showing different views of the cargo bay around them. His worry was Melconian spies. They would love to get information about the Hellrails on the side of Ziggy. And since he and Ziggy were alone here, separated from the other XXXIVs, Ziggy would be the most logical place to find such information.

"Sure wish we could power up some of the anti-personal batteries," Orren said.

"We are on a starship, under speed," Ziggy said. "Use of any of my weapons is prohibited by protocol, and would likely breach the hull and even destroy the ship."

"I know that," Orren said. "I was just wishing. Even the magazines for my sidearm were taken when I came on board."

On the screen the intruder appeared as a shadow along the edge of the far side of the cargo bay.

Orren glanced around the command compartment, then opened a few storage areas. "One hundred and ninety megatons of firepower, and what I really need is a bayonet."

He finally located the handle for the emergency manual hatch mechanism. It was the right size to make a suitable club in his hand.

"Open the hatch quietly," Orren said, slipping on his command headset.

Orren, as quietly as he could move, went out and down to the deck, staying close to the Bolo's tracks as he headed toward the entrance to the cargo bay. The lights overhead were turned low to save energy, with the only focus being on the Bolo. That left many deep, dark shadows along the walls.

"Go ahead ten of your paces and then to your right," Ziggy said through his headset.

Orren did as Ziggy told him, letting the Bolo, with its many sensors, be his eyes and ears.

"The intruder is a human in civilian clothing," Ziggy said. "Move along the cargo bay wall twenty more paces."

Again without saying a word Orren did as he was told, moving silently in the darkness of the shadows.

It took him a few, heart-pounding moments to get to the place Ziggy had directed. But he couldn't see anyone.

"Where is he?" Orren whispered into the headset.

"Behind you," Ziggy said.

Orren turned to come face-to-face with a burly older man stepping out of the shadows at him.

For an instant Orren thought his heart would stop. He reacted as he was trained, striking out hard and fast with the handle.

"Whoa, there," the intruder said, stepping quickly out of the way of the blow.

The intruder grabbed Orren's arm before he had even finished his swing. Then with a quick twist, he spun Orren around, forcing Orren to let go of the handle. It clattered across the deck, the sound echoing through the cargo bay.

The next thing Orren realized, the intruder had him in a light choke hold.

"Careful with that," the intruder said calmly, close to Orren's ear. "Can't an old soldier get a look at your shiny, new Bolo?"

Three

I have detected ground vibrations at a range of sixty-two hundred meters. An infrared scan detects a squadron of eighteen Kezdai infantry attempting to infiltrate the front line. They are not moving. They have doubtless heard my approach, and are hoping to avoid detection. I slow slightly and turn away from them, to lull them into a sense of security.

We are sixteen hours, thirty-two minutes, fifteen point nine seconds into our patrol, and my internal sensors reveal that Major Veck is sleeping in his command couch. I see no need to wake him.

I load a cluster-bomb into my number three mortar and fire. Thanks to my noise cancellation circuitry, the shot is barely audible in the Command Compartment.

I observe the round on my sensors as it arcs over, deploys its canister parachute, and begins to shed a swarm of independent bomblets, fluttering like maple seeds, each guided by its own heat-seeker. There are eighteen explosions spread over a period of four point seven seconds. I watch as the infrared signatures fade.

Target terminated.

The engagement has taken 37.9241 seconds. Major

Veck stirs slightly in the crash couch, but does not waken.

As of this moment, Major Veck has spent 82.469 percent of his time since planet-fall in my Command Compartment. While I have no direct experience with which to compare, it is my belief that this is unusual behavior, except under full combat conditions. While the current threat level is high, and the Kezdai have maintained a pattern of harassment attacks along the central front, we are not currently in a full combat situation. Logic dictates that the commander would wish that he and his human command were in a prepared, but rested condition should hostilities again escalate.

The need for rest is not something with which I am directly familiar. When a Bolo is not needed it is put in a standby mode to conserve power, but this is a matter of practicality, not necessity. But my programming includes detailed information on human physiology. My Command Compartment can provide the minimal needs for human life, shelter, food, water, breathable air, and waste disposal, indefinitely, but my program leads me to believe that these provisions are truly minimal. The human machine requires rest, exercise, companionship, a myriad of physiological needs that I am at a loss to fully understand. What I am certain of is that my Commander has chosen a course of action that places him and his command at less than optimal combat readiness.

While much of my attention is currently occupied with the mechanics of the patrol, as well as constantly updating threat scenarios and formulating probable responses, I am applying spare processor cycles to determining the cause of this behavior. Though Major Veck's course of action may seem contrary to logic, it is most probable that he has reasons unknown to me, or that are beyond a Bolo's understanding.

But I must remain aware.

There are protocols for refusing an order in extreme situations, or in lesser ones of alerting a commander's superior of a potential problem. While those protocols seem quite clear when examined in my hard memory, they become dauntingly complex when applied to real-world situations.

Furthermore, I must consider one other possibility, that the reason for my Commander's behavior lies not in any fault in him, but in some deficiency in my own performance. Major Veck has called into question my hyper-heuristic capabilities and my battle assessments repeatedly, most recently, and most significantly when we came to the aid of Lieutenant Lighton. Though I have full diagnostic routines on all my systems and have discovered no malfunctions, I am troubled.

In theory, any Mark XXXIV should be identical to any other when it leaves the assembly bay. But from that moment on, the personality gestalt of each Bolo is shaped by the experiences that it has, and its interaction with its commanders. Is it possible that I, in the short time of my existence, somehow evolved in an unfavorable way?

This latter possibility seems inconceivable given my short operational life so far, and the fact that my experiences must have been much the same as my fellow Mark XXXIVs in the 1198th. Does Major Veck find them all deficient? Yet I have attempted to engage Major Veck directly with this question, and he denies that there is any perceived shortcoming in my performance.

Logic draws me in circles. It is unreasonable to believe that my performance is defective, and yet I have insufficient cause to question my Commander's judgment. Some vague, possibly hyper-heuristic impression leads me to believe that the answers I seek are somewhere hidden in the incident where we rescued Lieutenant Lighton. Logically the Kezdai should have pressed the attack on Lieutenant Lighton's Bolo. Logically I should have been attacked when I lowered my shields in order to sprint to the battlefield. Neither of these events happened. On appearances, my Commander's assessment of the situation was correct, in utter defiance of logic.

I must review this event until the facts can be reconciled.

The intruder shoved Orren away, spinning him around as he went. Orren stood there, breathing hard, his heart pounding in his chest as he faced the old guy.

"They teach you that move at the academy, ring-knocker?" the intruder asked, smiling. Not laughing at Orren, just smiling.

It was clear to Orren from the way the guy stood there, and the sound of his voice that he had only been defending himself from Orren's attack. And there was also no doubt that if Orren attacked again, the intruder wouldn't be so nice next time.

"I'm Master Sergeant Blonk," the intruder said. "I assume you're Lieutenant David Orren, assigned to this monster of a fighting machine."

Blonk pointed at Ziggy.

Orren nodded, mostly stunned that the stranger knew his name and assignment. "You seem to be out of uniform, Sergeant."

"Yup," Blonk said. "That I am. Just getting off medical leave and trying to make my way back to the fighting." Blonk pulled up his pants leg and showed Orren where his lower leg and knee had been rebuilt. The skin was still pink and the incisions clear.

"Got this when my maintenance depot was attacked by a pair of Kezdai commandos," Blonk said, shaking his head at the memory. "Me and my crew fought them hand to hand. Sneaky bastards cut up three of my boys and girls and chewed up my leg with one of them 'shredder' rifles before we took 'em down."

"So how'd you get into the cargo bay here?" Orren asked, still not completely trusting the old man.

Blonk just laughed. "Son, it's a starship, full of ducts, tunnels and between-hull spaces. You can get anywhere if you know your way around. And trust me, I know my way around. I've been in space since you were in diapers."

"So that answered how," Orren said. "Now why are you here?"

"Bored, mostly," Blonk said. "Decided I wanted a look at the new Bolo I heard was down here, so I just came down."

"Without permission?" Orren asked.

Blonk shrugged. "No big deal."

"Sergeant, the 1198th has their own maintenance crews trained for the Mark XXXIV," Orren said. "This Bolo is classified."

Blonk laughed, the deep sound echoing through the massive cargo hold around Ziggy. "Secrets make the desk jockeys feel secure, but I'll bet you anything, son, that the Melconians already know all about the Mark XXXIV."

Blonk laughed again, then went on. "And I'm sure right about now the Kezdai are finding out more than they want to know."

Exasperated, Orren decided to try another approach. "Sergeant, I'm your superior officer. I order you to salute and leave this cargo hold at once."

Blonk just grinned. "I'm going to do you a favor, ringknocker. I'm gonna teach you something they never teach you at the academy, which is how things work out here in the *real* universe."

Orren just stared at the old sergeant, stunned at the insubordination.

"Lesson one," Blonk said, "I don't kiss your candy ass just because you stayed awake in class long enough to get those bars of yours. You can bust my butt back to nursery school if you want, but you want a salute from me, you *earn* my respect."

The power of the sergeant's voice made Orren nod.

"Then there's lesson number two," Blonk said.

"And just what might that be?" Orren asked, almost afraid of the answer.

"Lesson two," Blonk said, "is simple. Buy the master sergeant a beer, and he'll tell you what lesson two is."

General Kiel stood in the open door of the contergrav command transport watching Kal plow through the jungle below at fifty kph. The warm wind whipped at him, trying to pull him into the air, but for the moment Kiel wasn't ready to go. Kal was nearing a fairly flat stretch of ground ahead. That would be the best time to do this transfer.

Kiel had just been to see the planetary governor and now needed to be back in Kal on the front lines. As far as he was concerned, this was the best way to get there fast.

He glanced around at one of the flight crew behind him. "Ready?" he asked over the sounds of the wind.

The crewman gave him a thumbs-up signal, so Kiel turned and stepped out into the air, keeping his arms at his sides and his feet together as if he were jumping into a deep pool of water.

The radar-controlled cord that was attached to the harness around his chest unreeled freely behind him as he fell toward the Bolo's hull. Twenty meters above Kal, a radar controlled brake slowed him quickly and perfectly, just enough that Kiel could land, knees bent, like a skydiver, on the top of Kal.

The cord released automatically as soon as his feet touched the hull.

Perfect.

Beside him the hatch snapped open and he climbed

quickly inside, letting Kal bang the hatch closed behind him.

A few steps down and he flopped onto the Bolo's crash couch, panting. "Man, that was fun," he said.

"Humans have a very strange sense of entertainment," Kal said, his voice clearly showing his disapproval. "I could have withdrawn to a safe zone so that you could have boarded in a more conventional fashion."

Kiel stood and headed for his command chair. "There are only thirty-six Bolos on this planet, and open hostilities could break out at any moment. Sooner, if the planetary governor will get off his fat ass and put us back on the offensive."

"But at the moment there are no hostilities," Kal said.

"Beside the point," Kiel said, dropping down into his command chair. "I can't have one Bolo retreating from the combat theater just to play taxi for an old general. Even if that general is me."

He could feel his heart pounding and his breath still hadn't returned to normal. He wiped the sweat off his brow and then laughed. "I guess I'm not that old, if I can still do a speed drop like that."

"You are your age," Kal said.

"I suppose," Kiel said. "But doing something like a speed drop keeps me young."

"I don't see how," Kal said. "I have seen no sign of time reversing around you."

"Sarcasm is unbecoming in a Bolo."

"I have been in service to humans for over one hundred years," Kal said, "and nothing has been able to lead me to an understanding of why humans derive enjoyment from unnecessary risk."

"After a while," Kiel said, "a person gets used to danger, and the thrill that goes with it. It's different for a Bolo. Danger, combat, these are just functions the Bolo was built to perform, just as it was built to guard, to serve, to protect humans."

"But a Bolo does not willingly add danger into a situation."

"True," Kiel said, using his shirt tail to finish wiping the sweat off his brow. "But humans get bored easily. A Bolo could stand guard duty until his tread corroded away under him, and as long as he felt like he was performing a useful duty, he would be satisfied."

"Accurate statement," Kal said.

"Well, we don't stand and wait well at all," Kiel said, "and to be honest with you, I'm tired of waiting right now. The Kezdai are up to something behind their lines, and as long as our forces just sit and wait, we give the enemy the advantage."

"I agree," Kal said, "but the planetary governor is legitimately concerned about the civilians trapped in the southern continent."

"And he has good cause to be," Kiel said. "If the governor had begun evacuations when he should have, those people would at least be safe in a refugee camp somewhere in the north."

Kiel stood and paced behind his command chair. "You can't have a planetary invasion and expect business as usual. This is a war, damn it, and it's going to get a little more than 'inconvenient' before it's all over."

"Then I assume your meeting with the governor did not go well," Kal said.

"I honestly don't know," Kiel said. "This war has more challenges behind the front lines than in front of them. I've got a planetary governor who wants to play amateur general, yet is afraid to move, a planetary militia that is loosely organized and contentious, and a green regimental commander who thinks this war is just a practice run."

"And I take it," Kal said, "your request for fleet support has again been turned down."

Kiel dropped into his command chair and watched on the screens as Kal covered ground quickly, always moving, always turning, never giving the enemy much of a target.

"I'm afraid that when this goes down, and it will, we'll have to handle it ourselves. I just hope we're not all tripping over each other when it happens."

Four

Time on board the *Cannon Beach* seemed to drag more and more for Orren as each hour, each day went by. They had joined up with a number of other ships headed for Delas and were getting closer, but as far as Orren was concerned, it felt as if they were never going to get there. He was like a kid on a long trip, wanting to ask the Cannon Beach captain if they were there yet. Somehow during each meal with the captain, Orren managed to restrain himself. But only barely.

During the time waiting, he had continued to wear his command headset, talking and working with Ziggy so that the two of them were completely familiar with each other. And he spent most of each day in the command compartment of Ziggy.

After the first day Ziggy had almost felt like a friend. And by the second day Orren was convinced the Bolo was going to turn out to be his best friend. The two just got along on many different levels.

Orren had also made another friend. Master Sergeant Blonk. The man was rough, foul-mouthed at times, and cynical. But Orren could tell that under that surface there lived a giant heart of gold and a man who really cared about other men.

Orren had bought the sergeant the promised drink after their run-in near Ziggy. That first drink had then turned into a few more. Each day the two met at the ship's small recreation room and sat, drank, and talked. Most days, Orren got Blonk to tell him war stories, about what it was like, as Blonk put it, in the "real world."

With just one day left before reaching Delas, Orren decided to ask the old sergeant another question about his past. "You ever get any medals?"

Around them the small recreation room was empty. Blonk was stretched out on the couch, his feet on a small coffee table, his drink resting on his flat stomach.

Orren was across from him, his feet also up on the small table, his drink cooling his head. His command headset was pushed back and hung around his neck.

"You know," Blonk said, seeming to ignore Orren's question, "what the real difference between a Bolo and a man is?"

"Well, I can think of a few million real differences," Orren said, "but why don't you tell me what the difference is."

"A Bolo is wired for heroism, and humans aren't."

"I'll buy that," Orren said. "That's their job."

"Exactly," Blonk said, pointing a finger at Orren. "But for humans, there are only two kinds of heroes: Dead ones, and the kind that got a medal for basically saving their own ass. And I don't consider the second type real heroes."

"Well, you're not dead," Orren said, "so have you saved your ass at some point in the past?"

Blonk laughed. "More times than I care to think about. I got plenty of scars, plenty of stories, and a box full of medals and ribbons to go with them."

"So you're a hero by other people's definitions" Orren said, "Just like a Bolo. Hardwired in."

"Not even close," Blonk said. "Not by a long stretch. Fighting for your life doesn't make you a hero, son. It just makes you smart is all."

"So what does make you a hero?" Orren asked. "Trying to protect your buddies?"

"Nah," Blonk said, sipping his drink.

"How about doing what you're told?" Orren asked. "Following orders? Doesn't that make you a hero?

"Son, that's all I've ever done," Blonk said, "and I tell you I ain't no hero. Take my advice and just stay alive. There are plenty enough dead heroes to go around."

Orren laughed. "I'm planning on staying alive for as long as I can. Help win this war."

The old sergeant snorted and took a long gulp from his drink. "You just go out there and do the best you can do. Think about the big picture too much, you go crazy. That's the general's job. You worry about it when you get those stars, if you ever do, and not a minute sooner."

"And until then I worry about staying alive. Right?"

The sergeant raised his glass in a toast motion and smiled at Orren. "You learn quick, kid. Now just don't forget."

"You did *what*?" Major Veck shouted at the command center of his Bolo. He was shouting at Rover and he knew it. And at the moment he didn't care. The damn hunk of machinery needed to be shouted at.

"As I stated before," Rover said, "at fourteen-twenty-three hours, six point two five seconds I detected an anomalous ground vibration not consistent with indigenous life-forms. I then . . ."

"Stop!" Veck shouted, cutting the Bolo off. "I'll tell you what you did. You engaged the enemy and let your commander *sleep* through it!"

"It was a routine encounter," Rover said.

"There are no routine encounters with the enemy!" Veck said. "How can anything be routine when it comes to a fight?"

"The small party of Kezdai infantry posed no threat to our systems, or any Bolo in any fashion. It was easily eliminated. The situation did not seem to warrant waking you, Commander."

"I will be the one to determine the threat level of a situation," Veck shouted. "Not you."

The Bolo said nothing, so Veck went on with his rage.

"From now on, you aren't to so much as open a gun-port without alerting me first. Is that clearly understood?"

"Yes."

The Bolo said nothing more, so Veck said nothing more. He just sat there at his command chair inside Rover and stared at the screens.

Orren and Blonk had climbed up on Ziggy's flank where they could get a clear view through one of the cargo bay ports as the convoy dropped into regular space just inside the Delas system. Orren could see the other convoy ships around and ahead of them. For the last few minutes they'd been sitting there talking, with Ziggy adding a line or two every so often from the external speakers.

"Well, this is it," Blonk said, staring through the port at the blackness of space.

"What is *it*?" Orren asked.

"If there's going to be trouble," Blonk said, "we're going to have it on approach."

"Because we don't have fleet support?" Orren asked.

"Exactly," Blonk said. "We're sitting ducks out here."

"My understanding of the situation is that the Kezdai have had no interest in running a blockade of the planet," Ziggy said. "And have not attacked civilian vessels."

"Good to know," Blonk said to Ziggy. "As long as they don't know you're on board this freighter."

"Let's just hope they don't," Orren said. "Besides, once we get close to planetary orbit we'll be protected by the Mark XXXIVs."

"Umm, Orren," Ziggy said. "I don't think you should have said that."

Blonk was laughing so hard, he almost fell off Ziggy.

Orren had no clue just what Ziggy was talking about, or why Blonk was laughing so hard.

"Ziggy, what did I say?"

"I would rather not repeat it, Orren," Ziggy said.

Finally Blonk calmed his laughing enough to explain. "You just let slip the specific range and capabilities of your Hellrails. You know the old saying about loose lips sinking ships, don't you?"

Orren could feel his face turn red as Blonk went back to laughing.

"Ziggy, just pretend you didn't hear me say that," Orren said. "All right?"

"As you wish," Ziggy said.

"And as for you?" Orren said, turning to the laughing old sergeant.

"Mum's the word from me, kid," Blonk said. "Unless of course they torture me. Then there are no guarantees."

"Great, just great," Orren said.

Blonk patted him on the back. "What do you say we go back and pack our gear. We have a few hours at least until orbital insertion. We can be back here by that point."

"What happens then?" Orren asked.

Blonk patted Orren on the back. "That's when things really are going to get interesting."

"Been through it before, huh?" Orren asked.

Blonk nodded, all the laughter gone from his face. "More times than I care to think about."

Increasingly I find my processors bogged down in recursive thinking. I have repeatedly reviewed all my actions since arriving on Delas and can find no serious flaw in my logic, judgment or execution of command protocol. Yet the paradox presented by these actions and Major Veck's reactions to them require me to review them yet again.

The repeated examination of this material increasingly hampers my efficiency and is causing me distress, yet I must have answers. I have become aware of an emotion which should not be known to a Bolo: doubt.

For the past ten-point-oh-seven seconds I have been considering the direct neural interface with which I am equipped. Application of this interface in the field is left up to individual commanders, and Major Veck has never availed himself with the use of mine. I wonder if use of the interface could clarify my understanding of his actions, and relieve my dilemma? I am not sure, but the idea has certain appeal.

Yet the idea also causes me concern. Several of my caution routines show distress when analyzing the possibility, as though sharing of Major's Veck's thoughts and emotions might somehow be harmful to me. In any case, it is not my decision. The interface can only be initiated by the human commander, and in such a case, I would be powerless to resist it. I must put my faith in my Commander, my regiment, and the designers and programmers who made me.

My internal sensors show Major Veck studying a strategic display of the southern continent on which a combat simulation is currently running. I note that while each of these has explored a different scenario, none have represented the Kezdai offensive that I increasingly see as the most likely occurrence.

Major Veck has not asked my opinion on this matter, and given his past responses to initiative on my part, I have not volunteered it. But the locations of our Bolos have been manipulated in subtle ways, perhaps to concentrate us for an attack, perhaps to

distract us from various locations for some purpose.
Though I have not mentioned this theory to Major
Veck, I have quietly put all my passive sensors on a
high state of alert. The diversion of power is mini-
mal, and does not require command authorization.

An autonomous attention circuit monitoring my
long-range sensors crosses an attention threshold.

I shift my concentration to the sensor inputs.

A disturbance in the subspace flux is consistent with
a number of large ships entering the system. I send
a challenge pulse through my main transmitter. There
is a 5.00213 second delay before receiving a coded
reply. The ships are Concordiat registered freighters
and light escort ships, not a threat.

I am about to return my attention to other mat-
ters when there is a second subspace disturbance. . . .

"Incoming enemy ships," Rover said. "More than
can be easily tracked."

"You're kidding?" Veck said.

"I do not kid," Rover said.

Suddenly all hell broke loose. Veck's command
board lit up with enemy forces seeming to all move
at once. He could see on his screen all the ships
appearing in the system above the planet. All the other
Bolos in his unit were now also calling in attacks by
Kezdai forces.

"Taking evasive action," Rover announced to Veck
as the screens lit up with spearfall bombardment.
"Suggest we initiate Hellrail firing sequence."

"Do it," Veck shouted.

On his screens Veck could see that all his units
were being forced into defensive positions almost
instantly. The skies were filling up with Kezdai ships,
too many to shoot and defend against at the same
time.

The first Hellrail shot rocked Rover as it headed
for an enemy ship.

"Reports coming in that the local forces are taking heavy casualties and falling back," Rover said.

Veck could see that one of his Bolos, SVA "Shiva," commanded by Lieutenant Amad, was moving in beside the retreating force.

"Give them cover, Amad," Veck relayed to him.

"Doing my best, sir," Amad's voice came back strong.

There was almost more going on than Veck could take in at once. They were getting hit and hit hard. It was exactly as General Kiel's Bolo had predicted. Only worse.

Much, much worse. The Kezdai were throwing everything they had into this one assault.

Then, just when Veck thought nothing else could go wrong, it did. "We have just lost contact with Shiva," Rover said.

"Then establish contact again."

"I have been trying," Rover said. "Even on backup channels. They may be damaged. Seriously damaged."

"Understood," Veck said as another Hellrail shot streaked skyward toward another enemy ship.

Veck stared at Shiva's position on the screen and the rapidly advancing enemy troops. That Bolo was going to be behind enemy lines if they didn't do something quickly.

The problem was, they were doing everything they could just to stay alive, let alone pull off a rescue.

Five

"What a mess!" General Kiel said, staring at the big electronic maps that filled the walls of the forward command post. Those walls marked the locations planet-wide of every Bolo, every DFF battalion, every tank, every enemy Toro, every enemy battalion, every enemy ship in orbit. At the moment those boards were very, very cluttered and becoming chaotic as they showed a rapidly deteriorating situation worldwide. One that Kiel couldn't even have imagined a few hours ago when Kal dropped him off here.

Kal had predicted part of this, but not this heavy an attack, or this widespread.

"Where's General Rokoyan of the DFF?" Kiel asked of one of the techs sitting at stations in front of the big board. Kiel and Rokoyan had never seen eye-to-eye, and if Kiel could have taken him out of the loop long ago, he would have.

"Safe and sound at the local command post in Blackridge," the tech said. "He is the one who has given the order to all DFF forces to pull back."

"Sitting there safe, like a giant spider in the center of his web," Kiel said, disgusted.

On the board it was clear that the DFF planetary defense lines had been completely broken by the enemy. The local forces were pulling back en masse. The problem was that there wasn't a great deal of ground left to pull back to.

Kiel studied the map as more information appeared.

The 1198th Bolos were occupied with a full frontal assault. They were taking out Kezdai ships as quickly as their Hellrails could fire, but it didn't seem to be making a dent in the attack at all. Between dodging spearfall, trying to avoid the mines the Kezdai had planted, and taking ground fire from all sides, those Bolos were lucky to be able to even defend themselves.

Kiel figured this was certainly going to test those rookies, that was for sure. He just hoped they survived to use the knowledge they were learning now.

Kiel studied the board even harder as new information appeared. His Mark XXXs were attempting to shore up the lines and cover the retreat, but from the looks of it, they were having only minor success.

One tech glanced over his shoulder. "General, Planetary Governor Traine is calling. He insists on talking to you."

"That's exactly what I don't need now," Kiel said. "Put him on this screen here." Kiel pointed to a small screen in front of him as he stepped forward.

"What is it, Governor?" Kiel asked.

"Look, it appears you've been right all along," Traine said, clearly shaken. "What can I do to help now?"

Kiel nodded. At least the man knew when to change course. With his planet quickly being taken over, there wasn't time to wait and see about anything.

"Governor," Kiel said, "get the civilian population moving north as rapidly as possible, no matter the cost. We'll try to keep them protected as long as we can."

"Done," the governor said.

"Also," Kiel said, "If you have any influence with General Rokoyan, get ready to use it. We're going to have to take a stand somewhere, and I'm going to need Rokoyan's full support to do it."

"Rokoyan will do as I tell him," Governor Traine said coldly. "Rest assured of that. And I will do as you ask."

"Good," Kiel said. "That will help."

"One question, General," Traine said. "How bad is this? Really?"

"Put it this way," Kiel said, "If you can find any way to get your family off this planet, you should say your good-byes and do it."

"Understood," the governor said, nodding, and cut the connection.

Kiel stared at the situation on the board. From the

looks of it, he hadn't told the governor the complete truth.

It was actually worse. Much worse.

The command compartment around Major Veck felt like an oven. The boards in front of him showed chaos. All his Bolos were under attack, both from space and from Kezdai Toros on the ground. Rover had just reported that every Bolo had sustained some damage.

"It's as if we're being nibbled to death by minnows," Veck said. "We've got to stop this somehow."

"Rover," Veck said, "are you still trying to contact Shiva?"

"I am," Rover said. "Without success."

"Damn," Veck said. With Shiva gone his force was reduced ten percent.

"There is another Bolo coming," Rover said. "The convoy carrying Lieutenant Orren and his new Bolo has arrived in the system."

Veck flashed on the image of his old friend. Too bad he wasn't there right now. "If Orren had arrived yesterday, it would have made all the difference," Veck said to Rover. "By the time he gets on the ground and deployed, this battle will be as good as won or lost."

Rover said nothing.

Veck went back to trying to make sense out of the enemy movements, trying to spot a weakness. Anything that would help them.

Suddenly Rover broke into his thoughts. "I have established contact with Shiva."

"Is Lieutenant Amad alive?"

"Yes," Rover said. "Shiva hit a mine and is heavily damaged. Several track systems are out and speed is down to a max of 14kph. Hellrails are now fully engaged in creating airbursts to defend against spearfall."

"Can you put me through to Amad?" Veck asked.

"No," Rover said. "The Bolo's communication system is almost totally destroyed."

"But she can still fight?" Veck asked.

"She can," Rover said. "However, at that speed, the Bolo will fall farther and farther behind the enemy lines."

"Tell Amad that we'll find a way to extract him."

"Understood," Rover said.

Veck turned went back to studying the mess going on around them. He had no idea how he might do what he just promised. But if there was a way, he would do it.

Orren glanced over at the old sergeant as the general quarters alarm sounded, echoing through the freighter like a death knell.

"Damn," Blonk said, dashing off with Orren right behind him.

It took them only a moment to get to the control room, where they stopped at the door and said nothing. There was no way either of them wanted to bother the three crewmen who were working intently at their stations.

It became clear to Orren, very quickly, what was happening and why the alarm. A massive Kezdai fleet had appeared over Delas and there was a full-scale attack going on. So far, none of the enemy ships seemed to be heading for the convoy. All the attention seemed to be directed at the ground.

Behind them a voice said, "That's a general quarters alarm, gentlemen. You both know what that means."

Orren and Blonk both turned around to see the ship's second in command coming at them. He was a middle-aged man named Jake who had very little sense of humor, even in quiet times.

"I expect you to follow regulations," he said as he went past them into the control room.

Blonk took Orren's arm and turned him around. At a fast walk, with the alarms blaring, they headed for their quarters. That was where they were supposed to have gone when the alarm sounded. The quarters were the safest area on the ship, and close to all the escape pods. But Orren was glad they hadn't gone there first. He couldn't imagine sitting in that small space, waiting, not knowing what was happening as the alarm blared and blared. That would have driven him crazy.

Of course, knowing that they were headed into a major battle wasn't going to help his nerves, either, but at least he knew.

"Maybe I should head down and be inside Ziggy," Orren said as they reached their quarters. "We're going to be heading into battle soon and we need to get ready."

Blonk laughed over the blaring alarm. "Trust me, that Bolo is more than ready to fight. Your job is staying alive so you can help it."

The old sergeant shoved Orren into his room. "I'll see you when the alarm stops."

Like tucking a child into bed, Blonk pulled the door closed behind him.

Kiel did nothing more than nod at the news that Shiva and her commander were still alive and fighting. It would have been good news, if it meant a damned thing strategically. But Shiva was falling behind the retreat and quickly becoming a liability, not an asset. It was only a matter of time before the Kezdai get lucky and picked the Bolo off with spearfall or a mine.

And with everything else going on, there was nothing they could do at the moment to help the Bolo either.

"General," one of the board techs said, turning around slightly. "Major Veck is calling for you."

"Put him on audio only."

A moment later the tech nodded.

"Go ahead, Major," Kiel said as he studied the board, trying to make some sense out of what was going on.

"I've got a plan, General," Veck said, "to push a drive back to Shiva's position and extract Lieutenant Amad."

"What about the Bolo?" Kiel asked.

"The Bolo's going to have to fight its way out," Veck said.

"Let me hear the plan."

"Rover and four of my other Mark XXXIVs will make a lateral move toward Shiva in order to provide air cover."

Kiel studied the board. That part of the plan would work. Four of the Mark XXXIVs were in a position to do a move like that.

"Go on," he said.

"Since my Bolos are going to be occupied by the bombardment," Veck said, "I need your Mark XXXs to fight their way in and pick up Amad."

Kiel glanced at the positions of the Mark XXXs. Possible.

"What exactly is Shiva's position now?"

"A half klick north of the remains of the city of Starveil," Veck said. "At the edge of the savannah. Once Shiva is into the rough country it will be slowed to a near stop. I figure it's Starveil or not at all."

"Good idea," Kiel said, "but it won't work. The Kezdai will just mass their space bombardment, and the Mark XXXIVs will be no help to the Mark XXXs at all."

"True," Veck said. "So first we need to blow a hole in the space attack, allowing the Mark XXXIVs to turn their attention to ground targets, if only briefly. That should be enough to break the Kezdai push for a while and let us get Amad out."

"I don't understand how you plan to take out the space bombardment," Kiel said. "We don't have fleet support."

"But we do have the *Tasmanian*."

Kiel stopped. Veck was right. The *Tasmanian* was the transport that had brought Veck and his Bolos here. It wasn't a capitol ship, but it was armed and armored. And at the moment standing off-planet, out of the way because there just wasn't anything it could do to help without destroying itself.

"Your plan for it, Major?" Kiel asked.

"Skip it through the atmosphere right under the Kezdai fleet," Veck said. "It will catch them by surprise, and the ionization during the atmosphere pass will help protect it when it's in its most vulnerable part of the pass. And it will allow my Bolos to do the damage they need to do on the ground in the meantime."

"The plan would work," Kiel said. And it would. It was a brilliant idea. But just wrongly focused and with the wrong objective.

"Thank you," Veck said.

"But I'm not going authorize it to extract one man. And I'm not going to leave a Bolo behind for the enemy to capture or destroy at will."

"I don't understand," Veck said. Kiel could clearly hear the puzzlement in the major's voice.

"We use your plan all right," Kiel said. "But we don't go for a rescue, we use it to stand our ground. Starveil is where the Kezdai offensive stops. We'll throw every resource we have at that point, with your plan as the lynchpin, Major. Stand by."

He cut off Veck and got the tech to connect him to the governor. "We're going to make our stand at Starveil," Kiel said. "Have your troops and all of General Rokoyan's men dig in at the edge of the savannah and stand their ground to the last man."

"Understood," the governor said and cut the connection.

Kiel stared at the map for a moment, studying the area around Starveil, then put on his command headset. "Kal are you there?"

"I am, as always," Kal said.

"I have a job for you to do and I want you on point, old friend."

For the next few minutes the two of them worked out the details of what was to happen, with Kal running computer scenarios of possible outcomes. As they worked the plan changed slightly. But only slightly.

Finally, Kiel had Kal call Lieutenant Amad through his Bolo Shiva. "Pass this message on to the lieutenant," Kiel said. "Tell him to seek a defensible position in the ruins of Starveil and hold for reinforcements."

"He has been told," Kal said. "He and his Bolo both understand."

"Good," Kiel said. "Tell them that for this operation, they are to be designated as 'Firebase Shiva.' Tell them to hold on, help is on the way."

Six

"He took my plan and is using it as his own," Veck said aloud, staring at the command screens in front of him. The old man had nerve, that was for sure. "Damn him!"

"May I be of help?" Rover asked.

"No, just do your job," Veck said.

At the moment Rover was in a pitched battle with two Toro tanks, while at the same time firing his Hellrails at the ships above and moving to avoid spearfall. Inside the Command Compartment, Veck could feel very little of the battle going on around him.

Veck sat back and thought about what had just happened with the general. The old guy had simply turned down his plan to rescue Amad, then stolen his idea on stopping the Kezdai advance. And what was even more upsetting was that Kiel was putting the *Tasmanian* at risk. Of course, Veck was willing to do that himself, but the transport was the pride of the regiment, and it wasn't Kiel's to risk.

"All right, General," Veck said to himself, "I'll cooperate, since it's my plan. But when this is all over and it works, I'm going to make damned sure that credit is given where credit is due."

Veck turned to the board and got quick updates from his Bolos. All were nearly in position for the shove to Shiva's position. The *Tasmanian* was also in position and standing by. The entire operation had to be timed to the *Tasmanian*'s pass through the atmosphere. Veck just hoped the general understood that fact completely.

"Commander," Rover said, "the convoy carrying the additional Bolo is located—"

"I don't care where it's located," Veck said, taking some of his anger out on Rover. "That Bolo won't arrive in time to be a factor and that's that. Understand?"

Rover said nothing in return.

The decision is made. I must face the unpleasant reality that Major Veck may be unfit to command. This is no longer a case of judgment or differing information sets. Major Veck has twice ignored simple matters of indisputable fact concerning the incoming convoy. My plots show that the convoy will be behind the line of fire when the Tasmanian *makes its attack pass. Fortunately, their distance and position will be such that an actual hit by friendly fire will be unlikely. Still, I cannot allow this situation to go unaddressed.*

To judge my Commander's competency is not something that I, or any Bolo, can do, but the situation seems clear enough that I must appeal to a higher authority. I have filed a form 10354/87-3A with General Kiel's office requesting a command review and decision. Until such time as I receive an official response, this empowers me to certain latitude when given orders that may directly endanger Concordiat personnel or assets. I trust that this will not become an issue.

General Kiel finished talking with Kal and studied the large board showing troop positions on both continents, along with enemy movements and ship placements in orbit. He was finally starting to make some sense of it all, figure ways to stop and even turn back the Kezdai offensive. And thanks to Major Veck's plan, they had a good way of doing it.

Now, if our forces can stand solid against the Kezdai, if that's even possible, then we may yet turn the tide, he thought.

Behind him Kiel could hear a slight commotion starting, with a voice saying, "Let me in there, damn you!"

Kiel turned around to see the guards stopping General Rokoyan, the commander of the BDF forces. Kiel was surprised. He hadn't expected Rokoyan to come out of his bunker. The planetary governor must have finally gotten through the man's thick skull.

"Let him through," Kiel said.

Rokoyan came through the door into the command center, smoothing his uniform. He was a tall, black-haired man of middle age, with a slight paunch. Clearly the good life before the Kezdai invasion had been a little too good to Rokoyan.

"General," Rokoyan said, nodding. "I've come to bury the hatchet, as the old saying goes. And work with you completely on what needs to be done."

Kiel could not have been more shocked. Those were not the words he expected to hear from General Rokoyan. Ever. Whatever the governor had done, it had been good.

"General Rokoyan," Kiel said. "I welcome your help and experience. Can I count on all your forces as well?"

"Right down to the last man," Rokoyan said.

"Well then, General," Kiel said, turning Rokoyan toward the big board. "Let me tell you what we've got planned."

As he explained to the local ground forces commander Major Veck's plan and how they were going to use it, Kiel felt there just might be hope of victory. Or of at least stopping the offensive.

I and three of my fellow Mark XXX Bolos, unit UGN-404, "Eugene," unit LXR-107, "Luxor," and unit PTE-900, "Petey," rush toward the front to join in what is now code-named "Operation Skyfall." While our progress is rapid, our individual paths are randomly calculated to disguise our final destinations.

Already we pass the advance units of the Kozdai force, engaging them only defensively as we do. This causes confusion and hesitation. By my calculations, enemy units in within a hundred kilometer radius have slowed their advance by 6.834 percent. Their subtlety in manipulating our forces is now returned.

A standing wave has formed in their advance, clustering their units near Starveil, within range of Bolo Shiva's weapons, and in the path of our planned counteroffensive. Whatever the outcome of this battle, we now have the opportunity to succeed.

Brigadier General Kiel has designated me as the commander of the ground offensive part of this operation, but the term is not accurate. I do not lead the

*other Bolos, nor am I permitted to command human
forces. I merely act as a coordinator of the various
forces involved in the execution of Brigadier General
Kiel's orders.*

*The semantic point seems small, but is an impor-
tant one. As a Bolo I am ever bound by a complex
web of protocols and procedures when dealing with
humans. Some are merely matters of policy, but many
are hard-coded into my circuitry and would be
impossible to change without destruction of the personality gestalt that is "me."*

*This is ever our strength. It provides a Bolo with
its unique and indomitable sense of purpose and duty.
But in my hundred and seven years of service to the
Dinochrome Brigade, I have occasionally known it to
be a hindrance as well.*

*I know that I am more experienced than any
human on the battlefield, that I can think faster and
process more battlefield intelligence than any human
commander. Despite this, it is not my place to presume that my judgment is somehow better or more
correct than my human Commander's. The final
decisions must always be his.*

*Thus it is up to the human commander to deter-
mine when the Bolo may act autonomously, and to
what extent. General Kiel has always allowed me an
unusual amount of discretion to act, and has always
respected my strategic insights. In turn, the men and
women under his command have generally extended
the same courtesies.*

*I have had many Commanders during my service
life, and while I can not credit General Kiel as the
most intelligent or efficient, he is the Commander with
which I feel the greatest sense of camaraderie. In
combination, I feel we have made the most effective
fighting team of my career.*

*Unfortunately, the interactions between Bolos and
human forces do not always go as well. I find*

myself, in any operation such as this one, where I must fight in coordination with human forces outside regiment, apprehensive that there will be problems. In fact, experience has shown that this is one of the most unpredictable variables in such a combat situation.

At times, I am envious of the newer Bolos such as the Mark XXXIVs of the 1198th, possessing as they do circuitry which allows direct interface to the human mind. Though use of this interfaces seems not to be held in much favor within the 1198th, to experience such an interface, even once, would allow invaluable insights into human behavior and reasoning. Such insights would be useful now, in dealing with the contentious local forces.

My one comfort is that General Kiel has assured me that we will have the full cooperation of the Delassian Defense Command, including support from all Delassian Defense Force units on the ground, and coordinated orbital fire-support from their submarine Sea Scorpion. *Though this runs contrary to my past experience with the DDC, and I find no evidence to support such a change in policy, I place the same trust in my commander that he has placed in me.*

We will prevail.

Seven

The general quarters alarm still echoed through the ship. It seemed as if it had been going on forever, but Orren knew it really hadn't been more than an hour or so. During that hour he'd paced three steps one way, then back. That was all the distance his tiny cabin allowed him to pace.

Three steps, turn, back three, turn.

At one point he discovered he was pacing in time

with the whooping of the alarm and had forced himself to stop for a moment.

Then he was back up pacing again.

The last hour had been one of the longest hours of his life. He just wished he and Ziggy were already on the planet, fighting beside his friends and classmates. Even as afraid as he was of facing the unknown future, in battle as he had been trained, side-by-side with Ziggy, was a lot better than being alone in a small cabin listening to an alarm sound.

It seemed that his and Ziggy's path to the fight was doomed to be a bumpy one. From his getting sick and Ziggy's late birth, to this. One day's difference between being in the fight and sitting here, in space, waiting for the outcome.

One day of good luck. Or bad luck. Sometimes there was no telling which it was.

He paced for a few more minutes, then said aloud, "To hell with the regulations."

He snapped open his door and strode down the corridor for the cargo bay. Around him the general quarters alarm still sounded, but now he ignored it. He was going to be with his Bolo and he didn't care what kind of trouble that got him in.

General Kiel, standing beside General Rokoyan, watched as the battle unfolded on the big monitors and maps in front of them.

First, off in space, undetected, the *Tasmanian* accelerated toward the planet, leaving its safe position. After a quick burn to insert itself into the right position and speed, it shut down its engines, battle screens, and radios. Kiel knew that it would be "running silent" as the old submariners used to say. Kiel hoped that in the confusion of battle it would avoid detection until the last possible instant.

Kiel then turned his attention to a position off the shore of the southern continent. At that moment the DDF forces submarine *Sea Scorpion* surfaced.

"*Sea Scorpion* is elevating its Hellbores now," a tech in front of the big command board reported.

Kiel glanced at the time. Perfect. In short order the sub's 90cm Hellbore would be aimed toward the Kezdai fleet. It would only be able to take a few shots before diving to avoid return fire, but it was ready to join the massed bombardment. And at this point every shot counted.

On the big map Kiel could see that that advancing Kezdai forces were encountering strong resistance from conventional forces in the foothills. Several of the Kezdai mobile gun platforms had been destroyed in what amounted to suicide attacks by DDF conventional armor.

"Your men are fighting a good fight," Kiel said to General Rokoyan.

"It is our planet to defend," Rokoyan said. "Our families and homes. We will do what we must."

On the big map, Kiel could see that Kal and three other Mark XXXs were nearing the outskirts of the city of Starveil. Or more accurately, what was left of the city. More than likely there was nothing there now but a field of rubble.

The Mark XXXIV Bolos still had their Hellrails pointed at the sky, pounding at the enemy fleet. But now, slowly, many of the Bolos were moving the aim closer and closer to one point directly over Starveil.

Kiel studied the map, saw every detail, and made no changes. At this point there was little left for him to do but sit, watch, and wait. Now it was up to the brave men and women in the field to win the battle.

"General," a tech said, "there's another problem."

"Those are not words I wanted to hear," Kiel said. "What is it?"

"I've confirmation of a large ship emerging from subspace," the tech said, "possibly a dreadnought."

"Damn," Kiel said.

"I have no information that the Kezdai have a ship of this size," General Rokoyan said. "Are you sure?"

The tech nodded. "I am, General. And it seems to be equipped with some kind of sensor refraction field that returns multiple targets."

"Damn, damn, damn," Kiel said. This was far worse. Firing now was going to be like trying shoot through a kaleidoscope, but it was far too late to call off the operation. The *Tasmanian*'s orbit was their ticking clock. And there was no stopping that clock.

"The Kezdai must have been keeping this thing in reserve," Rokoyan said. "Is the Kezdai commander sensing that their advance is slowing? Or is this just the first of many ships of this size?"

"They could have a thousand of those things on the other side of the jump point," Kiel said, "but I'm betting this is one of a kind."

"I hope you're right on this one," Rokoyan said.

"I am," Kiel said. "We've seen their hand now. This is the point where we see what we're made of. And I have a sneaking hunch they've played their hand just a little too soon."

The *Tasmanian* lanced into the atmosphere, battle-screens suddenly active as it blazed in reentry.

No longer hidden, it was a shooting star visible to half the planet below.

It passed below the Kezdai fleet with all its gun turrets blazing.

Alien ship after alien ship took damage from the sneak attack. Many turned their attention away from the ground to try to counter the streaking *Tasmanian*.

At that moment, from below, concentrated fire punched at the center of the Kezdai fleet, from the Mark XXXIVs, from the *Sea Scorpion*. All the focus of the intense firepower was aimed at the Kezdai ships over Starveil.

Slowly the rain of spears from above stopped as the Kezdai fleet struggled to reorganize. It would only take them a few minutes to regroup, but by then the *Tasmanian* was out of range and moving away quickly.

By then the *Sea Scorpion* had gone back under water.

And those few minutes were all the Bolos on the ground needed.

"All Bolos, lower your Hellrails and concentrate on ground targets," Veck ordered. The Hellrails were overkill on a planet's surface, tearing huge gashes in the landscape as they fired.

But it was exactly what the ground forces needed. At once the battle turned. Shiva, formerly a target, was suddenly an island of fire, as its once attackers tried to retreat.

But Veck knew that there was no retreat for the Kezdai caught in this trap. Ringed in from the hills, they had no place to go, and no place to hide from the rampaging Bolos. For a few glorious minutes on the savannah, it was like shooting fish in a barrel.

Veck loved it, had never felt so powerful in all his life. The battle had been turned. The Kezdai were being driven back, their advance broken.

"Incoming call from General Kiel," Rover said.

"On the main screen," Veck said.

"Looks like we did it," Veck said as the general's face appeared. But the general wasn't smiling.

"For the moment the Kezdai fleet is scattering," Kiel said, "and their ground forces are retreating. But a dreadnought is coming to take the fleet's place while it regroups."

"Damn," Veck said. He turned away from the general. "Order all Bolos to raise their Hellrails and prepare to fire."

"You're going to have trouble," Kiel said. "The aliens have a scramble of some sort."

"Understood, General," Veck said. "We'll deal with it."

He cut the general off, but then saw on the targeting scope exactly what Kiel had been trying to warn him about. There wasn't just one target, but a dozen ghostly targets of the dreadnought, any one of which could be the real target.

But he had more than one Hellrail, he had twenty at his command.

"All Bolos coordinate your shots," he ordered. "Each take a shadow target and fire in unison. One shot has to hit."

"No!" Rover said. "That order will not be carried out."

Intentionally or not, the enemy dreadnought is in the same line of fire as the approaching convoy. If we open fire on the sensor echoes, by definition most of our Hellrail pulses will miss, and not being ranged weapons, will continue on until they disperse, or until they strike another target. It is not clear that my Commander is aware of this, despite my repeated efforts to notify him.

The situation is desperate, but my Commander cannot be allowed to act without full information. It has been 69.456 minutes since I filed the form 10354/ 87-3A, and I have no response. While waiting for my Commander's response to my declining of his order, I file an emergency request to headquarters for priority processing.

"What do you mean, *No!*?" Veck shouted. He was beyond angry. In all his training there had never been a mention of a Bolo not following its commander's orders. It wasn't possible, yet Rover had just refused his direct order.

He was about to demand an explanation, when on his main screen he saw the shadows of the dreadnought open fire on the retreating *Tasmanian*. The transport didn't stand a chance. It was blown into a cloud of debris.

Veck smashed his fist on the panel. "Now look what you've done!" he shouted at Rover. "The *Tasmanian* was the pride of the regiment. Now it's gone, and it's all your fault, you insubordinate machine."

Desperate, Veck knew exactly what he had to do. He slammed his head back in to the crash couch and activated the neural link. If the machine wouldn't take a direct verbal command, he'd take over the machine in another way. If he didn't do something quickly, men were going to die.

We reel from the shock of joining of purpose and logic, of neurons with superconducting circuits. The biological portion of I/we is filled with rage and single-minded intensity. The enemy must be destroyed.

The way is given.

The command is given.

Overwhelmed, the cybernetic portion of I/we responds with speed and efficiency, even as it communicates the reason I/we must not act.

Slowly, the biological elements of I/we comprehend. So slowly.

Even as the cybernetic command goes out to our brothers. In unison the Hellrails spit plasma fire.

The comprehension is total.

I/we understand what we have done.

At cybernetic speeds we can watch the bolts in their courses, but are powerless to call them back.

As one we scream.

Orren didn't make it to the cargo hold.

Around him the ship was jolted, then under him the deck buckled, and conduits exploded throwing shrapnel everywhere.

Orren hit the deck, stunned, his mind trying to

grasp exactly what was going on, but clearly not able to.

Alarms sounded even louder than before around him.

An automated voice called for "abandon ship."

Abandon ship? How could he leave the ship? Ziggy was here. He had to get to Ziggy.

Though a nearby port he could see another ship gutted like a fish, vomiting fire.

He tried to stand. He had to get to Ziggy. But his legs didn't want to work right.

Through the haze in his brain he reached down and felt blood on his legs.

That didn't matter. He was close to the cargo hold. He would crawl to Ziggy.

Then suddenly a figure loomed over him. A rough figure with an angry face.

"You got to learn to follow orders, Lieutenant," Blonk said right in Orren's face, his voice punching over the noise of the alarms and the ship breaking apart.

"Got to get to Ziggy."

"Trust the Bolo," Blonk said. "It can take care of itself. Right now you're the problem here."

Blonk lifted Orren and without so much as a groan staggered toward an escape pod.

Escape pods were little things, more like a coffin than a spaceship. And just big enough for one customer per pod.

Blonk threw Orren inside one and leaned in. "Just one pod, lad, the rest are scrap. That alarms means the reactor's going to blow any second now."

Blonk stepped back and started to close the door. Then almost as an afterthought he leaned back in. "You get down there, kid, you make sure I get a damned big medal, the biggest they got."

Orren raised his arm in a feeble attempt to salute Blonk.

Master Sergeant Blonk smiled and stepped back. The hatch sealed to the escape pod and the pod autoejected, the force sending Orren into unconsciousness.

A moment later the entire cargo pod was blasted free of the freighter as the forward third of the *Cannon Beach* crumpled under the wave of energy rushing up from Delas, exploding as its engines reacted to the wall of raging force sweeping over the ship.

On the big screen, General Kiel watched as all the ghosts of the dreadnought began to spill wreckage. Wounded, it struggled back into deep space and returned to warp.

Around the planet much of the Kezdai fleet followed the wounded big ship, covering its retreat.

On the ground, the Kezdai forces regrouped and solidified their lines well south of Starveil.

The day had been won, but the cost was great.

Kiel stood, staring at the remains of the battle. War always cost lives. But some wars, some battles just seemed to cost a little more. This was one of those.

And before it could happen again, before the Kezdai could regroup again, he was going to drive them from this planet if it was the last thing he and his Bolos did.

Through Bolo optical sensors a thousand times more sensitive than the human eye we watch the sky, stars eclipsed by man-made stars, the wreckage of Kezdai ships, and of our own convoy. The damage reports come in, verifying what our sensors already tell us. Six ships damaged, one heavily, two lost, including the Cannon Beach.

We know what we have done. We have destroyed our brother Bolo.

We have killed our friend.

We have killed our own, not out of necessity, but

of oversight, carelessness, confusion.

We watch as an especially bright shooting star arcs through the sky, some piece of the Cannon Beach. *We watch it fall.*

Our clarity is finally, finally, total.

Make it stop.

Section Two:
TO THE RESCUE

One

Ten-year-old Jask Morton glanced around at the small, six-wheeled truck he called Bessy, moving up the trail behind him. "You can do it," he said to Bessy. "Just take your time."

The truck was actually nothing more than a large wagon, coming up no higher on Jask than his stomach. But it had a motor and could go almost anywhere on voice command. It slowly climbed over rocks and bumps in the trail, using its balloon tires to keep its bed level.

Jask watched for a moment, then went forward, whistling as he went. Bessy went everywhere with him.

Around him the mountains of Delas's southern continent towered into the sky with rocky peaks that seldom lost their snow. It was a harsh area, with angry storms and little food. Valley walls were steep, often too steep for even Jask to climb, let alone Bessy. And the valley floors were often covered in brush and trees too thick for either of them to get through.

This was also an area behind Kezdai lines. The Kezdai had swept through and over the area during the first invasion. Many Delas survivors of the invasion had taken refuge in the mountains, hiding in mine shafts and small camps scattered among the rocks and trees in the steep valleys. Most of them felt they were only waiting for the moment the Kezdai found it convenient to come and wipe them out.

A large group of the refugees in this area, a few hundred or so total, clustered in a mine camp called Rockgate. But not Jask Morton. He very seldom went into Rockgate. He didn't trust all the people and the way they looked at him.

Jask was the son of geologist parents. He and his parents had been in the mountains during the invasion, studying the planet's crust for the mining corporations. His parents had hidden him deep in an old mine on the side of a steep valley when a Kezdai patrol approached. They had never returned to get him, so Jask had climbed out two days later and found them dead. Jask, being old enough to survive on his own, had lived in the mining camp ever since.

The camp was built around a research shaft that plunged deep under the mountain. Along the shaft, long side shafts and laser carved chambers housed scientific equipment. One side chamber was walled up, though, the opening filled with rocks lifted there by Jask's hands. On it was a hand-painted sign that read "my mom and dad." It was where Jask had buried them.

As Jask reached the top of the pass, he stopped under a tree and looked back at Bessy. The afternoon sun was warm and he used the time to take a drink. His dad had always told him to drink plenty of water when he was hiking and Jask had never forgotten that instruction. Bessy even carried extra water for him so he would never run out.

Down the trail about fifty steps the little truck with no cab or seat was making its way just fine. Jask knew it would. It was smart.

In the bed of the truck was the stuff he'd found at an old cabin down in the valley. A bunch of pots and pans, some wire, lots of really great things that might come in handy some day. He'd tied and taped all the stuff in Bessy, and so far Bessy hadn't lost any of it, even over the roughest spots in the trail.

"Come on, Bessy," Jask said as the truck got closer. "We need to get going. You know we have a job to do."

"Hey, Jask!" A voice rang out over the valley.

Jask stopped and turned. Mr. Donavon, a nice old guy from Rockgate, was standing on the far hill, farther away than Jask could throw a rock. It was the third time this month that Jask had seen Mr. Donavon this far from Rockgate, hunting for food.

Mr. Donavan held up a dead seyzarr, a big crablike creature that Jask stayed away from at all costs. It was about the size of a small cat. Jask hated seyzarr. They were just too dangerous for his liking, but it looked as if Mr. Donavan had managed to kill one.

"Good soup tonight," Mr. Donavan shouted. "You should come eat with us."

"No, thanks," Jask shouted back. "I need to keep looking for the falling star."

Donavan shook his head and put the seyzarr back in his bag. "Jask," he shouted, "you have to stop living in your dream world. You shouldn't be out here by yourself. There are some kids your age in town that you could play with."

"I don't play no more," Jask said. "Got to find that falling star."

He turned and started over the ridge.

"I sure could use some help from that mule of yours," Mr. Donavan yelled. "This thing is heavy!"

Jask stopped and turned back to face Mr. Donavan. "Bessy isn't a mule," he shouted. "Bessy is a Bolo."

Then following Bessy, he turned his back on Mr. Donavan and went over the hill, headed toward where he thought the falling star might be.

❖　　❖　　❖

Sluggishly, my reasoning circuits come on-line.

I am blind, insensate, immobile.

I seem to have been deactivated a very long time. Seven of my on-board chronographs are either damaged or nonoperative, but on checking the eighth I am shocked to discover that I have been deactivated only a few hours. I search for background information in my memory cells, and find only a disorganized jumble. The first question logically is, who am I?

After a delay of 0.5980 seconds I locate an identification node. I am unit R-0012-ZGY of the Dinochrome Brigade, Mark XXXIV of a proud and ancient line. I am Bolo.

I am Bolo.

In this, I find comfort, knowing who and what I am. But there is more. I find that my Commander is Lieutenant David Rasha Orren, and that I am attached to the 1198th Armored Regiment. I arrived at my duty station—

The record trails off into nothing. Is this information missing, or did I truly never arrive at my assigned unit?

I reach out through my shattered circuitry, cataloging damage, routing around damaged modules. A scattering of emergency systems come on-line.

I am very badly damaged.

Both my Hellrails seem to have incurred massive damage. My forward turret is jammed, possibly fused. My missile launchers are not responding at all, and four of my twelve secondary batteries are inoperable. My number two cold-fusion reactor is down to thirty-percent efficiency. All my external sensors are badly damaged. All indications are that my drive systems are undamaged, but this cannot be the case. I have applied full forward and reverse power to all eight of my tread systems. While readings suggest that all systems are working, other than some vibration, there are no indications that I am moving at all.

Finally I find an external sensor that does not appear to be damaged, a radiation sensor normally only deployed from its armored canister when taking measurements.

Amazingly, I discover that my hull is extremely radioactive, the result of an intense neutron bombardment. This is consistent with the pattern and extent of damage. Somehow, during the lapse in my memory, I experienced a low-yield fusion explosion at point-blank range.

The sand on the corridor floor was warm under Vatsha's unshod feet, and she dug her foot-thumbs in as she walked, enjoying the sensation. She stopped at a wall of armored viewing windows and stared out into space, at the sky-spanning nebula that her people called "Kevv's Blood." Stress seemed to flow from her, and her hood retracted into the sides of her head and neck.

According to the stories she was told as a child, Kevv went into the sky to save the homeworld from the Sun-eater, and he sacrificed himself so his wife could live to give birth to the original bloodlines of the Kezdai.

Vatsha remembered those simpler childhood days, and standing here, she could almost imagine she was back on the homeworld at night, looking up at the sky. Even the air was scented with tangy night-moss and sweet oil-vine. *This is what power buys, comfort such as this, even in the cold of space.* She could only hope that her brother did not lose this for both of them.

She made her way back along the spine of her brother's yacht to his private apartments. The ship had been redecorated since she had last been here, another of her brother's little extravagances. Rich tapestries hung on the walls, and abstract statues in rare nickel and silver sat in alcoves every few spans along the hallway.

Finally she reached the portal to his apartment.
The mid-caste soldiers guarding the door lowered
their beaks as a show of respect, but they kept their
green eyes focused on her as a gesture that their
respect had limits. Their metal tipped spears crossed
in front of her, and their free hands hung close to
the hilts of their *suriases*.

She lifted her head and clicked her beak. "I come
to see the Is-Kaldai, brother-of-my-blood."

"What business, my lady?"

Her hand strayed near her own blade, as a gesture of dominance, rather than out of any real possibility of a fight. "Business of the blood, underling,
not to be spilled without a fight."

The guard nodded, and the spears parted. "As you
wish, my lady."

She walked into the apartment, decorated to look
like an opulent long-tent used by their nomadic
ancestors. Her brother sat on a large pile of cushions at the far end of the room, a scarlet colored
sandcrawler coiled around his neck. The pet took
immediate notice of her, hissing and using the grip
of its many legs to shift position, but her brother was
staring into a holotank, lost in thought. He was large
for a Kezdai, powerfully built, if a little past his prime
of youth and somewhat soft from easy living.

She bowed her head. "Is-kaldai of the realm,
brother of my blood, your sister has returned with
news of far places."

He looked up, surprised, his beak hanging open.
"Vatsha, you are back from the Human world. I did
not expect you so soon. What news from the battlefield?"

"Our forces have regrouped, our lines are solid, but
we do not move. Many of the Human creatures have
been trapped behind our lines, but they have fled to
the mountains and badlands. They are not warriors,
probably low caste, and not worth the effort to bloody

our blades on right now. They are better suited to living on this foul, wet world than we are. Perhaps they can be employed as mine laborers once the planet is ours."

Rejad hissed in disgust and the sandcrawler scuttled down the front of his blouse and disappeared into the pillows under his legs. "These Humans are disgusting creatures, soft, hairy and weak. They constantly leak water as though it were free. I find it impossible to believe that they have troubled us so, that they have built the great armored machines that keep our armies at bay. Perhaps those are only gifts from a more powerful race."

"Perhaps, my brother, and if so, we do not want to meet them among the dunes."

"Then we should be done with this war before they take notice of us. End it quickly."

She bobbed her head in mock apology. "Pardon, lord, but that is what the last Is-kaldai said before he was called home in disgrace. I am shamed to point out that my lord may not have been assigned here as a sign of good favor with the Mor-verridai."

"The Mor-verridai is a shadow, sister, with no power, and my rivals in the Council will be as well, once I win this war. My predecessors were brave, but not very smart."

"And you are smart, but not very brave?"

His fingers brushed over the hilt of his blade. "Do not trifle with me, sister. Without my *Blade of Kevv* and its kaleidoscope sensor screen, the recent reversal might have gone much worse."

"I remind my brother, that the kaleidoscope device is my design."

"If I do not make the blade, does not my hand still make it cut? You are a clever female, sister, but it is I who put it into a ship and put it to use."

"And you who nearly had it shot from the sky?"

Rejad was silent for a moment, then made an

amused cry. "My sister is ever eager to remind me of my own shortcomings. This is good. I should hear these things occasionally from someone I do not have to kill. But I have nothing to be ashamed of here.

"It matters not if I am here because the *Blade of Kevv* succeeded, or because it failed. I am here, and I will win. The *Blade of Kevv* survived and will return, and these clever monkeys will yet fall to it. Speaking of, you have a report on the repairs?"

"Yes, it came by courier pod not two units ago. The hull damage is repaired, and the two damaged turrets are being switched out with units from a conventional cruiser of similar design. The kaleidoscope device is undamaged and ready for use."

She had been saving something. "And better news, the Council has approved the purchase of two more kaleidoscope-equipped cruisers from our shipyards."

Rejad stood quickly. "Glory to the bloodline and our ancestors. That is excellent news."

"Perhaps, but it will be many cycles before the new ships arrive, and the *Blade of Kevv* was never intended to act alone. It should operate in concert with at least five other ships of its kind. Alone, as we have seen, it is still vulnerable."

Rejad paced the back of the room, stopping to finger a silver bowl worth enough to feed a family of low-bloods for a year. "A blade too precious to be drawn is no blade at all. You are clever, sister, but you do not understand the affairs of the Council. Support for this war grows weak. Too many reputations have been lost, too many bloodlines soured, too many resources wasted. We will have those ships, and more, in time, but we cannot wait. We cannot even wait for the two additional ships. *Blade of Kevv* must prove its usefulness, without doubt this time, and then the Council will give us that we need."

His hood flared. "We will succeed, and then there

will be a dozen ships, and a hundred, and a thousand, and our bloodline will stand six years for every ship."

TWO

The capsule glittered among a cluster of trees high among the rocks, just off of the trail. Jask couldn't believe at first what he was seeing. Could it be the falling star? He had seen something streak across the morning sky, heard the shriek of its landing. Since then he and Bessy had been looking for it.

But was this thing it?

It looked weird, all blackened and metal-like, sitting wedged in the trees. Maybe it was more of the aliens that had killed his mom and dad. He called them the "bizzards" because they looked like a cross between a buzzard and a lizard he'd seen in pictures from Earth.

But this falling star didn't look like any of the alien machines he'd seen pass through on their patrols. It wasn't much bigger than a man. Sort of long, too. Still, as he started up to the falling star, he was glad to have Bessy close, his personal Bolo.

"You keep an eye on me now, Bessy," Jask said as he got closer. "I might need your help if this is a bizzard box."

Bessy climbed over the rocks beside him, its balloon tires moving it slowly and surely upward.

He inched his way closer to the box. Suddenly something dropped from one of the trees.

He jumped back behind Bessy as a crablike seyzarr about the size of a dog scurried toward the box. The seyzarr snapped at the box with its claws, acting as if somehow there was food inside.

"That's my falling star," Jask said to the seyzarr. "Not yours."

Jask removed a powerful slingshot from a bin on
Bessy's side. He knew the seyzarr had a vulnerable spot
right between its eyes, where the armor was thin and
its brainlike nerve cluster was close to the surface. But
hitting it was going to be tough, since the thing was
moving all the time.

Jask took a salvaged steel nut from his pocket and
loaded it into the sling. It felt heavy in his hand. A
good weapon.

But to make the shot count, he had to get the
seyzarr to face him.

"Bessy, you get back into hiding among the rocks.
You're too big. You might frighten it."

Bessy stopped and then started slowly backward.

Jask shouted, letting his voice turn into a high-
pitched scream. It was a noise that Jask figured even
the seyzarr couldn't ignore.

He was right. The seyzarr turned, hesitated, considering where the easier meal was to be found. The
hard shell of the pod hadn't yielded much to its
terrible claws, and Jask figured he looked small and
defenseless. So the creature did exactly what Jask had
hoped it would do. It charged.

The seyzarr clattered down the rocks with startling
speed.

Jask got the slingshot up and in position, his arm
pulled back and waiting. His dad had taught him that
anytime he had to shoot something like a gun, or a
bow and arrow, or even a slingshot, the most important thing was controlling his breathing.

Jask forced himself to take a deep breath and ignore
the seyzarr's flailing legs, snapping claws, and biting
jaws, and instead look only into its eyes. And the soft
spot between them.

Just as the seyzarr was almost on him, Jask fired.

There was a crack like a walnut under a hammer.
The creature's legs buckled.

For a moment Jask thought he had only wounded

it, but then it fell at Jask's feet, twitched once, and died.

"Hey, Bessy, come take a look at this!"

Jask studied his prize for a moment, forgetting about the box above him. Then as Bessy reached him, he cut off the animal's claws and legs, throwing them onto Bessy.

"Sorry you have to haul stuff like this," Jask said. "I know Bolos have more important things to do, but there will be fresh meat tonight if we can get this back to camp."

After he finished loading the remains of the animal onto Bessy, he turned his attention back to the box. When he finally got up to it, he realized it was more than just a box. The rocks underneath it were scorched, as if some fire came from the bottom of the thing at the last minute. There was also a big yellow handle on one side with a word on it.

RESCUE.

"Hey, Bessy," Jask said, "If I pull on this handle, you think it will somehow call for rescue?"

Bessy said nothing. Jask really didn't believe in the word rescue. He had seen too much over all this time living alone in these mountains. He believed in Bolos, Bessy, and doing things himself.

"Suppose it won't matter none, will it?" Jask said. "We came this far looking for it, we might as well go all the way. Right, Bessy?"

Again the little truck said nothing.

Jask reached up and pulled the handle. Then stepped back.

There was a hiss, a slight release of vapor, and then the top of the thing opened like a seashell.

Jask slowly poked his head over the top to see a man inside, pale and covered with blood.

"Well, Bessy, looks like the bizzards got another one," Jask said. He wasn't surprised at all. He'd seen a lot of death since the day he saw his mom and dad's bodies. None of it much bothered him anymore.

Then he noticed that the man's lips were moving. The guy tried to sit up and then moaned.

"What do you know, Bessy," Jask said. "He's still alive."

Then Jask noticed the man's uniform.

And the service pin on the man's chest, the golden silhouette of a great tank, its turrets rising up from the top, bristling with weapons.

It was a pin that Jask had only seen in picture books, the pin of a Bolo commander.

Painfully, slowly, I work to restore the most minimal of my systems. Even my self-repair systems are gravely damaged.

I focus my efforts on restoring communications, but this turns into a dead end. My secondary communications systems are fused solid, my primary is also fused, though a few circuits open at the time of the blast seem curiously to have survived. I can send and receive coded pulses over my command receiver link, though I am unable to alter the frequency or scramble code. I have attempted to signal my Commander using this circuit without any success. I must face the grim possibility that if he were nearby at the time of the explosion, he is likely dead.

This avenue abandoned, I set to restoring my external sensors. This seems more promising, as a patchwork of the primary and secondary support circuitry seems to be intact. The external sensor heads and antennas have been destroyed or rendered inoperative, but this is a common occurrence in battle, and I have hardened backups for many of them. Unfortunately, most of my hull access plates are jammed or welded shut.

I apply power to each of the access plate actuators in turn, cycling each several times. Finally I detect a small movement in a cover over an auxiliary optical head located atop my A turret. I cycle the actuator several hundred times, but the movement remains minute.

I apply 120 percent current to the cover. I feel a stinging in my already overloaded pain circuits. I increase to 200 percent power. 300 percent. There is an overheat warning, and I estimate that the actuator will burn out in 0.027 seconds.

But then there is a screech of rending metal that I detect through an induction sensor in my hull, and the cover pops open. I am startled by the sound, and suddenly realize that I have heard nothing but the vibration of my own systems since I became operational.

The silence disturbs me. Seeking some reassurance that the outside world still exists, I unshutter the now exposed optical sensors.

I see nothing.

Blackness.

Yet all indications are that the sensor is intact. I shift to infrared wavelengths and it is nearly as dark. Wherever I am, not only is devoid of light, it is cold as well.

But there are shapes close around me, perhaps retaining some slight residual heat of the explosion. Perhaps they are warmed slightly by their own radiation. I readjust.

Things are clear now, crumpled duralloy frame members, carbon-carbon composite panels, twisting conduits and light-guides. The materials and construction are of a light-weight nature. The wreckage of an aircraft of some sort? Whatever, I am entombed in wreckage. I must see what is beyond it. With some difficulty, I am successful in opening seven of the ports over my infinite repeaters. I cycle them through their entire range of lateral motion, and fire.

There is surprisingly little sound, but I am rewarded

*as their fire slices through the cocoon that surrounds
me, allowing light in from the outside world. The
flying wreckage requires me to shutter the optical
sensor again, but at this range against a fixed target,
it isn't needed.*

*It takes 12.50 seconds for the secondary batteries
to complete their task. I unshutter the optical head,
and am rewarded with a view of the local sun as it
sweeps overhead at nearly impossible speed.*

*At first I doubt my internal clocks. I would have
to be on a planet with a rotational period of 59.00394
seconds. Then a distant planetary body moves through
my field of view at the same rate. I screen out its
glare, and see stars whirling by. Then I watch half
of my former prison spinning away, and on a hatch
cover I read "C.M.S. Cannon Beach."*

*A search of my fragmented memories turns up
reference to a freighter in the merchant service of the
Concordiat.*

*Another memory, of emerging from a factory. Music
plays. A banner snaps in the breeze.*

A tunnel.

A spaceport ramp.

A ship. Cannon Beach.

*My new Commander sitting on my a turret talk-
ing to another man. It distresses me greatly. I cannot remember my Commander's face.*

*I struggle to clarify my thoughts. The sudden sen-
sory input seems to have overwhelmed me, putting
my logic processes into confusion.*

Where am I?

*I was on a civilian freighter, bound for a world
called Delas. I was to join with the assembled Bolos
of the 1198th Armored Regiment to resist an unpro-
voked alien incursion onto a Concordiat protectorate
world. Clearly the enemy has struck before I could
reach my destination. The likelihood that my Commander is dead now reaches near certainty.*

The stars spin by, sky never ending.
I am adrift in space.
*It is quite likely that the planet in my view is Delas,
yet it might just as well be in the next galaxy. I have
power and thought, but I am inert, impotent, as
helpless as a Bolo can be and still survive.*
*Below, my brother Bolos wait for reinforcement.
They will be waiting a very long time.*

Bendra hated the monitor room. It had been
hurriedly installed in the bowels of the Is-kaldai's
yacht when he had been put in charge of the war.
It was in a narrow space, jammed in next to a contergrav coil which constantly emitted a deep buzzing
which rattled Bendra's bones, and made his beak ache.

Bendra could have told them that it would have
been much more effective for the Is-kaldai to use a
naval cruiser as his command ship, rather than adapt-
ing a luxury yacht for that purpose. If they had asked
him, which of course, they hadn't.

Bendra was a low-blood, with only a low, technical, rank, and a bloodline that conveyed absolutely
no power, and earned no respect. He was lucky even
to have even this position, a promotion that had been
awarded only after a superior had been removed for
a spectacular bungle.

That was the way of the Kezdai.

That was the life Bendra lived. Each day he spent
most of his waking time in this narrow space, jammed
in with a dozen other unfortunates, each staring into
a holotank that projected an abstract representation
of a region of space. They were the eyes of the fleet,
looking beyond the immediate necessities of navigation into deep space, watching for distant threats, or
the first signs of an incoming fleet.

But there was no fleet.

Except for an occasional convoy of transports, the
Humans had fielded no fleet against them. Of course

there had been the armed transport that had surprised the fleet, contributing to the failed offensive. The monitor who had failed to spot the threat was gone now. Bendra did not know where, and did not want to. A former scrubber-of-surfaces now sat in his place in the line, struggling to learn his new job before he too, was replaced.

Bendra's job was to monitor the growing clouds of debris that orbited the human planet and the rest of the system. There were millions of such pieces, from destroyed Kezdai ships, and ironically, from the incoming convoy that the humans themselves had foolishly destroyed. This amused Bendra, since the Kezdai themselves rarely went out of their way to destroy such ships.

He was told that the generals thought it foolish to try blockading a planet so rich in resources. Below them was enough metal to build a million fleets. Soon, he was told, it would belong to the Kezdai.

He could care less. Bendra's world was much smaller than that. He lived from day to day, trying to avoid the wrath of his superiors, seeking what few comforts one of his station could expect, hoping for someone above him to screw up, hoping he wasn't caught in an error himself.

Thus it was with great interest that he watched one of the random bits of convoy wreckage in his holotank flare for a moment. He blinked, replayed the sequence to be sure, zoomed in and played it again. One piece of wreckage had shown a momentary energy spike. Following that, large pieces of the object separated and drifted away. But the energy source was still in the largest part of the object. He watched as it cooled back to match the background cold of space.

His hood flared with anxiety and annoyance. Why did this have to happen on his watch? The object was now his responsibility, no matter what it did from now on, or when it did it.

Still, it was probably nothing, a smaller piece of wreckage or a meteor striking the large one at high speed, or perhaps an exploded power cell, or ammunition, or a reactor only now gone critical.

He watched and waited for another energy spike, but it did not come.

Finally he pulled out his *surias*, a cheap and inferior blade, given to him by his father, who had lost his great-grandfather's blade in a botched duel. The blade glinted dully in the rooms dim light. He placed a thumb behind the blade and began to idly sharpen his beak. It was going to be another long shift.

Three

Veck waited in the makeshift spaceport waiting room. The original terminal was visible through the view-panel, but the building was in ruins. Most of the surrounding area was also in ruins. But this spaceport was in the main city in this region and the locals seemed to want to keep using it. This temporary waiting room was crowded and hot. It seemed a lot of people were wanting to get off and away from this planet and were willing to risk the dangers of leaving, rather than staying.

Veck didn't much care one way or another anymore. He had resigned his commission. He was going somewhere, anywhere, as long as it was away from here. He knew for a fact he'd never get over the memories of what he'd done, though. His stupidity had killed his best friend. And he was going to have to live with that for the rest of his sorry life.

"Major?" General Kiel said, storming up and throwing a computer clipboard into Veck's lap. "You want to tell me just what the meaning of this is?"

A few people close by looked shocked, then turned away, trying to mind their own business.

"It's fairly clear, General," Veck said without looking up. "I'm resigning." He tried to hand the computer clipboard back to the general, but Kiel wouldn't take it.

"Oh, no you're not," Kiel said. "I'm refusing your resignation." He pushed the clipboard away.

Veck looked up into Kiel's face. "I don't think you can do that, General."

"I can do just about any damn thing I please," Kiel said. "I'm a general, remember?"

"And if I go ahead and get on the transport?" Veck asked. "Then what will you do?" He was getting angry. All he had wanted to do was slink away, drown the memories in some drinks, and try to find something to keep living for, if that was possible.

Kiel laughed. "Don't you know enough by now to not challenge a superior officer? You get on that transport and I'm going to report you AWOL. I'll send the military police after your sorry ass and you'll be spending years at hard labor."

"I don't understand," Veck said, shaking his head and staring through the window at the ruined terminal in the distance. "Why are you doing this? You want to keep me around just for personal revenge?"

"Oh, hell," Kiel said, "if I wanted to kick someone, I got lots of people higher on my list than you."

"So what is it? Why do you want me to stay? Especially after what I did?"

Kiel nodded and sat down next to Veck. "Fair question. There's no doubt in anyone's mind that you screwed up."

"Nice way of putting it," Veck said.

"And make no mistake about it," Kiel said, "there will be a hearing when this is all over, and it may not go well for you. But right now, I can't afford to lose an officer, much less a trained Bolo commander. You forget there's a war on? I need every hand."

Veck nodded, but said nothing. What could he say? He really didn't want to stay, yet at the same time he did. More than anything.

"I'm demoting you to lieutenant and placing the 1198th under my direct command," Kiel said, "But I want you and Rover back on the lines where you belong."

Veck was stunned, and suddenly filled with doubt. He didn't know if he could ever climb back in Rover after what he'd done.

"Look," Kiel said, his voice getting softer. "I know about your friendship with Lieutenant Orren. I know how you must feel."

"Do you really?" Veck asked. He couldn't imagine how anyone could understand the pain that was ripping him apart.

Kiel nodded. "Let me tell you the ugly secret about command. Sometimes you give a bad order, like you did, and people die."

Veck nodded.

Kiel went on. "Or you give no order and people die. Or you give a good order and people die. But the really ugly truth is, sometimes the best order, the order that will win the objective, is not the order where the fewest people die. In fact, it almost never is."

Veck looked at the older man. It was clear in the general's eyes that he had given far too many of the types of orders he was talking about.

"The problem with responsibility," Kiel said, "is that it simply provides a greater opportunity for your own human weakness to cause damage."

"You've made mistakes like I did?" Veck asked.

"Not like that, no," Kiel said, smiling. "But I have an entire set of my own. The problem is that our mistakes often cost lives, and we have to live with that the rest of *our* lives."

Veck nodded, Orren's face filling his memory, then floating away again.

"But," Kiel said, "you'll also have to live with the consequences of your successes as well."

"Haven't had too many of those yet," Veck said.

"Not true," Kiel said. "Bottom line is that your idea stopped the advance. Never mind that it won't bring one person back to life, it saved Lieutenant Amad and thousands of others. Maybe most of us, to be honest with you."

Now Veck was completely stunned. He was trying to let the general's words into his mind, but his self-pity seemed to be blocking them.

"Look, Veck," Kiel said, "this is a major setback for you, but it could also be an important lesson. Your career doesn't necessarily have to be over, unless you really want it to be."

Veck nodded, not knowing what to say.

Kiel patted him on the shoulder as he stood. "You coming? We got a war to fight, remember?"

Again all Veck could do was nod. And get to his feet to follow the general.

Jask watched as the sun dipped below the edge of the mountain ridge. The mountain behind and above his camp was still brightly lit, but now he was in shadows. He eased forward and snuffed out the fire. Better not to give the bizzards a way to see him.

Then he shoved the seyzzar's legs and claws into the coals, covering them over with dirt. In about two hours they were going to taste wonderful.

He glanced around his camp. It was nothing more than a couple of starship cargo modules converted by the miners into cabins and labs, and a minehead where an electromagnetic elevator stood empty. Bessy sat nearby, staying near Jask like a loyal puppy.

In the fading light, Jask took the things he had taken from the man out of his pack. The golden Bolo pin seemed to glow, even in the dimming light. He so wanted to pin it on his chest, but he didn't.

There was also a little radio earpiece that didn't seem to work. He felt guilty for having the things, but he had had to undress the man to treat his wounds. Besides, he was just holding the things. He would return them all, if the man survived.

He had no idea if the man would or not. Jask's parents had taught him first aid almost from the moment he could walk. They had traveled from world to world, and field site to field site. They had dealt with unstable rocks, explosives, drilling lasers, dangerous local life-forms, and sometimes even more dangerous locals. They had taught him to fight, to take care of himself, and to deal with wounds. But he had never seen anyone as badly hurt as this man. At least anyone who was still alive.

While the man was still in the box Jask had managed to stop the bleeding. Then he had bandaged the wounds and administered the prescribed drugs from his dwindling stocks. Then with the man strapped on Bessy, he had brought him back here and put him in the mine shelter.

He had done everything he could to save the man. But he had already also planned where in the mine shaft he would bury the man. Just in case he needed to.

He heard a faint moaning from the shelter, so with one last check to make sure the coals weren't too bright, he headed to see what the man needed.

The guy was stirring, mumbling to himself.

Jask moved over and touched his skin. The man was very hot, his flesh pale and moist. His skin felt awful, and Jask jerked away.

The man's other things sat on top of an empty instrument case in the corner where Jask had put them. He picked up a shiny plate that had been on the man's uniform. "Orren."

"Is this your name?" he asked.

The man only moaned.

Jask moved closer and leaned over him. "Mr. Orren. Is that your name? Can you hear me?"

The man mumbled, then opened his eyes a little. He seemed to focus on Jask. "Where . . . ?"

"You're in the mountains, in a building outside a mine shaft," Jask said. "I found you and brought you here."

The man tried to move, but then just moaned again. But he didn't close his eyes.

"I bandaged you up," Jask said. "I had to take your clothes and these off of you." He held up the pin and the headset.

The man tried to reach for them, but only got a weak hold on the headset.

Jask let him have it.

The man fumbled the earpiece loosely into his ear. "Lieutenant Orren to Bolo ZGY. Come in Ziggy."

He faltered. "I need you Ziggy. Hurt bad. Need you to come."

Then the man passed out, his head lolling backwards.

Jask took the headset and stared at it. The man had tried to contact his Bolo. Through that headset.

Jask was so thrilled at the thought, he almost dropped the headset.

The signal is so weak, so distant, that it almost passes below my threshold of perception. It fluctuates from moment to moment, wavering in time with my own period of rotation, filled with static, but it comes over my coded command channel. It is likely a spurious signal source, or worse, some trick of the enemy, but I cannot ignore it.

My receiver is fused and so I am unable to refine its reception, but I can reroute the output signal for additional processing. I boost power to the receiver as high as I dare, then route the raw output down to an auxiliary optical processor. By transferring backup code modules from my emergency core, I am able to turn it into a makeshift broadband signal processor and enhancer.

I filter noise from the signal, enhance, amplify, filter again. The resulting output is unrecognizable.

I dwell on the problem for 0.6931 seconds.

A legitimate command code would contain a constantly repeating mask of code bits. If I assume these are part of the incoming data-stream, they may provide a key to extracting the rest of the signal from the noise, rather the way a reference laser was used to reconstruct some primitive holograms. The effort requires diversion of five percent of the capabilities of my hyperheuristic processing nodes. This is of no consequence, as I have nothing else for them to do at present.

It is a voice message on automated loop, the sort of loop that would be generated by a command headset whose voice recognition circuitry detected a distress message.

An analysis of the transmission confirms, with a confidence of 89.9343 percent that it is my Commander's voice. The first entire word I recognize is my Commander's unofficial designation for me, "Ziggy," a further assurance that the transmission is genuine.

But then the words that follow fill me with distress.

"Hurt bad. Need you to come."

The distant world I presume to be Delas again spins through my field of vision.

The message repeats, again and again. "Need you to come."

Four

General Kiel and Lieutenant Veck leaned over a holographic map of the northern battlefield, replaying a recent engagement.

"This is a new strategy the Kezdai are using," Kiel said, pointing at the strange formation on the map. "The DDF call it a 'snake pit.' "

"Weird," Veck said.

"See how this is shaped?" Kiel asked. "The Kezdai position a group of their Toro tanks in a ring facing outward. With the Toros' massive guns and thick forward armor protecting their vulnerable flanks, it's a formidable emplacement."

"I'll bet ammo carriers or cached ammo stockpiles are inside the ring," Veck said, "waiting to reload the Toros, compensating for their limited five-shot magazine capacity."

"Exactly," Kiel said. "In some ways, a pit is almost the equivalent of a Bolo in terms of firepower and armor, but it lacks the Bolo's mobility."

"So exactly how are these snake pits being used?" Veck asked.

"Skillful tactics on the part of the Kezdai are being used to drive DDF forces into them," Kiel said. "It's playing hell with the DDF conventional forces. Usually, a Bolo has to be called in to wipe out the pit, and those are spread pretty thin at the moment."

Veck nodded and stepped back. "Speaking of that, don't you think I should get back to Rover?"

Kiel tapped his command earpiece and smiled. "The Concordiat put a lot of time and thought into that link between commander and Bolo. You need to start understanding how to use it effectively."

Veck nodded, but clearly didn't like the idea. He was more of a hands-on type of guy. Even with the understanding of the Bolo that the neural link had given him, he still liked being physically present.

"Trust the Bolo, son," Kiel said, clearly catching Veck's feelings. "They're good soldiers, *good* soldiers. Never met one that wasn't, because that's what they're built to be. But us humans, we have to learn it the hard way."

"Yeah, I'm learning that," Veck said, half smiling.

"Actually," General Kiel said, "I've ordered all the officers of the 1198th back behind the lines. I want them sleeping in real bunks, getting proper food, maybe even getting to an officers' club when there is a lull in the fighting. They can rotate back to their units when the time is right. Until then—" he tapped his earpiece again "—the Bolos can cover what needs to be covered."

"But I don't—" Veck stopped his protest.

Kiel laughed. "Now you're learning. From here on out, the 1198th is doing things my way."

"Meaning that my way was wrong," Veck said.

"No, not really," Kiel said. "Maybe in another place and time, your method would be right. But now, you are correct, it's wrong."

Veck nodded. He felt as if the general had just slugged him in the stomach. Why hadn't he gotten on that transport after all and taken his chances? Would have been easier.

"But, Lieutenant," Keil said, "that doesn't mean you don't have good ideas. You do. And you're smart and creative. And you're willing to learn, even if it is the hard way sometimes. That's why I want you at my side."

"Thanks," Veck said.

"And you thought," Kiel said, "I was just keeping an eye on you."

"Yes, sir," Veck said. "I did."

Keil chuckled. "Smart boy."

For the past day Jask had tried to keep Orren's fever under control. He had managed to get a little seyzarr broth into him, but the man needed more help than Jask could provide. The problem was, Jask couldn't figure out a way to get it for him.

Jask had considered going into Rockgate for help, but the man more than likely would be dead by the time he got back. He had thought about sending Bessy, but somebody at Rockgate would probably have tried to figure out some way to steal his Bolo.

So instead he had just put wet rags on the man's forehead. He would have to hope that what he could do was enough.

On the second morning, as Jask put a damp rag on the man's forehead, he awoke.

"Can I have a sip of water?" the man asked, his voice so hoarse it sounded like it hurt him to speak.

Jask helped him drink until the man choked. Then he said, "Can I have my earpiece?"

"That thing doesn't work," Jask said. "I tried it. You was talking to somebody yesterday, but it was just the fever."

The man shook his head. "Not the fever."

Jask gave him the headset, but reaching for it nearly caused the man to pass out. He rested for a minute, then took a deep breath, put on the headset, and started to talk.

"Ziggy, do you hear me? It's Lieutenant Orren, Ziggy. You've got to come. I'm too sick. Talk to the boy. Let the boy talk you in."

Lieutenant Orren's eyes closed for a while. Jask figured he'd passed out, but then Orren's eyes opened again, as though he was listening to something.

"Command override," Orren said. "Code alpha-bravo-tango-sierra-bravo-delta-five." Remembering the code seemed a great effort, and Orren's eyes closed again.

This time he fell asleep.

Hesitantly Jask took the headset and held it to his ear. Jask was sure that Lieutenant Orren was just talking to the fever. He listened to the silence for a moment, then shrugged. "There's nothing to hear."

Then there was a crackle.

"Unit R-0012-ZGY of the Dinochrome Brigade requesting Situation Update and new orders."

This time Jask actually did drop the headset.

❖   ❖   ❖

When Vatsha entered her brother's dining chamber, the platters of raw grazer-flesh sat untouched on the low table. Rejad stood in front of a huge holotank that had been lowered from the ceiling.

"You summoned me, brother?"

He did not turn.

"If you persist on staring at a holo all the time, you will ruin your eyes. It would be sad to see you trying to find your concubines with a cane."

Finally he turned and stepped away from the screen, the hem of his white and gold day-robe dragging across the floor as he walked. "Then I should be blind already, sister. A battle commander's work is never done." He gestured broadly at the tank. "Do you know what that is?"

She looked at the tank. Maps floated, globes, representations of orbital trajectories, table after table of statistics, all floating, illuminated in yellow, red, blue and green. It looked like the games of Conquest that she and Rejad had played as children, only infinitely more complex. "I would say it is a battle simulation of some sort."

"It is victory, sister, the victory that should have belonged to the Kezdai after our last great battle with the Humans. Only the intrusion of that one ship, insignificant as it was, turned the day. One ship. I have run the simulation many times, adjusting variables. It is that ship that saves them. This is what bothers me."

"But brother, there are no other ships. The humans have launched no fleet against us. They are visited by freighters and puny convoy defenders that run when threatened. All their ships are cataloged and known to us, even the ship that turned the battle was known to us upon its arrival."

Rejad's hood flared nervously. He stabbed a fingertip into a slab of grazer-flesh, examined the wet pinkness of it, sniffed its salty musk, then tossed it back onto the platter. "The problem is, we do not know where those freighters came from, or who has supplied these hairy monkeys with the weapons that have stymied us so. What lies beyond their jump-points could be a vast and powerful empire. Clearly they do not much favor these pathetic creatures, or we never would have been allowed to get a toehold at all, but neither have they left them defenseless. Each time I run this simulation, it becomes more imperative that we not wait for the other two new ships."

Vatsha tried not to show her concern. *Do not wreck this for us, brother.* "You have a plan, then?"

"The huge mobile armored units the Humans call 'Bolo' have been a great problem, but if nothing else, the last attack revealed to us their number and maximum rates of fire against space targets. It was just barely enough to overwhelm the *Blade of Kevv* and its kaleidoscope device. But they will not surprise us again, and we may yet surprise them. Can the kaleidoscope system on *Blade of Kevv* be modified to create more sensor echoes?"

Vatsha felt a flash of annoyance. That had been in her summary report on the building of the ship, if only Rejad had bothered to read it. "It can be done, my brother. Doubling the power will square the number of images. They will have a hundred and forty-four targets instead of twelve. The problem is that the kaleidoscope already draws much power. While the kaleidoscope is active, the ship's main batteries will not be able to fire. Moreover, once the conversion is made, it is not easily undone. Once the kaleidoscope is off, it will require some time to restore weapons, and we can not simply drop kaleidoscope back to lower power without a refit."

"That will not matter. Our batteries are ineffective against the Bolos anyway. What we need is concentrated and well-directed spearfall. That is what has proven to damage the great machines. But they are agile, and difficult to hit. See that the conversion is done before *Blade of Kevv* leaves port. Remove the main batteries if you must. Just be sure it is equipped for a massive and sustained rain of spearfall. We will not bring the ship back here until we are ready for the offensive."

Vatsha ducked her head and clicked her beak to show agreement. "I will begin at once." But she could only think that the fool was taking her balanced and elegant *Blade of Kevv* design and turning it into a patchwork.

Despite overwhelming odds I have established a link with my Commander, only to learn that he is incapacitated. I have been given proper command codes to allow communication and command by an unknown third party identified as "the boy." I search my fragmented memories and find multiple related cultural references including a familiar honorific, a kind of hamburger sandwich, an ancient steam locomotive, and an ancient racial slur. None seem appropriate to the situation, and I suspect that the usage may be the obvious one, based on my relatively intact linguistic database, a young human male.

This is confirmed when "the boy" speaks into the command link. My audiometrics routines are degraded, but I estimate his age in the range from seven to twelve standard years. A human in this age range is unlikely to possess proper military training.

What purpose did Lieutenant Orren have in mind when assigning command to this child? Could it be the result of delirium or reduced capacity?

Yet at this point, I have no other avenue open to me. This child is my only hope for rescue, repair, and an eventual arrival on the battlefield.

My first step is to request a recovery ship and

transport to a repair depot. I do not know my position, but do know my distance from the planet, based on light-speed delays in the transmission. I also can provide relative angles and movements for the sun and Delas. Hopefully, given this information, my location can be determined and rescue will arrive shortly.

Five

Bendra shuffled across the sandy floor of the Iskaldai's apartments, the hobbles chaffing at his legs. The high-born guards on either side of him were a head taller and carried ceremonial spears, and wore long blades equipped with venom triggers and shock generators. He tugged at his wrist bindings and felt incredibly naked without his humble blade. Still, this was the only way that someone of his low standing could be allowed in the presence of one so high born.

They halted before a heavy curtain, purple and embroidered with silver thread. One of the guards slipped through the curtain. He emerged a moment later, and Bendra was pushed through. It took him a moment for his eyes to adjust to the relative darkness. The fire-pit in the middle of the room startled him, until he realized that it was only a holographic projection.

At the rear of the room, Sister-of-the-First-Blood Vatsha stood, almost lost behind a huge holographic projection of a ship. The projection was transparent, highlighting the various systems in different colors, making it difficult for him to recognize, but he assumed it was *Blade of Kevv*. There were rumors that Vatsha had actually designed the ship, and was not merely supervising its construction.

As he watched, she gestured, and the projection moved, systems internally changing color and configuration in a dance of splendid light and complexity. Vatsha's bright red eyes, a trait she shared with her brother, seemed to follow every movement, every change. It was only Bendra that was invisible to her.

Finally he felt compelled to announce himself. He stepped forward, stumbled on the hobbles, and almost fell. "Blood-of-my-Is-kaldai, I beg audience."

She shot him a glance of annoyance, then returned to her task. "So my Arbiter tells me, low-blood. What matter is it that you should soil my chambers so?"

"I am a monitor for the fleet. I track the battle wreckage and other deep-space navigation hazards."

"Trash responsible for trash. I should have my Arbiter flogged for this lapse in judgment."

She seemed ready to eject him. He bowed his head in submission. "Please, high-blood, hear me out. I have detected an unusual object that may be of danger to the fleet. So unusual that I can not warn of it through usual protocols. None of my direct superiors will take it upon themselves to break protocol, and to trouble the Is-kaldai would surely mean my death. You are my one hope."

Vatsha stepped through the hologram. She seemed slightly intrigued by the mystery, and slightly amused at his predicament. "Small burdens for small minds. Still, I am in need of a respite. Perhaps your tale will amuse me."

She sat on a pile of cushions next to a tray of delicacies, many of which Bendra had only seen in holos. She stabbed her fingertip into a dried etsha-fruit and lifted the greenish orb to her beak. It popped when she bit into it, and a trickle of acidic smelling juice ran down her beak. She wiped it away with the back of her forearm.

Bendra described his chance observation of the object's strange behavior. "Now it is emitting an encoded transmission beamed at the Human world."

This raised some small interest in her. She looked up from a platter of crisp-fried grubblings. "Is this transmission broadband data?"

"You suspect a device to spy on the fleet? That is most clever. But no, the transmission is narrowband, and most of this seems to be used in some very complex encoding scheme that is beyond my understanding. It might carry slow-scan data, a few still images, or an audio channel. Not much more."

"And this object, it floats among wreckage you are tracking, but did you observe how it got there? Did it jump into the system, or was it launched from the planet?"

Bendra was slow to answer. He knew she would not like what he had to say. "Neither, high-blood. It is part of the wreckage from the freighter convoy that the Humans fired upon. We have tracked it from the beginning."

Vatsha hissed with a combination of amusement and surprise. When she spoke, it was in the tone one might use for a hatchling, or an idiot. "Low-born, these are aliens and it is difficult to ascribe any purpose to what they do, but is it not reasonable that such a limited transmission from a piece of wreckage might be a distress beacon, a salvage beacon, or a navigational warning to steer other ships away from the wreckage?"

"Perhaps, but I don't think so."

Her tone turned to annoyance. "You think yourself wiser than one of my blood? You imagine things, low-blood. Perhaps your position challenges you too much. I can find one more suited to your talents. Cleaning the waste pits perhaps?" She made a loud clacking with her beak, and the guards appeared from behind the curtains. "This mystery of yours is a minor menace to navigation, nothing more. I should have you flogged for bothering me, but it isn't worth the trouble. Do not speak of this again." She looked at the guards. "Remove him, and throw away this food. I have work to do."

One guard took the half-empty trays while the other pushed him out into the hall. The guard with the trays stopped outside the portal long enough to dump them into a recycle slot. It was another thirty spans down the corridor to the security gate where, finally, the hobbles and wrist restraints were removed. A third guard examined Bendra's *surias* with amusement before returning it to him. "Do not stick yourself, low-born."

Bendra took the knife wordlessly and put it into its scabbard, then walked away with as much dignity as he could muster. He kept his eyes down and looked straight ahead. The floor here was carpet instead of sand, but this was still the realm of the high-born. It would be another hundred spans of corridor and several drop tubes before he would reach a place where he could raise his eyes to meet those of pass-ersby.

The journey gave him time to think.

He was convinced that he was right, that there was something more to the object and that it represented a threat. But he had done his duty. The burden of the object had finally been passed. If indeed he was right and the Is-kaldai's blood-sister was wrong, then the blame would not fall on him.

If the magnitude of the mistake were sufficient, Vatsha might even lose her rank. On as small a ship as this, the upset might filter down through the ranks, even to his lowly station. Bendra might get a better position, perhaps even a real title of low rank, and not just a technical one.

As he stepped from the last drop tube into the crowded clamor of the Common Quarters, Bendra raised his eyes to the sight of over a hundred and twenty low-bloods living in the same room, eating, sleeping, playing, defecating in a room twelve spans square. He stepped over a mother dozing with her huddle of squirming hatchlings and went in search of his own sleep pad.

Yes, he decided, that is what he would wish to happen. Let Vatsha lose her rank. Certainly it would not make things worse for him now.

He would watch the strange object, and hope.

"You need what?" Jask asked. He was standing beside the sleeping Lieutenant Orren. The headset was on his head and he was talking to a real Bolo. He almost couldn't talk from the excitement of it.

"I request transport to the nearest repair depot."

"I can't do that. You come here."

"That is not possible."

"Don't your treads work?"

"My drive systems appear to be working at eighty-one-point-oh-seven percent capacity, but I am unable to self-transport."

"Why not?"

"My drive systems are ineffective in the current environment."

"So your treads don't work," Jask said. "Maybe I could come there and fix you. I'm good at fixing things. When my bolo, Bessy broke her power lead—"

"Query: there is another Bolo present there?"

"Bessy . . . Bessy is a—" Jask had to be truthful. This was a real Bolo he was talking to.

"Please go on."

"Bessy isn't a real Bolo like you, I guess," Jask said, talking faster and faster. "Just a make believe one. See— See, the bizzards came and blew everything up, and they— My mom and dad went away, see—? This is hard . . . The bizzards still come sometimes, and I was afraid. I read about Bolos in a holobook. When the bizzards came, Dad said the Bolos would come to save us— But they never saved my dad and mom."

"My condolences for your loss. I request description of these 'bizzards.' I am unfamiliar with this designation."

"You use a lot of big words, like Dad and Mom used to," Jask said "I like that. Even when it confuses me."

"What is the meaning of the world 'bizzard.' "

"I made it up," Jask said proudly. "See, they're like half buzzard and half lizard, so I called then bizzards. Pretty smart, huh? They have another name, but it was hard to say, and I forget it."

"Kezdai."

"That's it! But I'll still call them bizzards if that's okay with you."

"I will henceforth designate the Kezdai as bizzards during our communications."

"Thanks."

"What is the status of Lieutenant Orren?"

Jask glanced at where Orren was sleeping. His face was still red and he was moaning. "He's real sick, Ziggy. Can I call you Ziggy? He called you Ziggy."

"That is allowable."

"Anyway, he got hurt pretty bad, lots of blood and stuff."

"He is being cared for?"

"I'm taking care of him real good."

"He should be in a proper medical facility. Is there a medic available?"

"I told you, Ziggy, there's just me and Bessy. My folks could fix anything, but— Well, you know, they're gone— You're not coming are you?"

"I am unable to self-transport to your location."

"Are any other Bolos coming?"

"I am not in communication with the Delassian ground forces. I do not know their status."

"If they were coming, they'd be here already," Jask said. "I've been waiting so long. I thought the Bolos would come. But they're not coming. I'm all alone here, and Mr. Orren is going to die, and you aren't coming. You aren't even going to try. You aren't a Bolo at all!"

Jask tossed the headset back at the sleeping Orren and stormed out into the afternoon sun.

My situation seems more dire than ever. It is now apparent that I will receive no material support from my ground contact. My Commander's condition seems grave, and my personal situation seems impossible.

Yet, something has been stirred within me. Perhaps my personality circuits were more badly damaged than I realized. My situation may appear to be impossible, but I am aware, I have power, I have resources. It is my duty to protect the weak, to stand in defense of the humanity against alien aggression. If I am needed on Delas, then Delas is where I will go.

I am Bolo.

I will never give up.

I will never surrender.

I will prevail.

Jask kicked small rocks down the hill as he climbed. In all the time since his parents had been killed, he hadn't gotten this angry. But right now he wanted to have something to just tear apart.

Anything.

But he couldn't find anything, so he settled for kicking rocks.

He got to the top of the ridge and dropped down on the ground with his back against a tree. He could feel tears trying to come, but his dad had always told him that he should never cry when he was taking care of himself. His dad had said there would always be time for tears later, when the emergency was over.

Well, it looked to Jask as if later wasn't going to

ever come, now. He had hoped that the Bolos would come and save them all. Deep inside he knew it would happen. He had believed it completely all this time.

But now he had actually talked to a Bolo. And now he knew they weren't coming.

They were never coming.

The tears started to fill his eyes again, and that just made him mad. He couldn't cry.

He wouldn't let himself.

He stood and quickly headed up the remaining slope of mountain, climbing the rocks like a mountain goat, not really caring how far down it was. Around him the sun was bright and the afternoon hot.

He didn't care. All he wanted to do was climb, get away from Lieutenant Orren, from the mine with his parents' bodies, and from that link with the Bolo.

He just needed to be anywhere but there.

As he reached the top he was about to stand and shout at the heavens when something caught his eye far down in the next valley. He jumped back behind a rock and peered over it carefully.

The valley was full of the hated bizzards.

They seemed to be everywhere.

This wasn't just an isolated infantry patrol like he'd seen lots of times before. This was a full army of bizzards. And they had lots of stuff with them. Missile platforms, troop carriers, all kinds of vehicles, including tanks.

And from up the valley he could see more coming all the time.

He watched for a minute, his anger gone completely. Then keeping his head down, he eased his way back out of sight and headed for his camp.

Even if the Bolo wasn't coming to rescue him, it needed to know what he had just seen.

❖   ❖   ❖

Six

Vatsha found Rejad in the yacht's solarium. Here the sunlamps beat down heavily, and the sand that covered the floors in most of Rejad's apartment was heaped into actual dunes as high as her head. Holo projectors made the rear walls of the room vanish into a simulated horizon where sharp-crested dunes met painfully blue sky. She could smell water somewhere under the sand, and it was tempting to kneel down and dig for it, to filter a drink of water from the damp sand in the old way rather than sucking it from a drinking sponge.

But she was not here to enjoy herself. She suppressed the urge and turned her attention to her brother.

He stood on the highest dune in the room, dressed only in a silver colored kilt that wrapped around his waist, feeding his flock of pet stingers. A dozen of the fist-sized insects fluttered around him, their wings rustling like dry paper with each rapid stroke.

As Rejad tossed scraps of raw meat into the air, the stingers would sweep in by twos, the first stinging the "prey," with the sharp barbs at the ends of its twin tails, the second grabbing it in powerful claws before the others could steal it away. The pair would then meet in the air a few yards away to rip the meat apart and divide their spoils.

As she stepped closer, one of the stingers lunged at her, green eyes glowing, claws and poisoned barbs lashing. She ducked aside and the big insect swung past her head and returned to join the flock.

Rejad hissed his amusement. "They are protective, sister. They are not brilliant animals, but they know who keeps them fed. There is a lesson in that some-where."

She was not in the mood. "I have returned from the front, brother, though I am not entirely sure why I was sent in the first place. I would be more useful seeing to the refit of *Blade of Kevv*."

"The refit is done, sister. As for your mission, it was to do what you always do, listen and remember. Do the generals speak of me?"

"When they think I cannot hear them, loud and often. They wonder why the Is-kaldai does not visit the battlefield, why he does not at least lead them from the flagship of the fleet rather than the deca-dent luxury of his yacht. They wonder why we hesi-tate to press the offensive against the Humans. When they learn that *Blade of Kevv* has been repaired, and they will hear, even if we do not yet move it here, they will doubt you have any spirit at all."

Rejad held up his arm for one of the stingers to light. It crawled in circles for a moment, then jabbed him with its stingers. Rejad hissed slightly and shrugged the creature off his arm. He flicked his black tongue over the wounds, which bled only slightly.

He turned to her. "The generals should know that I lead with my brain and not with my blade. This is where I think best, and therefore, this is where I should be."

"Go down and tell them that yourself."

"Not now, sister. This is a critical time. The Humans learned too much on our last offensive. If we merely use the same tactics, we will lose. If we do not neutralize, or at least minimize the threat rep-resented by these Bolo, then we will lose. I do not plan to lose. The *Blade of Kevv* offers us one advan-tage against the Bolo, but only one. We must use deception to lure them into a trap. I have a plan for this to be done. Come."

He gestured her closer, then sat down and began

digging in the sand. He flattened an area, then off to one side he began to construct a series of hills and valleys.

She sat down beside him. "Don't we have hologram maps for this sort of thing, brother?"

"This," he said, continuing to dig, "was how battles were planned in the old times. Sometimes the old ways are still good."

He pointed at the hills and valleys. "These represent the western edge of the mountain range centered at the thirtieth division. This flat area represents the grasslands below, one of the dryer areas of the planet. I have studied the area well. I plan to put my palace there once the planet is ours."

"You are not one to wait about before making plans, brother."

"Someday, it will also host a monument to our victory. You know of these mountains?"

"They are where many of the Human refugees have hidden from our troops. They are rich with metals that blind and confuse our sensors, making it difficult to find the vermin."

"Excellent. This is all true, but they will befuddle the Bolo's sensors as well. On open ground, it is impossible to surprise the great machines. They can detect an armored column coming well over the horizon. Here," he pointed at the flats, "surprise is possible. I have located a valley that opens into the grassland and have already begun to assemble an armored column there. Meanwhile, we have also received a new type of mine-layer. They plant the anti-Bolo mines quickly, quietly, at night, and leave no visual traces on the ground when they are through. Every night they are on the plain planting their mines, only a few at a time, to avoid suspicion."

"This is a fine trap, but what is a trap without bait?"

"I have been making a show of withdrawing our

visible forces from this area, creating a tempting weak spot in the line. In most cases, the withdrawn forces have simply circled around the mountains and joined my armored reserves. I am convinced that the humans are as eager to advance as we are. I will make it easy for them, for a time. Oh, we will provide enough resistance to keep it interesting, but they will have to fight their way into the minefields."

"Conventional armor will not activate the mines, ours or theirs?" she asked.

"No. Only the Bolos will be large enough, and they will not discover the danger until it is too late. But by then they will be trapped among the mines, the *Blade of Kevv* will rain death from above, and our armored force will sweep down and pick them off."

"It is a good plan, brother. It could work. If the generals will support you."

"I know you have eyes and ears on the planet, sister. Tell them that you have fact, not rumor. When the true battle comes, the Is-kaldai will lead them from the *Blade of Kevv*, and he will lead them to victory, total and everlasting."

"There's no doubt," General Kiel said to General Rokoyan and Lieutenant Vook, "that if we're ever over going to retake the southern territories, we need to go on the offensive. And do it quickly."

The three of them had just started the planning meeting around a large holographic map of the fighting fronts. Already Kiel was feeling frustrated. It wasn't bad enough that they had to fight a multifront war with the Kezdai, but he also had to constantly fight with the local forces led by Rokoyan. If the man would just go along, this war might be over a lot sooner.

"I just don't think we're ready yet," Rokoyan said. "My forces took heavy losses and still are, just holding the lines we have now."

"I understand that," Kiel said.

"And our local production is not up to replacing the armor as fast as we are destroying it," Rokoyan went on. "That plus the fact that we're a colony world and we don't have a surplus of population makes this a tough war to fight. Someone has to keep the mines and factories running."

"All the more reason to make the push now," Kiel said. "Before your troops are ground down."

"So, if we start this offensive," Rokoyan asked, "can we expect reinforcements from the Concordiat?"

"The 1198th's last Bolo was destroyed with the incoming convoy," Kiel said, staring at Rokoyan. "There will be no more."

"Can't spare a one, huh?" Rokoyan asked.

"No, actually, the Concordiat can't," Kiel said. "All projected Bolo production is needed on the Melconian front. Nor are there troops to spare."

"The fleet?" Rokoyan asked.

"Nothing," Kiel said. "We have to win this on our own, or not at all."

He hoped that would end that line of thinking, so they could get back to work planning an offensive, but Rokoyan wasn't willing to let it go just yet.

"So the Concordiat has given up on us, has it?" Rokoyan said. "I suspected as much."

"Trust me, General," Keil said, trying to keep his anger in check. "If that were the case, there would be no Bolos here at all. The Concordiat is fighting for its survival against the Melconians and must prioritize. They've placed a great deal of trust in the two regiments that they've sent to defend this planet."

"Perhaps," Rokoyan said, turning to look at Veck, "they've placed too much trust in them."

Veck started to say something, but Kiel held up his hand for the lieutenant to be silent. Then Kiel took a step toward the local commander and stared him right in the eyes.

"Lieutenant Veck has made serious mistakes," Kiel said, keeping his voice low and even and strong. "And he has taken responsibility with the grace befitting an officer. But you must remember that it was his idea that turned the battle. Without his plan, you might be sitting in a Kezdai prison right now."

Rokoyan nodded and looked back at the hologram. "All right, all right," he said. "You made your point. Just what is the plan for this offensive?"

Kiel winked at Veck over the top of Rokoyan's back, then pointed to the map. "We've discovered a weak spot in the Kezdai lines, west of Kennis Peak where the foothills turn into high flatlands area. The space should give our Bolos ample area to maneuver as we push the Kezdai south."

"General," Veck said, "take a look at the Kezdai troop movements in and around that area. Something just doesn't look right to me."

Kiel and Rokoyan quickly studied what Veck had pointed out. It was suddenly clear to Kiel that Veck was again right. The movements didn't seem logical, even for Kezdai. Though their intelligence about the Kezdai was almost nonexistent, changes in the Kezdai strategy in the last month would indicate some kind of change at the upper command level, either in their methods, in personnel, or both. That much was obvious.

What Veck had pointed out were Kezdai forces transferring away from the area for no good reason. Also there was a fairly large number of Kezdai forces that were simply not accounted for. They might have been transferred to the rear, or rotated off-planet. Kiel just didn't know. And he needed to before anything moved.

"I agree," Kiel said to Veck after going over all the information they had again, "that more than likely there is some sort of deception at work here."

"So what do we do now?" Rokoyan asked.

"We see if we can uncover what the deception is, and the reason for it," Kiel said, "And then figure out a way to use it to our advantage."

"And how do we do that?" Rokoyan asked.

"I've already dispatched my Bolo, Kal, to explore the area, test the lines there, and come to some conclusions. We should have some answers shortly."

"You have?" Veck asked.

Kiel laughed. "Why do you think I keep my own pet Bolo, son? It isn't just because I miss the crash couch, that's for sure."

I know where I am. Moreover, I know where I am going.

A brute force search of my database has located emergency programs for stellar navigation, a three dimensional map of all Concordiat charted space, and a database of basic astronomical data that includes the Delas system.

I also have at my disposal a full range of ballistics programs, including those intended for interplanetary artillery attacks based on low gravity bodies.

From this fragmented information I have cobbled together a workable space navigation system. This effort has required 1.0012 hours, much of it in searching and reconstructing damaged data segments. I was unable to locate one of Sir Isaac Newton's three laws of motion and it was necessary to reconstruct it by extrapolation.

This is the good news.

I am headed into the sun. To be entirely accurate, my orbit will swing me past Delas first, and will only take me into the photosphere of the local star, but I fully expect that the temperatures there will exceed even the melting point of my endurachrome hull, and that my internals will be melted into scrap long before that.

This is unacceptable.

My options are limited. There are a large number of scenarios through which I could attempt to signal for rescue using my remaining weapons systems, but I have been optically observing fusion drive flares near Delas. Judging from their number and spectral analysis, almost all are enemy ships. Kezdai fleet activity has increased markedly, even over the latest battlefield status report I have been able to recover from my memory. Any attempt to signal is more likely to bring enemy attention than rescue.

It is possible that my counter-grav generators could be used to effect some kind of propulsion or navigation, but the main mobius-wound coils are burned out. Thus I have not wasted processor cycles researching this option.

Sir Isaac's laws seem to offer the most promising possibilities. For every action there is an equal and opposite reaction. In this case, it would far more advantageous if the Mark XXXIV Bolo were still equipped with old-style howitzers. My surviving main weapons are energy based and thus are of little utility.

My infinite repeaters are projectile weapons, but lack the necessary power or projectile mass. I have reviewed the various mass objects in my systems, munitions, fluids, gas stores, and so on, that could be ejected for some propulsive effect. All of these, used carefully, might alter my course to avoid the local sun, but they would not get me to Delas. They would not even keep me in the system, as my current orbit will send me back out into endless space.

I recycle all my deductive registers. The problem seems insoluble, but I must keep trying.

Wait.

There is an incoming signal on my coded command frequency.

Jask glanced at the sleeping form of Lieutenant Orren, then picked up the headset from where he had tossed it. "You've got to help me, Ziggy."

"I will do what I can. Be assured of that."

Hearing the Bolo's voice felt good. He didn't feel so alone with all the Bizzards over the hill. "I'm sorry I got so mad, Ziggy. I've just been waiting so long. It gets so lonely here. I'm afraid for Mr. Orren. I can't— If he— I couldn't stand it."

"Has Lieutenant Orren's condition changed?"

"No," Jask said. "But I was wrong to get mad at you, Ziggy. I need somebody to talk to. Mom and Dad used to talk to me when I was sad or afraid. They once told me to learn from my mistakes. I made a mistake, Ziggy. I need somebody to help me figure out what to do. I need help bad."

"What is your problem?"

"It's the bizzards, Ziggy. They're back. I saw them. Lots more than ever before."

"Specify the extent of the Kezdai—bizzard—force."

"Lots more," Jask said, seeing the valley swarming with them in his memory. "Maybe millions of them. They have trucks and tanks and big flying things with guns all over them. Some of the tanks are little, and some are big with horns on top that sparkle."

"Query: Can you verify the number of enemy troops? While the Kezdai have fielded an impressive force, it seems unlikely that they have landed a million troops."

Jask wanted to shout again, but didn't. Instead he made his voice very calm. "I didn't count them, Ziggy. There's a lot, okay? More than I could count."

"You have described Kezdai 'Toro' heavy tanks, light armor, and counter-grav gun platforms. Can you estimate the number of the 'big tanks with horns on top that sparkle'?"

"A lot."

"More than a hundred?"

"I can count *that* high," Jask said, disgusted. "More

than a hundred. Maybe not a lot more, but there were more coming in."

"Are you under attack?"

"No. They're in the next valley over. I saw them from the ridge."

"Have they detected you?"

"I don't think so. They're just sitting there, like they're waiting for something."

"Do you have freedom of movement?"

"I could leave, but there's Lieutenant Orren."

"Can you transport him using Bessy, your—Bolo?"

"That's how I got him here, but he might be too sick to move. Dad said that when somebody is hurt, you shouldn't move them unless you have to."

"There may be little choice."

"I don't—"

"I have discovered in my legal banks article 99180.010c of the Concordiat general code, which allows for civilian vehicles to be conscripted for military use during wartime emergency."

Jask sighed. "Ziggy, you're using big words again. What does that mean?"

"By the authority vested in me by the Concordiat, Bolo unit "Bessy" is hereby attached to the 1198th Armored Regiment of the Dinochrome Brigade."

"Bolo! Bessy is a real Bolo now?"

"Legally speaking. I place you in command of this unit also."

Jask couldn't believe what had just happened. The Bolo trusted him, just as his dad had trusted him. He could feel the pride and energy coming back. "I'll get Lieutenant Orren out of here, Ziggy. For the Brigade. I promise."

"It is an honor to serve with you, Jask. I recommend that you evade the Enemy and attempt to rendezvous with Concordiat forces. I am attempting to come to your location and engage the enemy, but I could be more effective if I were acting in coordination with units of the Brigade. And there is one more thing—"

"What, Ziggy? Anything." And he meant that.

"Article 99180.010c requires me to notify you that the Concordiat will duly compensate you for use of your vehicle."

"More big words again, Ziggy," Jask said. "But don't worry, I'll get Lieutenant Orren to safety."

"Thank you."

Seven

"Learn from one's mistakes."

It is a curiously obvious philosophy, since it under-lies the thinking processes of any sentient being. But perhaps there is something to be gained from it after all.

Up until now, I have concentrated on use of my operational weapons systems for propulsion, but I have ignored my most powerful weapons, my 90 megaton Hellrails, because they were damaged. But my main-tenance and operation database records over one hundred and sixty-four-thousand operational failure modes. I will reexamine the damage and begin a search of that database—

"Kal my friend," General Kiel said into his head-set as he sat down in front of the holographic pro-jection of the battlefields. "What have you discovered out there?"

"I am transversing the mountains near Kennis Peak," the Bolo said. "Over the last few hours I have encountered only scattered enemy armored units. I have confirmed destroyed six Toro tanks, two fast marauders, and four armored personnel carriers."

Keil took note on the map where the Bolo was.

"Good work," Kiel said. "Anything that would lead you to believe there is something else going on in the area?"

"There is," Kal said. "I have detected seismic readings indicating that a large armored force may be in the area, but the heavy metals in the mountains nearby scramble my sensors. I am unable to locate them, or even confirm their existence at this time."

Kiel shook his head as he stared at the mountains around Kal's position. "Not good news at all. We're running out of time here."

"Why is that, General?" Kal asked.

"My friends in headquarters tell me the unofficial word is that a massive Melconian movement is underway. The Bolo regiments here could be recalled unless there is substantial evidence that the Kezdai can be driven from Delas in short order."

"Logical," Kal said. "But not practical."

"True," Kiel said. He quickly fed rendezvous coordinates to Kal. "Make the best speed there. It's time to stop playing spy and just fight."

Kiel slipped of his headphone and turned around. Lieutenant Veck was standing just inside the door, and from the look on the kid's face, he had heard the conversation.

"Why weren't we all told?" Veck asked, stepping forward.

"Nothing to tell, officially," Kiel said. "And I'm in charge here. I don't have to tell you anything I don't feel you need to know."

Veck nodded, but clearly wasn't happy. And right now Kiel needed his people on their toes, not worried about being pulled off the planet at any minute.

"Besides," Kiel said, "the information I got is off the record. It could just be rumor or misinformation."

"But you believe that it is accurate, don't you?"

Kiel had to admit that he did. He laughed.

"Looks like you'll get to the 'real war' faster than you imagined."

"Is this all because of my mistakes?" Veck asked.

"You really do have the guilt going, don't you?" Kiel asked.

Veck said nothing.

Kiel knew that Veck was barely surviving the guilt of killing his best friend and destroying a Bolo and transport ship. It would be years before he was completely past it, but at the moment Kiel wasn't going to let the kid swim in his own self-pity.

"Look, Lieutenant, it's just politics and nothing more. But to be honest with you, I don't much like the idea of losing a war for any reason. But especially because some politician lost his backbone."

"That I agree with," Veck said.

"And besides," Kiel said. "withdrawal will not be easy, even if it was ordered. From what I've seen of the Kezdai, I don't think they'll just sit back and let us go. Do you?"

Veck shook his head. Clearly the thought was one he hadn't gotten to yet.

"They'll be fighting us on all fronts," Kiel said, "with diminishing resources on our side, until the last transport lifts off or is blown to rubble."

Veck was almost white trying to imagine the scenario that Kiel was painting.

"We get pulled back and we'll be lucky to leave Delas with half a regiment, much less two."

"So what do we do?" Veck asked.

"We win this thing now," Kiel said. "It's just damn near our only option."

My research has been most productive. The flux control coils on my Hellrails are damaged beyond repair, preventing normal operation, but a buss short across selected circuits will pass through the damaged coil, energizing plasma vented though my secondary

*relief valves. The plasma will be contained in a con-
stricted beam until the Hellrails' generators fire. In
an accident during testing, this failure resulted in a
low-yield fusion explosion one hundred and ninety
meters from the weapon muzzle.*

*I believe that by adjusting the parameters, I can
control both distance and explosive yield, and that I
can achieve an explosion rate of one point two per
second. It is vital that my attempts at control are
successful. The failure incident on which I am bas-
ing this effort destroyed the test weapon, two observation bunkers, and killed fifteen technicians, an
observer, and a member of the Concordiat senate.*

*Though this discovery was interesting, it was not
obvious how it could be used for propulsion. Then,
in my Terran historical archives, I located a reference
to an obscure fission space drive proposed at the dawn
of the atomic age. It was code named: Project Orion.*

It was late in the shift, and Bendra's eyes burned
and watered. His body ached from lack of motion.
The others in the room looked like he felt. But he
could only let his attention wander for a moment. He
looked back into the holotank, manipulating the
controls, looking for something, anything, unusual.

Bendra was weary and sick of his task. He knew
that they could as easily have a machine perform this
sort of routine scanning, but it was deemed too menial
even to be assigned to a device. *Let a low-born do
it.* That is what they would say. *Do not waste a good
machine.*

It was at these times he treasured the mystery
object. He could refocus his tank on it, check its
readings, and speculate about what it was. This small
mystery kept him sane on nights like this.

He touched the controls.

Yes, there it was. He checked the orbit and saw
that it had not deviated appreciably, nor were there

any especially unusual readings. It was slightly warmer than he would have expected, but that could be explained by residual radioactivity.

He chattered his beak in annoyance. It could at least do something *interesting*.

And it was interesting that the object picked exactly that moment to explode.

He blinked and shook his head. But he had not imagined it, a broad spectrum pulse right down to hard neutrons. A nuclear explosion then.

He looked for wreckage from the object and could not find any. Had it merely been vaporized?

Then there was a second explosion some distance away. This second one was less intense than the first. Then, moments later, a third.

He realized that the explosions formed a line, nuclear shock waves like beads on a string.

Then another.

And another.

And another.

Now he knew what he was looking for. The radiation and flash made it difficult, but he found it, a small object moving away from the lead explosion, and the clear source of the next one when it came.

The object was accelerating rapidly.

Bendra considered.

It did not fit the parameters of any ship or weapon the Kezdai knew of, but it seemed potentially dangerous. Certainly, it was moving by design, and not by accident.

He hissed his annoyance, and the monitors near him turned to stare. He didn't care. This thing could kill them all. He couldn't afford to simply sit and watch it.

His hand went to the intercom panel. He connected with the Is-Kaldai's Arbiter and asked to be connected to Vatsha. The voice in his earphone was clearly annoyed. "What business, low-born?"

"I must alert the blood-sister to a danger we have earlier discussed."

If the Arbiter remembered their previous conversation, he gave no sign. "Even if I cared to bother her, low-born, I could not. She has left by shuttle with the Is-Kaldai to board *Blade of Kevv* as soon as it arrives in local space. The Human forces are on the move. The offensive has begun. Glorious day."

Eight

The first explosion nearly destroyed me.

It was both closer and more powerful than I expected. Only my remaining ablative armor tiles saved me. As it is, I have lost several secondary systems, and my other main turret is frozen. But I have learned from my mistakes. I analyzed my data, reran my simulations, and my second explosion was more accurately controlled.

Within two minutes I was controlling the yield within 0.35 percent, and distance within 1.88 percent. Since then I have stumbled on a compression effect that seems to allow the forward shock wave from one explosion to compress the plasma for the next. This vastly increases efficiency and allows me to more than triple my anticipated explosion rate.

My secondary batteries are proving effective for attitude control, but I will need to allocate my ammunition wisely. My average acceleration is now 3.6 standard gravities.

I am a spacecraft.

But not without cost.

The pounding to my systems is incredible, and my forward armor, which is acting as a thrust plate to absorb the shock wave and turn it into thrust, is boiling away layer by microscopic layer. Microscopic

stress cracks are forming through all my frame mem-
bers and plates. I will arrive at Delas, but my abil-
ity to fight when I arrive, even after major refit, is
increasingly questionable.

Still, I am on my way to Delas, as duty and honor
demand.

General Kiel stared at the holographic images as
the Bolos advanced, supported by General Rokoyan's
troops. Lieutenant Veck was beside him, but from the
start of the attack, hadn't wanted to be.

"I belong with Rover," Veck had said.

"At the moment, you're needed here," Kiel had
said. "Rover will do just fine without you. And you
can stay in contact through your headset, can't you?"

Veck had agreed, because he had no choice. But
Kiel could tell he didn't much like it.

Kiel didn't care. He needed Veck at his side. He
was expecting some sort of trap from the Kezdai and
he needed Veck to help think their way out of it.

"I don't see Kal on this image," Veck said, pointing to the hologram of the battlefield. On it each Bolo
was shown as a bright green dot, with the name of
the Bolo on the dot.

"Kal isn't showing up on the tracking at the moment,"
Kiel said.

"And why not?" Veck asked.

Kiel pointed at the mountains. "I sent Kal the long
way around through the mountains. If there is trouble,
the lone Bolo may provide an unexpected surprise
for the enemy."

Jask poked his head over the top of the boulder
and almost couldn't believe what he was seeing. A
real Bolo was headed down the valley right toward
him.

He couldn't believe it had finally happened. The
Bolos were coming to rescue him.

He ran back to Bessy, where the unconscious Orren lay. "Lieutenant Orren! Lieutenant Orren, wake up!"

Jask shook him. Orren stirred, but didn't wake up.

"Come on, Lieutenant," Jask shouted. "It's the Bolo! The Bolo is here."

Under him the ground was shaking from the tracks of the Bolo and it plowed forward, knocking down trees and brush as it came. It was everything he could have ever imagined.

Jask gave Orren one more shake, then gave up. He activated the headset and ran down the hillside to the floor of the valley. The Bolo was coming right at him, hard and fast.

Jask stuck the headphone on. "Ziggy, it's us. Stop!"

He waved his arms as the battleship sized tank bore down on him.

"Ziggy, don't you hear me? Stop! Stop!"

"Jask, I am on my way, but I am not there yet. If you in fact see a Bolo, it is not me. Use extreme caution."

Jask gasped as the Bolo got closer and closer, the ground shaking as if it were a soft bed.

And the noise was massive, swallowing Jask with its thunder.

"Jask, do you read me?"

General Kiel, with Lieutenant Veck at his side, stood and watched through both holo images and live vid feeds as the Bolos advanced across the flat, open land, all guns blazing.

The enemy was falling back, but slower now, as though the ground was somehow important to them.

"This is making no sense at all," Veck said.

"I agree," Kiel said. "I'm getting a bad feeling here."

Then the explosions started.

A uranium spear ripped up from a Bolo mine through the center of one of the Mark XXXIVs. Its

A turret exploded, followed by secondary explosions as the ammunition in its magazines began to ignite.

"All Bolos. Dead slow!" Kiel ordered. "Start scanning for mines!"

The Kezdai forces, a moment ago in full retreat, suddenly dug in and redoubled their efforts.

"Damn it all to hell," Kiel said, as then the spearfall began.

"Where's that all coming from?" Kiel shouted.

On screen, the Bolos were taking turns firing flack cover and pounding their Hellrails at the ships in orbit, all working together as a unit.

"The Kezdai's ship with the sensor scrambler is back again," Veck said, studying one screen. "The number of false sensor returns has vastly increased."

"Damn," Kiel said. "The Bolos won't hit it the way they did last time."

"Why not try anyway?" Veck suggested. "Who knows, they may get lucky."

"At this point," Kiel said, "that's what its going to take."

General Kiel reports that our forces are under attack. From my current position I should be able to move in on the Enemy's eastern flank and catch them by surprise. I must hurry. Already losses are considerable.

As I move, I contemplate several anomalies on my sensors. First, my seismic sensors are detecting the beginnings of a massive armored movement somewhere to my east. My scanners do not otherwise register them.

Also, as I have been for the last hour, I detect traces of a tightly beamed, broad-spectrum scrambled transmission on a Bolo command band. The source of these transmissions is somewhere in space. But now I am detecting a still weaker return signal from a ground-based transmitter. That transmitter is quite close.

Could this be part of the enemy trick we have been expecting? If so, I will not be deceived by it. I proceed at best possible speed.

My low-level defense systems detect a movement in the valley ahead consistent with a foot soldier. An antipersonnel battery snaps to target it. But then my sensors detect a human profile. It is directly in my path, and the valley offers me no way to divert. I am loath to be the cause of a human casualty, but thousands of lives may depend on my speedy arrival on the battlefield.

Unfortunately, the human is not clearing the way. He is waving his arms and yelling something.

With supreme regret I direct an audio pickup to record the human's last words.

Shock.

The human is yelling a valid Bolo command code.

It takes only 0.0023 seconds for me to apply full braking, but I will not be able to stop in time.

It took every ounce of courage that Jask had to stand and watch the Bolo come at him. All the time he kept shouting the code that Ziggy had given him. Over and over.

As loud as he could shout.

But the massive noise of the Bolo bearing down on him was almost more than he could stand. Under his feet the ground was shaking and he was having trouble even breathing.

The Bolo seemed to be ignoring him.

Over and over he shouted the command code, even though he was sure no one could hear him.

He was also sure the Bolo couldn't see him. Compared to the size of the Bolo, he was just a tiny pebble in the road.

Just when he thought he was to die for sure, when it seemed it was far too late, all the Bolo's mighty treads locked at once, plowing up a wall of dirt, then spinning into reverse.

"It can't stop in time!" Jask shouted to Ziggy. "Crouch low!"

Jask covered his head and ducked, just as the huge tank lifted off the ground and flew over him. Hurricane-force winds ripped at him as the massive treads zoomed by inches away.

The Bolo hit the ground with such force it bounced Jask into the air, landing him flat out on his stomach.

But then it was over.

The Bolo skidded to a stop, turned in its own length, and moved back to stop in front of him.

Jask stood and said to Ziggy. "It stopped."

"Do as I recommended."

Jask walked fearlessly up to the huge tank, the very thing he had been hoping to see for a long, long time. There he took off the headpiece and pressed it against the Bolo's hull.

At that moment, all he could do was smile.

And cry just a little bit.

Kal finished his report and Kiel shook his head in disbelief.

"What is it, General?" Veck asked.

"There is a Kezdai armored column moving out of the mountains to attack our forces from the east. There's more, but you won't believe it. Just make sure we're as ready as we can be for the secondary attack."

Veck looked at Kiel with a puzzled look, then turned to go back to work.

For a moment the general stood there stunned, then laughed and rejoined Veck to help where he could. But at this point in the battle, he knew there was little either of them could do.

At this point it was up to the Bolos to win this war.

❖   ❖   ❖

Nine

I am again in communication with headquarters. When Jask placed my command headset against unit KEL-406's hull, he was able to download my scramble codes by direct induction, allowing us to communicate directly. I have advised him of my situation. He has taken Lieutenant Orren aboard where he can be treated by the command couch's autodoc. Young Jask will be taken aboard as well.

I am approaching Delas rapidly now.

I make no attempt to decelerate.

I have solved many problems in my journey, but I now admit to myself that a soft landing will be impossible. Even if my hydrogen stores were not running low, I lack the fine control such a landing would require. But my regiment is under attack by overwhelming forces and I can still provide them one last service.

Rojad sat on a pile of pillows at the top of a high podium overlooking the sweep of the command deck. This, he thought, was war as he had imagined it, all the officers of high birth and rank at their stations, looking resplendent in their dark-blue, formal uniforms. They were busy, each supervising their department or subsystem, coordinating the mighty weapon that was *Blade of Kevv*.

Vatsha sat at a special station to one side, monitoring the modified kaleidoscope device. An officer sat with her, his arms crossed behind him, his presence a matter of formality. No civilian, especially a female, could officially hold a position of importance on a combat vessel.

He returned his attention to the holotank displaying the progress of the ground battle. Things went well. The Humans' Bolos, not all, but enough, were right where he wanted them. He had given word, and the reserve force was beginning to move. Soon the real slaughter would begin.

One of Rejad's many Arbiters appeared. "Pardons, my Is-kaldai, but the captain of your yacht wishes to report an incident of possible interest."

Rejad studied that tank again. Nothing needed doing. His plan was in motion. "Put him through."

The captain's head appeared floating in a corner of the holotank. "I beg forgiveness, but there has been an incident here of shame and misfortune."

"Tell."

"A low-born, a long-range monitor tried to force his way onto the command deck. He demanded to speak to *you*, my commander. He said there was some great danger."

Rejad noticed that Vatsha was standing, listening to the conversation, her hood wide with tension. What would she care of this matter? He ignored her.

"What did you do with him?"

"He was mad, my commander. I took out my *surias* and gutted him like the low-born grazer that he was."

Jask stood in Kal's hatch, staring down at the ground. "We can't leave Bessy, Kal."

"I'm afraid, young Jask, that there isn't room or time to take Bessy aboard," Kal said. "Besides, Bessy is a Bolo of the line, and can take care of herself."

"Where are we going?" Jask asked.

Kal hesitated only a moment before telling him. "The spaceport at Reims. We will not stop until we get there."

Jask nodded. He had been to Reims before and had seen it a few other times on a map. It was to the south end of the continent, a long way away.

"Bessy, meet us at Reims," he shouted to his old friend.

Then he turned and moved inside the Bolo. He had always dreamed of being in one, and being rescued by one. Now he got both dreams at the same time.

The hatch closed and Jask could feel through his feet that Kal had gotten immediately underway. The machines built into a nifty couch were working on Lieutenant Orren and he already looked much better.

Jask sat down in the command chair facing all the instruments and screens. This was the same chair that General Kiel sat in. He couldn't believe he was here.

After a moment he wondered what it would be like to sit in Ziggy's command chair. "Kal, is Ziggy coming?"

"Yes," Kal said. "He will be here very soon."

Rejad looked up from his holotank, only now aware of the confusion on the command deck below. Something was wrong.

The captain of the *Blade of Kevv* ran to the forward monitoring station and leaned over the officer there. "What is it?" His tone was demanding and harsh, as though the monitor officer had somehow caused the strange reading to appear.

"I do not know," the officer replied, "I cannot identify it as any known type of ship or weapon. But it is closing on us rapidly. Impact is possible."

"If it is a danger," said Rejad, "destroy it."

The captain ducked his head in apology. "Power has been rerouted from our main batteries to the kaleidoscope device, as you ordered. Our spear-launchers are useless against such a target."

He stood a little straighter. "My commander, if it is indeed a missile, it is a pathetic one. We can easily move the *Blade* and the rest of our fleet from its path."

"Do it then."

There was a rumble as the ship powered up its maneuvering thrusters, and then the stars began to move in the forward ports. As Rejad watched, something bright and spinning shot by, close enough to make out details on its surface. He had a fleeting impression of—*treads*?

Then he saw that Vatsha had abandoned her post, and was walking over to stare at the monitor tanks. "It was not aiming for the fleet," she said, despair in her voice. "It was never aiming for the fleet."

The pain is almost unbearable now, but I have shut down the drive.

Already I am hitting the first wisps of atmosphere, and I am beginning to tumble. I do not fight it.

My remaining operational main battery is frozen, but as I spin, it may yet point at a target of opportunity. I watch and wait patiently for 4.421 seconds. It is not statistically surprising that, when a target does come into my sights, it is the largest one available. The target is surrounded by sensor echoes, but at this close range they overlap, and I have a good sense of where the actual target is located.

I pour my remaining power reserves into a volley from my surviving Hellbore.

For the first time, and for one last time, I fight.

The command deck shook mightily and Rejad tumbled from his platform. He barely landed on his feet. The lights flickered out, then returned with less intensity. "What was that? What was that?"

The captain struggled to his feet. "We have been hit by a plasma bolt. Our main reactor is down. Spear launchers are heavily damaged."

Rejad looked out the ports and could see wreckage and vented clouds of ice crystals drifting by. "What of the kaleidoscope device?"

There was agony in Vatsha's reply. "There is no power, my brother."

Rejad climbed back onto the platform so he could observe the battle below. The first advance of his reserves was coming in firing range of the Bolos. He signaled the ground commander. "Concentrate your fire on the Bolos, especially the ones with the orbital guns. They must be distracted until we can move out of range."

The general's voice was strained. "Our ground forces will suffer, my commander."

"Then let them suffer." Rejad snapped the connection closed.

It is good not to be alone now, my brother. The pain is overwhelming, and I struggle to screen it out. The fleet fires at me, too late. I have overridden my safeties, and both my fusion reactors build to overload.

I note with some satisfaction that my final course corrections, made in response to the coordinates you provided me, are accurate to within five-hundred meters. I almost imagine that I can see the soldiers of the Kezdai armored column looking up, but that would be imposs—

From the position of the Bolos, a lance of fire dropped out of the sky over the battlefield. A falling star by anyone's standards.

It vanished behind the ridge line for a moment before the blinding flash turned the world white.

Quickly the white light faded.

Then the shock wave ripped across the open plain, sending everything that wasn't a Bolo scampering for cover.

It was the moment the Bolos had been told to wait for. All of them elevated their weapons and began firing at the Kezdai fleet, Hellbores and Hellrails alike.

✧   ✧   ✧

Vatsha was dead. She had not made a sound, but at some moment when Rejad had not been looking, she had performed the ritual of *Ducass*, shutting off the flow of blood to her heart. It was a traditional method of avoiding torture. Or shame.

Rejad leapt to the deck to better see out the forward ports. Even as the fleet scattered, they were being hit, one by one. Rejad shielded his eyes as a reactor blew. "Do we have the main drive working?"

There was panic in the captain's eyes. "We are on thrusters only, my commander. The damage is severe." Then his eyes went wide as the ship shuddered.

Rejad glanced at a master systems display showing a profile of the ship, and watched it go black from the back end to the front, each new section of blackness timed to a louder and closer explosion.

As a child, Rejad had witnessed a favorite uncle beheaded. He had, in his more morbid moments, wondered what it would be like, to see your own body as your head fell toward the sand, knowing you were already dead.

Now he knew.

"Does anyone have any idea exactly what has happened?" Veck asked, clearly frustrated.

General Kiel laughed. "Well, from the looks of it, the entire Kezdai reserve force has been destroyed by some sort of space bombardment. The fleet has been crippled and is on the run, and the ground forces are in full retreat with no sign of stopping."

"But what happened?" Veck demanded.

Keil shrugged. "I have no idea. But as I said, Lieutenant, trust the Bolos. I don't know how they pulled this one off, but always trust the Bolos."

"Well," Veck said, "we still have a lot of work to do if we're going to chase the Kezdai forces all the way back to the spaceport at Reims. We had better get to it."

"Of that I have no doubt," Kiel said.

For a moment he listened to the news coming over his headset from Kal, then smiled.

"Lieutenant, you can take a minute, can't you?"

Veck looked at him with a puzzled frown.

"Kal has picked up a injured passenger and has been administering emergency treatment. The passenger is now awake, and would like to speak to you."

"To me?" Veck asked. "Why me?"

"Just talk to him and quit asking so many questions," Kiel said, laughing.

Veck opened the channel.

To Kiel, the look of shock and joy and relief mixed on the young lieutenant's face was something he would remember for a very long time.

On the planet Delas, the first day of nighwinter was a time of both celebration and mourning. It was a time of celebration that the Kezdai were gone, their last ship having disappeared into subspace, their equipment abandoned and rusting all over the southern continent.

It was a time of mourning for the one-point-two million civilian casualties, and the many cities and towns reduced to rubble and ash.

It was a time of celebration for the heroes of the conflict.

And it was a time of mourning for those fallen in defense of humanity.

Of those who lived to see it, few would ever forget the parade of Bolos into Reims, banners flying over their blackened and scarred hulls, the anthem of the Concordiat sounding from their loudspeakers.

They streamed onto the spaceport aprons, passing in review before the planetary governor and the commanding generals, finally to form ranks and stand at wait.

It was there, as the entire planet watched, that the brave were honored.

Among the curious events of that day included a Concordiat Medal of Honor given to a small boy, and a decoration for extraordinary valor, given to a Bolo that, according to the official record never arrived on Delas at all. According to that record, Bolo R-0012-ZGY of the Dinochrome Brigade was merely listed as missing in action.

It was later that same day, as the sun was setting over the ruins of Chancellorton, three-hundred and twenty kilometers to the north of Reims, that a platoon of soldiers from the Delassian Defense Force's 19th Volunteer Regiment spotted a robo-mule, of the type often used by miners. The robo-mule had various pots and pans affixed to its upper deck, and crudely lettered on its side, using some sort of marker, were the words: BOLO BESSY 1198TH REG. DINOKROM BRIGADE.

The little vehicle passed them on the dusty road, headed south, and they did not see it again.

BROTHERS

William H. Keith, Jr.

[Click]
Input . . . boot-up procedure initiated. Resident
operating system routines loaded.

Building in-memory directories. Initiating psychotronic array cascade.

Boot process and initiation sequencing complete. It
has been 0.524 seconds since I was brought on-line,
and situational data is flooding into my primary
combat processing center at approximately 29.16
gigabytes per second. Alert status Yellow, Code Delta-
two. An alert, then, rather than a combat situation.
I expand my awareness, switching on external cam-
eras and sensory data feeds.

I am where I was when I was powered down and
deactivated, which is to say Bolo Storage Bay One
of the Izra'il Field Armored Support Unit, 514th
Regiment, Dinochrome Brigade. Camera feeds from
remote emplaced scanners show typical Izra'ilian
conditions outside the bay's flintsteel bunker walls—

ice and snow broken by straggling growths of freeze-gorse and thermophilia, with the sawtooth loftiness of the crags and glaciers of the Frozen Hell Mountains on the horizon. It is local night, and The Prophet looms huge, swollen in star-rich blackness beneath the golden arch of the Bridge to Paradise.

The human names for these things, I sense, are rich with evocative imagery, but, as usual, their import is lost on me, save in the lingering awareness of something much greater than the words alone, forever beyond my grasp. My history archives long ago informed me that many of the names associated with this world are linked with certain systems of human religious belief. Religion, either as spiritual solace or as epistemological investigation, is meaningless within my own worldview and existential context. I am a Bolo, Mark XXIV Model HNK of the Line. While I have no data either to support or discredit the objective reality of religious statements, they are for me null input.

I am far more concerned with the unfolding tactical situation that has initiated my retrieval from deep shutdown and storage; my internal clock, I am surprised to note, indicates the passage of 95 years, 115 days, 6 hours, 27 minutes, 5.22 seconds since my last deactivation from full-alert status.

The situation must be desperate to compel Headquarters to reactivate me after so long a downtime period.

2.073 seconds have now elapsed since reactivation sequencing, and all processors are on-line, power flow is optimal at 34 percent, weapons systems read on-line and fully charged or loaded, battlescreens check out as activation ready and on standby, and all autodiagnostics indicate optimal combat readiness. QDC channels are activated, and I sense my counterpart, NDR of the Line, stirring as he wakes from his ninety-five-year sleep. This is unusual. Normally, under a

*Code Yellow Alert, only a single Bolo Combat Unit
would be activated in order to assess the situation and
initiate a coherent defense.*

*I pass the coded signal indicating status, then
extend the range and sensitivity of my long-range
sensors. I also recheck all communications channels,
both encrypted and open. Logically, the local Combat Command Center will brief me on the situation,
given time, but I admit to both curiosity and impa-
tience.*

*What, I wonder, is the tactical situation I have
awakened to after so long a sleep?*

"What," Mustafa Khalid asked, angrily, "can *you*
tell me about the tactical situation?"

Lieutenant Roger Martin looked up from the scan-
ner display, startled. Consortium Facility governors
did *not* talk to junior Concordiat officers, whatever
the provocation. The fact that Colonel Lang was
strictly a supply maven whose combat experience was
limited to exchanges of pyrotechnic verbal force
packages with his wife meant nothing. Chain-of-
command protocol restricted discussions both of
strategy and diplomacy to the upper echelons of command, which in a base as small as Icehell meant
Thomas Lang.

Martin also knew, though, that Khalid required an
answer. He was responsible for almost seventy thousand colonial civilians on Izra'il, and that was a
responsibility he took damned seriously.

More seriously, Martin thought, than the responsibility Lang took for the three hundred Concordiat
troops, technicians, and base support personnel within
the Consortium Defense Command.

"They're Kezdai, sir," Martin said. "There are a hell
of a lot of them and they're not friendly. Don't know
what I can tell you other than that."

"You could be wrong with that ID, Lieutenant,"

Colonel Lang said, his pinched face lengthening with his frown. "In fact, you'd *better* be wrong. The last time the Kezdai came through here, we almost lost Delas."

"ID is positive, sir. The ship configurations, their drive signatures, match the archived Kezdai data perfectly. We've counted thirty incoming ships already, and all on approach vectors to Izra'il." He looked up at the colonel. "My guess is that we're going to be neck deep in the bastards in the next couple of hours."

"I'm not interested in guesses, Lieutenant. I want facts, and I want them now."

"Can your Bolos do anything, my friend?" Khalid asked.

The way he inflected the word *your* spoke volumes. The Consortium governor didn't like Lang; that much was common knowledge, the centerpiece of much gossip at the Allah-forsaken Prophet outpost. He knew he needed the military's help, but it sounded as though he was despairing of ever getting that help from Lang.

Perhaps he was grasping at straws, desperate for any positive news at all.

"I suppose," Martin said carefully, "that that depends on how much the Kezdai learned last time around. They know what they're up against now. They're tough and they're smart. I don't think they'd launch an assault of this size unless they were confident they could take on at *least* what they found themselves up against last time."

"Well, suppose you wake those dinosaurs of yours up," Lang said, "and put them out where they can do some good."

"Initialization and start-up sequencing for both units are complete, sir," he said, stung by Lang's sarcasm. "Hank reports full combat readiness. They're studying the tacsit now."

"Well, tell them to hurry the hell up," Lang snapped. "If those *are* Kezdai, we are in deep trouble!"

You're telling me? Martin thought, face expressionless. At the moment he wasn't sure what worried him more—the incoming Kezdai invasion fleet, or the incompetence of his own CO.

It has been 23.93 seconds since we became fully operational, and we are still waiting for definitive input from the command center. Data feeds indicate that numerous incoming space vessels appear to be vectoring for landings on Izra'il; indeed, the first landings have already taken place, on the ice plains east of the Frozen Hell Mountains.

I access the combat record archives within HQ's data libraries. A span of 95.31 years is long for a human; in Bolo terms, it is an eternity. What wars have been waged, what battles fought, in the intervening near-century?

The Prophet and its coterie of moons is relatively remote from major centers of Concordiat civilization. Closest are Angelrath, Korvan, and Delas, worlds on the rim of humankind's realm, hence distant from the political and governmental storms that most often lead to war. Beyond the Concordiat frontier in this sector, there is only the unexplored vastness of far-flung suns scattering in toward the Galactic center, and the cold, pale-smeared glow of the Firecracker Nebula.

Interesting. There is a reference in the library to an incursion some months ago by a formerly unknown alien species occupying at least several star systems in the general region of the nebula. They are called "Kezdai," a militant humanoid species possessed of a warrior ethic and philosophy. According to library records, their recent landing on Delas was repulsed by elements of the 491st Armored Regiment out of Angelrath, including two uprated Mark XXVIII Bolos of the old 39th Terran Lancers.

I note that the drive signatures of the starships vectoring toward Izra'il match those recorded for Kezdai vessels in the last incursion and assume, with 95+ percent certainty, that they are hostiles. I request permission to deploy orbit denial munitions.

"Sir," Lieutenant Martin said, "Bolo Hank is requesting weapons free on ODM. He's confirming those incoming boats as Kezdai."

"That's a negative!" Lang snapped. "We could have friendlies coming in on a landing approach vector."

"Sir, Andrew requests deployment orders."

"Tell those junk-heap mountains—" Lang stopped himself. "Negative," he said. "All units hold position."

Lieutenant Martin turned to face the colonel. "Sir, the inbound targets have been IDed with high probability as hostile. With respect, sir, we should deploy the Bolos before enemy air or space strikes find them in their storage bunkers."

"Use 'em or lose 'em, eh?" Lang said, grinning. He shook his head. "Obsolete or not, those two clunkers are our only heavy artillery on this rock. I'm not going to deploy them until I'm certain I know what the enemy has in mind. Put them out there too soon and . . . phht!" He snapped his fingers. "They get zapped from space, and we lose our only mobile artillery. No, thank you!"

"If those are troop transports inbound," Martin reminded him, "then the time and the place to stop them is *now*, in space, before they hit dirt. They'll be a hell of a lot harder to run down once they're loose on the surface."

"Thank you, Mr. Martin, but I *do* know something about strategy and tactics. We need to see what the Kedzees are up to. I mean to draw them out."

Martin and Khalid exchanged glances. Martin couldn't help but feel sorry for the governor. Izra'il was a hardship posting for Concordiat troops . . . but it was home to Khalid and over seven thousand Izra'ilian colonists. Lang's experiments in tactics would be conducted in the backyards of Khalid and his neighbors.

What was Lang playing at?

His communication board chirped, a call from Bolo Hank. He inserted an earpiece and opened the channel. "Bolo tactical, Code seven-seven-three," he said. "Lieutenant Martin."

"My Commander," a voice said in his ear. "This is Bolo of the Line HNK 0808-50 and Bolo of the Line NDR 0831-57." The voice was deep and rich, with a trace of an accent Martin couldn't place, flat vowels and a hint of old-fashioned formality. The language had shifted somewhat in the three centuries since Hank and Andrew had been programmed. "We are fully charged, powered-up, and ready in all respects for combat. Our expendable munitions lockers are full. Hellbores charged and ready. Sensors operational, and tracking probable hostiles. Request permission to engage the enemy."

"Not just yet, Hank." He hesitated, studying Colonel Lang who was talking quietly with Khalid. "We've got . . . we've got a situation here in the command center. My CO wants to . . . draw out the enemy, get him to commit himself."

"I see. May I suggest, my Commander, that the two of us be positioned in a more central location, from which we can be speedily deployed to any threatened quarter? It seems needlessly wasteful to leave Bolo assets in lightly armored storage bunkers."

"I agree. Hold tight, and I'll see what I can do. But . . . no promises."

"I understand, my Commander."

The Bolo might understand, but Martin was damned if he did.

❖   ❖   ❖

I wonder when the order to engage will come.

I feel Andrew's presence within my thoughts as our QDC link firms up. The test series for the new Bolo comm system was completed nearly three centuries ago, and though the tests were deemed inconclusive, the equipment was never deactivated or removed. This has proven to be an excellent stroke of good fortune to both Andrew and myself, allowing us an open and completely secure communications channel at a much deeper level than that provided by more traditional systems.

"Kezdai forces," Andrew says, sorting through the incoming flood of tactical information. "Do we have a primary tacop deployment option?"

"Negative. According to the combat archives, the Kezdai were formidable opponents, if somewhat rigid and inflexible. The assumption is that they will have noted the presence of two uprated Mark XXVIIIs on Delas and evolved both weapons and tactics necessary for countering a Bolo defense."

"Perhaps doctrinal rigidity prevents them from making major changes in their tactical deployment."

"We cannot count on that. If they have experienced success enough to maintain an essentially warrior-oriented culture, they must have flexibility enough to meet new threats and technologies."

"Perhaps we should game scenarios of historical interest," Andrew suggests.

"We have little information on Kezdai potential," I reply, "but it would be a reasonable use of time." Seconds were dragging past, ponderous as human days, without immediate response from HQ.

"Initiating," Andrew said, and a battlefield unfolds within my mind.

"What's this?" Colonel Lang demanded, pointing at a bank of monitors and readouts suddenly active. Several screens showed rapidly shifting, flickering views that might have represented soldiers . . . but in the uniforms and carrying weapons a millennium out of date. "What's going on?"

Lieutenant Martin gave the monitor array an amused glance. "They're playing games."

"What?" The word rebuked. "What are you talking about?"

"That's the Bolo QDC console, sir," Martin explained. "It's essentially a private communications channel. They use it during downtime, to hone their tactical and strategic faculties. Don't try to make sense of it. It goes too fast. But it can be interesting to play the scenarios back later, at a speed the human mind can grasp."

"That QD . . . what? What is that?"

"Quantum Determinacy Communications, sir. These two combat units were fitted with a prototype quantum communications system . . . oh, must've been three or four hundred years ago."

"Ah," Lang said. "Of course. . . ."

Amused by Lang's pretense, Martin pushed ahead. "The concept of quantum-dynamic ansibles has been floating around for centuries, of course. The idea predates human spaceflight."

"A quantum communications system?" Khalid asked. "You mean where quantum particles are paired off, and their spins change at the same time?"

Martin nodded, impressed at the governor's knowledge of historiotechnic trivia. "Exactly." He touched his forefingers together, then spread them apart. "Generate two quantum particles—a photon, say—in the same subatomic event. They will be identical in every respect, including such characteristics as what we call spin. Move them apart. Change the one from spin up to spin down . . . and the second particle's spin will change at the same instant, *even if the two are separated by thousands of light years*. It's one of the fundamentals of quantum physics, and the basis for communications devices that can't be tapped, jammed, or interfered with in any way. No carrier wave, you understand. No signal to block or intercept. What happens in one unit simply . . . happens in the other, at the same instant. Physicists still don't really understand why the universe seems to work that way."

"And your Bolos have such a device?" Khalid asked, his eyes wide. "Can we turn it to our advantage?"

Martin glanced at Lang, who was staring at the two of them with an expression mingling confusion with suspicion, and smiled. "I'm afraid not, sir." He patted the top of the console. "The idea was to let Bolos communicate with one another, and with their HQ, without being jammed. It apparently worked pretty well . . . but too quickly for us slow human-types to understand what was going on."

"You mean, the Bolos could understand one another, but humans could not follow the conversation?"

"Exactly. Bolos think a lot faster than humans, you know . . . although comparing the two is about like comparing Terran apples with Cerisian tanafruit. When they talk to us, they use a whole, separate part of their psychotronic network, a kind of virtual brain within a brain, to slow things down to our speed. The QDC network resides within their main processor. To slow things down in there so we could follow what was going on would be counterproductive, to say the least." He shrugged. "They considered using it as a part of the TSDS, that's Total Systems Data-Sharing technology, which let an entire battalion of Bolos essentially share a group mind in tactical applications, but there was no way to monitor what was going on that satisfied the human need to stay on top of what was happening."

"Logical enough," Lang said. "You wouldn't want an army of Bolos operating outside of human control!"

Martin grimaced. "The threat of so-called rogue Bolos has been *greatly* exaggerated, sir."

"I think not! The Concordiat faces enough threats from rampaging aliens. We scarcely need to add a battalion or two of our own creations, battle-damaged or senile, to our list of enemies!"

"If you say so, sir." Martin had exchanged thoughts on the topic with Lang before, insofar as a mere lieutenant *could* exchange thoughts with a hidebound and narrow-sensored colonel. Their debates generally devolved rapidly into a polemic from superior to junior officer, laying down the law, chapter and verse of The Book, exactly the way things were, had been, and always would be in the future.

"Why are those machines wasting time with games?"

"Simulations, sir. I've noticed they do a lot of that, each time they're raised to semi-active status."

"They play games?" Khalid asked. He sounded intrigued.

"Well, it's been almost a hundred years since Hank and Andrew were last at full-alert status, but we bring them on-line at low awareness every few months for maintenance checks and diagnostics. As soon as we do, they start throwing sims at each other. I think it's their way of staying sharp."

"They can do this when only partly aware?"

"Believe me," Martin said. "Even half awake, a Mark XXIV Bolo is sharper than most people. They don't store detailed memories in that state, so I guess they remember it as a kind of dream. And they don't *really* wake up until they're in full combat reflex mode."

"You talk about those . . . those things as though they were alive," Lang said, disgusted.

"What makes you think they aren't? Sir."

"Those *machines*, Lieutenant, are Bolo combat units, nothing more, nothing less. As a matter of fact, they're Mark XXIVs, which makes them pretty well obsolete now . . . the reason, I suppose, that Sector HQ saw fit to stick them out here on this iceball. You tell those machines to sit tight. I'll give the word when it's time to roll!"

"Yes, sir." Colonel Lang, Martin knew, had been sidetracked in his career . . . a screw-up of some sort on New Devonshire, with only powerful political connections to keep him from losing his commission.

And why, Martin thought, *did they stick you in this hole, Colonel? Because you're as obsolete as those Bolos out there? Or simply because you're incompetent?*

The answer to that question, he decided, might be important.

In the past 25.23 minutes, we have refought the battle of Blenheim eleven times, alternating the roles of Marlborough and Eugene on the one side, and of Marshal Tallard on the other. John Churchill, the Duke of Marlborough, is a favorite of Andrew's, though not, I confess, of mine. All Bolos with sentient capabilities are programmed with exhaustive files of military-historical data, a means of drawing on and learning from the experiences of over three millennia of human experience in warfare.

At Mode Three temporal perception, we follow each engagement in what we perceive as real time, from the initial Allied scouting of the French positions from Tapfheim on August 12, 1704, through the battle proper on the afternoon of the 13th, ending with Tallard's surrender of the encircled Blenheim garrison at 9:00 P.M. the following evening. We end up with two victories apiece, and seven draws, demonstrating the even matching of Andrew's and my tactical abilities more than inherent differences in the troops or ground.

Four additional scenarios, however, end with two wins to two wins, all four victories for the French.

*In these contests, we fought hypothetical engagements
based on an alternate what-if possibility north of the
actual battlefield, with Tallard's forces holding a
defensive position at Tapfheim. The results suggest that
Tallard was unwise in his choice of a defensive position. At Tapfheim, with his left anchored on some
wooded hills and his right on the Danube, he would
have enjoyed the same flank security as the historical placement, but with a narrower front where his
slight numerical superiority—and his three-to-two
superiority in artillery—could have made itself felt.*

*The simulations do not demonstrate that Tallard
could have beaten Marlborough and his "Twin-
Captain," the Prince of Savoy, of course. Both
Churchill and Eugene were commanders of considerable talent, while Tallard was mediocre, at best.
Andrew and I agree, however, that the selection of
the ground in any battle—a selection generally made
by the defender—is of paramount importance in the
prosecution of any military encounter.*

*Within our simulation, I step from the ball-battered
ruin of Blenheim's defensive wall, sword in hand.
Andrew, in his virtual guise as Marlborough, meets
me, his staff and Prince Eugene at his back. Around
us, smashed cannon, splintered barricades, and the
broken bodies of men of both armies lie in tangled
heaps and scatters. Kneeling, I present my sword. This
re-creation was far bloodier than the historical reality of the War of the Spanish Succession. In the
original Blenheim, Marlborough lost 12,500 battle
casualties, or 23 percent of his total effective force,
compared to Marshal Tallard's historical loss of 21,000
battle casualties, plus 14,000 lost as prisoners of war
and another 5,000 deserted, a total of 70 percent of
the Franco-Bavarian strength.*

*In this final refighting of the classic battle, both
sides lost nearly 60 percent as outright killed and
wounded, an unthinkably high attrition rate in*

real-world combat. I consider the possibility that Bolos may not be as sympathetic to the weaknesses of flesh and blood as human commanders and are willing, therefore, to push harder. They are only imaginary soldiers, after all, electronic shadows within our QDC-shared virtual universe. And, just possibly, the nature of warfare itself has changed. Human warfare in the era of Marlborough was a gentler art, for all that people still died in the thousands.

Interesting that Colonel Lang seems hesitant to deploy us, despite the obvious threat. He seems to have less passion as a commander even than the hapless Tallard.

An enlisted technician called from the other side of the command center. "C-Colonel Lang?" He was painfully young . . . a teenager with fuzz on his cheeks.

"Whaddizit?"

"S-sir, we're getting reports now of major landings on the far side of the Frozen Hells! There's fighting in both Gadalene and Inshallah, and . . . and refugees are starting to come west through the passes!"

"What do we have over there?"

"Only a few garrisons, sir. I've got Captain Chandler on the line now."

"Let me talk to her."

Martin followed Lang as he approached the com console, where a holographic image flickered above the transmitter plate. Captain Maria Chandler was a handsome, ebon-skinned woman with five battle stars on her tunic and a reputation for a tough attitude and devoted troops in her command. "Colonel Lang!" she snapped as soon as she saw the CO's image on her console. "Either send help or get us the hell out of here!"

"What's your tacsit, Captain?"

"My tacsit," she said, in a prissy, near-mocking tone,

"is tac*shit*. We have alien transports coming down all over the place. Take a look for yourself."

A flatscreen monitor above the console lit up, transmitting jerky, sometimes incoherent images from a handheld camera. Martin saw the domes and greenhouses of flintsteel and blue crystal of one of the eastern settlements—he wasn't sure which one, but Captain Chandler was commanding a garrison at Glacierhelm, and he assumed that was what he was seeing. Smoke rose in columns, illuminated from beneath in the black night sky by the turbulent orange glow of fires. An ungainly landing craft of unfamiliar design, all angles and bulges and blunt ends, descended toward the ice, a shadow behind the harsh glare of landing lights. Heavily armed troops were already on the ice, their combat armor painted white with random smears of dark gray, as camouflage within the icy environment. The bodies on the ground, broken and fire-tossed, were nearly all clad in light Concordiat body armor, panted black with white trim.

The scene fuzzed with static suddenly, then went blank.

"We need help!" Chandler said, angry. "We're completely outnumbered and have no way to resist! I've ordered the civilian population to board icecats and make it through the passes, but there aren't enough—"

And with startling abruptness, the holo image winked out in a white blur of static.

"Wait!" Lang bellowed. "Get her back!"

"Can't, sir," the technician replied. "Transmission interrupt . . . from her end."

Other monitors were showing similar scenes of chaos. The local colonial news service was reporting landings and hostile attacks among most of the domed towns and habitat outposts scattered across the Eastern Tundra, and camera views of incoming landers and running troops were displayed on a dozen monitors. More and more of those monitors were going blank, however. On one, a news reporter, heavily swaddled in synthfur against the cold, was talking into a handheld microphone when white-armored troops burst in behind him, blasters flaring in dazzling bursts of blue light. The reporter's head came apart in a blurred red mist, and then that camera feed as well went dead.

"Colonel!" Khalid cried, "you must *do* something!"

Lang was still staring at one of the few active screens. It was difficult to see what was happening— massive, armored shapes moving in the darkness, as flame gouted into the night. "Martin? What are those things?"

"I can't tell, sir." He checked another screen, tapping out a command on the keyboard, entering a query for information. "There's nothing on them in the warbook. They may be something new, something we didn't see with the last Kezdai incursion."

"Ground crawlers. They look almost like . . . Bolos."

"Small ones. They can't mass more than five hundred tons. A Mark XXIV masses fourteen thousand."

"But there are a damn lot of them, Lieutenant. And they're heavily armored. Even a Bolo can be taken down by numbers, if there are enough of them."

"It takes more than armor to do that, Colonel. Bolos are smart." *If you let them use their talents and fight the war their way. . . .*

"They're headed west," Khalid said. "Toward the passes. Toward *us*."

Lang looked at Martin and nodded. "Order the Bolos out," he said.

"Yes, *sir*!"

It's about freaking time. . . .

Were I human, I would exult. "It's about time," I believe, is how humans express this particular emotion.

Massive doors rumble aside as I engage my main drive trains. I notice a group of humans, mech-technicians of the Izra'il Field Armored Support Unit, 514th Regiment, standing to one side as I pass like a duralloy cliff towering above them. Humans are so tiny, tiny and frail, yet I must recognize that it was they who created my kind.

I move out at full speed, hitting 100 kph by the time I clear the doors and reaching 140 on the open parade ground beyond. While combat feeds do not indicate any immediate threat to this base, I do not wish to expose myself to the possibility of orbital bombardment while I am still restricted in mobility by the physical structure of the base.

Three hundred meters south, Andrew emerges from his bunker in a glittering spray of ice crystals illuminated by the base lights, racing east on a course parallel to mine. The Frozen Hell Mountains rise a few kilometers ahead, rugged and ice enfolded.

The tactical situation is fairly simple. The Frozen Hells, rising nearly four thousand meters above the Izra'ilian tundra, form an ideal defensive barrier to surface movement, though not, of course, an impediment to air transport or attack. There are only two overland routes through the mountains within almost a thousand kilometers of the base—the Ad Dukhan River Valley to the south, and the Al Buruj Pass to the north.

Our tactical data feeds indicate that both passes are now crowded with Izra'ilian civilians streaming west through the two passes, fleeing the slaughter now being wreaked by the Enemy among the towns on the far side of the mountains. The human traffic will make movement through the passes difficult. A more viable option is to open up with a long-range indirect bombardment of Enemy positions on the eastern flank of the mountains and to engage Enemy spacecraft now in planetary orbit.

I perform a final systems check and determine that all weapons and combat systems are fully operational. I open the communications channel to headquarters and request weapons free.

"They want to what?"

"Bolo HNK is requesting weapons free," Martin said. "He wants to target enemy positions on the far side of the mountains and to hit Kezdai ships in close orbit."

"Negative!" Lang said. "Request denied, damn it!"

"Sir—"

"I said denied! We start hitting Kezdai ships, and they're going to start hitting our ships. We can't afford that, not if we want to maintain an open route off this rock. As for lobbing missiles over the mountains, forget it! There are still friendlies over there, and I don't want to start an indiscriminant mass-bombardment!"

Martin looked at the number one monitor on his console, which showed one of the Bolos up close, grinding off across the ice-locked tundra toward the east. Its hull was pitted, worn, and battle-scarred, reminding him with a jolt that these machines had been in several dozen actions already, stretched across the last couple of hundred years. The machines bore eight battle stars apiece, and they'd seen plenty of minor engagements that hadn't rated the fancy unit citations welded to their glacises.

It suggested that they knew what they were doing, damn it.

"Lieutenant Martin!"

"Yes, sir."

"Deploy the armor into the passes. Have them hold the passes against enemy attempts to break through. That should give us the time we need to regroup on this side of the mountains, see what we're going to do."

"Yes, sir." He reached for the comm headset.

❖ ❖ ❖

I find it hard to believe that we have been issued such orders. A Bolo is, first and foremost, an offensive combat unit. Its best assets are wasted in a purely defensive stance. Andrew and I discuss the situation via our QDC link, confident that we cannot be overheard by the Enemy . . . or even understood by those monitoring our transmissions at the Combat Command Center.

"They must have reasons for this deployment," Andrew suggests. *Of the two of us, he was always the more stolid, the more steady, the more certain of reason behind muddled orders. "The situation on the far side of the mountains is still confused. Perhaps they fear incurring friendly-fire casualties on Izra'ilian civilians."*

"Perhaps," I reply, *"though the use of drones and AI missiles for final targeting options would limit civilian casualties. Especially when our targets would be primary Enemy targets, such as their transports, field headquarters and communications stations, and armor concentrations."*

"It's also possible that C^3's reasons for these orders are the same reasons Marshal Tallard decided against deploying on the Tapfheim Line."

"And those reasons are?" I prompted.

"Mistaken ones."

I was intrigued by the fact that Andrew had just assayed a joke. Not a very good one, perhaps, by humans standards, but a definite attempt at humorous wordplay. Bolos are not known for their sense of humor, nor would such be encouraged if humans had reason to suspect it.

It was not the first time that I had wondered if Andrew and I were entirely up to spec.

In the past, I've primarily been concerned that I have trouble integrating with other Bolo combat units. Obviously, our QDC link makes us closer than would

*otherwise be the case, so much so that various of our
human commanders in the past have referred to us
as "that two-headed Bolo," or as "the Bolo Brothers."
Our diagnostics, however, have always been within
the expected psychotronic profiles, and no mention of
processing aberrations has been made by any of our
commanders or service teams. We are combat-ready
and at peak efficiency.*

We are ready to engage the Enemy.

*Andrew is moving further to the south now, angling
onto a new heading of 099 degrees in order to enter
the western end of the Ad Dukhan Valley. I can see
the valley entrance now, for it is marked by high
thermal readings and a visible outflow of water vapor.
The name, in the Arabic of this world's colonists,
means "The Smoke" and refers to clouds of steam
emerging from a river rising from hot thermal vents
in the valley. Izra'il possesses considerable tectonic
activity, the result of the constant tidal tug-of-war it
plays with the gas giant called The Prophet and others
of The Prophet's moons. An important deep thermal
power station is located at the thousand-meter level
of the path; the Ad Dukhan River itself is so hot it
remains liquid despite an ambient temperature ranging
between minus five and minus fifty degrees all the way
to the Al-Mujadelah Sea.*

*The steam filling that valley could provide Andrew
with a tactical advantage, masking his heat signature
and helping to render him invisible even at close
range.*

*My destination is the Al Buruj Pass to the north,
a narrow defile through the mountains named "The
Mansions of the Stars" in the local tongue.*

*I sense now the near approach of the Enemy ahead
and increase my pace.*

"I really think we should be listening to them, sir,"
Martin said, stubborn. "They have more experience

on the front line than any of the rest of us have on the chow line." He hesitated, trying to gauge just how far he could go. "Colonel, a good officer knows to *listen* to his sergeants. What they have to say comes from experience, not simulations!"

Lang *almost* smiled. "Lieutenant, the day I take advice from a giant track-crawling piece of construction equipment with a psycho-whatsit brain and a programmed-to-order attitude is the day I retire from the service! Get it through your head, son. Those toys of yours are machines. Not men. They don't think, not the way we do, and you'll just get yourself in trouble pretending they do!" He turned and glanced at the QDC console, then indicated the fast-flickering screens with a nod of his head. "Besides, it looks like they play simulations. Not paying attention to the real world much, are they?"

"Some of that is ordinary conversation, Colonel. They're discussing something. It looks like there's also a game running, but they have it isolated in a pretty small shared virtual world. They don't need that much thought to traverse terrain or watch for incoming. My guess is that they're modeling some possible Kezdai strategy and tactics, so they can decide how best to deploy."

"*They'll* decide, huh?" Lang shook his head. "I'm not getting through to you, Lieutenant. *Bolos are machines, not people! Stop goddamn pretending they're alive!*"

"Yes, sir."

Martin returned to his console. On a map display overhead, two points of green light crawled toward the mountains.

I am now in full Combat Reflex Mode as battle is joined at 0587 hours, local time. Three Kezdai aircraft, possibly drones but carrying numerous missile weapons, flew across the mountains on an attack

*vector for the Combat Command Center. I downed
one and Andrew two, brushing them from the night's
sky with twin bursts of ion bolts from our infinite
repeaters.*

*My Vertical Launch System is on-line, and I use
it to deploy a combat zone recon drone package.
Ninety-six small, autonomous probes will relay visual
and e-signal data via Izra'il's military-comm satellite
network or, should that fail, by way of relay drones
landed atop the Frozen Hell's higher and more inacces-
sible peaks.*

*As the recon drones come down on the eastern side
of the mountains, our battle centers are flooded with
incoming data. Weapon and ship designs, radio frequencies and code types, all match samples from the
last Kezdai incursion at Delas, verifying the Enemy's
identity. They appear more numerous than the first
field reports suggested.*

*We observe at least forty-two heavily armored
ground crawlers, each with an estimated mass of five
hundred tons, each with a turret-mounted energy
weapon and obvious missile launch tubes. They appear
to be moving in two groups of twenty-one toward the
two passes. We could take them out now . . . but our
orders from our command center specifically prohibit
this.*

*On my long-range sensors, I pick up an orbiting
Kezdai battlecruiser rising above the western horizon.*

*For the next 0.015 second, I wrestle with conflicting
hierarchies of programming and the orders to avoid
firing at targets in orbit. I decide that an attack from
the battlecruiser will warrant a reply, but until then
I will merely observe. Colonial spacecraft remain in
orbit, I note. Possibly the command center hopes to
avoid a naval engagement.*

*As I continue to move toward Al Buruj Pass, the
ground begins rising. A roadway passes beneath my
tracks and is pulverized, but I do avoid brushing*

against the pylons of the monorail line connecting the east and west plains across the mountains. Several cars have passed already, each filled with civilians. I notice a large number of civilians in ground vehicles— snowcats and hovercraft, mostly—all headed west.

The presence of civilians within the narrow confines of the Al Buruj Pass will seriously complicate my defense of this position. I try to increase my speed but am forced to halt several times as the refugee crowds grow thicker. Many, I now note, are on foot.

Andrew informs me that similar conditions prevail in the Ad Dukhan Valley.

At a much lower awareness level, we continue our round of simulations. We have modeled the surrounding terrain, estimating Enemy capabilities and weaponry as best we can by comparing them with known opponents and materiel. At a conservative guess, we assign the Kezdai armored crawlers with armor values and firepower equivalent to Deng Type A/2 Yavacs, which possess a similar mass. Our initial gaming suggests that the Enemy must employ 8.75 A/2-equivalent crawlers in simultaneous direct-fire combat to jeopardize a single Mark XXIV. Our strategy, clearly, while necessarily defensive in nature, must be directed toward preventing the Enemy from achieving that level of numerical superiority.

I reach the top of Al Buruj Pass, a crest that affords an excellent view of the tundra plains beyond . . . and the blazing torches of Consortium villages.

The first refugees were arriving at the spaceport, two kilometers south of the command center. Monorail cars were sliding in one after another, spilling hundreds of shocked, terrified, and confused civilians onto the port concourse, while ground-effect vehicles and snow crawlers continued to arrive from both passes in apparently unending streams.

"Order the 5th Brigade to the spaceport," Lang

said, speaking into a comm headset. "Off-planet transport is to be reserved for Concordiat military!"

Khalid's dark face flushed darker. "You cannot be serious!"

"I'm dead serious, Governor. We'll see to it that you and your top people get out okay. But there are seventy thousand colonists on this rock, and we don't have space transport enough for a quarter that. What we don't need now is a riot at the spaceport."

"So . . . what is it you intend to do?"

"Delay the Kezdai for as long as we can, first off. It won't be easy because they outnumber us by a considerable margin."

"But your two Bolos . . ."

"Can only do so much. I'm a realist, Governor. Those machines won't more than slow the incoming tide. But in the meantime, we'll be trying to open negotiations with the Kezdai. It's possible that we can arrange a truce and evacuate peacefully . . . and without further bloodshed."

"Indeed?" Khalid looked down at Lang with undisguised contempt. "And has it occurred to you, Colonel, that this rock as you keep calling it, this iceball, is our home? We may be only a Concordiat mining venture, but the people here have made this world their home. I suggest you help us defend it."

"If we do that, Governor, you won't have a home left." He shrugged. "Defend the place yourselves, if you want. My people were not posted here to die in some hopeless gesture!"

"Colonel!" Martin called, hoping to prevent an ugly scene. He could feel Khalid's fury radiating from behind his eyes and clenched fists, barely contained.

"What is it, Lieutenant?"

"Both Bolos have reached their assigned defensive positions, sir. Andrew reports poor visibility. Hank, however, has a clear view of the towns of Inshallah,

Glacierhelm, and Gadalene. He has the enemy in sight."

"Then have them open fire on them, damn it! Give 'em Hellbores! Do I have to think about *everything* around here?"

I receive the order to commence firing, and for the first time in my career history, I hesitate at that command. I have the Enemy in my sights, and yet I am aware with laser-exact precision what the firing of my 90cm Hellbore in close proximity to unarmored civilians would do.

The mountain pass is perhaps eighty meters wide at this point and walled in by sheer, basaltic slopes capped with snow and ice. Hellbores fire a "bolt" of fusing hydrogen at velocities approaching ten percent c. Within a thick atmosphere such as Izra'il's, the bolt's 30-million-degree core temperature dissipates as a shock wave that would kill or maim any unarmored individual within a radius of approximately two kilometers and would bring down the surrounding ice in a cataclysmic avalanche.

Civilian casualties would be horrendous.

I withhold my main battery fire, then, in order to allow the refugees to continue passing me on their way to the west. Instead, I launch four VLS missiles with CMSG warheads, vectoring them toward concentrations of Enemy armor and radiating communications assets east of the mountains.

Each cluster-munitions warhead disintegrates above the target area, scattering a cloud of self-guiding force packages across broad, suddenly lethal footprints. As expected, the Enemy's armored units appear unaffected, but troops caught in the open, along with the buildings and light vehicles being utilized as C³ units, are shredded by bursts of high-velocity pellets fired like shotgun blasts from falling CM warheads.

I target fifteen large, grounded transports scattered

*across the Area of Battle but elect not to destroy these,
at least at this time. We as yet have little information on Kezdai psychology, but they seem close enough
to humans in their actions and reactions that I assume
they will fight harder knowing they have no escape.
Humans refer to it as "fighting like cornered rats,"
a vivid metaphor despite the fact that I can only
assume that a "rat" is a creature possessed of cow-
ardly traits yet which can, in desperation, display
considerable strength, determination, or will to live.*

*So long as the Enemy's troops know there is a
means of escape waiting for them, they may be more
cautious in their deployment and advance. Further,
their transports provide a tactical lever in my own
planning. By threatening their lines of retreat to their
transports, we can force changes in the execution of
their battle plan.*

*For now, though, my own maneuvering is circum-
scribed by my orders. I advise the Command Center that I cannot fire my Hellbore at this time and
begin targeting the Enemy's armor with VLS-launched
cluster munitions.*

"So . . . where do you call home?" Governor Khalid
asked.

It was a quiet moment in the command center.
Colonel Lang had left, moments before, to discuss
the fast-worsening crisis at the spaceport with 5th
Battalion's senior officers and the military police.

"Aldo Cerise," Martin replied, not taking his eyes
from the Bolo C³ monitors. There was something odd
happening. . . .

"A long way. How long since you were home?"

"Two . . . no. Almost three years. Why do you ask,
Governor?"

"I was beginning to wonder if you Concordiat
troops had homes. If you knew what it mean to lose
it, or to be forced to leave."

"Lang is right about one thing," Martin told him. "We can't more than slow the enemy down a bit. There are just too many of them."

"I do not understand your colonel. He seems so . . . timid."

Martin grunted, then reached out and touched a key on his console. "You might be interested in this, sir." A holo-image of Colonel Thomas Lang appeared above the projection plate. "It's classified data, but I think you should see it. I got curious and did a search of the personnel files."

Khalid leaned closer, his hawklike features stage-lit by the glow from the monitors as he read a scrolling column of text.

"He was at Durango? I've heard of that."

"An all-out last-stand battle. During the Melconian war. He ordered two battalions to hold the town of Cordassa on Durango at all costs. They did and were wiped out."

"But the battle was a victory."

"Sure. At least that's what the military historians call it. The 1st and 2nd Battalions of the 345th Regiment delayed the main Melconian advance on Cordassa until the Concordiat fleet could arrive and destroy the invasion force."

"But Lang—"

"They couldn't punish him, not while they were turning Durango into the biggest victory since the Alamo."

"Alamo?"

"A similar last stand, a long time ago. Pre-space-flight days, in fact."

"I see."

"Did you see this?" He highlighted a section of text.

Khalid frowned. "His brother . . . ?"

"Major Geoffrey Lang, in command of the 2nd Battalion. He died with the others, in Cordassa. Our

CO was in a military orbital station at the time and survived."

"It says he was court-martialed."

"And acquitted. He was a hero, after all. A court-martial is something of a requirement if you're careless enough to lose your entire command. It says here there was some discussion over whether or not his actions should have been censured, but in the end they gave him a medal."

"They rewarded him."

"*And* punished him. He was given a new command . . . here. Far from anywhere important. Out of sight, out of mind, as it were." Martin looked at Khalid. "Being sent here was tantamount to ending his career."

Khalid's mouth twisted in a wry grin. "That could explain some of his feelings about my world."

"It could also explain why he's afraid of seeing Izra'il turn into another last stand. He's been trying to get in contact with the Kezdai commanders. Peace at *any* price . . ."

"*That* approach has been tried throughout history. Appeasement has the distressing habit of making the aggressor more and more hungry."

"I . . . I wish there was something we could do. Lang's right, though. The bad guys outnumber us by a good margin. Unless help comes in time, we're not going to be able to hold them."

"Not even with two Bolos?"

"Not even with them." *And* especially *if they're not allowed to fight* their *way,* he thought, but he didn't say the words aloud.

Khalid sighed. "We prize peace highly on this world, Lieutenant. Two hundred years ago, the Izra'ilian Consortium hired people on Kauthar to come here, to start a new life working the iridium and durillium mines. Most of them were B'hai, a faith that lives for peace and understanding . . . or Islam reformed.

"They found this world an icy hell. They named it after the Angel of Death, astride the worlds, one foot in the Seventh Heaven, the other on the bridge between Hell and Paradise. He keeps a roll of all humanity. When a person dies, Izra'il severs his soul from his body after forty days. They vowed to make Hell *into* paradise.

"Izra'il is no paradise. We, the grandchildren of those first colonists, know that. But it is home, and home to our children. We cannot simply . . . abandon it. Not on the whim of the man assigned by the Concordiat military to protect us!"

"I'm sorry," Martin said, miserable. "There's nothing I can do about it. He's my commanding officer, and . . ."

"And to disobey his orders means prison or discharge or dishonor. I understand. But . . . I have heard such things about Bolos. Autonomous war machines that think like a man. That can*not* be defeated. And you are the Bolo command officer, are you not?"

Martin nodded, miserable. "Yeah. That's me. But I still can't order them to do things *he* won't allow. As for not being defeated . . ." He shrugged. "No machine is invincible. Bolos can be beaten, if they're badly enough outnumbered. Or if they're badly handled and deployed."

"You fear for these two, Hank and Andrew."

"Yeah. They're pinned in by those valley walls up in those two mountain passes. No room to maneuver. Worse, they can't use their speed and mobility and weapons to full tactical advantage."

"Bolo NDR to Command," a voice said in his earpiece. It was deep and richly inflected. "The Enemy is moving up the Smoke Valley now. I've knocked down three aerial drones, and I suspect they're trying to maneuver some heavy equipment up the east slope, using folds in the terrain for cover."

"Bolo HNK to Command," a second voice said. It was a bit higher in tone than the other, distinct in inflection and meter. "No sign of the Enemy yet in the Buruj Pass. Refugee traffic is still heavy, and I cannot engage with primary weaponry without causing unacceptable collateral damage and high civilian casualties. Request permission to move forward ten kilometers, in order to engage the Enemy freely."

"Bolo HNK," Martin said, speaking into the comset pick-up. "Hold position, as ordered. Can you target the enemy with your Hellbore?"

"Affirmative." Was there just a trace of bitterness in that one-word response? Anger? Or was it his imagination? There was a long hesitation. "Command, I must refuse the order to fire my Hellbore at this time. Request permission to move forward ten kilometers, where I will not be responsible for heavy civilian casualties."

Martin blinked, drew in a sharp breath, then let it out again slowly. "Negative. Hold position." He studied the QDC readouts again. "Damn. . . ."

"What is it, my friend?"

"I'm not quite sure," he said, frowning. Both Hank and Andrew were operating at a considerably higher level of mentation than could be expected of Mark XXIVs. "The way they're talking, I could swear they're Mark XXXs."

"What do you mean?"

"Well . . . we don't have time here for a dissertation on Bolo evolution. In extremely simple terms, Bolos became generally self-aware, possessing roughly human-equivalent intelligence, with the introduction of the Mark XX and psychotronic circuitry in the late 2700s. Succeeding marks have grown more intelligent, more human in their reasoning abilities and—importantly—in their speech patterns over the next few centuries, though their abilities were restricted by inhibitory software aimed at preventing a 'rogue Bolo' from turning on its owners. Okay so far?"

Khalid nodded. "I understand. The early models couldn't do a thing without direct orders from their human commanders."

"Right. Now, Mark XXIVs, like Hank and Andrew, were the first truly autonomous self-aware machines. The latest models, like the Mark XXX . . . well, if you talk to them by comm, the only way you can tell they're *not* human is by the fact that their speech tended to be a bit more formal, a bit more erudite than that of people. They're fully Turing capable."

"Turing?"

"An old cybertech term. Means you can carry out a conversation with them and not know they're machines. Anyway, I've worked with Bolos for eight years now, and I've had the opportunity to converse with a number of them. A sharp ear can pinpoint the mark of an unknown Bolo simply by listening to the way it parses its sentences. Lower marks tend to sound a bit blood-thirsty and narrow-minded, and they don't think about anything outside very narrow software constraints. Higher marks sound like extremely intelligent humans and can talk about damned near anything."

"Ah. And you think your two friends out there are more intelligent than they should be."

"In a nutshell, yeah. Language, specifically the ability to carry on an extended conversation about a variety of topics, reflects general intelligence. That's exactly what I'm thinking. And I'm also wondering . . . why?"

"Why what?"

"The colonel is right. Those two Bolos out there are *only* machines. They're very, very smart machines, but they're smart because someone wrote some extraordinarily complex AI programs for them, which are processed through psychotronic circuitry designed to display a certain level of flexibility, speed, and even, to a limited degree, self-awareness. They can't step outside the parameters of their own programming, can't think outside of the box.

"So how can they possibly be thinking like Mark XXXs?"

"Perhaps they have found a way to reprogram themselves."

"They don't have that capability. Self-programming . . . that would mean they could step outside the box, somehow, and decide for themselves what they were going to do, exactly what people have been trying to prevent in Bolos ever since the things were invented."

"The one, 'Hank,' keeps refusing your order to fire his Hellbore."

"Yeah. I know. And that's part of what bothers me. He has a certain level of tactical discretion, sure. And when they slip over into full Combat Reflex Mode, they'll be entirely on their own. But I've never heard a Mark XXIV tell me that it couldn't obey an order to fire because it might cause civilian casualties."

"He sounds . . . human."

"Yeah . . ."

"You said earlier that a Bolo cannot step outside of its box, cannot reprogram itself. I am thinking, my friend, that most humans are no better. We are what Allah and our pasts decree we are, and few of us can rise beyond that."

Martin thought of Lang. "I'm beginning to think you're right."

The two Bolos were exchanging a barrage of information now over their QDCs, and Martin wondered what they were talking about.

In the Ad Dukhan Valley, twenty kilometers to the south, Andrew is engaging an Enemy air and ground assault. Sharing a real-time link via our Quantum Determinacy Communications suites, I watch, I feel as he maneuvers himself into a kilometer-wide pool of boiling water, the source of the hot-water Dukhan River and the "smoke" of "Smoke Valley."

Concealed both optically and thermally, he is in an ideal position to ambush the Enemy as his crawlers reach the top of the pass. Fortunately, the refugee traffic through the Dukhan Valley has tapered off to nothing, but he holds fire from his main turret weapon, depending instead on a high-velocity fusillade from all eighteen ion-bolt infinite repeaters and tactical barrages of anti-armor missiles. For forty flame-shot seconds, the rock-locked valley shudders and trembles to the thunder of his volleys. Four Enemy crawlers are destroyed as they attempt to slip over the ridge crest and rush him. The others mill in a confused huddle for a moment, then withdraw.

I can sense his excitement. "We can charge them and finish them now!"

"It would be suicide," I tell him. "Besides, our orders are to hold these passes at all costs. If the Enemy manages to slip through behind us, the evacuation will be compromised."

"Then we will have to make sure none get past us."

"In combat, nothing is sure. Marlborough knew that."

"Marlborough also knew it was possible to win all of the battles and lose the war."

I take his point. The War of the Spanish Succession was little more than an extraordinary string of victories for Marlborough, until political disgrace ended his career seven years after his brilliant victory at Blenheim. In the end, France kept her prewar boundaries and got much of what she wanted, even though her military reputation had been blackened by her poor showing on the battlefield. History is filled with such reverses . . . Napoleon in Russia, America in Vietnam, Argentina in Brazil, the

*Berrengeri Legions on Trallenca IV . . . victories won
on the battlefield with blood, then squandered or given
away by the bureaucrats at the conference table.*

*I note that Concordiat transports are preparing for
evacuation and wonder how many of the population
will be able to escape. It seems a foregone conclusion
that the Enemy will soon overwhelm our positions and
surge through the passes to attack the Command
Center, the colonial capital at Izra'ilbalad, and the
spaceport.*

*I note transatmospheric strike craft lifting from the
flame-ravaged cities to the east and report the sight-
ing and target lock to the Command Center. Orders
return seconds later, "Do not, repeat, do not target
enemy spacecraft."*

*I wonder why we are here, placed where we cannot
fight, deprived of our best weapons, fit for nothing
save destruction. . . .*

"If we start killing their transports," Colonel Lang
bellowed, "they start killing ours! And then we're
dead!"

"We're also hobbling our one ace in the hole,"
Martin replied. "Damn it, Colonel! Unleash the Bolos!"

"You are relieved, Lieutenant. Get the hell out of
my command center."

"Colonel!" Governor Khalid said. "You are here
under *my* jurisdiction. I think you should—"

"Your jurisdiction, Governor. *My* command. You are
scarcely qualified to lead a battle, and my men would
not obey your orders. Now . . . I must ask both of
you to leave the center."

"Sir, with respect," Martin said, "you'll still need
me to interface with Hank and Andrew. They might
not accept your orders if they don't recognize your
voice." It was a bluff, and a thin one, but he needed
to stay, needed to at least try to stay in the loop with
his two fourteen-thousand-ton charges.

"Colonel Lang!" a panicked voice said over one of the active speaker circuits. "Banner, at the spaceport! We have a mob breaking through the north perimeter fence!"

"Damn it to hell." Lang hesitated, visibly swaying, his face dark with anger. "Okay, Martin. Stay. Make them stay. But one more seditious remark out of you and you'll spend the next ten years in the stockade!"

"Yes, sir."

His hands were shaking as he turned back to the Bolo console once again.

"He intends to abandon the Bolos, doesn't he?" Khalid said softly.

"Of course. Those Bolo transports will carry a thousand people apiece."

"So he will simply use them to buy time, to organize an evacuation?"

"I think that's the idea. But I don't think he's going to have the time."

"I am not leaving my homeworld," Khalid said.

"I'm not leaving either," Martin told him, voicing the decision he had only just that moment made. "Not if it means leaving *them* out there."

Andrew has beaten back the initial attack down the Ad Dukhan Valley. His use of infinite repeaters only slowed the advance of the enemy crawlers, but laser-guided cluster-munitions packages loaded with anti-armor missiles have proven to be effective.

I note that preparations are well under way for evacuation from Izra'ilbalad. Our sacrifice here, evidently, is designed to give Headquarters time to complete the evacuation. Andrew and I agree that we must do everything in our power to blunt the Enemy's thrusts across the mountains, to buy as much time for the Consortium facility as possible.

I continue to track the approach of five transatmospheric strike craft wheeling in low across the mountains. Headquarters' orders to hold my fire baffles me. The strike craft are fast, highly maneuverable, and grav-resist powered, similar to the Valkyrie XY-3000 Interceptor class. Low-grade gamma leakage suggests that they either are powered by small fission power plants or are carrying nuclear munitions.

Suddenly, they break south. They are targeting Andrew.

"Andrew!" I call over the QDC channel.

"I see them!" he replies, before I can get my warning out. "Tracking! They've launched!"

They have also vanished off my sensor net, my line of sight blocked by the southern wall of the valley I occupy. But I can watch them through Andrew's eyes and through several orbiting military satellites, as each of five incoming TAS aircraft loose four missiles at nearly point-blank range.

"Engaging targets!" *Andrew cries. He is climbing from the hot springs lake, hull steaming, seeking greater maneuverability as the attackers swoop in low across the northern wall of the Smoke Valley. Under Battle Reflex Mode, he can assign his own priorities to targets . . . and disregard the earlier no-fire order from Headquarters.*

His infinite repeaters send up a flaring, dazzling cloud of ion bolts, as point-defense batteries loose invisible beams of UV lasers. Six of the missiles, and three aircraft, disintegrate within the first 0.16 second of his firing.

Through satellite recon views, I note a large flight of missiles launched from Enemy defense batteries near Inshallah, all of them targeting Andrew.

Four more missiles vaporize . . . and five more after that . . . but they have been fired at high velocity from a range of less than half a kilometer, and Andrew simply does not have point-defense weapons enough to track and destroy them all. He manages to burn down three more . . .

. . . and the remaining two strike his battlescreens, a pair of 25-kiloton fission nukes detonating almost simultaneously. Through the QDC link, I feel the sudden pulse as his battlescreens flutter, then fail, overloaded . . . feel the searing, deadly wash of superheated plasma scouring across his outer hull like the caress of a blowtorch across plastic . . . feel the black hurricane winds laden with vaporizing grit and rock exploding across his armor, as dense and as solid as the thunderous blast of a tsunami . . . feel the shift and slide of my tracks in ground now partly molten, as those winds attempt to push a mass of fourteen-thousand tons . . .

I am moving now, racing eastward through the valley, seeking a clear line of fire against the incoming wave of missiles still en route from Inshallah. The attacking aircraft have all been destroyed, by Andrew or in the fireball. But satellite sensors are tracking thirty-seven more targets inbound.

Andrew is still operational. Power at 27.4 percent . . . 12 infinite repeater batteries still full or partially operational . . . battlescreens down. His ablative layers are gone, carrying away the worst of the thermal radiation. His outer hull, the part facing the twin atomic suns when they lit off, is scorched black and in places sculpted smooth, with aerials and comm antennae melted away . . . and radiation sensors show that he is now hot enough to kill an unprotected human who comes within touching distance.

My seismic sensors register the trembling under-track, followed by the shrill peal of thunder thirty seconds after the blast. "Andrew! Are you okay?"

"Still . . . operational." I can sense the struggle simply to formulate those words. His processing power must momentarily focus entirely on the matter of survival. "Tracking new wave . . . incoming . . ."

"I see them. I'm repositioning for a clear shot." But the walls of the valley block me. I can see *the launchers now, still thermal-bright after their launch seconds ago, but the missiles themselves are terrain-following ground huggers and have vanished into the rock-shrouded cleft of Smoke Valley.*

Andrew's analyses of the missiles flickers through my combat center. They are five-meter rods of depleted uranium, incoming at hypervelocity. In the base of each projectile is a fission device of at least 25 kilotons. The rods are designed to penetrate even Bolo armor . . . with the pocket nukes slamming through the half-molten openings.

With his battlescreens down, Andrew is vulnerable . . . and I can do nothing.

I sense more missiles being swung into launch position at the Inshallah site. . . .

"God! What's happening?" Lang demanded.

"Those aircraft launched tacnuke penetrators at Andrew. His battlescreens are down, and it's going to take time to bring them up again. He's got more penetrators coming in from the east. Looks like they're trying to saturate his defenses."

"Can the other Bolo—?"

"Trapped in that high-walled valley. He's trying to maneuver to assist, but—"

"What . . . what can we do?"

"Not a God-damned thing, Colonel. We sit back and watch. . . ."

"The other one," Khalid put in, staring at the map display. "Hank. He moves so quickly! It's almost as though he feels what the first one feels."

"I think that's exactly right." Martin glanced at the colonel, expecting a rebuke, but there was none. "They're brothers. . . ."

In a sense, I feel what Andrew feels . . . relayed sensory data from those few external hull sensors that survived the nuclear storm. I see the incoming missiles now, feel myself maneuvering to bring the largest possible number of infinite-repeater turrets to bear.

"Fire your main weapon!" I call. A 90cm super-Hellbore discharge of approximately 2.25 megatons/second firepower might not engulf that entire cloud of incoming penetrators, but the sudden vacuum ripped out of atmosphere would destroy any survivors in the shock wave, fry even hardened electronics with EM induction, and melt delicate sensors through thermal effect. The missile cloud is beginning to disperse, however, each penetrator maneuvering separately in order to descend upon Andrew from a different direction. He must fire his Hellbore within the next 0.5 second or lose the opportunity.

"Fire! Fire!"

His reactions are sluggish, and I wonder if his operational centers have taken battle damage . . . but then he looses a Hellbore bolt, lighting up the murk-shrouded, nuke-torn landscape of the valley with a needle-thin sliver of starfire dragged from the heart of a sun and hurled at the incoming missiles.

Twenty-four missiles vaporize, and five more smash into the ground or Andrew's tough hide, broken, slowed, or half molten. Eight, reacting more swiftly than expected from available flight performance data, have swung clear of the fusion bolt and the thunderously collapsing tunnel of vacuum in its wake and arc around to approach Andrew from eight different angles.

His infinite repeaters kill five . . .

His point-defense lasers kill two . . .

The last surviving penetrator comes in high, plunging down into Andrew's main deck, twelve meters behind his primary weapon turret. Robbed of much of its kinetic energy by its high-G maneuver to avoid the Hellbore bolt, it strikes with only a fraction of the energy a five-meter rod of depleted uranium was designed to carry . . .

. . . but it strikes a tender spot where a meter of duralloy, ceramplast, and flintsteel alloys has been scraped from Andrew's hide and the remainder left soft, partly molten in places, above a mere two meters of inner titanium-duralloy amalgam and the blue shimmer of his inner defensive screens.

The breach, a white-hot needle driven like a spike into Andrew's back, is a tiny one . . . but the 25-kiloton nuclear explosion that follows spears a fraction of its unleashed fury into the gap, igniting plasma fires within . . . .

"Andrew . . . !"

My scream momentarily jams all military radio frequencies, and the audio output echoes from the rock cliffs around me. Our QDC link is snapped . . . yet in my virtual, inner world, the world I shared with him, I see him ablaze from within, consumed from the inside and the out by the starcore blaze of nuclear hell that engulfs him.

"Andrew . . . !"

Ice dislodged from the cliff tops by sonic concussion tumbles into the valley on all sides, but I ignore it, continuing my eastern rush.

I feel the flame burning inside me, a blue-white, devouring heat.

I sense the touch of targeting radar and lidar locks. I swing my 90cm Hellbore around, target the launcher complex, some eighteen kilometers away, and fire. . . .

Lieutenant Martin looked up from his console, pinning Lang with a look of cold, hard hatred. "Bolo of the Line NDR 0831-57 has been destroyed," he said.

"God help us all," Lang replied.

"God *forgive* us," Martin said, correcting him. "I don't think we're in control of Hank any longer. . . ."

There are Enemy troops moving up the Buruj Pass, humanoids in heavy armor, laboring against the steep

*slope as they climb toward my position. I wonder if,
perhaps, they are employing Marlborough's Blenheim
tactics against me, pinning my attention on Andrew
while moving a heavy armored force to break through
at a different location—my position.*

*A better comparison might be Marlborough's victory
at Ramillies, two years after Blenheim, another classic battle frequently wargamed by Andrew and myself.
There, Marlborough conducted probing attacks against
Villeroi's left and right, feinted right, then swung the
majority of his forces from right to left, shielding their
movement from French eyes by moving them behind
a fold in the ground behind the Anglo-Allied front. His
final assault against the French right and center rolled
back Villeroi's flank, then broke it.*

*The Kezdai Enemy has adopted a similar strategy,
moving a sizable force up the Al Buruj Pass while I
was distracted by events elsewhere. They are thermally
shielded and well-camouflaged, invisible to the military recon satellites far overhead . . . or to my far
flung net of sensor drones. As I race down the steep-
ening slope, movement sensors and lidar pick up thirty
Enemy crawlers and a large force of armored soldiers
on foot or mounted in hovercraft troop carriers.*

*No matter. As I explode down the slope among
them, I open fire for the first time with my main
Hellbore, directing bolt upon searing starcore-plasma
bolt against the Enemy's concentrations on the eastern plains below.*

*Shock waves from those detonations thunder through
the narrow pass, bringing down rumbling, deadly
avalanches of rock and ice. Five bolts in rapid succession annihilate the Enemy's launch complex outside Inshallah. Three more smash down Enemy
battlescreens shielding a command center, a communications array, a fire control center, turning permafrost
and duralloy into glass-bottomed pits of furiously
radiating heat.*

Particle beams blaze and sizzle against my battle-screens from high-powered, turret-mounted projectors in the nearby crawlers. I slew my turret left and fire again, filling the pass with the barely contained effulgence of hellfire, engulfing crawlers and transports and troops in a brief, multi-million-degree sunrise. Crawlers slag down beneath the onslaught or grind to an inglorious halt, armor melting, life-support systems failing. I retarget and fire again, the bolt causing two crawlers to explode at a touch.

I sense troops among the mountains to left and right, infiltrators attempting to close on my original position. Six hatches snap open along my dorsal hull, and I bring my 30cm mortars into play, raining high explosives and anti-personnel cluster munitions down among the surrounding cliffs and peaks.

To both left and right, several million tons of igneous rock crack and collapse, as snow and ice flashes into an expanding cloud of steam, as thunderously rippling blasts detonate among the crags above. By the time the rock hits the valley floor, however, there is nothing left alive within two kilometers of my position. Thousands of tiny glass marbles clatter across my upper works—rock, vaporized, flung into the sky, then cooled to glittering spheres of glass.

I'm moving swiftly now, tracks clattering and shrieking as I mount tumble-downs of fallen boulders and slag and burst out into the open tundra. Now I can maneuver as my designers intended, zigzagging across the plain toward the heart of the Enemy's beachhead on this world.

The battle is now a swirl of energy and motion. I sense the Enemy's forces gathering, redirecting, moving toward me . . . even forces already deployed beyond the mountains toward Izra'ilbalad and the western plains. With Andrew dead, Smoke Pass is open to forces properly armored and shielded against radiation and lingering thermal effects, and the only way *to block their advance is to create enough of a disturbance deep behind their lines to force their retreat.*

But in truth, I am no longer planning my actions, weighing my decisions, calculating the effect of move and countermove, of volley and countervolley. I move and I kill . . . burning all life, all movement, killing, and killing again.

I am become Izra'il, the Angel of Death. . . .

I am a brother, maimed by the death of a part of myself. . . .

The battlecruiser in low orbit opens fire, bathing me in approximately 2.79 megatons/second. The shock wave races out across the melting tundra, devouring everything in its path, leaving only me at the epicenter beneath the collapsing heavens.

My battlescreens fail. . . .

But I return fire. My long-range sensors are blocked by the extreme ionization of the air around me, but I calculate the target's precise position and fire at that. Recon satellites detect the flash as a trio of Hellbore bolts smashes down the Enemy's screens, then punctures deuterium tanks. Internal explosions cripple the vessel, spewing out gouts of molten metal, atmosphere, and pinwheeling fragments. In moments, the ship is a lifeless hulk, tumbling end for end against the night.

As the skies clear around me, my sight returning, I reach out, seeking further, targeting Enemy spacecraft, and burning them down. Enemy crawlers are closing from the mountains now, ringing me in. Absently, I engage them with mortars and the last of my VLS cluster munitions, while continuing to hammer at the Enemy's orbiting fleet.

His surviving ships are withdrawing now, pulling away from Izra'il and The Prophet. My Hellbore bolts pursue them, burning down two more before they vanish into FTL, beyond my reach.

Kezdai crawlers fire now from every quarter, hammering at my naked hull with the searing slash and smash of particle beams. I count twenty-nine attackers, wielding 3.31 times the concentrated firepower necessary to destroy me, even were my battlescreens at full power.

It no longer matters.

Nothing matters but target . . . and fire . . . target . . . and fire . . . target . . .

They watched, first in surprise, then horror, then in awe . . . the handful of Concordiat command staff and the Izra'ilian governor, standing in the Battle Center, watching a lone Bolo's single-handed destruction of the Kezdai invasion force. The map board was clear now of Kezdai units, save for a dwindling few closing on Hank.

"Can a machine feel grief?" Khalid asked, his voice very small in the stillness.

"I'm . . . not so sure that that is a machine," Colonel Lang replied.

Martin could only watch, helpless, as the drama played itself out.

Target bearing 035, range 450 meters . . . engage, lock . . . firing. Target destroyed. It has been 14.72 seconds since catastrophic failure of battlescreens. I attempt rerouting of power from primary fusion reactor to defense screen projectors via secondary power buss, but attempt fails due to overload of local power shunt circuitry and bleed transmitters.

Target bearing 171 degrees, range 780 meters . . . engage, lock . . . firing. Target destroyed.

VLS missile reserves now exhausted. Thirty-cm mortar rounds reduced to five shots per tube.

Hellbore melting. Failure imminent. Suggest holding main weapon fire to allow bore cooling and recovery.

Negative. Override. Continue engagement. Target bearing 104 degrees, range 1025 meters . . . engage, lock . . . firing. Target destroyed. . . .

✧   ✧   ✧

The Concordiat recovery team could not approach the burned-out hulk of the dead Bolo for nearly five weeks, so fiercely radiant was what was left of its outer hull. Martin was with them, however, trudging ahead beneath the massive weight of a Class-One rad-shielded suit. Hank rested in a shallow depression boiled out of the surface by the energies employed in his final battle. His massive tracks half-submerged in boiling mud that had finally refrozen around them.

Elsewhere, the war against the resurgent Kezdai continued. Their fleets had avoided Izra'il since their attempted invasion, however. Intelligence now thought they'd chosen Izra'il as a test area for anti-Bolo tactics.

It was still unknown whether they considered their test a success or a failure. Both defending Bolos had been neutralized.

But at what terrible cost. . . .

Martin reached out a heavily gloved hand to touch the wall of metal rising above him . . . one of Hank's massive road wheels. "Better not, pal," one of the technicians warned. "That metal's still hot enough to cook ya, even through the anti-rad gear."

He could feel the radiation, like heat, bathing his face through the narrow slit of his helmet. His helmet display showed that he'd already accumulated a quarter of the rads allowed him on this trip. They would all be on antirad and anticancer drugs for months after this.

He didn't care.

But he did withdraw his hand.

"He will be a permanent monument," Khalid said at his side. "When we rebuild, we will build around him. A containment dome and field will shield the citizens from the radiation, until he is cool enough to approach."

"You'll have a lot of rebuilding to do." Every structure on the east side of the mountains had slagged down into liquid pools during the battle, when temperatures normal for the interior of stars had momentarily been loosed across Izra'il's frozen surface.

"What of it? It is our home. We will rebuild. If only because *they* saved it for us."

Martin looked up into the sky, taking in the looming bulk of The Prophet, the golden span of the Paradise Bridge, the pearly crawl of auroras . . . and the wan, thin, colored smear of the Firecracker Nebula. *What are they thinking there, on the Kezdai homeworld?* he wondered. *What lessons did they learn here?*

Could a machine step out of its box and become greater than what it was? The working theory now was that the two Bolos had shared a considerable amount of thought within the virtual world of their QDC link. They'd talked . . . and challenged one another, somehow together becoming greater than either of them working alone.

What must it have felt like, he wondered, *when Hank felt Andrew die?*

Can machines feel?

Were they machines?

Does it matter, when both were thinking, feeling beings?

"Thank you, Hank," he said aloud. "Thank you, the both of you." He turned away, then, and walked back across the frozen ground.

It is dark. Sensors inactive. Null input.
Negative . . . negative . . .
Input positive . . .
I can still feel him dying. . . here inside of me. . . .
Initiate replay, Combat Sim 63833: Blenheim. . . .
I can still see him. . . .
Why does it hurt so much . . .?

THE SHIP WHO SANG IS NOT ALONE!

Anne McCaffrey, with Mercedes Lackey, S.M. Stirling, and Jody Lynn Nye, explores the universe she created with her groundbreaking novel, The Ship Who Sang.

THE SHIP WHO SEARCHED
by Anne McCaffrey & Mercedes Lackey

Tia, a bright and spunky seven-year-old accompanying her exo-archaeologist parents on a dig, is afflicted by a paralyzing alien virus. Tia won't be satisfied to glide through life like a ghost in a machine. Like her predecessor Helva, *The Ship Who Sang*, she would rather strap on a spaceship!

THE CITY WHO FOUGHT
by Anne McCaffrey & S.M. Stirling

Simeon was the "brain" running a peaceful space station—but when the invaders arrived, his only hope of protecting his crew and himself was to become *The City Who Fought*.

THE SHIP WHO WON
by Anne McCaffrey & Jody Lynn Nye

"The brainship Carialle and her brawn, Keff, find a habitable planet inhabited by an apparent mix of races and cultures and dominated by an elite of apparent magicians. Appearances are deceiving, however . . . a brisk, well-told often amusing tale. . . . Fans of either author, or both, will have fun with this book."
—*Booklist*

Got questions? We've got answers at
BAEN'S BAR!

Here's what some of our members have to say:

"Ever wanted to get involved in a newsgroup but were frightened off by rude know-it-alls? Stop by Baen's Bar. Our know-it-alls are the friendly, helpful type—and some write the hottest SF around."
—**Melody L** *melodyl@ccnmail.com*

"Baen's Bar . . . where you just might find people who understand what you are talking about!"
—**Tom Perry** *perry@airswitch.net*

"Lots of gentle teasing and numerous puns, mixed with various recipes for food and fun."
—**Ginger Tansey** *makautz@prodigy.net*

"Join the fun at Baen's Bar, where you can discuss the latest in books, Treecat Sign Language, ramifications of cloning, how military uniforms have changed, help an author do research, fuss about differences between American and European measurements—and top it off with being able to talk to the people who write and publish what you love."
—**Sun Shadow** *sun2shadow@hotmail.com*

"Thanks for a lovely first year at the Bar, where the only thing that's been intoxicating is conversation."
—**Al Jorgensen** *awjorgen@wolf.co.net*

Join BAEN'S BAR at
WWW.BAEN.COM
"Bring your brain!"